S0-BAZ-166

BLOODFORGED

She sprang into the middle of them before they could move, whirling around with the iron bar and cracking skulls and snapping arms. A handful fell away, howling and clutching themselves, but the rest leapt in, screaming. She smashed a man with a hatchet in the neck, lifting him off his feet and sending him crashing into the wall of the ramp. Two more hacked at her legs with swords. She dodged one, but took a cut from the other, then ran him through.

More darted in, slashing and chopping. She pulled on the iron bar. It was stuck in the swordsman's ribs. A dagger gashed her back. A club smashed her shoulder. A sword grazed her arm.

Ulrika snarled, enraged, and shot out her fangs and claws as her vision turned crimson and black and a roaring filled her ears. The men around her gasped and cried out. She inhaled their fear and leapt at them, leaving the iron bar where it was. She didn't want a weapon now. It would only keep her at a distance from her victims.

More Nathan Long from the Black Library

Ulrika the Vampire

Book 1 – BLOODBORN

BLACKHEARTS: THE OMNIBUS
(Contains the novels *Valnir's Bane*, *The Broken Lance* &
Tainted Blood)

More Vampire novels from the Black Library

VAMPIRE WARS: THE VON CARSTEIN TRILOGY
by Steven Savile

(Contains the novels
Inheritance, Dominion & Retribution)

THE VAMPIRE GENEVIEVE
by Jack Yeovil

(Contains the novels *Drachenfels, Genevieve Undead,
Beasts in Velvet & Silver Nails*)

Gotrek & Felix

GOTREK & FELIX: THE FIRST OMNIBUS
by William King
(Contains books 1-3: *Trollslayer, Skavenslayer &
Daemonslayer*)

GOTREK & FELIX: THE SECOND OMNIBUS
by William King
(Contains books 4-6: *Dragonslayer, Beastslayer &
Vampireslayer*)

GOTREK & FELIX: THE THIRD OMNIBUS
by William King and Nathan Long
(Contains books 7-9: *Giantslayer, Orcslayer & Manslayer*)

Book 10 – ELFSLAYER
by Nathan Long

Book 11 – SHAMANSLAYER
by Nathan Long

Book 12 – ZOMBIESLAYER
by Nathan Long

A WARHAMMER NOVEL

ULRIKA THE VAMPIRE

BLOODFORGED

NATHAN LONG

BLACK LIBRARY

For Lili, because she liked the first one.

A BLACK LIBRARY PUBLICATION

First published in Great Britain in 2011 by
The Black Library,
Games Workshop Ltd.,
Willow Road, Nottingham,
NG7 2WS, UK.

10 9 8 7 6 5 4 3 2 1

Cover illustration by Winona Nelson.

Map by Nuala Kinrade.

© Games Workshop Limited 2011. All rights reserved.

The Black Library, the Black Library logo, Games Workshop,
the Games Workshop logo and all associated marks, names,
characters, illustrations and images from the Warhammer
universe are either ®, TM and/or © Games Workshop Ltd 2000-
2011, variably registered in the UK and other countries around
the world. All rights reserved.

A CIP record for this book is available from the British Library.

UK ISBN13: 978 1 84970 013 9
US ISBN13: 978 1 84970 014 6

No part of this publication may be reproduced, stored in a
retrieval system, or transmitted in any form or by any means,
electronic, mechanical, photocopying, recording or otherwise,
without the prior permission of the publishers.

This is a work of fiction. All the characters and events
portrayed in this book are fictional, and any resemblance to real
people or incidents is purely coincidental.

See the Black Library on the internet at
www.blacklibrary.com

Find out more about Games Workshop
and the world of Warhammer at
www.games-workshop.com

Printed and bound in the UK.

THIS IS A dark age, a bloody age, an age of daemons
and of sorcery. It is an age of battle and death, and of the world's
ending. Amidst all of the fire, flame and fury
it is a time, too, of mighty heroes, of bold deeds
and great courage.

At the heart of the Old World sprawls the Empire, the largest
and most powerful of the human realms. Known for its engineers,
sorcerers, traders and soldiers, it is
a land of great mountains, mighty rivers, dark forests
and vast cities. And from his throne in Altdorf reigns
the Emperor Karl Franz, sacred descendant of the
founder of these lands, Sigmar, and wielder
of his magical warhammer.

But these are far from civilised times. Across the length and
breadth of the Old World, from the knightly palaces of Bretonnia
to ice-bound Kislev in the far north, come rumblings of war. In
the towering Worlds Edge Mountains, the orc tribes are gathering
for another assault. Bandits and renegades harry the wild southern
lands of the Border Princes. There are rumours of rat-things, the
skaven, emerging from the sewers and swamps across the land.
And from the northern wildernesses there is the
ever-present threat of Chaos, of daemons and beastmen corrupted
by the foul powers of the Dark Gods.
As the time of battle draws ever nearer,
the Empire needs heroes
like never before.

CHAPTER ONE
CHANGES

'YOU WILL NOT return to Sylvania,' said Lady Hermione. 'And you will no longer be Countess of Nachthafen.'

'But – but, why?' asked Gabriella.

'Because *she* has ordered it so,' said Hermione.

Everything was changing, Ulrika thought sourly as she watched Countess Gabriella struggle to maintain her composure, but everything remained the same.

Ulrika had done all this too often before – had stood here in attendance in the drawing room of Lady Hermione, the leader of the Lahmian vampires in Nuln, had suffocated beneath a long wig and layers of dresses and petticoats, had listened to her mistress, Countess Gabriella, have words with Hermione, and had wished she were anywhere else in the world. The only difference betwixt then and now was that Lady Hermione had a new name, and a new disguise to go with it, and it appeared Gabriella was about to be given the same.

Three weeks had passed since the monstrous Strigoi, Murnau, and his army of ghouls had attacked the Lahmian sisterhood at Mondthaus, Lady Hermione's country estate, and since Witch Hunter Templar Captain Meinhart Schenk had come within a hair of discovering the sisterhood's true nature – three weeks also, since Gabriella had killed Witch Hunter Friedrich Holmann when Ulrika had refused to do it. In those three weeks prodigious amounts of work had gone into making it appear the sisters had all died, and to establish new identities for each of them.

They had faked their deaths after Countess Gabriella and Lady Hermione had decided that continuing in their current identities was impossible. They were certain Schenk and the witch hunters would never stop wondering if they were vampires, even if nothing could be proved, and their every action would be scrutinised.

And so, the day after the attack, women were found who bore some resemblance to Gabriella, Hermione, Ulrika and the beautiful Famke, Hermione's protégée. They were dressed in appropriate clothes, then torn apart as if by ghouls, with special care taken that their faces were shredded and unrecognisable.

Then began a great shifting of behind-the-scenes resources. Bank accounts were closed and money transferred, titles and deeds to houses and other properties changed hands, always through third parties, and wills and birth certificates were forged and ancient family trees pruned and grafted so as to bear fresh new fruit.

At the end of this process, an old man appeared on the doorstep of the recently deceased Lady Hermione von Auerbach, claiming to be the grieving Lord Lucius von Auerbach, a distant cousin to whom Hermione had willed her properties. With him were his two beautiful young daughters, Helena and Frederika.

Lord Lucius claimed the family had come to Nuln to mourn the passing of their cousin, and afterwards decided to take up residence in her mansion. In reality, of course, Lord Lucius was a mere blood-swain – a slave of Hermione's, chosen for his sad, noble face – and his two young daughters were none other than Hermione and Famke themselves, remade with paint and henna and the subtle illusions that were the Lahmian sisterhood's stock in trade. Lady Hermione's hair, which had before been a rich chocolate-brown, had been straightened and lightened to a honey-blonde, while Famke's hair, which had been the colour of white gold, had been darkened to the same shade and given a more youthful cut. This and a change of dress, manner and voice appeared all that was required to make Nuln think them entirely different women, and Ulrika had to admit that, even though she was in on the game, when they were in public, she had a hard time remembering they were the same women she had known since she had arrived in Nuln the month before.

'The Queen wishes me to stay in Nuln?' asked Gabriella.

'Yes,' said Hermione. 'With the deaths of Rosamund, Karlotta, Alfina and Dagmar, she believes we are shorthanded here, and as you performed so...' Here Hermione pursed her lips and looked as if she would rather eat a decomposing rat than continue. 'So admirably, she has decided you will stay and take over Dagmar's position, opening a new brothel in the Handelbezirk and continuing her work gathering information there. You, I and Mathilda will be the Queen's eyes here for the foreseeable future.'

'But my place is in Nachthafen,' said Gabriella, upset. 'Sylvania cannot go unwatched.'

'I am informed that someone will be found,' said Hermione. 'And Krieger is dead now. A new threat will not arise so quickly again from that quarter.'

'We can only hope,' said Gabriella, sitting back. 'I do not like this change.'

'You can be sure I like it even less,' said Hermione,

sniffing. 'But as the Queen commands, so must we do. Now we must come up with a suitable name and guise for your new position.'

Ulrika turned towards the window that looked into Hermione's back garden, their words fading away as she stared into the moonlit night. So they would stay in Nuln. It was the last thing she would have wished for. Too many things she would rather have forgotten had happened here. Sylvania, for all its isolation, had at least been simple and ordered. When they had come here things had become complicated.

The murders of the vampiresses Rosamund, Karlotta, Alfina and Dagmar had threatened to expose all the Lahmians, and the hunt for their killer had set them at each other's throats. Hermione had suspected Mathilda of attempting to take her position, and had accused Gabriella of being a von Carstein spy, out to weaken the sisterhood. There had been betrayal, bloodshed and death, and Gabriella and Ulrika had lost nearly everything, including their lives.

None of these things, however, pained Ulrika as much as the death of Templar Friedrich Holmann, and the worst of it was, she could blame no one but herself for the misery it had caused her. They had met by chance, both on the trail of the killer, and had Ulrika been wise, she would have killed him the moment she saw him. She had not been wise. She had been weak. She had tricked him into thinking she was a vampire hunter and left him alive, and as their paths continued to cross during the investigation, she had come to like him, so much so, that at a moment when he was overwhelmed by ghouls and might have died, she had exposed her fangs and claws to save him.

Like her, Holmann had found himself weak, and was unable to kill her, and that had been his downfall. He had defended her against other witch hunters, and was too ashamed to return to his order. He had intended to run away, to leave the Empire, and Ulrika would gladly have let him, but Countess Gabriella would not allow it. She had told Ulrika that, having revealed her true nature to Holmann, she had left herself only two choices – she could kill him, or she could feed on him and make him a blood-swain.

Ulrika could not bring herself to do either. She could not kill a man who had saved her life, and she would not make a slave of him – for that was what became of those upon whom a vampire fed. They lost their will, and became addicted to the pleasure of being bled. She had liked Holmann for what he was, for his strength and sadness and honour, and the idea of turning him into a lapdog who pawed at her knee and showed his throat nauseated her. So she had refused to make the choice, and Gabriella had done the deed instead, feeding on him, then snapping his neck. Things had not been well between Ulrika and the countess since.

A movement out of the corner of her eye turned Ulrika's head. Through the diamond panes of the window, she saw Famke beckoning to her from a stone bench set against the balustrade of the veranda, a lute in one hand. Even with her hair darkened and sitting in moonlight, the girl looked like a sunny summer day – a strange thing to say of a vampire, but undoubtedly why her mistress had chosen her to be one.

Ulrika looked back at Gabriella and Hermione, still deep in discussion about Gabriella's transformation, then slipped out of the room to the corridor and through the back door to the garden. It was a cold clear spring night, but Famke didn't mind the cold any more than any vampire did, and was dressed only in a light gown of rose-coloured silk. Her feet were bare.

'Good evening, sister,' Ulrika said, bowing and crossing to her. 'Will you play me a song?'

Famke grimaced at the lute. 'I am practising my scales. Lady Hermione says a Lahmian must be a perfect courtier, and a perfect courtier must be skilled in all the arts.'

'Then I am far from perfect,' said Ulrika. 'All I know are Kossar drinking songs, and those aren't fit for court.' She pulled off her long wig, revealing her short sand-coloured hair, and sat down beside Famke with a sigh. 'Did you hear? We shall be staying in Nuln.'

Famke nodded. 'I am glad. I would have missed you. But perhaps you are not so pleased. You looked so sad staring out the window.'

Ulrika paused, then shrugged. 'I... it was nothing.'

Famke put a hand on her arm. 'You will forget him.'

Ulrika looked up, chagrined that she was so easy to read. 'I hope so,' she said.

Famke smiled sympathetically. 'Of course you will,' she said. 'He was only a man.'

Ulrika murmured noncommittally as the girl bent her fingers awkwardly around the neck of the lute, trying to make a chord. Famke had been sorely abused by her father and other men before Hermione had rescued her and given her the dark kiss. She could see no good in man, any man.

'It's only that he dealt with us honourably,' Ulrika said after a moment. 'And I wish I had been allowed to deal with him honourably in turn. I understand the need for secrecy, but–' She paused, looking over her shoulder at the drawing room's bright window. 'Sometimes I wonder if she killed him out of spite. She...' A flash of memory overwhelmed her – the mob in the Industrielplatz surging around their coach, howling for their blood. Gabriella throwing the maid, Lotte, to their savage embrace, so she and Ulrika might escape. 'She can be cruel.'

Famke nodded, then also glanced warily at the

window. 'When Hermione turned me,' she whispered, leaning close, 'I thought she was the most beautiful, wise, wonderful woman in all the world, but now–' She shook her head, her eyes faraway. 'She seemed to go mad during the trouble – attacking your mistress, thinking everyone was against her. It frightened me.'

'Aye,' said Ulrika, combing out her wig with her fingers. 'I know it is a struggle to survive, but there must be a way to do it... differently.'

She slouched back against the balustrade. Famke did the same. Their shoulders touched.

'I keep dreaming of running away,' said Ulrika. 'Leaving them and all their cat-clawing intrigue behind and living free.'

Famke gasped and turned her head, her lips almost touching Ulrika's ear. 'I've dreamed the same thing!' She motioned towards the house. 'I get so tired of walls. Even the garden is a little box.' She sighed. 'I used to love the outside. Before. Now, even with all the nice things mistress gives me, I sometimes feel I'm in a coffin – dead after all.' She laid her head on Ulrika's shoulder. 'Wouldn't it be a wonderful adventure to run away together, like two princesses in a book.'

Ulrika smiled and looked over the garden wall, and over the walls and rooftops of the houses beyond it. 'Aye. Two horses and the open road, just as my father and I used to ride on the oblast. No destination, no obligations, our swords at our hips, and the horizon a hundred miles away.'

'We would need a little more than that,' said Famke, laughing. 'A coach to protect us during the day, a driver, I suppose, a swain or two so we could feed.'

Ulrika grunted, feeling as if every item Famke added were being piled onto her back. 'Then we might as well not leave at all,' she said, hotter than she meant to. 'We would be bringing the coffin with us.'

'But travelling without them would be folly,' said Famke. 'What if we were to be far from shelter at sunrise?'

'I know, I know,' Ulrika sighed. 'And this is why we stay in walled gardens and airless rooms, but it ruins the fantasy a bit, don't you think?'

Famke smiled sweetly. 'Well, if it is just a fantasy, then we shall have winged horses instead of a coach, and shall sleep on Mannslieb so we will never see the sun.'

Ulrika laughed, but before she could make a reply the veranda door opened. Ulrika and Famke looked up, then sprang apart, guilty, as they saw their mistresses glaring at them from the doorway.

'Ulrika! Come along,' said Gabriella sharply. 'We are done here. It is time to go.'

'Famke, what are you doing?' snapped Hermione. 'You are meant to be practising.'

Ulrika and Famke rose quickly from the bench and curtseyed, saying 'yes, mistress,' at the same time, but as Ulrika hurried to follow Gabriella, she stole a glance back to Famke and exchanged a secret smile with her.

I wish you winged horses, sister, she thought, then went into the house.

CHAPTER TWO
THE GILDED CAGE

'I WILL BE leaving you at home,' said Gabriella as Ulrika rode in the coach with her through Nuln to their temporary quarters. 'I must go on to the Handelbezirk to meet with Madam Dagmar's old employees, to familiarise myself with procedures and client lists. You will find it boring.'

Ulrika made no reply. She just stared out the window.

'I have a surprise waiting for you at home,' Gabriella continued. 'I think you will be very pleased.'

Ulrika still said nothing, and finally Gabriella sighed.

'I am sorry I raised my voice to you, beloved,' she said. 'But I cannot have you speaking with Famke.'

'Why is that?' asked Ulrika, turning from the window. 'Why shouldn't I speak to her?'

'Why is that, *mistress*,' said Gabriella. 'You must not forget yourself because I gave you some autonomy during the recent troubles. The crisis is over now.'

'Why is that, *mistress*?' said Ulrika through her teeth.

'Much better,' said Gabriella. 'Because, though we are now supposed allies, Hermione is still actively working

17

against me. She does not want me in Nuln any more than I wish to be here, and she is deathly afraid I will be promoted above her. Therefore she will try her best to ruin my name and reputation while I am here.'

'And what does that have to do with Famke, mistress?' asked Ulrika.

'Don't be dense, girl,' said Gabriella. 'Famke is her creature. She is a spy for Hermione as surely as you are a spy for me, and will report anything you say to her mistress. You cannot trust her.'

Ulrika clenched her fists until her nails bit into her palms, but she couldn't contain her fury. 'Must I see no one but you?' she cried at last. 'You killed Holmann! You deny me Famke! Who am I to talk to?'

Gabriella blinked, bemused. 'You may of course speak to me any time you like, dearest,' she said. 'But if you require other playmates, there will be swains aplenty once the new brothel opens its doors. We will have a score of handsome gentlemen to guard us, and the most beautiful women in the Empire at our beck and call.'

'I don't want swains!' Ulrika barked. 'Have I not said? I let Holmann die rather than make him my slave. I want equals! I want true friendships, not the servile fawning of besotted fools!'

For a moment, Gabriella looked like she would reply in kind, but finally her face softened. 'Then I'm afraid you will often be lonely amongst us, child. Though I have had good friends over the course of my centuries in the sisterhood, they have been few and far between. There is too much vying for position for most sisters to be true friends. Only when some outside force attacks us do we unite.' She paused at that, smiling wryly. 'And sometimes not even then.'

She patted Ulrika's knee. 'Our position will not always be so precarious, dearest,' she said. 'There will be a time when I will be able to allow you to find true companionship outside my house, but until then, I will do my best to be the friend you require.'

Ulrika turned back to the window, unconsoled. 'A friend I must call "mistress",' she said.

They made the rest of the trip in silence.

GABRIELLA'S TEMPORARY HOME was in the Kaufman District, a quiet neighbourhood of rich merchants south of the noble Aldig Quarter. It was an unassuming little half-timbered row house, maintained by Hermione for just such situations as this – as a residence for visiting sisters who could not be seen staying at her own house. It had two floors, two bedrooms, a butler, a coachman and a maid – all blood-swains, of course.

Gabriella and Ulrika had lived there since they had crept back into Nuln after leaving the artful carnage to be found at Mondthaus, and to Ulrika it felt more like a prison – a well-furnished prison, to be sure, with heavy oak furniture and coloured glass in the windows and carved and painted ceiling beams, but a prison nonetheless. While Gabriella, Hermione and all her minions were busy arranging new identities and hiding old ones, Ulrika had more often than not been left to cool her heels there with nothing to do except read and pace and brood about the turn her life had taken since she had died.

The maid let them in from the small yard at the back, and Ulrika made to go directly to her room, but Gabriella laughed and caught her hand, holding her back.

'No no, beloved,' she said. 'I will not have you sulking. Come to the parlour. I must go in a moment, but have a surprise for you, remember?'

Ulrika curtseyed but kept her eyes on the floor. 'As you wish, *mistress*.'

Gabriella sighed and smiled sadly. 'I know you are chafing against the edges of our life just now, but it will get better, I promise you.'

'How will it get better?' asked Ulrika, looking at her at last. 'We will change this coffin for a bigger one, with whores in it. It will still be a coffin.'

Gabriella frowned. 'You are determined to be offensive, but you will not bait me. Come.'

She led Ulrika into the tidy little parlour. On the Araby rug in the middle was a great trunk, stood on one end, with brass fittings at the corners, and a key sticking out of the lock.

Gabriella gestured to it. 'Open it.'

Ulrika hesitated, then stepped forwards and turned the key. The lid swung out, almost of its own accord, revealing that the trunk was a neatly constructed miniature armoire, with a rail to hang clothes on, and little compartments for accessories, shoes and toiletries – and it was packed with male clothing.

Ulrika struggled hard to remain unimpressed, and to cling to her anger, but she couldn't resist taking one of the doublets off the rail and holding it up. It was beautiful – black velvet embroidered with grey thread – and with slashed breeches and hose to match. There were three more doublets on the rail, in deep shades of burgundy, green and grey, as well as a black cape, a few lace-trimmed white shirts, and tucked below them, a pair of thigh-high black riding boots made of supple Estalian leather, and an exquisite Tilean-made matched rapier and dagger set, complete with sword belt and sheaths.

'I took the measurements from your ruined riding gear,' said Gabriella. 'I know you are more comfortable dressed so, and since you did me such great service as my "drake", I decided you must be rewarded.'

Ulrika turned to Gabriella, holding the black velvet

doublet to her breast. She wanted to shuck her dresses and wig right then and there and try it on. 'Thank you, mistress. This… this is a great gift.'

Gabriella smiled. 'I hoped you would like it. You will of course still wear your skirts when we make formal calls,' she continued. 'But when you are at your leisure, you may dress as you like.'

Ulrika bowed. 'Thank you, I…' She looked up suddenly at Gabriella, her eyes lighting up. 'May I come with you, now? Will you wait while I change?'

Gabriella pursed her lips. 'As I said before, it will not be to your taste. I am meeting with the procuress and the kitchen staff, and I am late already.'

'Then may I go out?' Ulrika asked. 'On my own? Just a walk around the neighbourhood? To the park in the Aldig?'

Gabriella's lips became a hard flat line. 'Don't be silly, my dear. It is too dangerous. You know we must be invisible now. The city has quieted somewhat, but the vampire mania has not subsided entirely. All that is required is one spark and we are back to where we were before.'

'But no one will know what I am,' protested Ulrika. 'Do you think I'm fool enough to reveal my claws and fangs? I learned that lesson.'

'They will know you are unusual,' said Gabriella. 'A woman in male attire. The unusual attracts attention, and we cannot afford attention, do you not see?'

Ulrika stared at her, rage beginning to simmer within her again. 'Then precisely when am I allowed to wear these clothes? You say I may not wear them when we go calling, and I may not wear them in public, but only at my leisure. Do you expect me to stay at home and march from room to room in them?' She snatched up the boots and held them up. 'These are for riding, mistress. When may I ride?'

Gabriella drew herself up. 'Do not take that tone with me, child. I am merely thinking of your–'

Ulrika cut her off. 'Do not call me child! I am a grown woman. I have travelled the world from Kislev to Middenheim to the Worlds Edge Mountains. I have fought the hordes of Chaos. I have led men in battle. And you will not let me leave the house?' Her rage was at full boil now, and the world turned red around her, as if she saw through crimson lenses. Her arm twitched with the desire to hurl the boots at a statue of a noble lady with a knight kneeling at her feet that sat on a table across the room, but she held back, and forced herself to speak in an even tone when she would rather have spit the words in Gabriella's face. 'You think of me as some kind of doll, to be dressed up first as a girl, then as a boy, then left under the bed when you have tired of playing. Well, I am not a doll, and I am not a child. I will go where I wish to go, and I will speak to whom I wish to speak.'

'Ulrika–' said Gabriella.

Ulrika did not slow, and despite her attempt at control, her voice began to rise. 'I owe you fealty for saving my life and teaching me the ways of your sisterhood, and I will serve you faithfully because of it, but I am not your slave. I am not your dog.' She laughed bitterly. 'Ha! You said I was your friend. Does a friend say "sit and stay", and expect one to be happy with a bone and a bowl of water?'

'Enough!' snapped Gabriella, then softened her tone. 'It is because I am your friend that I do this. I know you feel confined, and I know it is cruelty to offer you clothes and no opportunity to wear them, but as I said before, these things will come.'

'When?' cried Ulrika.

'Soon,' said Gabriella. 'We live a long time, beloved, and eventually all things happen. When we are established, when we have the measure of the authorities, then we may allow ourselves more leeway. If you have patience, friends will come, freedom will come, you will ride where you wish to ride, and come and go as you please, but not now. Not for a while yet. I am sorry.'

Ulrika trembled with frustration, crushing the velvet of the doublet in her fists, but then she slumped. 'I am sorry too, mistress,' she said. 'I know we must be cautious. I know I must be patient. It is only that…'

'It is only that you are not bred to this confinement,' said Gabriella, stepping to her and folding her in her arms. 'I know. You are a child of the wide Kislev plains, and I believe the cloistered nature of Lahmian life pains you more than the shedding of blood.' She kissed Ulrika's cheek. 'I promise you, dearest. You will ride again, but–' She lifted Ulrika's chin and looked her in the eye. 'But you must make a promise to me as well.'

'What is it, mistress?' asked Ulrika.

'You must promise to obey me now,' said Gabriella. 'You must promise to bide here in the house until I give you leave to depart. You must let me be the one who decides when it is safe to go out, and with whom it is safe to speak. These strictures will not last, but until I lift them, I would have your word that you will obey them.'

Ulrika hesitated. She felt like Gabriella was stuffing her into the trunk with the doublets and boots and closing it tight. She wanted to run. She wanted to see the moons. But at the same time, she knew the countess was right. It was too dangerous now. They were on unfamiliar ground, and the population was still too unsettled. With a sigh she nodded her head. 'Very well, mistress. I will obey you. You have my word that I will stay in the house, and that I will only speak to whom you allow.'

Ulrika felt Gabriella's arms relax around her. She

smiled and stroked Ulrika's cheek. 'Thank you, dear one,' she said. 'I will make it up to you one day, you will see.'

With another kiss on the cheek, she stepped back and collected her gloves. 'I wish I could speak to you further on this, but I must go. I will return before daybreak. Feed from the maid if you wish, and I asked the butler to bring new books from the bookstalls. You shall have plenty to occupy you.'

'Thank you, mistress,' said Ulrika, and walked with her to the back door, where the maid waited with Gabriella's cloak. 'Take care.'

'I will,' said Gabriella.

The maid fixed the cloak around her shoulders, then opened the door and curtseyed her into the yard. Ulrika turned away as the girl closed the door again, then paused as she heard the key turning in the lock.

She turned back. The maid had no key in her hand. The door had been locked from the outside.

CHAPTER THREE
ESCAPE

ULRIKA STEPPED PAST the maid to the door and tried the latch just to be sure. It was locked. Her skin prickled with terrible premonition, and she hurried through the house to the front door. It was locked too.

She turned to the maid, who had followed her, wide-eyed, from the rear vestibule. 'Fetch the butler. Tell him to bring his keys.'

The girl scurried off, and Ulrika paced the entryway, her long skirts shushing on the polished wood floor until the butler arrived, looking sleepy and holding his ring of keys.

'Open the door,' said Ulrika.

'Yes, m'lady,' said the butler.

He inserted the key in the lock and tried to turn it, then turned back and bowed to Ulrika. 'It appears the countess has set the wards, m'lady. The lock will not open.'

Ulrika cursed and looked around. 'Wards? There are wards? Does she always do this?'

'Usually only when she sleeps, m'lady,' said the butler.

'We must be able to go in and out, to go to market, to deal with tradesmen and–'

Ulrika snatched the key from him, then tried it herself. With her unnatural strength, she bent it, but could not budge the lock. She cursed again and strode to the back door. She had the same result there.

'Damn her!' She threw the keys away, then stomped back into the parlour. There were floor-to-ceiling windows there, heavily curtained. She threw open the curtains and fumbled with the hasp that held the windows closed. It opened, and she breathed a sigh of relief, but as she pushed against the windows, they did not move. It felt as if she were pushing against a stone wall.

With another curse she drew back a fist and punched at a square leaded pane. Her knuckles stopped a hair's width from the glass, blocked by the same invisible stone wall. She snarled and jumped back, then picked up a heavy oak chair and flung it at the windows. The thing bounced back and thudded to the ground, the windows untouched. Ulrika glared at them, fists clenched at her sides.

'Mistress,' said the maid softly. 'Mistress, are you well?'

Ulrika turned. The girl and the butler had edged back to the dining room door, watching her warily.

'I am fine,' she said. 'Go to your rooms.'

They ducked their heads and hurried away, relieved. Ulrika righted the chair, then kicked it savagely, then paced and kicked it again, smashing it into a table.

The countess had locked her in. Ulrika had made a solemn pledge to her that she would not leave the house, and she had *still* locked her in! Ulrika snarled. Now she knew what Gabriella truly thought of her. For all her petting and soft words, she did not trust her to keep a vow. She believed her nothing more than a child, without honour or brains or sense of duty. It was a slap in the face – an insult to her integrity.

Rage filled her again, crimson clouds blurring and warping her vision until the room seemed at the bottom of a stormy red sea. She kicked the chair again, upsetting it. When Gabriella returned there would be a reckoning. Ulrika would not be lulled once again by smooth talk. She would demand her release, and if the countess refused, she would fight her way out, or die trying. She could not allow herself to serve such a duplicitous witch for one second longer. Ursun's teeth! If she could break the wards that trapped her, she would leave now and never come back. To hell with all this Lahmian intrigue, with its rivalries and subtleties and airless rooms. She wanted out!

A tiny voice in Ulrika's head reminded her of her vow to Gabriella, but she roared at it and it retreated into a corner, cowering. When the countess had turned that key, she had removed any obligation Ulrika owed to her. There was no dishonour in breaking a pledge to someone without honour.

She leapt at the window, claws and fangs bared, and slashed and clawed at it. It rebuffed her as before, and she fell back panting, but her anger was too hot to let it be. She turned, growling under her breath. If there was a way through the wards she would find it, and if there wasn't, the countess would return to find her tidy little home torn to shreds.

Ulrika sprinted up the stairs to her room, darted around her canopied bed and crossed to the heavy curtains on the wall that faced the street. She gripped them in her claws and tore them down – and was faced with a blank wall. There was no window behind them. She stared, nonplussed, then ran across the hall to Gabriella's room and tore down her curtains too. Again there was no window, only smooth plaster.

Ulrika stepped back, mind churning. She was certain she had seen upper windows on the outside of the house. They must be false, to give the impression of normality, while protecting Lahmian guests from exposure to the sun. Quickly, she tried every room on the floor, tearing down the curtains. None had windows.

Ulrika kicked the wall in frustration, then stopped, panting. What about a fireplace? Could she climb up a chimney and out? She ran back to Gabriella's room and ducked her head under the mantelpiece. No such luck, the inside of the chimney was hardly big enough to admit her head, let alone her shoulders.

With a snarl, she snatched up the poker and slashed at a cherubic marble caryatid that held up one end of the mantel. Its little stone head bounced across the room and stopped below where the window should have been. She laughed and crossed to it, meaning to hurl it at something, then paused, looking again at the wall. There was a shadow on the plaster – a very faint vertical line. She stepped closer. It looked like the impression left on a blotter after one had lifted away the paper – an almost imperceptible tracery of what one had written. She ran her hand over it. There was a shallow depression in the wall, and to the right of it, another. She looked up. An arched line connected them, as faint as the rest.

Her skin tingled with excitement. This house had not been built for the Lahmians. It had been refitted to suit their needs. There had been a window here once. Indeed, there still was, on the outside. The question was, how sturdily had they closed it up?

She raised the iron poker, then paused. This window faced the street. Breaking through it would attract attention. She hurried to the study at the back. Yes. The same shallow grooves in the wall. She smashed it with the poker. The plaster cracked and crumbled. She struck again and made a hole. With her claws she tore at the edges, ripping away the smooth painted veneer until she could see what lay beneath. Only lathing and gravel fill!

She went at the lathing with both hands, ripping out the thin strips of wood and letting the pebbles they held in place spill to the floor. Buried only two inches deep was a wooden window frame. Ulrika ripped and tore until the whole frame was exposed. A thin black-painted wood panel had been set within. She pried at the edges and pulled it out, and saw moonlight. The window looked out into the carriage yard.

Ulrika reached out with the poker, hardly daring to hope, and thrust at a diamond pane. The tip popped through it with a tinkling of glass. There was no ward. She was free!

In her eagerness to be out of the house, she almost leapt through the window then and there, but then caught herself and stepped back. If she were truly to strike out on her own, she must prepare. Suddenly she smiled. How nice of Gabriella to have had the fore-thought to provide the things she needed the most.

She ran back down to the parlour and stripped out of her plaster-dusted dresses, then pulled on a shirt, the black velvet suit, the leather boots and some gloves. They were all a perfect fit. Next she strapped on the beautiful rapier and dagger, then took the grey suit from its hanger and folded it up. There was no pack, so she slipped the suit into one of the voluminous shirts, tied off all the holes, then knotted the sleeves together and slung it over her shoulder like a bag.

What else would she need? Money. She jogged back up to Gabriella's room and ransacked her bureau and armoire, taking every piece of jewellery she could find. Under a hat box she discovered a small iron coffer which was filled with fifty golden Reikmarks. She scooped them up and filled the purse that hung from her sword belt. Now she was ready.

Part of her wanted to wait until Gabriella returned, just to confront her with her leaving, but that would put her much too close to morning, and she would have to be far away and under cover before then.

She hurried to the study and the window. A last moment's hesitation overcame her as she looked out into the yard. It was an enormous thing she was doing, leaving the woman who had saved her and taught her how to get along in her new life. There might be no going back. And who knew what lay before her? Death might catch her that very morning as the sun rose. She shrugged and kicked through the glass. Better to die free than to live caged.

A thrill ran through her as she leapt down into the coachyard and the night wind ruffled her hair. Already she felt better. She padded past the carriage house to the back fence. Now to find a way out of Nuln. If only she could have said goodbye to Famke before she left.

She paused. Why say goodbye? Hadn't Famke said she wanted to run away too? With a mad laugh, Ulrika vaulted the fence and struck out through the sleeping Altestadt for Hermione's townhouse.

SHE WASN'T SO inclined to laugh as she observed the place from a rooftop across the broad, mansion-lined Aldig Quarter street upon which it sat. It was a three-storey palazzo in the Tilean style, with elaborate stonework and twisting columns flanking the doors and windows. But for all its filigree it was as sturdy as a fortress, with bars on the windows and a four-inch-thick oak door, and though there were no guards visible, Ulrika knew Hermione's 'gentlemen' were inside, and there were likely wards and heavy locks too, stronger than those that had protected the little safe house. No wonder the Strigoi, with all its strength, had preferred to kill the Lahmians outside of their houses when it could. It would take an army to break down Hermione's defences.

Of course, it wouldn't take an army for Ulrika to enter. The maids and men-at-arms knew her, and some little lie would be enough to get her through the door. The difficulty would be getting Famke out again. She was sure Hermione could lock the doors and windows with a snap of her fingers, and then she would be trapped inside. Hermione might kill her for trying to steal her protégée from her, or worse, bring her back to Gabriella.

But perhaps she wouldn't have to enter the house. Perhaps Famke was still in the garden. With renewed excitement Ulrika dropped down from the rooftop to a narrow side street and circled the block until she reached the back wall of Hermione's estate. Her heart surged as the tinny strains of an inexpertly played lute reached her ears. That could be only one person. Ulrika tiptoed to the wall and made to spring to the top of it, then paused. What if Hermione was with Famke? Or some of her gentlemen? She strained her senses. No heartbeats, but Hermione might still be there. Ulrika would have to spy it out.

She jumped up and caught the top of the wall with her fingers, then pulled herself up slowly until she could just peer over the wall. Trees and shrubs and statues of lovers dying in each others' arms screened off much of the house, but by craning her neck and leaning to the left she could just see the veranda, and Famke.

She was alone on the bench where Ulrika had left her, her golden hair gleaming silver in the moonlight as she bent assiduously over her lute, wrestling with a Bretonnian melody – and losing.

Ulrika breathed a sigh of relief, then slipped over the

wall and dropped down into the garden. She padded through the trees and shrubs to crouch down at the edge of the lawn, not wanting to step out where she would be in view of the windows.

'Famke!' she whispered.

Famke looked up, peeking through her long straight tresses.

'Who?' she asked, her playing faltering. Then she saw Ulrika and stopped altogether. 'Sister! What are you doing here?'

Ulrika put a finger to her lips and beckoned to her. 'Shhh,' she said. 'Come here.'

Famke looked back towards the house, then stood and hurried down the steps and across the lawn. 'What is it, Ulrika? Why are you sneaking around like a thief?'

Ulrika grinned. 'I have run away. The countess revealed herself to be without honour or respect, so I have decided to strike out on my own, and I've come to take you with me.' She took Famke's hand. 'Come. We haven't much time.'

'You… you've run away?' asked Famke, stunned.

'It was that or die.' Ulrika stood. 'Now to the wall, before anyone comes looking for you.'

Famke pulled back. 'Ulrika, I… How can we do this? It was only a joke. A dream.'

'It is no joke for me,' said Ulrika, impatient. 'Not any more. I tore apart the countess's house and robbed her blind. There's no going back.'

'But it's impossible!' said Famke. 'We will need a coach, and blood-swains, and places to stay.'

Ulrika hefted the purse at her belt. 'We'll buy all that. Now, come on!'

Hermione's voice rang from inside the house. 'Famke? Famke, where are you?'

Ulrika turned back to Famke. 'Come, sister,' she whispered. 'Before it's too late.'

Famke shook her head, looking as if she would cry were vampires able to shed tears. 'I cannot. It won't work. I'm sorry.'

Ulrika stepped out of the bushes towards her, anger growing in her breast. 'What is the matter with you? Do want to live under the thumb of that horrible woman for the rest of eternity? How can you stand to be shut up like this? You are like a doll in a box. Wouldn't you rather die free than live caged?'

Famke hung her head. 'I'm sorry, Ulrika. I am a coward.'

Ulrika groaned, and considered slinging the girl over her shoulder and carrying her over the wall by force, but just then the veranda door opened and Lady Hermione stepped out, two of her gentlemen at her back. Famke squeaked.

'What goes on here?' asked Hermione coldly as she stepped down to the lawn.

Ulrika fought down the instinct to attack, and bowed instead. 'For-forgive me, Lady Hermione. I heard Mistress Famke playing while I was walking, and thought I would pay my respects.'

'I see,' said Hermione, swishing forwards through the grass as her men spread out behind her. 'A social call, over the garden wall.'

'Ah, yes, mistress,' said Ulrika. 'I-I know I should have presented myself at the front door, but I thought I would surprise–'

'So you were only being social,' said Hermione, cutting her off, 'when you asked my darling Famke if she would rather die free than live caged?'

CHAPTER FOUR
THE WALLS OF NULN

ULRIKA STEPPED BACK, keeping her hand away from the hilt of her rapier with difficulty. Famke shrank back too.

'I–I'm afraid you misheard me, mistress,' said Ulrika.

'Did I?' asked Hermione. 'Then what *did* you say?'

Ulrika opened her mouth. Nothing came out. She cursed herself. Had she been the countess, the lies would have flowed like wine. Gabriella was never at a loss for words, but Ulrika had not been trained in parlour fencing. She shot a look at Famke, but the girl seemed paralysed with fear.

'I… don't remember,' she said at last.

Hermione shot her a withering look. 'If you are going to come wooing my ward for Gabriella, you really should be better prepared.' She held out her hand as more men filed out of the house behind her. 'Surrender your sword. You will be held here until the countess can be sent for.'

Ulrika took another step back and felt the bushes pressing into her back. The garden wall was close.

'Of course,' she said. 'I–'

With a sudden spring, she shoved Famke into Hermione, then turned and bolted through the shrubbery.

Hermione shrieked in anger, then started chanting an ear-blistering incantation while her gentlemen bellowed and plunged into the bushes. Ulrika didn't look back. It would only slow her. A tree before her offered a low branch. She leapt up and kicked from trunk to branch to the top of the wall like a cat, but the air above the wall rippled and thickened as Hermione's incantation neared its conclusion. It dragged at Ulrika as she struck it, holding her in mid-air and slowing her like a fly caught in honey. The gentlemen burst from the bushes and leapt and flailed below her, trying to catch her ankles.

Ulrika fought against the thickened air, pushing through it with her arms and pushing it away with her mind. Let me go! she screamed to herself. Let me be free!

Suddenly she *was* free, and crashed down ungracefully to the cobbled alley, landing hard on knees and elbows. She scrambled up and ran as the voices of Hermione's gentlemen roared from behind the wall.

'Lower the wards, mistress!'

'She's escaped!'

'Fetch lamps, someone!'

'Goodbye, Famke!' Ulrika shouted over her shoulder, then turned left at the end of the alley and sprinted away, twisting and turning through the deserted streets without thought for where she was going. She heard no sounds of pursuit, but that was no guarantee. She had no idea of the extent of Hermione's powers. For all she knew, the lady could fly, though it seemed likely she would be too concerned with appearances to go flitting over Nuln in her fancy dresses. That was not the Lahmian way.

No, Ulrika thought with a tremor. The Lahmian way was to use their influence and position to get what they wanted. Hermione wouldn't hunt her. She would ask the authorities to do it. Suddenly Ulrika felt the walls of Nuln closing in on her. She had to get out before Hermione blocked off her routes of escape, and she had wasted too much time already, running around like a headless goblin.

She stopped and looked around, getting her bearings. She was in the Temple Quarter, with the towering spires and battlements of the temples of Sigmar, Shallya and Myrmidia looming all around her. Fool! She had run almost to the Garden of Morr – completely the wrong direction. She turned and started south, moving this time at a swift but measured pace, and praying to the gods who would no longer hear her that she was not too late.

A FEW MINUTES later, she came to a stop near the High Gate, the main portal through the wall which divided the rich Altestadt quarter from the common commercial vulgarity of the Neuestadt. She had climbed the wall once before, coming the other way, and had almost been caught. She was loath to try it again.

And perhaps she didn't have to. She had climbed before because she had looked like a scruffy and disreputable foreigner whom the guards would have been unlikely to let into the Noble Quarter in the middle of the night. Looking down at herself now, in her handsome black doublet and expensive boots, she wondered if she might risk the direct approach. She looked like a noble now, and she was only going into the Neuestadt, and the guards didn't care so much about that.

She looked ahead. All was quiet at the gate. The guards in their black uniforms and breastplates trudged through their duty as if half-asleep. It was now or never.

She strode forwards, chin high. As she approached, the guards looked up, peering at her, then straightened and grounded their spears when they saw the cut of her clothes.

She nodded coolly to them and they pushed open the pedestrian door beside the larger gates.

'Evening, mein herr,' said the bearded gate captain, saluting.

'Evening,' said Ulrika, stepping into the narrow tunnel that passed through the wall.

Out of the corner of her eye she saw the captain do a double-take. Either her face or voice had told him she was a woman. She kept going, forcing herself not to increase her pace. She could feel his eyes boring into her back, but he said nothing as she stepped out of the other side of the little passage into the Neuestadt. One gate down. One more to go.

But just as she let out a sigh of relief and began to stride away, there came a clatter of hooves behind her. She looked back and saw four horsemen ride up on the Altestadt side of the gate, calling for the captain to open it. Ulrika froze. She recognised the men. They were all Hermione's dandies. She stepped into the mouth of an alley and listened.

'We're looking for a thief,' one of them was saying. 'A woman disguised as a gentleman. She stole my lady's jewellery.'

The captain gaped. 'We just let her through, seconds ago!' He turned and shouted to his men. 'Open up! Open up!' then peered through the bars of the opening gate. 'She's just – why. she's gone! Where could she have got to!'

'We'll find her, captain,' said the first horseman, and plunged through the gap with the others behind. 'Bergen, Standt!' he cried. 'Warn the other gates! Folstad and I will search here.'

'Aye, m'lord!' called the men, and thundered off into the Altestadt as the leader and the other went more slowly, looking into every doorway and alley.

Ulrika shrank deeper into the shadows and watched them pass by, groaning to herself. She was fast, but not so fast as a horse. They would reach the gates long before she could, and then she would be trapped. Was there another way? Could she climb out? She had climbed the Altestadt wall, but the exterior walls were another thing entirely - heavily patrolled, and much higher. The drop to the ground would likely break her ankles or legs, inhuman strength or not.

No. The walls were not an option. She must find some other way out of Nuln, and quickly, for it was too confined a place to hide for long. It would only be a matter of time before Hermione and Gabriella or the witch hunters tracked her down.

She started down the alley, avoiding reeking puddles and keeping an ear out for horses, while cudgelling her brains for an escape route. If she were human, she could just disguise herself and slip through the main city gates once they opened in the morning and the crowds began to stream in and out, but that was impossible for her, for she would burn to a cinder under the sun's angry rays. Worse, this would never change. Every night the gates would close, trapping her inside Nuln at the only time she was able to move around, and then open again just after she was forced to seek shelter indoors. Aristocrat of the night? What a joke! More like prisoner of the night.

But then, in the middle of the Handelbezirk, just as she was about to give up and start to seek shelter for the coming day, she walked into a thick, spreading fog, and the rank, wet stink of the river hit her. Her head came up as she inhaled it. The river! Now there was a gate that was difficult to guard.

She cursed as she started through the muffled streets towards the docks. Why hadn't she thought of it sooner? She and Gabriella had travelled from Eiche-shatten to Nuln in a riverboat stateroom and never once had to fear the sun. Of course, booking passage on a passenger ship, even under an assumed name, was not wise. If the Lahmians came asking after her, Ulrika did not have a face and manner a purser was likely to forget. She would have to stow away. But that was even better. No sun ever reached the holds of cargo ships. She could get away in perfect safety, and she wouldn't have to wait until tomorrow night to do it.

EVEN BEFORE SUNRISE, the riverfront was acrawl with industrious activity – both legal and illegal. Captains and harbourmasters checked manifests by lantern light and pried off the lids of crates to inspect the goods inside, while skulking figures made more furtive exchanges in the shadows of the grey wood warehouses. Longshoremen loaded cargo nets and rolled barrels up gangplanks, while in the dark places between the bigger docks little skiffs, hidden by the fog, offloaded contra-band directly into the broken-gated outflow pipes of the sewers, through which it would be distributed to a hun-dred destinations across the city. Women with little wheeled grills rolled them up and down the quayside, selling river trout and hot chowder to the crews, while women in more colourful clothes sauntered at a slower pace, ready to sate the men's baser appetites. Beggars clutched at Ulrika's cloak, moaning for coins, as she edged through the crowd, and hard-looking men eyed her fine clothes and beautiful rapier as they lounged in the doorways of the dockside taverns.

The furious bustle of it all surprised her. She had expected the wharfs to be quiet at this time of day, and had hoped to be able to climb on board an unmanned

ship and slip down into the hold without much difficulty. But there were no unmanned ships. All of them
were swarming with men.

She glanced to the east. There was a definite orange
glow to the fog in that direction now. If she didn't get
on board something soon she would have to give up
and try again tomorrow. Then she saw her way – the
grill women. When they trundled their little barrows up
before a ship and called their wares, the men aboard
would drop their work and hurry forwards for a hot
mug and a quick bite. All she had to do was time it
right.

She began trailing a woman who pushed a bright red
barrow and wailed, 'Hot chowder! Couldn't be
prouder! Hot chowder! I'll sing it louder!'

The men from a long, flat riverboat got the nod from
their bo'sun and filed down off the gangplank, rubbing
their hands and calling cheerful vulgarities to the grill
woman, who answered in kind.

Ulrika sidled casually up to the boat and looked over
its rail. A yawning black hatch was open in the centre of
the broad deck, a pallet of blackpowder barrels hanging
over it on a rope and tackle. She looked back at the
men. They were all crowded around the grill woman,
jostling and making jokes. Unfortunately, the bo'sun
had stayed on board, pacing and going over a sheaf of
papers on the aft deck.

Ulrika clenched her teeth. She would have to risk it –
just as soon as he turned his back. There! With a swift
leap she was over the rail and light-footing across the
deck, then dropped into the hatch.

She landed with a soft thud in a dark, cavernous hold,
her shoulders tensed as she waited for cries of surprise.
They didn't come, and she relaxed. The hold was as long
as the boat, and stacked with blackpowder barrels and
wooden gun-crates with the brand of a local forge

burned into their sides. The stacks were covered in heavy canvas tarps, and stretched all the way back to the aft bulkhead. Ulrika crawled over the piles until she was as far from the hatch as she could get, then wormed under a tarp and nestled amongst the barrels.

A thrill went through her as she pulled off her makeshift pack and made a pillow of it. She had done it. She had escaped Gabriella and Hermione and found a way out of Nuln. She was free. She could go where she pleased, do what she wanted to do, be who she wished to be!

The thought brought her up short. Where *did* she want to go? What did she want to do? Who did she wish to be? She had been so concerned with getting free, she hadn't until this moment given any thought of what she would do with her freedom once she had gained it.

When she had thought Famke would come along, she'd had some vague idea of going off and starting a new life with her outside the confines of the sisterhood, but she hadn't imagined any specifics, just a few jumbled images – galloping down a winding road on a pair of chargers, sleeping in some farmer's hayloft, finding some out-of-the-way place they could live in peace – all storybook nonsense, now that she thought of it. It would have been nothing like that.

The boots of the crewmen thudded on the deck above her, and she heard the calls of rough voices and the squeal of the winch as the pallet of barrels was lowered into the hold and men climbed down after it to roll them into place. Good. They would be off soon.

She returned to her problem. Now that she was on her own, she had no idea what she wanted to do, or where to go. She didn't even know where her boat was going. Should she go to Altdorf? She'd never been to the Empire's capital before, and had always wanted to see it. Should she return to Middenheim, where she knew the graf? Perhaps not. She certainly couldn't renew the acquaintance, and Middenheimers were even more suspicious and fanatical than other Empire folk. It would be a dangerous place to be a vampire. Should she leave the Empire entirely? That was an attractive notion. She could go to Marienburg or Bretonnia, or Tilea, where it was warm and she knew no one, and could start again from scratch.

Then, with sudden clarity, she knew precisely where she wanted to go – where she *must* go. Her rebirth and re-education as a vampire, and the nightmare of Murnau and the murders of the Lahmian sisters, had taken her mind from the things that mattered most to her before her death, but now she was her own woman once again. Now she could do the things that were important to *her*, and nothing was more important to her than the defence of her homeland.

At the time Krieger had stolen her from Praag, the Chaos armies that had besieged the city had just withdrawn for the winter in disarray. But it had been a certainty in everyone's mind that they would return in the spring, and this time the battle would truly be joined. It was the month of Jahrdrung now. Spring was less than two months away. If she started north immediately, she would make it just in time to help in the defence.

She smiled to herself at the thought. She was stronger now, and faster – deadlier than she could ever have imagined. She might not be able to fight side by side with the defenders, but she could do better things. She could sneak into the enemy's camp at night and slit the throats of their leaders. She could turn their troops into mindless swains who would do her bidding instead of theirs. She could sabotage and spy and slaughter, and drown her pain in the blood of battle. It was a perfect plan.

Of course there were dangers in going to Praag as well, both physical and otherwise. Felix and Gotrek and Snorri and Max Schreiber had certainly returned there after they had left her in the countess's care in Sylvania. Gotrek had come close to killing her then. He might not show such forbearance if they met again. And Felix and Max – she had loved them both, and thoughts of them still warmed her and filled her with desire. But these days desire was conflated in her with violence and feeding. More than once she had dreamed she was making love to one or the other of them, only to tear his throat out and drink him dry. What would happen if they actually met?

Despite these dangers, she found herself longing for such a meeting. The dour dwarf, the worldly magister and the moody poet had been her rock for some time. They had given her advice and comfort, and had led by example. They were practical, unflappable men, with little of the narrow-mindedness and fear that was all too common among the peoples of the Empire and Kislev. Hadn't Gotrek allowed her to live, despite the fact she had become a monster in his eyes? Hadn't Felix allied himself with the countess against Krieger, though he knew her true nature?

Suddenly she wanted more than anything to pour out her troubles to them, to tell them of Templar Holmann and the pain that had come when she knew she didn't have the courage to save him from Gabriella. She longed to ask them what she should do, how she should live, how she was to resolve the black knot of conflict that twisted her cold dead heart. She was alone now, and it frightened her. She didn't want to face the world by herself. She wanted companionship.

A mad spark of hope flared at the thought. Perhaps she and Felix and Gotrek and Max could travel together again – have adventures again. She had heard of it happening before. Hadn't a vampire taken up with a great lord years ago and fought an evil sorcerer at his side? Hadn't she even won the favour of the Emperor? Or was that only a story?

A cry of 'Cast away!' and a sideslipping lurch woke her from her thoughts and she looked up, even though there was nothing to see above her but canvas. They were away. She had made her escape. She was free!

It wasn't until she closed her eyes and laid her head back on her makeshift pillow that she discovered, to her horror, that she was growing hungry.

CHAPTER FIVE
THE TYRANNY OF HUNGER

ULRIKA'S EYES FELL open as the immensity of the problem hit her. It was full daylight now – she could feel it – and she was on a boat, with no knowledge of where or when it would next land. She might be trapped for days. On top of that, she had no blood-swain to feed upon, and so must find a victim – something she had never done before.

Panic tightened her chest, and the mad red rage that had sustained and driven her since she had realised that Gabriella had locked her in evaporated in an instant. Why hadn't she thought this through more thoroughly? Famke had been right. It wasn't going to work. She was completely unprepared. From the moment she had been reborn a vampire, her protectors – first Adolphus Krieger, then Countess Gabriella – had given her willing victims to feed upon. She had never had to worry about where her next meal was coming from, and rarely had she been faced with taking blood from the unwilling – such as when Gabriella had told her she must feed on Holmann. She had refused to do it then, for she had felt strongly for the templar, and had not wanted to turn him into a mindless swain. But could she feed on some other man? A stranger? In the end, of course, she would have to – indeed, once her blood hunger consumed her, she would not be able to stop herself. She would become an animal, without conscience or rational thought.

She did not want that to happen. She had sworn to herself and to the memory of her ancestors that she would never lose control again. The beast would not rule her. She would rule the beast. That being the case, she had to make up her mind how she was going to conduct herself while she still had mind enough to think.

She snorted. The situation was ridiculous. What she was doing here was nothing less than laying out the parameters by which she meant to live the rest of her eternal life. What a joke that she was doing it *now*, in the hold of a riverboat, with hunger gnawing at her mind, when, had she been less impetuous, she might have pondered the moral intricacies of the question in the comfort of Gabriella's townhouse, and *then* struck out on her own.

The thought made her suddenly long to go back, to beg Gabriella for forgiveness, to return to the cocoon of comfort it had seemed so important to abandon only a few hours before. But how could she? She couldn't even get off the boat, and even if she could, and could find a way back into Nuln, would Gabriella take her back? Would Hermione let her live? Could she live with herself, with the shame of having given up on her freedom at the first hardship?

No, she couldn't. She wouldn't. She was damned if she would. So, regardless of the inopportune time and place, she had to make a decision.

Her hunger growled that she should feed on whoever

came to hand, that her needs were more important than those of the cattle who surrounded her. She fought it down. She did not want to be like Krieger, her loathsome blood father, who drained innocent girls and left their corpses in alleys. Nor did she want to be like Gabriella, who had killed Templar Holmann with a cold pragmatism Ulrika could not accept. Even feeding on willing swains repelled her, for their slavish devotion to those who had blooded them was sickening to see. But what did that leave her?

If she truly hated what she had become so much that she would not feed at all, then she should kill herself and have done with it. The sun was up. She could end her dilemma instantly by walking up on the deck and burning to ashes, but she knew from experience she hadn't the courage. There had to be another way. If only she could feed just on those she felt deserved it – the wicked, the cruel, those who had become beasts themselves.

Her brain stopped suddenly, stunned at the simplicity of the solution. Why not? Why couldn't she? She could feed without dishonouring her past, or pricking her conscience, and at the same time, she would be doing mankind a service. Nor was there any fear of going hungry by keeping to this moral diet, for the Old World would never run short of evil men. She smiled, baring her fangs. Going to Praag seemed like an even better choice now – a never-ending feast of marauders and madmen. She would feed every night.

But…

Her euphoria crashed to the ground as swiftly as it had risen. *But*, what did she do until then? Upon whom did she prey as she travelled? Upon whom did she feed tonight? Was there a wicked man aboard this boat? How did she find out? Was she supposed to question her victims about their morals before she attacked them? It was laughable. Ridiculous.

She growled to herself, furious at her own foolishness. This waffling was human weakness – self-destructive nonsense. She should have left it behind when she died. She was asking herself to behave in a way that was completely antithetical to her nature.

And yet, how was that different from when she had lived? As a warrior, she had walked the knife-edge of savagery all her life, always on guard against the siren call of slaughter that had lured many a good man to the worship of the Dark Powers. She had resisted then, and she could resist now.

Yes.

She would refuse to make her new nature an excuse to abandon the principles of honour and mercy and restraint she had sworn by while she lived. It would be difficult, but easy things weren't worth doing, and a vow meant nothing until it was tested. She would find a way to live without hurting the innocent, even tonight, even while trapped on this boat. There would be some way. She was sure of it.

She folded her arms across her breast and closed her eyes, relieved to have come to a decision. Now she would sleep, and gather what strength she could to face the challenge that awaited her when the sun went down.

It was not a peaceful sleep, for her hunger grew like a living tumour with each passing hour. Many times during the day, she woke to the baying of it and had to fight it with all her strength before she could find unconsciousness again. Finally, there was no slipping back under. The emptiness in her breast was too painful, and she lay awake, staring at the canvas in front of her face and gripping herself with her claws. She could sense the heart-fires of the crew as they moved around the ship above her. There were five of them, and regardless of the vow she had made, she wanted nothing more than to fill the bare hearth of her cold heart with their warmth.

Why had she not fed upon Gabriella's maid before she had quit Nuln? The girl's blood would have held her for at least two days. When had she last fed? Two nights ago? Longer than that? Even if all had been calm since, she would have been feeling the pangs by now, but her exertions of the night before – escaping Gabriella's house, fleeing from Hermione, racing across the city – had wrung her dry. Her veins ached with want. Her tongue felt as if it were turning to powder. Even her eyes felt dry.

Again she cursed herself for not thinking her escape through more thoroughly. What was wrong with her? It wasn't like her to act without thinking. She was a grown woman and a veteran soldier, experienced in the necessities of travel and well versed in the preparations required before a dangerous journey. She had been in such a tearing hurry to be gone. The red rage that had overcome her had practically dragged her out of the house by her collar.

And that was it, wasn't it? The red rage.

For all her talk of maintaining control of her savagery, Ulrika was so lost in it she didn't even know when she was under its spell. Her actions since the turning of Gabriella's key in the lock had not been those of a woman of the world, but of a petulant child, of a spiteful cat who shreds her mistress's things because she has been left alone. A rush of shame came over her as she remembered her rationalisations for breaking her vow to the countess not to leave the house – and rationalisations were all they had been. Gabriella's actions didn't matter. A vow was a vow, and Ulrika had broken one for no better reason than wounded pride.

She was disgusted with herself, and baffled as well.

She felt as buffeted by emotion now as when she had been fifteen and thought the world a hateful place full of know-nothing adults and locked gates. Why had she reverted to such childish behaviour? Was it because Gabriella treated her like a child? Was the red rage some symptom of her new unlife? Would it cool at some point and allow her to think? She prayed to her father's gods it would be so, and soon.

After a time she crawled out from the tarp and raised her head over the cargo. A lattice of red light slanted down through the grate that covered the hatch. Sunset. Less than an hour to go, but even an hour seemed unbearable. She sat with her knees up and her back to the bulkhead, watching the slow fading of the light because there was nothing else her mind could focus on.

Finally, the last dull purple drained away and everything became shades of grey. She pushed herself to her feet, feeling a hundred years old, and crept unsteadily to the hatch, her head swimming and her limbs trembling with weakness.

She found a ladder lashed to a support post and propped it against the underlip of the hatch, then climbed up to look through the wooden grid of the cover. There was a simple latch – an iron ring with a wooden pin pushed through it to hold it closed – but no lock. She breathed a sigh of relief. That was another thing she hadn't thought through. What if she had been locked in the hold for days or weeks? She couldn't imagine the agony of it.

She extended her senses. The heart-fires of the crew were all at either end of the boat. There were none in the middle near her. She reached her hand up and tugged the pin out of the latch, then listened. No alarm. She put her shoulders to the underside of the hatch and pushed. It was heavy, but despite her weakness, she was still stronger than a man. She lifted it enough that she could edge out onto the deck, then lowered it silently back into place with shaking arms. Still no clamour. She looked around.

The boat was hugging the south bank, a dense black wall of forest that hung out over the river, and looking north, Ulrika saw why. A large flotilla of Imperial warships was cruising down the centre of the river, pennons waving, and all the other water traffic had given them a wide berth. Ulrika's boat and many others were sidling along in the muddy shallows, waiting for them to pass.

Most of the crew were huddled around a cauldron at the back of the boat, eating from wooden bowls and talking amongst themselves. Behind them, a man kept a hand on the tiller. In the prow, another man scanned the river. Ulrika's head throbbed as she looked at him. She could smell his blood, and hear it rushing through his veins. A quick pounce and she would be sated. The agony of her empty heart would go away.

She took an involuntary step towards him, then forced herself to stop. Did she care so little for her vow? Would she break it on a whim like she had her vow to Gabriella? She did not prey on the innocent – and even if she did, how could she feed on him while trapped on a boat? If she let him live, he would tell the others. If she killed him, they would know they had a predator on board. Unless, she thought, she threw him overboard. She forced the thought away. She was *not* going to feed on him. She had to find another way. She had to think. The situation couldn't be impossible.

She crouched in the shadow of the mast and looked back at the men sitting around the cook pot. Perhaps she could sneak close enough to listen to them, and determine who was the most wicked. The hypocrisy of the thought made her cringe. Would she feed on someone because he was a mere bully, and tell her conscience she had done a noble thing? Such self-deceiving rationalising made her sick. It would be more honest to just bleed one and start keeping her vow on the morrow. Aye, honest, but weak.

She growled under her breath. What a stupid thing her conscience was. This morning, when the hunger had only begun to wake, it had been easy to say, 'I will be virtuous. I will only prey on villains.' Now, with blood tantalisingly within reach, and madness and death waiting for her if she did not feed, the words seemed the babblings of an idealist. She must survive, and feeding on men was as natural to her as feeding on cows was to men.

'Henneker!' called the man in the bow. 'Rocks ahead. Turn it north–'

His words cut off as he noticed Ulrika peering from the shadows, and his hand dropped to the club at his belt. 'Stowaway!' he shouted, starting towards her. 'Captain! We got a sneak!'

Ulrika cringed back and turned, but there was nowhere to go. The men in the aft were setting down their bowls and hurrying forwards too, clubs and gaffs in their hands.

'No one stows away on my boat,' growled their leader, a grizzled captain who held a cutlass and a lantern.

'He's a toff by the look of 'im,' said the lookout. 'Look at them boots.'

'Hoy, it's a lass!' laughed another man.

'Why so it is,' said the captain, holding up his lantern as his crew surrounded her. 'Hold still, girl. Let me have a look at you.'

Ulrika backed towards the rail, shielding her face. So close, the smell of their blood overwhelmed her. She couldn't bear it. She wanted to kill them all. She wanted to bathe in their blood. 'Get away!' she shouted. 'Leave me be!'

She tried to push through them, but two grabbed her arms. She snarled and lashed out, tearing at them. They fell back, shouting and clutching bloody wounds, and the rest backed away, staring and terrified.

'Sigmar! She's got fangs!'

'She's a fiend!'

'Kill her!'

Ulrika dropped into a crouch, howling, the beast urging her to attack – to slaughter and feast. But a tiny kernel of pride held her back. She would *not* be slave to her hunger! She would not let it choose the time or place or victim! Those were her decisions to make!

The captain raised his cutlass. 'All together, lads,' he said. 'In Sigmar's name.'

The men surged forwards, finding courage in their numbers, and Ulrika sprang, but not at them. Instead she leapt back on the rail and ran along it, weaving like a drunk in the throes of her weakness.

'Keep back!' she cried. 'Put me ashore! Ashore!'

A great, juddering jolt rocked the ship, slewing it sideways. The rocks! In the excitement, the steersman had forgotten them. Ulrika staggered and grabbed for a rope, but missed. She toppled from the rail and plunged into the swirling black water of the river.

The pain as the waves closed over her head was worse than any she had felt since her rebirth – worse than the ache of blood hunger, worse than the blistering caress of the sun, worse than any wound she had ever taken, live or undead. A bubble of memory pushed through her panic as she fought to reach the surface again – Gabriella afraid of travelling in an open boat, saying that vampires feared water. She knew it from tales told around the fire in her youth as well, but in her frenzy to keep away from the boatmen she had forgotten it.

It had been a fatal lapse. The water was killing her, and all her flailing wouldn't save her. The current was flowing through her body as if she were a ghost, and dragging at her essence. Ulrika could feel it ripping, like a flag in a high wind being torn from a pole. Little translucent tatters of self frayed off and floated downstream, taking with them memories, emotions, joys and sorrows, and each one hurt like her arm being twisted off.

She heard the men from the boat shouting as her head broke the waves again, but she couldn't understand them. She couldn't think. She couldn't see. Then a rank, loamy scent came to her. Earth! The shore! She thrashed towards it, praising the gods that had abandoned her that she could still smell.

The water made her clothes heavy and dragged her below the surface again. As a vampire, she had no need to breathe, but it wasn't drowning that would kill her, it was the merciless current, trying to separate her essence from the undead body to which it unnaturally clung. It sucked at her like a leech, sucked the strength from her arms and the will from her heart. More pieces of self ripped away, taking faces and feelings with them. An insidious voice whispered that the pain would stop if she just gave up and died, but she knew it was a lie. Vampires clung to life so tenaciously because they knew the eternal torment that waited for them with the true death, and she was still too much of a coward to face that.

She struggled on, though in her blindness she had no idea if she made any progress at all. Then her boots struck bottom. Had she sunk, or had the riverbed risen to meet her? The current dragged her sideways along it. She kicked forwards, digging in with her heels, and found she was slogging up a submerged slope. She was nearing the bank.

She reached out her hands and struck what felt like a tree branch. No. A root. She clung to it, trying to draw herself out of the river. The current fought to keep her, tugging on her clothes, weakening her fingers, sucking at her soul, but finally she pulled herself out and collapsed on the bank, blind and shivering uncontrollably, her mind a whirling jumble of pain and broken thoughts.

But one thought remained whole – she had to keep moving. She couldn't stay in the open. The men might come back, the sun *would* come back. She had to hide, but how, when she could not see or stand?

The rancid scent of man came to her nose – sweat, shit and alcohol, faint and faded, and the sharper reek of fish. A fisherman? Was his shack nearby? Was he in it? Would she be able to feed on him? Would she at least be able to hide from the sun? She turned after the scent, like a blind mole sniffing through the earth after grubs, and inched along on her stomach, fingers digging weakly into the dirt and leaf mould.

Every yard seemed a mile, and nausea and vertigo racked her with each slow movement, but after pushing through bracken and pulling herself over the roots of trees, her head struck something flat and hollow. She struggled not to vomit, then reached forwards and ran her hands over the obstruction. It was wooden, and curved, and covered with flaking paint.

Ulrika sobbed. It was a boat. There was no shack, and no fisherman to feed from, just a weathered old skiff pulled up into the trees and turned upside down. She slumped against it. She could go no further. She was too weak to search any deeper into the woods. With the last of her strength, she pushed her way under the boat and curled up on the ground and closed her eyes. She had never been so cold in her life.

SHE STOOD NAKED next to her father's blazing pyre, knee-deep in Sylvanian snow and trying to weep for his death, but the heat from the fire dried the tears before they could be shed. Then, like paper curling as it was eaten by a flame, her father rose up, his hair and beard a mane of fire and his skin melting.

'Join me, daughter,' he said beckoning. 'You must die for what you have become.'

She backed away from him, terrified, but he stepped down from the burning logs and staggered stiff-legged after her, bits of blackened flesh falling from him with each step.

She tripped and fell backwards in the snow, and suddenly it wasn't her father that was closing in on her, but Gotrek the Slayer, the runes on his fell axe glowing cherry-red.

'It won't be quick, girl,' the dwarf growled, as he lowered the axe closer and closer to her throat. 'You don't deserve it.'

The heat from the glowing rune burned her face and chest as she shrank away from the axe's razor edge.

The axe touched her skin.

She screamed.

AND WOKE TO the smell of burning flesh.

A tiny crack in the bottom of the boat was letting in the smallest needle of sunlight, and it had worked its way across her clothes as the sun moved, to the exposed flesh of her neck.

She jerked away and bumped into the side of the boat, then lay gasping and shaking and mewling in pain. She was still shivering with cold, but at the same time burning up as if with fever. The bright glare of the sun showed under the edges of the boat all around her, blinding her, and the heat of it beat down on the overturned bottom, broiling her. Her limbs felt made of twigs, and looked it too. Her wrists, where they stuck out of her velvet cuffs, were nothing but tendons and veins, and her fingers were bone-thin. She couldn't move, couldn't lift her head. If the little lance of light followed her to the side of the boat, she wasn't sure she'd be able to escape it again.

How had she come here? Why was she under a boat? Who... who was she? Fresh panic welled up inside her as she realised she could not remember her name or who she was. She didn't know where she was or why she had come there. The stifling heat and the bone marrow cold had taken all that away, leaving only pain.

She struggled to recall the dream she had just woken from, hoping it would give her clues to who she was. She could not remember. There had been snow, and a burning man, and another with an axe, but she couldn't see their faces. She didn't know their names.

The only thing she did know was she was hungry, a black, empty ache worse than the cold, worse than the heat. It made her want to throw aside the boat and hunt through the forest for blood, but some instinct told her that would be death, that the sun would kill her, burn her like the man on the pyre, so she just lay there, baking and shivering, with her ravenous heart eating her from the inside, watching as the needle of sunlight carved a slow path across the shadowed ground under the boat.

MORE DREAMS CAME, each stranger and more unsettling than the last – Felix burying her, though she called out to him that she wasn't dead, Adolphus Krieger and Countess Gabriella feeding on Friedrich Holmann as Ulrika fought to break free of a cage over a fire, and more delirious wakings, where the boat and the ground spun around her in nauseous loops, and her shivering grew so strong her teeth chattered and she could not lie still.

Then, after a mad dream where her veins broke

through her skin like earthworms and nosed off in all directions in search of sustenance, she woke to find that the sun and the heat had gone and all that was left of her was cold and hunger. The cold was worse than ever, but the hunger was even stronger. Her sickness had disorientated the beast for a time, but now it was back, and would not be denied.

Ulrika cursed it. She was too weak to move. She was too broken in her mind. She couldn't even begin to think of hunting for food, but the beast howled and clawed at her insides, uncaring, and she found she had strength to move after all.

Trembling and limp, she crawled out from under the boat and pushed herself to her knees, then fell as she tried to stand. Her legs wouldn't support her. She crawled instead, away from the river and the boat, deeper into the dark wood, bushes raking her face and rocks stabbing her palms. She could barely see where she was going. Her unnatural vision, which usually allowed her to see in the dark, had grown dim, and the world was nothing but looming tree shadows and river fog.

A while later, the clatter of many hoof beats reached her and she shrank back, fearful. The hooves thundered past somewhere ahead of her, then faded away to the right. Was there a road? She crept forwards again, and moments later found it. She turned in the direction the hooves had gone and inched along in the ditch beside it. If there was a road, there might be a town, and if there was a town, there would be men, and if there were men, she could feed.

SOME ENDLESS TIME later she saw firelight in the distance. At first she thought it was a house, but then she saw it was a coaching inn, a great black shape hunched beside the road with a flickering lantern hanging above its door. She licked her lips. There would be men inside. There would be blood.

She paused to collect herself. Though her mind was still fogged, she knew she would never get close to her prey if she remained on her hands and knees. They wouldn't let her in the door. She gathered her strength and levered herself painfully to her feet, then stood swaying for a moment, fighting swirling vertigo. When she had found some semblance of balance, she lurched forwards, throwing one leaden foot ahead of the other as if it were made of granite.

As she got closer, the heart-fires of the people inside the inn called to her, promising comfort and warmth. Her veins ached at their nearness, and her steps quickened with need. Unfortunately, they grew no more graceful and, as she reached the stable yard gate, she toppled forwards to land on her face on the cold dry ground.

A cry of surprise came from the yard, and she struggled to get up and away, but she could go no further. She could not rise again. She was too weak, and the pain was too great. She pawed uselessly at the dirt as heavy footsteps drew nearer.

CHAPTER SIX
MERCY'S REWARD

'OLD MAN,' SAID a male voice. 'Old man, are ye well?'

Ulrika didn't know who the voice was talking to, and didn't care. All she cared about was getting away. With a supreme effort, she got her elbows under her and dragged herself an excruciating inch.

A hand cupped her shoulder and rolled her over on her back. She squinted up at the round face of a sturdy middle-aged groom. 'Old man,' he said. 'Are ye havin' a fit–' He started back, frightened, and made the sign of the hammer. 'A-a lass? Sigmar preserve us, girl, you gave me a fright. Skin and bones and pale as death. What's wrong with ye? Are ye sick?'

Ulrika could do nothing but moan. His blood scent was overwhelming. She reached for him, trembling with hunger.

He edged away, unnerved, then a calculating look came into his eyes. 'Well, ye look rich enough, though. What have ye done? Run away in yer brother's clothes? Mayhap yer people'll pay t'have ye back. Aye, mayhap.' He took her hands, then tsked. 'So cold. Yer near frozen through.' He knelt down and scooped her up in his arms like she weighed nothing. 'Can't have ye dyin' can we? No money in that. Come on.'

Ulrika clung to him as he carried her through the yard to the stables, her head resting on his shoulder. His bare neck was only inches from her teeth. She strained to reach it, but he put her down on a pile of hay bales next to a little iron stove and turned away. As he rummaged through a cupboard, Ulrika could hear the stamping and shifting of stabled horses to her right.

'Soon have ye bundled up,' he said, 'Then I'll fetch ye some broth from Frau Kilger's kettle. That'll warm yer insides.'

He turned back to her, his arms full of horse blankets, then proceeded to drape them over her one at a time until she felt as if she was being buried. She wanted to curse the simpleton and tell him, 'These won't warm me. I need blood!' but all she could do was moan and struggle futilely.

Finally he stepped back and shook his head. 'What must have happened to ye to turn yer hair white so young? Ah, it's a wicked world, a wicked world.' He tsked again, then turned for the door. 'Broth's coming. Won't be a moment.'

Ulrika frowned as he padded off across the yard. Her hair wasn't white. It was dirty blonde. She worked her arm laboriously out from under the heavy strata of blankets, then reached up and tugged down a wet lock. It was just long enough for her to see the ends of it, and it was white as milk.

Panic and uncertainty welled up in her. When had this happened? Had she always had white hair? Did she just not remember? She tried to think back to the last time she had seen herself. She couldn't. She couldn't even remember what she looked like. Who *was* she? The pain in her head wouldn't let her focus long enough to work it out.

The groom's heart-fire re-appeared at the edge of her senses, and after a moment he came back through the door, balancing a bowl of steaming soup on a plate.

'There we are,' he said soothingly as he crossed to her. 'Hot from the pot, and I brought ye some bread too.' He set the bowl down on the hay bale next to her and pulled a wooden spoon from his belt. 'Now then, have a sip of that. Er, ye are from money, aye?' he asked, pausing with the spoon hovering over the bowl. 'Not some damned play actor?'

Ulrika swallowed convulsively. The smell of the soup did nothing for her, but his blood scent once again filled her nose, and she could think of nothing else. The voice of her pride admonished her not to break her vow, but it was weak and faint and she squashed it like a cricket. She must feed. It was that or die.

With the hand that was free of the blankets she beckoned to him.

'C'm 'ere...' she murmured. 'Cl'ser.'

'What's that yer sayin', lass?' he asked, and put his ear to her mouth. 'I can't hear ye.'

With strength born of need, Ulrika clamped her hand around the back of his neck and pulled him down, her fangs shooting out. He grunted in surprise, then yelped and reared back to his feet as she bit deep into his neck.

'What are ye doin'?' He shrieked. 'Get off! Get off!'

Ulrika came up with him, clinging like a limpet, and sucked in his blood in great gulping swallows, her senses reeling with the taste and power of it.

The groom staggered around the stable, cursing and struggling to push her away, but with each mouthful of crimson elixir she grew stronger and stronger. All her senses came back to her. The dark corners of the stable became clear, and her mind sharpened. She wrapped her legs around his middle and held tighter, drinking all the while. Then, revoltingly, his struggles slowly turned to caresses, and he moaned and crushed her to him.

'Yes,' he murmured. 'Kiss... more...'

Ulrika's stomach turned. It was always the way, and she hated it. The victims got as much pleasure out of feeding as she did, which was a kindness, she supposed, but their mewling revolted her. Even disgust, however, was not enough to stop her feeding. Her veins begged for more, and still more, and she could not deny them.

Only when the groom collapsed and sprawled on his back did she wake to the fact that she was close to draining him entirely, and even then it was hard to pull away. Finally, however, she shoved back, gasping and cursing, and knelt over his prostrate form, blood dripping on his broad chest from her wet red mouth. She had broken her vow, but at least she could refrain from killing him. With no mistress around to feed his desire, he would recover eventually from the kiss, at least she hoped so.

'I'm sorry,' she mumbled. 'I'm sorry.'

She reached for the purse on her belt, thinking to pay him for what she had done, but it wasn't there. She had lost it somewhere during her long crawl, or maybe even before. Had she had it while under the boat? Had she ever had a purse?

A door slammed as she wiped her mouth. Footsteps and heart-fires were coming out into the yard from the inn, accompanied by hearty voices and slurring laughter. She froze, praying they would go away.

'Ho, Herman!' called one of the voices. 'Our horses!'

'And ye better have that stone out of Cecile's shoe,' said another. 'She's miles to go by morning.'

'By the hammer,' swore a third. 'Where *is* he?'

The footsteps started towards the stable. Ulrika surged up, ready to flee, but then collapsed on top of the groom again, nauseous and dizzy. She had drunk too much too fast. Her belly felt as full as a wineskin. Her head throbbed and her vision blurred. She pushed up again, fighting down the urge to vomit.

A man loomed in the open stable door. 'Herman! Where–?' He stopped dead when he saw Ulrika hunching over the unconscious groom. 'Sigmar's beard!' he gasped, and backed away, clawing for the pistol he wore at his belt. Ulrika saw the badge of Wissenland on his right shoulder. He was a roadwarden.

'A fiend!' he cried. 'A vampire!'

Three more wardens crowded the door behind him and cursed in their turn, drawing swords and pistols. Ulrika staggered up then dived aside as the first warden fired. The shot was deafening in the small space and the horses reared and whickered in their stalls.

'Shallya's tears,' a warden cried as they pushed through the door. 'It's killed Herman.'

Ulrika looked around as she scrambled for the shadows. She'd trapped herself. There was only one exit from the stables, and the roadwardens were standing in it. There was nothing here but stalls and horses.

She heard another hammer draw back and threw herself into an empty stall just as a second pistol thundered. She groaned and clutched her bloated stomach. All she wanted to do was lie down and sleep. She was too sick to fight.

'Did you get it?' asked a warden.

'Might have winged it,' said another. 'Reload and go cautious anyhow.'

Ulrika looked up. Perhaps she could leap over the wall of the stall when they reached her, and get around them that way. But wait. There was a hole in the ceiling, leading to the hayloft.

'Ready?' came the first warden's voice.

'Aye,' said the others.

Ulrika heard more hammers drawing back, and gathered her legs under her, preparing to spring and praying her belly and wobbly limbs didn't betray her.

'Now!'

The roadwardens charged forwards. Ulrika jumped to the top of the dividing wall as they fired blindly into the stall. She teetered, dizzy, then leapt for the hole in the ceiling.

The edge caught her painfully in the ribs, but she dug her claws into the straw-covered planks and pulled.

'Where's it gone?' rasped a warden.

'Above us!'

A blast shot between Ulrika's feet just as she scrabbled out of the hole. She collapsed, groaning, on the loft floor, and this time she did vomit, splashing a flood of blood across the weathered boards and watching it vanish down the cracks between.

'Blood! We've wounded it!'

'Fetch a ladder!'

She pushed to her hands and knees and looked around. The walls angled to a peak above her head, and there was hay stacked all around. At the far end was the hay door, through which they winched the bales when they put them up for storage.

A ladder slapped against the edge of the hole, and she heard it creak as someone started to climb.

Ulrika lurched to her feet and stumbled towards the closed door, but just as she reached it, she heard a soft voice croak from below. 'Masters, don't kill her. Please.'

There was a general swearing, and then the first warden spoke. 'He's alive, poor fellow.'

'Aye, that's worse,' said another. 'Have to kill him now, before he turns.'

Ulrika stopped, the hay door half-open. What nonsense was this? He wouldn't become a vampire. She hadn't given him the dark kiss. She turned back, wanting to go down and kill them all to protect the groom from their ignorance.

A warden rose through the hole in the floor and fired. A hammer-blow impact punched her backwards through the hay door. She fell, flailing, then slammed hard on her shoulders in the cold mud of the yard, a sick, burning pain blossoming in her shoulder as her body rang with shock and the world dimmed and wavered.

There were shrieks and feminine cries from nearby, and then the voice of the shooter calling from inside the stables. 'I hit it! It's fallen into the yard!'

Ulrika's vision cleared and she struggled to sit up, hissing in pain. People were pouring out of the inn, drawn by the sound of the pistol shots, and gabbled and pointed at her. From the stables came shouts and the thudding of boots.

She forced herself to her feet and ran unsteadily for the fence at the back of the yard – and the dark stand of trees beyond it. The wardens roared for her to stop, and a pistol ball whizzed by her as she vaulted the pickets and crashed through a thick cover of brush into the trees.

A few yards in, she crouched down behind a broad trunk and puked again, spilling more of poor Herman's blood, then wiped her mouth and looked back. Two of the wardens were on top of the fence, one leg slung over, and staring into the woods as they reloaded their pistols. Neither, however, looked eager to venture into the darkness, and after a moment they turned back and dropped back into the inn yard.

Ulrika let out a sigh of relief and slumped down against the bole of the tree, then winced in pain. They would likely come after her soon, but she had a few moments while they gathered lanterns and torches, and she could not move on until she took the ball from her shoulder. It ground against her clavicle with every move, and if she left it where it was, her swift healing, fuelled by the blood she had ingested, would seal it inside her.

She pulled off her doublet and shirt, and winced at the sight of her emaciated arms and her ribs showing through her skin. It seemed it was going to take more than one feeding to return her to her old self. Then, pressing against the tree to steady herself, she extended the claws of her left hand and probed gently into the wound until she found the little lead nugget. The pain of her exploration was nothing compared to the agony of digging behind it and pulling it out through torn shoulder meat, but the relief when she threw it into the brush was exquisite.

As she tore her sleeve into strips to make a bandage, her mind, fogged and confused since she had crawled from under the boat, began to clear at last. She knew who she was again. She knew who she had been and what she was now. She knew where she was heading. But there were terrifying gaps – faces with no names, names with no faces. Was her father dead? She thought so, but couldn't be sure. Had she made love to Max Schreiber, or had they only been friends? She no longer knew.

The biggest hole was the most recent. She could remember the pain of sinking in the river, and crawling from it to the little boat, but the last clear memory she had before that was fleeing from Hermione's house and running through Nuln. How had she got from there to the water? She had vague flashes of lying for a long time in a confined space, and others of men shouting at her, and of falling, but that was all. The rest was gone. She had no idea what had transpired.

She was just tying off the bandages when she heard a muffled pistol shot and ducked, then looked around. No one was shooting at her. There was no one outside the inn yard fence. Who were they firing at?

Then she understood. The roadwardens had just shot Herman to keep him from turning into a vampire. She snarled, baring her fangs. Stupid men! She had spared him! She had done her best to honour her vow and let him live, and it had still come out wrong! Why was she so concerned about not killing men when they seemed to have so little compunction about killing each other? She was tempted to go back and prove herself the monster the wardens thought her, but she forced herself to be calm. She needed no more pistol wounds, and the night needed no more death.

With a last venomous glare in the direction of the inn, she pulled on her now-sleeveless shirt and her holed doublet, slung her makeshift pack over her shoulder and limped deeper into the woods, wondering if she would ever find a way to live without causing misery everywhere she went.

CHAPTER SEVEN
THE MIDNIGHT ROAD

ULRIKA CREPT TOWARDS the highwaymen on silent feet. There were two, both on horseback, looking down on a lonesome stretch of moonlit road from the top of a low hill, and she was coming up behind them through a stand of slender trees. They were hard men, in shabby leathers and patched cloaks, with faces scarred by war, weather and drink, but one of them affected a bright feather in his broad-brimmed hat.

'I tell ye, young Ham,' that one was saying. 'Style matters. Style will keep y'from the gallows.'

Ham, an ugly, lumpen young fellow, guffawed. 'G'wan, Nikko. How's a feather in yer cap gonna save y'from the drop?'

"T'aint just the feather, laddie,' said Nikko. 'It's the whole thing. Why, if y'go in crackin' skulls and makin' widows of all and sundry before y'grab their loot, they hate ye, y'see. They scream to the wardens and call for the jaggers, and pretty soon yer on the wrong end of a foxhunt. But–' he reached up and tapped the brim of his hat, 'if ye swan in with a fancy bow and a merry, "stand and deliver!" and ye pay compliments to the ladies as ye take their purses and pearls, why then, they almost love ye for it. They've got a grand story to tell their friends – robbed by a dashing gentleman of the road – and they ain't so inclined to go to the chasers.'

Ham grunted. 'Sounds like a lot o'bother. And what if some coachman unloads with a pair of barkers. Am I supposed t'kiss his hand, then?'

Nikko shrugged. 'Y'can kill any number of coachmen and outriders and wardens as ye like. The marks want t'know yer dangerous. Gives 'em a thrill. Y'just can't kill the quality. Nobody cares if a few peasants gets it – not even t'other peasants – but ye kill a nob and they'll chase ye from here to Marienburg.'

A distant rumble brought their heads up, and they looked to the south. Ulrika looked too. A coach flashed past a break in the trees, winding along the road that would pass below the hill.

'Here we go,' said Ham, lifting a crossbow from a hook on his saddle.

Nikko jammed his hat down firmly on his head and drew a pistol. 'Just don't shoot 'til they show fight this time, aye?'

Ulrika rose from her crouch. It was now or never. She'd lose her prize once the coach came into range. She stepped from the woods, directly behind them, unarmed. 'Stand and deliver, gentlemen.'

The highwaymen almost jumped out of their saddles. They spun to stare at her as she strode between their horses.

'Who in Ranald's name are you?' asked Ham.

'Get away,' snarled Nikko. 'Yer spoilin' our game.'

'You,' said Ulrika, 'are my game.'

With a lightning hand she caught Ham's arm and jerked him from his horse to slam on the ground. Nikko cried out and swung his pistol at her. She ducked and twisted it from his hand, then cracked him on the temple with it. He slumped to the ground beside his companion as their horses danced nervously aside, eyes rolling.

Ham was on his knees, drawing his dagger from his belt. 'Ye mannish bitch,' he snarled. 'I'll have yer liver for this!'

Ulrika kicked the dagger from his hand and hauled him up by the front of his leather jerkin, though he was nearly double her weight. He tried to throw a fist, but she caught it.

'Leave off!' he shouted, struggling. 'Leave-'

His words died as she opened her mouth and let out her fangs.

'Sigmar protect me,' he whimpered.

'You, murderer?' said Ulrika, raising an eyebrow. 'I doubt he cares.'

She sank her teeth into his neck and drank, closing her eyes as the soothing warmth of his blood filled her and his struggles quietened.

She fed with perfect control. Taking only enough to give her strength, but not so much as to bloat her or make her drunk with it. And when she was done, she killed with perfect control. A quick twist to snap his spine, and Ham sagged to the ground, limbs asprawl, a beatific expression on his ugly face.

She turned to Nikko, who stared groggily at her from where he had fallen.

'Mercy,' he whispered, crabbing backwards. 'Mercy! I won't tell a soul.'

Ulrika hesitated, considering. Nikko was no brute like Ham. He was handsome for his years, and had a friendly way about him. She could give him mercy if she wished. She would be far away by morning, once she had stolen his horse and ridden north. Even if he told, they would never catch her. But then she thought of his callous words, how he was willing to kill any number of coachmen and outriders because peasants didn't matter. She snarled. A dashing feather could hide a vile heart.

'Aye,' she said, drawing her rapier. 'You won't.'

He screamed and tried to run, but her blade lashed out and decapitated him before he gained his feet. His head bounced free of his hat and began to roll slowly down the hill, just as the coach thundered by.

Ulrika watched it out of sight, then knelt and searched the highwaymen, taking from them what coin and gear she could use, and stuffing it all in a sturdy pack she had stolen from a previous victim. It was more than two weeks since the incident with Herman and the roadwardens, and she had made good progress towards Praag, but the journey had by no means been easy or pleasant.

Ulrika could not have imagined before she left Nuln how difficult travel would be for a creature of the night. For a start, even after she had filled out again and regained the appearance of health, she had neither the face nor hair nor manner of dress that lent themselves to blending in. No matter where she went she was noticed, and noticed was the last thing a vampire wanted to be. A Lahmian sister, dressed as a great lady, or a servant, or a harlot, might be catalogued and dismissed, forgotten as soon as she was seen, but people didn't stop looking at Ulrika. They were always taking another glance, trying to work out what she was. Was she a woman or a man? Old or young? A bravo or a dandy? And if they looked too long, they might notice something else – the pallor of her skin, the coldness of her touch, the inhuman something that made dogs bark fearfully when she was near.

So she'd learned to find shelter away from places where humans congregated, in farmers' barns, in ruined towers, under haystacks and curled up in roadside

shrines. But as she'd continued further north, and travelled deeper into the Great Forest, even such meagre
shelters were not always available, and she'd had to,
more than once, burrow under the leaf mould of the
forest floor and pray nothing disturbed it before the sun
went down.

Even more difficult was the challenge of feeding regu-
larly. After the shame and tragedy of poor Herman,
Ulrika had become more determined than ever to master her hunger, and to feed only on those that deserved
it, so she was forever seeking out the worst of humanity
and luring them to their doom. On her journey so far
she had drunk from bandits and thieves, from murderers and pimps, from cultists, rapists, poisoners and
thugs. Such hunting had been relatively easy in the
towns of the south – though she had twice been seen
and chased from a village by peasants armed with
torches and pitchforks – but again, the further into the
northern forests she went, the harder it became. Even
along the major coach roads, she sometimes went a
night without seeing a single man, let alone a villain.

Because of all these dangers, she had grown more cautious and methodical. Now she began looking for
shelter hours before sunrise, rather than scurrying
around in a mad rush while the sky grew pink. Now she
made sure to feed before venturing off into desolate
areas, and always enquired the distance to the next
town. Now she kept an ear out at inns, listening for
rumours of bandits and plundered wagons. Now she
cut the throats of the men she fed from, in order to hide
the telltale bite marks she left.

Still, for all that she had got better at it, it was a hard,
unpleasant life, and she often dreamed of returning to
Gabriella and begging forgiveness so she could be snug
and safe again in the comforting nest of Lahmian luxury. But every time she was tempted, she reminded

herself of the countess saying she might have slaves but not friends, and of the deaths of Friedrich Holmann and Lotte the maid, and the spaniel-eyed fawning of the blood-swains, and it strengthened her resolve. She would not trade honour for comfort. There had to be another way to be a vampire.

There *had* to be.

Ulrika picked up Nikko's wide, feathered hat from where it had fallen and tried it on. It was a good fit. With the rough leather jerkin and heavy patched cloak she had acquired along the way, she imagined she looked a proper vagabond now – which was all to the good. A ragged traveller was much less conspicuous than a white-haired dandy in black velvet.

She tied the leads of Ham's horse to Nikko's saddle, then mounted and turned to the north.

IN ANOTHER TWO weeks Ulrika was across the Kislev border, and two weeks after that, she was within sight of the towers of Praag, far in the distance across the flat plains of the central oblast. Travel through them had been even more difficult than through the forests of the Empire, because towns were even sparser, and cover in an almost treeless land even harder to find.

She'd lost the two horses just after Kislev, when she'd been caught feeding and had had to flee without going back to where she'd hitched them. Since then, she had made her way by following a supply caravan – a mile-long procession that was bringing timber, grain, guns and cavalry remounts to Praag to support the remains of the Ice Queen's army there, as well as food and arms for the siege that was sure to come when the hordes returned in the spring.

The caravan moved slowly enough that Ulrika could make up at night whatever distance it had covered during the day, and it was always surrounded by ne'er-do-wells and villains – men who attempted to steal the supplies, cheat the soldiers who guarded them, or lure away their camp followers for evil purposes, so she had a steady supply of predators to prey upon no matter where they were. She did her best to pick men of such evil and unreliable reputations that no one would care or wonder if they went missing, but even so, by the end of the first week the camps were whispering about a monster that followed them, and dragged away men in the night.

She didn't feed every night – that would have been too dangerous – and to her pleasant surprise, she found she no longer needed to. Where once missing blood for even a single day had been agony, now she found she could go sometimes as much as three days before the pangs became unbearable. She didn't like to leave it too long, however, for it wouldn't do to be weak and desperate if something went wrong, or if she became separated from the caravan, so she tried to feed every third night and never from the same campfire twice in a row.

As the caravan had got closer to Praag, Ulrika had begun to see reminders of the Chaos invasion of the previous year – burnt towns, abandoned farms, mounds of earth covering hastily dug mass graves, and gaunt peasants whose fields and stores had been raided twice, once by the invaders when they came south, and a second time by the Ice Queen's armies when they had arrived to push the hordes north again.

She also saw signs that some marauders had not retreated. Columns of Gospodar winged lancers often thundered past, their eagle-wing banners snapping in the wind, and sometimes with barbaric severed heads impaled on their lance tips. Rumour flitted around the campfires that this or that caravan had been raided by crazed northerners who came howling out of the night and vanished again with captives and plunder, none knew to where. Ulrika saw a farm burning on the horizon one night, and passed through the smouldering ruins of a little town the next, its citizens butchered and violated in unspeakable ways. She snarled with patriotic loathing at each atrocity. Her homeland had been defiled, and worse was yet to come. She almost relished the return of the hordes in the spring. It would give her opportunity for vengeance.

Finally, that morning, just before she had bedded down in the root cellar of a gutted farmhouse, she had seen the distant onion-domed towers of Praag glittering in the first pink rays of the rising sun, and now that it was evening there was only one last march to go. She would be in the city before daylight, and then... and then...?

Her spine tingled with fear and excitement. In only a few hours she might be seeing Felix and Max and Gotrek again. Should she do it? Could she? Could she not? And what would be the aftermath? She might be dead the next instant, killed by the Slayer's dread axe. Worse, she might be shunned. They might turn from her in loathing. Perhaps that was better. She would know where she stood. And if Felix or Max welcomed her with open arms, could she control herself? Would she love them, or feed on them?

With a snort of impatience she picked up her pack and crawled out of the cellar. She had come too far to turn back now.

It was only a few hours later when Ulrika heard the screams. They drifted to her over a rise in the road, faint upon the wind. She picked up her pace, and as she reached the crest she heard clashes too. There was a battle somewhere ahead of her, hidden by intervening hills. She licked her lips. A battle meant blood, and it would be wise to feed before entering the uncertainty of the city. She hurried on, pack bouncing on her back, and after a long run over the rumpled landscape, came over a hill and saw, in the cup of a valley, a scene of savage slaughter.

A marauder warband, huge gaunt men, their half-naked bodies painted in purple woad and pierced all over with strange bone fetishes, were swarming a caravan – *her* caravan, the one she had travelled with since Kislev – while the soldiers and mercenaries who guarded it fought in a swiftly dwindling circle, outnumbered two to one. Mutated war hounds, their hides like armour and their muzzles dripping red, fought beside their barbaric masters, tearing out throats and intestines, while the leader of the band, a scarred bald gargantua on a hellish black horse, dealt death with axes in both hands.

A blistering rage gripped Ulrika at the sight. She had protected these people since Kislev, picking off the human wolves who would have thinned their ranks, and now, almost within shouting distance of Praag, they were attacked? How dare these northern scum touch her flock! They were hers to cull!

She whipped her rapier and dagger from their sheaths and sped down the hill, aiming for the giant on the horse. The marauders did not notice her as she charged their backs, and she killed four before they knew she was amongst them. Even when they turned, howling with outrage, they could barely stand against her. Her blades were so swift, and her arms so strong, that she could knock their attacks away and run them through almost at will. What a thrill to fight this way! Her reactions were twice what they had been when she was alive, and her strength even greater. Marauders fell back from her with neat little holes in their tattooed chests, dying with almost no blood spilled. Others lost hands and arms to her questing blades. She was a whirlwind!

But soon even her inhuman prowess was not enough to counter their numbers. They swarmed in behind her as she pressed forwards, and battered at her from all sides. A sword cut her back. Another sliced her over the eye. A mace stunned her shoulder. She staggered and nearly stepped into the swipe of an axe. This was madness. Had she thought she could fight a hundred men at once? Her bloodlust had caught her once again. She would not be able to reach the leader. She would have to get out.

She slashed around wildly with her rapier, then drove for the edge of the battle, running one marauder through the neck and opening the lean belly of another with her dagger. A third swung a stone maul at her. She pierced his ribs as it whooshed over her head, then vaulted his toppling body and ran for the brush by the side of the road.

Four marauders howled after her while the rest turned back towards the beleaguered defenders. Ulrika smiled. Four she could deal with. Four she could make use of.

The marauders crashed through the low scrub after her as she turned to face them. She killed the first as his feet got tangled in twisting roots, then ran the second through as he leapt over his dying comrade. Unfortunately, he crashed down on top of her and she had to twist aside to avoid being knocked flat. The third took advantage of her awkward position and aimed a slash at her unprotected back. She just blocked it with her dagger, spun and took his head off with her rapier.

The last, a towering brute with painted black lips and purple cord sewn through the flesh of his chest like the laces of a corset, came in roaring and swinging an enormous axe, and leaving himself wide open for any number of death thrusts. Instead Ulrika only disarmed him, gashing his fingers as another clumsy blow whistled past her and making him drop the weapon.

He howled and drew his dagger from his belt, but she knocked that out of his hand too, then threw down her weapons and leapt on him, claws extended, like a mountain cat attacking a bear. Her hands caught his throat and she clamped down on it as he roared and battered at her with heavy fists, trying to knock her away. A punch to the temple and a knee to the groin stopped all that, and he sagged to his knees, moaning.

She shoved him onto his back and straddled him, never breaking her grip on his throat, then leaned in and showed him her fangs. A glimmer of fear finally flickered in his mad eyes.

'This is my land, Norse,' she breathed. 'I will defend it with sword and knife and tooth and claw. I will feed on any who defile it. I will–'

Her grand speech was cut off by a tantara of horns and the thunder of two hundred hooves. She looked up. Pouring down into the valley from the direction of Praag was a full company of Gryphon Legion cavalry, lances lowered and feathered banners cracking in the night wind.

CHAPTER EIGHT
ON THE WINGS OF GRYPHONS

CONFLICTING EMOTIONS SWIRLED within Ulrika as she saw the Gryphons galloping towards the melee – pride in their martial glory, relief for the poor caravanners and love for one of the great symbols of her land, but also worry. Would they see her before she could feed? Would they attack her?

Her painted captive took advantage of her distraction and threw her off, scrambling for his axe. She caught him by the ankle and brought him down again, then pinned his arms to his sides and looked back. The Gryphons were fighting the marauders, and hadn't the advantage of her nocturnal vision. They were unlikely to see her and her prey in the thick brush. She would risk it.

As the marauder struggled in her embrace, she sank her teeth into his dirty neck and drank, then immediately jerked back, spitting and cursing, as crimson sprayed her face and clothes. His blood tasted as dirty and rank as he smelled, but if it had been only that, she would have drunk her fill. The taste, however, was the least of it. There was a taint within his blood, a sickening, dizzying wrongness that sparked mad whisperings in her mind and sent feathery tendrils probing through her veins like poison-winged moths looking for places to lay their eggs. The marauders had been feeding so long at the teat of Chaos that they were now carriers, and anything that fed on them would become as twisted and mad as they. She dared not drink more.

The marauder got an arm free and punched her. She caught it and pinned it under her knee, then grabbed his head and twisted. His powerful neck muscles fought her, but her strength won out and she snapped his neck and he subsided. She leaned over him, cursing and shoving her finger down her throat to try to puke out the mouthful of vile blood she had swallowed.

Before anything came up, however, heavy hoof strikes shook the ground. She looked up. A handful of marauders were fleeing towards her, with six Gryphons bearing down on them from behind, lances lowered.

Ulrika cursed and rolled, dragging the marauder on top of her as his comrades bounded past her and the Gryphons thundered over her. Had they seen her? Had they seen what she was doing?

The Gryphons ran the marauders down, impaling them on their lances, then wheeled back towards the main battle, and straight for Ulrika. Ursun's teeth, they were going to find her! And she was covered in blood!

But what of it?

Suddenly she saw possibilities. Hadn't there been a battle? Wasn't she wounded? Blood was to be expected. And now that she thought of it, getting into Praag at night by herself might be just as hard as getting out of Nuln had been. If the Gryphons were stationed there, perhaps she could ride in with them. She smiled to herself. Now she was thinking like a Lahmian.

She wiped the blood from her mouth and chin, then

struggled under the marauder as if she were fighting him. The patrol was almost upon her.

'Help, brothers!' she called. 'Help me!'

The Gryphons turned, but as they started for her, Ulrika grunted in dismay, realising she had made a mistake. The marauder's neck was a torn ruin. They would see it! Where was her dagger? There! She clawed for it.

One of the Gryphons, a dashing young Gospodar with a proud nose and magnificent moustaches, slid from his saddle and stabbed the marauder in the back with his sabre, then pulled him off. Ulrika snatched up the dagger at last, then rolled with the corpse and straddled it, stabbing wildly at the bite wound in its neck, as if mad with rage and fear.

'Filthy savage!' she cried. 'Monster!'

'Easy, fellow – er, madam,' said the Gryphon, catching her arm. 'He's dead now.'

Ulrika reeled back and let herself slump against him. 'Thank you,' she murmured. 'There were too many.'

The Gryphon helped her to her feet, giving her an appreciative once over, then waved his fellows away. They turned their horses, smirking, and galloped back into the melee, which still raged around the surrounded caravan.

'There now,' said the Gryphon, picking up her rapier and returning it to her. 'Are you hurt?'

She shook her head. 'I don't know. It… it all happened so fast.'

'Let me have a look at you.' He held her at arm's length and gave her another longish head-to-toe, then returned to business and squinted at the gash over her eye, tsking softly. 'Well, it's bloody, but not very deep. Listen, I must get back, can you make it on your own to our field surgeon? He'll be setting up just there on the hill. I'll come check on you after.'

'Thank you, sir,' she said. 'I believe I can, and I am most obliged to you.'

He looked back at the corpses of the marauders as he mounted his horse. 'You gave better than you got, that's certain,' he said approvingly, then dug his spurs in and galloped after his comrades. 'See you soon!' he called over his shoulder.

Ulrika waved after him, then turned and made her way around the edges of melee towards a little pony cart that had drawn up on the low hill. She watched enviously as the Gryphons wheeled and charged in formation, trampling the disorganised marauders like so much wheat. Her blood rage was still upon her, and she wanted more than anything to join in the slaughter, but she didn't dare. In the frenzy of battle she might forget herself and reveal her unnatural strength, or let out her fangs and claws. Besides, she had written herself a part as a nobly wounded maiden, who needed the care and attention of a brave man, and it wouldn't do to let her 'saviour' see her back in the fray, fighting like a whirlwind.

IN LESS THAN a quarter of an hour it was finished, and the Gryphons were victorious. As the rescued caravanners crept out from behind their circled wagons to thank the white-bearded Gryphon captain, and a few selected squads chased down the last of the fleeing marauders, the rest began the dirty work of collecting the corpses of their fallen comrades and heaping the bodies of the Norsemen onto piles for burning.

Ulrika watched it all from the Gryphons' field hospital, where the surgeon and his assistants bandaged and stitched up lancer and caravaner alike, and the screams of the wounded almost drowned out the hiss of hot pitch being applied to the stumps of amputated limbs. She sat as far away from the surgery as she could, for the

swallow of tainted blood she'd had from the marauder
had not sated her hunger in the least, and the scent of
honest human blood was making her head swim.

A while later, as the wounded and the dead were
being loaded onto any wagon that had room, and the
lancers and caravanners were sorting out their order of
march and making ready to move out, the dashing
Gryphon at last rode up the hill to where Ulrika still
waited, and the surgeon and his assistants were packing
up their cart.

'You look a proper veteran now,' he said, grinning at
the bandage she wore wrapped around her head. He
glanced again at her leather jerkin and boots. 'You really
are a very martial sort of girl, aren't you?'

'I am from a riding family on the border of Troll
Country, sir,' she said, standing. 'Everyone fights there,
daughters as well as sons.'

The Gryphon looked at her with new respect. 'Your
family serves with the march wardens? They are brave
fellows. Good with a lance.' A thought came to him. 'Listen, some men from those lands make their camp near
us. What is your surname? Perhaps your people are
among them.'

Ulrika tensed. She was on dangerous ground. If she
gave a name he knew, she could be caught in a lie. If she
gave her real name, he might know it. Worse, he might
try to bring her to the north country camp, and there
was a very real danger that her father's old rota might be
there. The last people she wanted to see were Yuri or
stern old Marek.

She shook her head. 'I believe my family was wiped
out trying to hold the northern passes. I… I was in
Kislev, visiting relatives, when word came of the invasion, and I was stuck there all winter. Now I am going
north to… to learn if any still live.'

The Gryphon looked grave. 'I am sorry to hear it, lady.

I hope you have good news.' He looked her up and down again, then put his hand to his chest. 'I am Petr Ilanovich Chesnekov, of Volksgrad, at your service. If there is anything I can do to help…'

Ulrika hung her head to hide a smile. The Lahmian way seemed to be working quite well. 'Ulrika Magdova… uh, Nochivnuchka,' she said, remembering at the last minute not to use her real name. 'An honour to meet you, Petr Ilanovich Chesnekov, and I would not impose on you more than I have, but…'

'Speak, Madam Nochivnuchka,' he said. 'If it is in my power, I will do my best to serve.'

She paused, as if hesitant, then continued. 'I have a cousin within Praag who might be able to tell me more of my family. It would be a great weight off my mind if I could enter the city tonight to speak to her. I cannot bear another moment of uncertainty, but I fear the gates are closed.'

Chesnekov beamed. 'Not for the lances of the Gryphon Legion, they are not. It will be an honour to escort you into Praag, madam.' His eyes glittered eagerly. 'In fact, you may ride with me if you wish.'

'I would be most grateful, sir,' she said, stepping forwards. 'Thank you.'

She almost vaulted up behind him, but then remembered who and what she was meant to be. So instead she waited while he dismounted, held the stirrup for her, assisted her in climbing up onto the horse's rump, then at last remounted.

'There,' he said. 'All comfortable?'

Ulrika circled her arms around his waist and pulled in tight behind him as he nudged the horse forwards. 'Very comfortable, thank you.'

She smiled to herself as she felt his heart start hammering in his chest. Yes, she thought. She was getting better at the Lahmian way.

Chesnekov returned to his company and filed in at the rear as they kicked their horses into a canter and thundered down the road towards Praag. As they rode along, Ulrika began to wish she had been able to find some way to feed before mounting up with him. Spending so long in such close proximity to the lancer's bare neck and the heat of his blood was going to be difficult to bear. Her lips kept inching forwards towards the pulsing vein beneath his skin, and she had to forcibly pull herself back to keep from nuzzling and biting him.

After more than an hour on the road, the cavalry company approached Praag's towering red walls. Ulrika looked with wonder upon them, amazed that, having taken such damage, the city remained undefeated. The great outer bastion was horribly scarred and smashed, riddled with black pockmarks where the vile missiles of the daemon cannons had struck it, and where the massive rams and towers had crashed into it. In places it was down entirely, with wide gaps where it had been reduced to mounds of rubble. Around these, rickety scaffolding had been erected, and men worked through the night to pile the fallen stones on top of one another again.

'I hope they are in time,' Ulrika said in Chesnekov's ear as they rode closer. 'Spring is almost upon us. The hordes will return soon.'

Chesnekov looked over his shoulder at her, then turned back and frowned. 'They'll be in time. The hordes aren't coming. Not this year at least.'

Ulrika blinked, baffled by his words. 'What? Of course they're coming. They vowed to destroy us.'

'Then they lied,' said the lancer. 'The army has watchers from here to Black Blood Pass. No one has seen them. They haven't even started massing. If they were coming in the spring, they would be on the move already. They are not.'

Ulrika's skin prickled with dismay. The world seemed to shift beneath her. 'But... but I don't understand. What happened?'

Chesnekov shrugged. 'No one knows. Some say it was the death of their leader, Arek Daemonclaw – that without his strong hand, the other leaders fought amongst themselves. Some say it was the disappearance of his twin sorcerers – that only their magic had held the alliance together. I heard an ice witch say something had happened with the winds of magic. Some great balance had shifted, and they had receded, and the hordes receded with them; at least, most of them did. Whatever the cause, there will be no invasion – at least until the next time.'

Ulrika still couldn't quite believe it. 'But the supply caravans, the troops. Why would they keep marching north if there is to be no war?'

Chesnekov laughed. 'Oh, Duke Enrik isn't fool enough to tell Tzarina Katarin the invasion's off. If he did, she'd cut off all the money that's coming to Praag. There's plenty of rebuilding and resupplying to be done, and plenty of marauders still to hunt – as you've just seen.' He shrugged. 'No, we need what the Tzarina is sending, make no mistake. But if she thought there was no longer any threat, she'd find other uses for the money, so Enrik keeps sending dire warnings south, begging her to help rebuild the "Great Bastion of the North" before it's too late.'

Ulrika hardly heard the half of what he said. The hordes weren't returning. Her biggest reason for coming to Praag had vanished. She had planned to lose herself in blood and slaughter, to fight for her people and her land, now it seemed there was nothing for her to do. She had travelled across two countries for naught.

'You seem disappointed,' said Chesnekov. 'Are you not relieved?'

Ulrika shook herself from her misery. 'I had hoped for vengeance. I wanted to make the hordes pay for the death of my family. Now… now I don't know what I will do.'

Chesnekov nodded solemnly. 'You have a warrior's heart. Well, there are still chances for revenge. Indeed, one of the warlords still lurks in the hills to the north – a mad, perverse thing known as Sirena Amberhair, neither man nor woman – who leads the debauched reivers we fought just now. If you wish to apply to my captain, I will put a good word in for you. You won't be the first she-Gryphon. The northern families have sent us daughters before.'

Visions of riding with the lancers and cutting down swathes of marauders from horseback flashed through Ulrika's head, and she suddenly ached for it to be possible, but of course it wasn't. A vampire could not live among men. The Gryphons bunked together, ate all their meals together, and patrolled in the sun. She would be discovered in an instant. And even if she wasn't, her hungers would not allow it. She was having trouble keeping her teeth from Chesnekov's neck as it was. Imagine being surrounded by an entire barracks full of heart-fires. No. If she was going to fight the marauders, she must do it on her own, in the shadows, away from temptation.

Memories came to Ulrika as they rode under the imposing arch of the Gate of Gargoyles and into the city at the tail of the lance company. She recalled standing on the walls with Max and Felix and the Slayers, watching Daemonclaw's endless horde advance on the city, the vortex of black energy his sorcerers had summoned swirling above them in the sky. She remembered the siege towers spewing forth their cargo of hideous beastmen, and fighting them while slipping in pools of their blood.

The devastation continued inside the walls as well – collapsed tenements, burnt-out homes, shops and workshops of the Novygrad all reduced to blackened rubble. Markers had been raised here and there in the debris, honouring the lost and the dead, and decorated with mementoes from their lives – a broken sword, a horse-shoe, a spray of wilted flowers, a stuffed doll.

With each turn of Ulrika's head came more memories – the hordes breaking through the outer wall and rampaging through the streets, the duke's men closing the Old Town gates on the survivors in order to keep the invaders out, the terrible fires. She shivered and upbraided herself for having selfishly wished the hordes would come again just to assuage her discontent. Her few brief moments of glory and violence would mean months and years of slow death by starvation, exposure and disease for those who actually lived here.

And yet, there were signs amongst the ruins of rebirth. Here and there new timbers were laid over old, patching smashed windows and doors. Half-built houses and tenements rose out of the wreckage, their pale, naked frames like saplings growing from the ashes of a forest fire. A tavern with no roof and no doors had 'Open for Business' scrawled on its soot-smudged wall in the Kislevarin alphabet, and shadowy figures huddled around an open fire within it, dipping their mugs in an open keg of kvas.

Ulrika's chest swelled with pride to see such activity. Praag had always rebuilt. Even after the Great War against Chaos, when the very buildings had screamed and wept blood from the nightmarish energies unleashed during the final battles, the city's indomitable spirit had not faltered. Though the very walls were filled with ghosts, though ruins like the Old Palace and the towering Sorcerers' Spire remained malignant tumours of madness and mutation, the people had built again, exorcising what spirits they could, and ignoring or living with the rest.

She wondered if Praag would ever be long enough at peace that it could lay all its ghosts and become a normal city again. Somehow she doubted it.

Not far inside the gate, a few square blocks had been cleared of rubble, and a vast military encampment had risen in their stead. The banners of rotas and companies from across all Kislev rose from a multicoloured sea of tents, with a parade ground lined off in the centre for drills and inspections. It was to this camp that the lance company was headed, but as they approached it, Chesnekov smiled over his shoulder at her.

'Where does your cousin live?' he asked. 'I will deliver you to her doorstep.'

Ulrika froze for a moment. She had almost forgotten her earlier lie. She had no address to give him, and she didn't want him to know where she intended to go. 'Uh, could I impose you for a moment longer before we go there?' she asked.

'But of course, madam,' he said. 'What do you require?'

'I… I am famished, and I wouldn't like to wake my cousin in the middle of the night and immediately ask her to feed me. If I could beg from you a little bread, or something to drink?'

Ulrika saw the faintest cast of doubt enter Chesnekov's eye, as if he wondered if she had befriended him just to get a meal from him, but he inclined his head politely and turned his horse after his fellows. 'The mess is for troopers only, but if you will consent to wait in my tent, I will bring you something.'

Ulrika hid a smirk. In his tent, was it? Bread for bed, then? Fair enough. At least it made it easier for her to get away. 'I thank you, sir. You are most kind.'

They followed his company through the camp, at this

hour silent and still, most of the soldiers asleep in their tents. Only a few lonely sentries watched their passage down the central avenue to a roped-off enclosure with the red and gold standard of the Gryphon Legion rising at the front.

As the troopers entered and trotted through the ranks of tents to a stable area at the back, Chesnekov slowed to a stop before a tent.

'Wait inside,' he said as he handed her down. 'I'll return shortly.'

'I will,' she said. 'And thank you again–' But he was already cantering after the others.

She saluted him, smiling wryly, and turned to leave the camp, but then paused, looking down at her leather jerkin and shirt. She couldn't walk through Praag covered in blood. She stretched her senses towards his tent. There was no one inside it. She ducked through the flap and looked around in the darkness. A cot sat on either side, with battered trunks at their feet and bits of gear and horse tack scattered everywhere.

Ulrika crossed to the cot that smelled like Chesnekov and opened the trunk. A second uniform and a neatly folded pile of civilian clothes lay within it. Ulrika pulled out a voluminous white shirt and held it up. Perfect. She quickly shucked her coat, jacket and blood-soaked shirt. There was a washbasin on a stand between the two cots. She filled it from the jug, washed her leathers, face and hair until the water no longer turned pink, then put on the new shirt.

She cocked an ear as she reassembled the rest of her costume, listening to see if the lancer was coming back. He was not. She sighed. The poor fool would return with bread and sausage and something hot to drink, expecting an amorous trade, and she would be gone. Ah well, at least he could eat the sausage. She turned to the tent flap, then stopped. If she had made the decision

that thieves were p[...] prey, she could not a[...] was only something a[...]

She took out one of [...] from the bandits she ha[...] it onto the pillow of C[...] than pay for another shi[...] path of honour, which wa[...]

She bowed to the em[...] Ilanovich Chesnekov,' she [...] me a great service. May you[...] and peace for Kislev.'

And with that, she turned and[...]

CHAPTER NINE
OLD FRIENDS

IT WAS WELL after midnight, but though the ruins of the Novygrad were quiet, and the soldiers in the camp asleep in their cots, much of the rest of Praag seemed wide awake. As she wandered through the Merchant Quarter, people spilled into the street from taverns ablaze with lamplight and loud with manic laughter and singing. Young men argued philosophy on the corners while rich merchants and their wives rolled by in open carriages, bundled in furs and surrounded by well-armed escorts, and mercenaries from all over the Old World swaggered the streets, calling out to harlots, and women who only dressed like harlots.

But side by side with all the frivolity were scenes of abject misery, and painful contrasts assaulted Ulrika everywhere she looked. In high windows, noble men and women, their faces hidden behind elaborate masks of enamel, gold and velvet, stuffed their faces with imported delicacies, while in the alleys below them, starving refugees, displaced by the devastation of the horde's passage, huddled in makeshift tents, making meals of rats and cockroaches. In the taverns, strutting dandies toasted the duke and his great victory over Chaos, while in the streets, weary watchmen guarded barricades behind which whole neighbourhoods had been evacuated because of the spectral horrors that had risen from the bloody cobbles during the Chaos attacks, and which had not yet been laid to rest. In the squares, wild-eyed priests of Ulric and Ursun prophesied doom at every hand, while boys with rouge on their cheeks and girls wearing their corsets on the outside of their dresses laughed at them and sang rude songs.

Music was everywhere. Every tavern and kvas parlour had a singer or a group performing for the crowd. Raucous drinking songs rattled the windows of crowded inns. Sharp-faced poets sang scathing satirical ballads to groups of laughing students. Refugees crooned sad lullabies while rocking their hollow-cheeked children to sleep. Even on quieter streets, Ulrika heard snatches of wild melodies on the wind – a strummed lute, a drunken flute, the haunting keening of a mournful violin. In a dark courtyard, she saw a barefoot young refugee girl dancing to some song only she could hear, as silent tears streamed down her cheeks.

And the musical madness seemed to reach even the highest ranks. As Ulrika moved through the crowds, she heard that the ruler of Praag, Duke Enrik, a distant cousin of hers, was putting on a victory concert at the Opera House in a week's time. It was to be the social event of the season. Ulrika found it offensive. It was indeed a great thing that the hordes had retreated, but to claim one's armies had defeated them and won a valiant victory when in reality the invaders seemed to have destroyed themselves with infighting and then retreated in the face of a brutal Kislev winter, was exaggeration on a grand scale.

Ulrika shook her head. From the duke to the lowliest

beggar, the people of Praag seemed to her like drunks dancing on the edge of a precipice, and putting on blindfolds so they couldn't see it. Had the city always been like this? She didn't remember such wild merry-making going on before. But of course, when last she had been here, it had been in the middle of a crippling siege. Perhaps, after the fear and horror of the long, terrible winter, Praag had only gone mad with relief.

Finally she arrived at the place she had been edging towards since she left Chesnekov's camp – the White Boar Inn. It had been inevitable she would come, but even as she'd headed for it, she had dragged her feet, and spent more time than was necessary watching the passing parade. At the same time, though her hunger had grown ever more insistent, she had put off feeding to come here, wanting to see the business to the finish before she did anything else.

The White Boar had been where she and Felix and Max and the Slayers had spent all their time while waiting out the siege. It had been here that she had fallen out of love with Felix, and into love with Max. It had been in a room above the taproom that she had nearly died of plague before the wizard had used his powers to drive the illness from her body. If her old companions were anywhere in Praag, they would be here. Just a few more steps, and she could be reunited with them.

She hesitated on the threshold, wondering again if that was what she wanted. Would they welcome her? Would they fear her? Would they attack her? Was she ready to fight them if they did?

A burst of harsh laughter came from within the tavern. She thought she heard a deep dwarfish guffaw amidst it. They *were* here. Knowing it, she almost turned around and walked away, but then she straightened. With the hordes not returning, she had lost one of the reasons she had journeyed to Praag. She wouldn't give up on the other out of fear. Thrusting out her jaw, she pushed open the door and stepped in.

The taproom was just as she remembered it, dark, smoky and filled with soldiers, mercenaries, and the women who made their living from them. Gospodar lancers with drooping moustaches stood in one corner, toasting each others' girls with kvas. Squat Ungol tribesmen hunched around a table, drinking fermented mares' milk and murmuring to each other. Men in uniforms from Kislev, the Empire and beyond crowded the long bar. Ulrika saw Tilean pikemen, crossbow men from the Reikland and Hochland long gunners, all talking to each other at the top of their voices.

'Another one gone, I hear,' said a mercenary with an Erengrad accent as Ulrika eased past him. 'That little beggar gal who sang so sweet down by the bridge. Hasn't shown up at her patch for three days now.'

'That's the fifth I heard of this week,' said a man who might have been a winged lancer once. 'Too bad. I liked her. Gave her a coin for luck every time I passed. What d'ye suppose is happening to 'em?'

'Who cares?' said a third companion, a dour-looking swordsman in Praag's colours. 'Good riddance, I say. Filthy refugees spreading disease and stealing our food. Why don't they go back where they came from?'

'Because it isn't there any more, y'clot,' said the ex-lancer.

A loud cheer drowned out his friend's reply, and a deep voice bellowed. 'Harder! Strike harder!'

Ulrika turned towards the voice and saw, in a room at the back, a crowd of hard-faced mercenaries surrounding a short broad figure who sat on a bench and gripped the table before him, while a man with a hammer stood behind him, raising it over his head. There were too many men in the way for Ulrika to see exactly what happened next, but she saw the hammer swing down at the skull of the short figure as another cheer went up.

'Good!' cried the deep voice. 'Once more to set it!'

Ulrika started across the taproom, alarmed. What was going on? As she walked up the three steps to the back room, the man with the hammer stepped back and raised it one more time, and she got a clear view at last of the figure sitting on the bench. It was Snorri Nosebiter, Gotrek and Felix's ugly Slayer companion, and he was having a nail pounded into his head.

Ulrika stared at the sight. She knew it was not the first time Snorri had had nails pounded into his head. A row of three rusty spikes had jutted from his skull in lieu of the traditional Slayer's crest since before she had first met him, and he'd still had them the last time she saw him, when he and Gotrek, Max and Felix had left her in the care of Countess Gabriella, in the ruins of Castle Drakenhof. Now it seemed he was adding to his collection. Four lesser nails, some bent, had been interspersed among the spikes, and he was in the process of adding a fifth.

He sat hunched, naked to the waist, his massive arms braced on the table before him, while a trickle of blood welled from the base of the new nail to run down between his bushy black eyebrows and drip off the end of his bulbous, oft-broken nose. A puddle of red was spreading between the mugs and plates on the table. Neither Gotrek, Felix nor Max was among the witnesses to this act of decoration.

The man with the hammer struck again, and the new nail sank another quarter of an inch into Snorri's skull as the men around him cheered and raised their fists and mugs.

'That's it!' called the hammerer. 'It's set! Your crown is complete, Slayer!'

'Snorri will be the judge of that,' said Snorri, and reached up to grip the nail. Ulrika winced as he tugged experimentally at it, but he seemed to feel no pain. He nodded, satisfied.

'Good!' he said. 'Now Snorri needs a drink!'

'Then Snorri better go get a drink,' said a big man with a cheerful, red face and a kerchief around his neck. 'For 'tis his round.'

Snorri wiped the blood from his brow with the back of his hand, then frowned. 'Wasn't it Snorri's round last time?'

'Aye,' said the man, who looked to be the leader of the others. 'But ye wagered it would take four strikes to pound that nail through yer thick skull, and it only took three, so ye owe us. Ye don't remember?'

Snorri shook his head. 'Snorri doesn't remember that.'

The man with the neckerchief laughed. 'Well, who would, if they'd just been hit on the head with a hammer. But it's Ranald's truth, ain't it, boys?'

The boys all agreed it was indeed Ranald's truth, and laughed and pounded Snorri's back, calling him stout fellow and old friend.

Snorri grinned and shrugged. 'Well, Snorri guesses it must be true, then. Snorri will get the drinks.'

Ulrika shrank back as the Slayer stood and stumped past her, roaring for the barmaid to take his order. She wasn't certain she wanted to renew her acquaintance with him. Particularly not at that moment. Even if he didn't want to slay her for being a vampire, he was just the sort to blurt it out at the top of his lungs in public. Unfortunately, he caught her motion out of the corner of his eye and looked her way. At first he didn't seem to recognise her, for his eyes moved away again, uninterested, and she breathed a sigh of relief, but after five heavy paces he slowed to a stop, then turned back, frowning thoughtfully.

Ulrika shot a glance at the Slayer's companions, who were joking amongst themselves now, and not paying any attention. She didn't want them seeing him coming back to her, so she stepped to him.

'Hello, Snorri Nosebiter,' she said, keeping a hand on the hilt of her rapier in case he attacked. 'It's good to see you again.'

'Snorri knows you,' said Snorri, still frowning. 'You are young Felix's girl.'

'Y-yes,' said Ulrika, a bit stunned he had taken the reappearance of a woman he had last seen as a vampire so calmly. 'At least I was. Ulrika Magdova, Ivan Straghov's daughter.'

Snorri's ugly face split into a wide grin. 'Now Snorri remembers!' He turned and continued on towards the bar. 'Ivan is a good man! How is he?'

Ulrika paused, uncomfortable, then followed him. 'He… he's dead, Snorri. He died in Sylvania.'

Snorri's face fell. 'Oh, yes. Snorri forgot. That's too bad. Snorri liked him. He was always very generous with his kvas.' He frowned again and peered up at Ulrika. 'Snorri remembers something happened to you too. Something bad.'

Ulrika blinked. Snorri had taken her reappearance so calmly because he didn't remember she had become a vampire. What a stroke of luck.

'Y-yes,' she said at last. 'Something bad. I became sick, and had to go away. Now I'm better. But listen.' She hurried on, not wanting him to think too long on it. 'I'm looking for Felix and Max. Are they here in Praag? Do you know where they're staying?'

Snorri pushed through the crush at the bar and pounded on it for service. 'Drinks for Snorri and his friends!' said Snorri as the barman turned his way.

The barman began filling mugs, and Snorri turned back to Ulrika. 'Max is here,' he said. 'But young Felix went through a door with Gotrek Gurnisson and never came back. Snorri misses them.'

Ulrika frowned, confused. 'They went through a door? What do you mean? What door? And why didn't they come back?'

Snorri shrugged. 'A door in a hill, in Sylvania. Max and Snorri waited outside that door for a long time, but Gurnisson and young Felix never came back out. Max couldn't open the door again, and neither could Snorri. His hammer couldn't touch it. And then there were beastmen again.'

Ulrika was even more confused now that he had answered the question. A door in a hill? What did he mean? Was it some sort of magic?

'Are they dead?'

'The beastmen? Oh yes. Snorri killed them.'

'Not the beastmen. Felix and Gotrek,' said Ulrika, fighting for patience. 'Are they dead?'

Snorri shook his head. 'Snorri doesn't think so. They just didn't come back.'

Ulrika sighed. She wasn't going to get anything sensible out of the Slayer. She would have to find Max and ask him what had happened.

'But you say Max is here?' she asked. 'Where?'

Snorri began to fumble in his belt pouch for coins as the barman set a brace of mugs on the bar in front of him. 'Max is staying with his fancy friends. They have a foolish manling house on the street with the statue of the lady with the big hat.' He snorted, disgusted. 'A house with seven towers, and none of them big enough to put a stairway in, let alone mount a cannon on. Snorri thinks it's stupid.'

Ulrika nodded. The statue of the lady with the big hat must be the monument to revered Miska, Mother of all Kislev, dressed in her ancient armour. She knew where that was – an intersection in the Noble Quarter – and finding a nearby house with seven ornamental towers shouldn't be too hard.

'Thank you, Snorri,' she said. 'I'm going to look for Max now. It was good to see you again.'

'Snorri thinks it was good to see you too, Ulrika, Ivan's daughter,' said Snorri, pushing his coins across the counter to the barman. 'Goodbye.'

Ulrika turned to go, then paused, shooting a look towards the mercenaries, who were laughing and miming pounding nails into one another's heads.

'Listen, Snorri,' she whispered. 'Your friends are taking advantage of you. They're cheating you. They're making you buy drinks for them when you shouldn't, and probably worse besides. If I were you, I'd find other friends.'

Snorri frowned at her. 'Ragneck wouldn't cheat Snorri,' he said. 'He's a good man. He drinks almost as much as Snorri, which is pretty good for a manling.'

Ulrika sighed, then fished in her coin purse, still bursting with stolen gold. 'Well, you can't say I didn't try,' she said, then dug out enough coins to cover Snorri's round, and then some. She put them in the Slayer's hand as he was reaching for the mugs. 'Here. At least let me pay for the next one.'

Snorri beamed at the gold in his hand, then grinned at her. 'Snorri thinks that is very nice of you.'

'It's nothing,' said Ulrika. 'Goodbye, Snorri. And good luck. I hope you find your doom soon.' And before those villains rob you completely blind, she added to herself.

'Goodbye,' said Snorri as she turned to go. 'And good luck to you too.'

It was much too late for that, Ulrika thought. Her luck had died in Sylvania, at the same moment she had. She pushed through the crowd to the door, then stepped out into the cold night.

As she turned towards the Noble Quarter, her hunger tugged at her again, like an eager dog straining at its leash, but she again pulled it to heel. She had to find Max first. She had to know. Everything else could wait.

THE HOUSE WITH seven towers was harder to find than Ulrika expected. Towers were all the rage amongst the rich of Praag at the moment, and no mansion was complete without a handful of unlikely spires and cupolas poking from the roof, and as Snorri had said, none were even remotely practical. They served only as pedestals for glittering, mosaic-covered, onion-shaped domes of every size, colour and description.

Finally, after prowling all the streets in the vicinity of Miska's statue and counting the towers of every house, she had found one that had seven, and also looked as if it might house sorcerous occupants. There were dwarf runes set into the walls protecting the grounds, and she could see strange sigils and symbols ringing the tops of all the towers. Extending her senses, she could detect invisible barriers overlapping every wall. They didn't feel very strong, but she was certain pushing against them would be enough to alert the dwellers within.

Ulrika briefly considered just brazenly knocking on the front door and inquiring if Magister Schreiber was at home, but quickly dismissed the notion. For one thing, it was long past midnight now, and even though some lights still burned in the upper floors, it was much too late to make a polite call. For another, she had no idea who Max was staying with. A wizard of some kind, almost certainly, but she had no way of knowing their temperament or abilities. Would they sense what she was? Would they attack her instantly because of it? She had no interest in finding out.

She sighed. She needed to get Max alone. She knew he was even-tempered enough to at least listen to her before he made any kind of decision about her. He had agreed, after all, to allow Countess Gabriella to take care of her. It would be wisest for her to come back the next night and wait for him to come out, but she was impatient. She wanted to know what had happened to Felix. She wanted to see somebody she cared for. She wanted some part of her arrival in Praag to go the way she had thought it would. Maybe she could work out which room was his and get his attention somehow. Would a thrown pebble wake the wards?

A watch patrol appeared at the end of the street, and she melted into the shadows as they trudged by, then stepped back out when they had passed, and raised herself on her toes, trying to see over the walls of the mansion into the windows. Most were curtained, and those that were not held nothing of interest. Even the lit one showed nothing but the corner of an armoire and a bit of table. Perhaps around the back.

She circled the block, looking for the back of the property. It butted up against another mansion that fronted the next street over, but fortunately that house had no wards, and she leapt the gate and padded around to the back garden without raising any alarms. The rear of the sorcerous house was very close to the shared garden wall, and the windows were tantalisingly near. One, high up, glowed with warm light.

The garden wall was warded, of course, but there was a tall tree on Ulrika's side of it. She shot out her claws and climbed it like a cat until she was level with the window, then edged out on a branch and crouched down. Through the glass she could see a beautifully appointed bedroom, done in dark woods, with white draperies and alabaster vases set upon intricately carved ebony dressers and, half-hidden behind the window frame, the curtains and posts of a canopied bed, a candle burning on the bedside table.

She was about to hop to another branch to get a different angle on the room when a pale figure in a robe of ice-blue silk stepped into view. Ulrika stopped and watched. It was a woman of perhaps forty years of age – tall, slender and beautiful, with a regal bearing and skin so white Ulrika might have thought her another vampire, but for the fact that she could sense the heart-fire pulsing in her breast. She could also sense the woman's power. It was her magic that guarded the house, a cold crystalline energy that seemed to well up from the ground like hoarfrost.

The woman untied her gown and let it slip from her shoulders, exposing a slim, exquisite body, then stepped to the bed and pulled aside the curtain. A naked man lay on his side within the canopy. He rolled over, blinking sleepily, then opened his arms to her and smiled.

It was Max Schreiber.

CHAPTER TEN
SONGS OF HOME

ULRIKA STARED AS the pale woman sank into Max's arms and kissed him deeply. His hands slid down her back to grip her waist, then the curtain fell closed again and they vanished from sight.

Quivers of rage made Ulrika's arms shake, and her claws dug deep into the bark of her branch. A growl started low in her throat and she crouched forwards like a hunting cat. How dare he take another lover! Hadn't she come a thousand miles to see him? Hadn't she run away from a life of luxury to be with him? And this was how he repaid her? She wanted to tear him apart. She wanted to tear both of them apart. She would leap through the window in a shower of glass and rip them limb from limb! She knew there were wards on the house. She didn't care. As angry as she was, she would tear through them like they were mist, and strike before either Max or the woman could prepare incantations.

She tensed to spring, the muscles bunching in her legs, but then a small voice inside her head laughed at her and told her she was being ridiculous. What did she have to be jealous about? She and Max had never been lovers – at least she had no memory of it. It was possible they might have been, given time, but Adolphus Krieger had intervened and stolen her away.

Ulrika tried to ignore the voice. Perhaps they never consummated their love, but she had been in love with Max, and he with she. She knew it! And it had only been four months. Had he got over her so quickly?

Max had remained true longer than she had, sneered the voice. Hadn't she given herself to Krieger not two weeks after he had kidnapped her?

Yes, but Krieger had used his unnatural charisma to weaken her will, Ulrika argued. She hadn't been herself.

Oh? And what was her excuse with Friedrich Holmann? He hadn't seduced her. Just the opposite in fact. She hadn't spared many thoughts for Max then, had she? He hadn't even entered her mind. And what did she expect, anyway? Max knew she had become a vampire. Did she truly think he would pine away for her for the rest of his life – a woman he would never see again, and could never have?

Ulrika's cat crouch collapsed and she hung her head. The faint notes of a far-off violin came to her on the wind. It seemed to be laughing at her. She agreed with it. She was a fool. Why had she come? Every reason she'd had, every hope for what Praag would give her, had crumbled to dust as soon as she looked at it. The hordes weren't coming, her homeland wasn't in danger, Felix was lost, perhaps dead, and Max had moved on. There was nothing for her here, not even her father's grave, for he had been burned on a pyre in Sylvania.

She flopped back against the trunk of the tree, hollow and lost. Praag was to have given her a purpose, something to do for the endless years of her eternity. What would she do with them now? She had no friends – nowhere she fit. She couldn't live among humans, and couldn't stand to live among vampires. What would she do? Where would she go?

A muffled cry of ecstasy and a billow of the curtains of the canopy bed made her look through the window again, then away. With a sigh, she climbed down the tree. She might not know where she wanted to go, but she knew she didn't want to stay here. She couldn't bear it.

ULRIKA WANDERED AIMLESSLY after that, her mind numb and listless. She was too lost to think, too glum to face her dilemma. Not even hunger could pierce her mood. She took streets at random, drifting through clusters of refugees and beggars and drunks like a ghost – unseen, unseeing, and untouched by the misery and madness around her. She walked past a clutch of poets who, for only a pulo, would write a poem of mourning for one's relatives lost in the war. She walked past an entire company of soldiers, armed to the teeth, who were descending, one by one, down a hole into the sewers, while corpsmen were winching dead soldiers up out of the same hole and laying them in neat piles on the street. She walked past the Opera House with its statues and its scars, and around the barricades that walled off the Sorcerers' Spire, the huge destroyed tower which had once been home to Praag's college of magic, and which was sometimes known as the Fire Spire because of the huge explosion that had destroyed its upper reaches during the Great War.

Stepping out of the tower's long moonshadow, she crossed the Karlsbridge over the River Lynsk into the western half of the city, skirting the enormous park that the long ago rulers of Praag had dedicated to Magnus the Pious after his victory over Asavar Kul, and into the area of shabby, garreted tenements and cheap taverns that surrounded Praag's famed Academy of Music and its College of Art, both of which were situated in the north-west corner of the park.

The streets in the student area were narrow and winding, and emptier than those of the Merchant Quarter. Many of the taverns were boarded up, as were quite a few of the shops that sold or repaired instruments or printed sheet music. Their walls were crudely painted with 'out of business' and 'temporarily closed' signs. But though the streets might be deserted, the air was still filled with music. It spilled from the few taverns that remained open, it shrilled from the tin whistles of beggars squatting in the shadows and it murmured from the throats of watchmen making their lonely rounds.

Ulrika was too trapped in the bleak whirlpool of her thoughts to pay attention to this cacophony. Should she stay in Praag? Should she go to some other city? Should she go back to Gabriella? She couldn't. She had sworn she wouldn't. But what else was there? Should she go looking for Felix? Where would she start? And what if she found he had moved on to someone else, as Max had? Would she kill him? Kill herself? She didn't know.

Then a voice pierced the darkness – a girl's voice, high and clear, singing softly in the distance. At first Ulrika paid it no more mind than any of the other music that assaulted her, but then the melody caught her ear. It was a song the peasants on her father's estate used to sing in the evenings – a sad old Ungol folk ballad about a boy who went to war and a girl who stayed behind.

Ulrika paused, turning her head to hear better. She remembered old Anatai, her father's cook, singing the same song as she shuffled around the kitchen, preparing the evening meal. She remembered a wounded young horse soldier singing it at the campfire after a deadly battle against trolls. She remembered singing it herself as she left her father's lands to travel to the Empire for the first time. She swallowed. The song tugged at her like it had reached into her chest and wrapped fingers around her heart.

As if of their own volition, her feet started in the direction of the song, turning corners and crossing streets until she came at last to a run-down kvas parlour in the middle of a block. Its sign was a blue jug hung from a string over the door, and despite the bitter cold of the early spring night, Kossar soldiers in fur hats and fingerless gloves sat outside it on three-legged stools, drinking from little clay cups.

Ulrika squeezed past them and ducked under the low door. Inside was a big square room with trestle tables all around. It was nearly as deserted as the streets outside. A few old men slouched at the bar, and a few robed students and tawdry women huddled at the tables, but that was all.

Ulrika didn't give them a second glance. Her whole attention was taken by the source of the voice, a slight, olive-skinned figure that sat on a bench on the stage, an old balalaika in her lap. She was a striking young girl, with the thick dark hair and almond eyes of an Ungol, and the straight nose and high cheekbones of a Gospodar – a beautiful half-breed. Her clothes were old, and oft mended, but clean and seemly – the clothes of a farm girl – though Ulrika doubted she had ever done much farm work for, from the way the singer held her head as she sang, she was certain the girl was blind.

She brought the song to an end with a last high quavering note, and there was appreciative applause from the students and their women, as well as a few gruff salutes from the old men at the bar. Some of the students tossed coins into the balalaika case that sat open at the blind girl's feet, and she bowed her head appreciatively as she heard the coins clink against one another.

'Thank you, masters,' she said, in a strong north

country accent, and then began another song.

Ulrika knew this one too. Her mother had sung it often before she died, and it had made her father cry ever after when anyone else sang it – a tale of a young bride called from her marriage bed by something in the woods and never heard from again, though her bridegroom searched all his life.

Ulrika found a table in the shadows, far from the other patrons, and listened as the girl sang ballad after ballad in her pure sweet voice. The songs hurt to hear. Each one was a knife in the heart, but Ulrika couldn't stop. The pain was terrible, but the memories that spilled from the wounds were exquisite, and well worth the agony – sitting on her father's lap in the big dining hall as the musicians played a wild reel and the peasants danced their complex circles, being sung to sleep by her mother after a nightmare, riding out with the lancers when she was barely big enough to sit on a horse, and singing along in her squeaky little voice as they bellowed out a marching song, kissing Yusin, the farrier's boy, behind the forge as his father whistled a tune in time to the clanging of his hammer, dancing with Felix before he went off to the Wastes with his dwarfen companions, reuniting with her father after the siege of Praag as the streets rang with songs of victory.

The songs were a bright window to a world she could never return to, a world closed to her by a poisoned kiss. It had never been a perfect world. The shadows of death and destruction had loomed over it since her birth – constant companions to any child born so near the madness of Chaos – but still it was a world that had allowed for hope, for sunshine and love and family and true companionship. Now her world was darkness without hope of light, love was a blood-sport, her family were backstabbing intriguers, true companionship seemed impossible, and it would last for all eternity.

The longing to step through the window to her old life was so strong she felt her dead heart might burst from her body and vanish into the songs. If she could have cried, she would have, but tears were another thing her new world was without.

It was therefore something of a relief when the girl took a short break to have something to eat and drink. Ulrika too was feeling hungry, the urge to feed she had put off for so long returning stronger than ever, but she could not leave before the girl finished singing. If she sang until dawn Ulrika would gladly walk out into the sunrise and die content, so she forced her hunger back into its cage and looked around for something to take her mind off it until the girl resumed.

Near her, some of the students were arguing over their kvas about the singer.

'You're mad,' said one with a scruffy beard. 'Training would ruin her. She's a pure talent, as wild and free as a horse of the oblast. If you tamed her, she would be just another Opera House donkey.'

'But she can barely play,' said a round-faced one with a tiny hashmark moustache. 'Her singing's lovely, but she's clamming one note in five.'

'You want to take away her charm – her passion,' said the first. 'You'll make her like Valtarin. Look what happened to him when old Padurowski took him under his wing.'

'He got better,' snapped his friend.

'Better? Aye, he's the finest violinist in Praag now, but all his heart is gone. His playing is all just technique and posturing. It's like he's lost his soul.'

The round-faced boy laughed. 'I'd part with my soul too, if I could play like that.'

'That would assume you had one to part with in the first place,' sniffed the scruffy boy.

After that their conversation dissolved into friendly

name-calling and Ulrika became more interested in the pulse in their necks than their words. Perhaps she would have to feed now after all, but just then the blind girl returned to the stage, a small boy guiding her by the arm, and Ulrika's hunger faded as she once again sat down to play.

Ulrika let herself drift back into memory on the wings of the songs, forgetting her despair as they called up images of the broad plains and vast painted skies of her youth, of riding and hunting on snowy mornings, of wheat fields and pastures on golden afternoons, of sunsets never to be seen again.

Her reverie was momentarily disturbed as three toughs came in through the back door and leered at the blind girl as they passed the stage, and then again a little later when raised voices came from the bar and she saw the same men were arguing with the barkeep.

'Please, Shanski. Business is still slow,' he was saying. 'The Academy is barely open since the siege. So many young men gone to fight and not come back.'

'Your lack of business is not our business, Basilovich,' the leader of the toughs replied. He was a short, heavy-set gangster with rings on every finger. 'Now pay up.'

Ulrika glared at them for a moment, wanting to tell them to be quiet, then returned her attention to the singer and they were forgotten again.

The girl was singing a soft old ballad about Mother Miska saying goodbye to her children and riding off into the north to her destiny. Ulrika knew it from the womb, and was mouthing the words along with her, when the gangsters intruded again. As they filed out the back door, the leader, the one the barman had called Shanski, stopped beside the stage, grinning and making rude gestures at the blind girl. She of course saw nothing and continued to sing, but Ulrika growled in her throat. What an ass.

She relaxed as Shanski opened his belt pouch and took out a coin. At least he was going to pay for his fun. But no, the gangster was cleverer than that. He dropped the piece into the blind girl's case with one hand, making sure it clinked against another, while at the same time scooping up more coins with the other hand.

The girl bowed as she heard the telltale coin chime, and said, 'Thank you, master,' without breaking her rhythm.

There was an angry hissing and muttering from the crowd of watchers, but it all died away when Shanski turned and glared at them, hand on his sword. He sneered at their cowardice then strutted out the back door after his men, stuffing the stolen coins into his pouch.

Ulrika snarled with anger, then paused and smiled to herself. It was time to feed at last.

CHAPTER ELEVEN
THE SHEPHERDESS

ULRIKA ROSE AND sauntered out the front door – it wouldn't do to be seen following the gangsters out the back – then trotted down the street, looking for a way to get behind the building. There was an alley up ahead. She sped towards it.

As she turned into it, she saw a man hunching along it in front of her, looking this way and that and calling into the shadows. 'Lushaya! Lushaya, are you here?'

He looked up as he noticed Ulrika coming towards him, and held out pleading hands. 'Have you seen my daughter, m'lord? Have you seen my Lushaya?'

'It's "m'lady",' said Ulrika as she shoved past him and pushed her senses ahead of her to search for the heart-fires of the gangsters. She found them off to her left, and turned down a side alley after them. The man behind her cursed her, then started calling for his daughter again.

Ulrika caught up to the three gangsters a block further on, just as they were entering the service yard of a small inn. She waited in the shadows until they all went in, then scaled the back wall of a rickety three-storey tenement that rose beside the yard and catted silently over its roof so she could look down on them from above.

Shanski rapped on the inn's back door, and after a moment it cracked open and an older man handed out a small coin purse, then made to close it again. Shanski stuck his foot in and stopped him.

'Hang on, Grigo,' he said. 'Let me count it first.'

'It's all there,' said the man in the door. 'I'd never cheat Gaznayev. You know that.'

'I know the boss'll have it out my hide if it's short,' chuckled Shanski, shaking the coins into his palm. 'So…'

The man looked around, nervous, as Shanski methodically counted the money. Finally he nodded and returned it to the pouch. 'Very good, Grigo. Wish all our clients was as reliable.'

'Just go, can't you?' said the man, and closed and locked the door as the gangster removed his foot.

Shanski shook his head. 'You'd think, with the service we give 'em, they'd be happier to see us. Ingrates.'

He tucked the bag into his fur coat, then motioned his two bullies towards the alley again. Ulrika wasn't about to let them reach it. She tensed at the edge of the roof, letting her anticipation peak, then leapt silently down into the yard. The men cried out in surprise as she landed on her toes and fingertips amongst them and shot out her fangs and claws.

'Leeches,' she whispered, rising and drawing her rapier and dagger from their sheaths.

'Kill him!' barked Shanski, backing away wide-eyed.

The two toughs lurched in, swinging iron-banded clubs. She dodged them easily, then slashed left and right. They howled as her blades cut their shoulders and flanks. She could have killed them instantly, but she didn't want to. All the night's frustration boiled up suddenly within her – all her anger at Max, all her disappointment that there would be no war to fight, all her anxiety over the fate of Felix – and exploded in a whirling fury of violence. She cut the toughs' hands and legs to ribbons with her rapier, gouged out their eyes with her dagger, tore their bellies, kicked and slapped and ripped them until they collapsed in blind, moaning heaps.

Shanski, paralysed at the gate during her frenzy, shrieked and fled into the alley as she raised her eyes to him. She impaled the blubbering toughs with two lightning thrusts, then sprinted after him. He shouldered through the gate of a potter's yard next to the tavern and slammed it behind him. She vaulted it as if it weren't there and kicked him face-first into the mud.

He rolled over on his back as she stood above him.

'Spare me!' he wept, digging desperately in his coat. 'Please, I have gold!' He held a double handful of little drawstring pouches up towards her.

Ulrika nearly hacked his hands off just to hear him scream, but then checked herself. She had no need of gold, but she knew someone who did. She sheathed her dagger and snatched a few of the pouches from his upstretched hands.

'You will repay what you stole,' she said, tucking them into her leather jerkin.

'Yes, yes!' he babbled. 'Everything.'

'But *I* want something else.'

She hauled him up by the collar, then, before he could guess her intent, sank her teeth into his neck and drank. He shrieked and struggled, but grew quickly weak, and his grunts of fear turned to moans of pleasure. She moaned too, for though his blood tasted of cheap kvas and burnt meat, it was warm and rich and heady, and filled her veins with strength and fire and contentment.

She had almost drunk her fill when voices and lantern light came from the yard where she had killed his guards. She paused, and lifted her lips from Shanski's neck.

'You didn't hear it?' said Grigo's voice. 'I thought I heard – light of Dazh! Look at that!'

'Ursun protect us,' said a second voice. 'What did that? An animal?'

'It's Gaznayev's boys. I... I just paid them!'

'You don't think he'll think we...?'

'Hell! I hope not,' said Grigo, groaning.

'Where... where's that fat bastard Shanski?' asked the second voice. 'Didn't you say...?'

'Aye. We better look. If he's alive he can tell Gaznayev it wasn't us. Get Mikal's pistols and come on.'

There was a moment of shuffling, and then two sets of footsteps started through the yard to her right. Ulrika cut Shanski's throat, then silently lowered his body to the ground and looked around. If she went into the alley the men would see her, and they had pistols. But the back of the pottery workshop was half-timbered – easily scalable. She ran to it and leapt, then flew up it like a cat.

Just as she reached the roof, Grigo's voice came from the alley. 'What's that? Up there! Shoot it!'

Ulrika dived over the peak as a pistol-crack echoed behind her, then scrambled to the edge that looked over the main street. The front door of Grigo's tavern was below her, and men were going in and out. That wouldn't do. She ran low along the row of buildings until she reached the end of the block and looked down again – a little side street, narrow and empty. Much better. She landed on the unpaved street with an almost noiseless thud, then cocked her ear. In the distance she heard Grigo and the other man calling to each other, but they seemed to be going in the other direction. Good. She stood and looked down at herself. Fortunately she had done all her butchery at longer range this time, and seemed unbloodied. She wiped her mouth with a hand-kerchief just to be sure, then pulled out one of the payment pouches she had taken from Shanski and spilled its contents into her hand.

That would do nicely.

THE BARMAN AT the Blue Jug was collecting mugs and jars, and the students and old men gathering cloaks and hats, by the time Ulrika returned. On the stage, the blind girl was wiping down the neck of her balalaika with a rag. Ulrika grunted with relief. She was in time. She crossed to the stage and slipped the handful of stolen gold into her instrument case. She tried to be quiet about it, but the girl heard, and seemed to know how many coins she'd dropped. She looked up with wide eyes.

'Th-thank you, master,' she said.

Ulrika almost corrected her, but then paused. She didn't want to talk to the girl. She didn't want to dis-cover she was common, or silly, or grasping. She wanted her to remain what she appeared when she sang, a pure and perfect spirit of home, untouched by the dirty real-ities of making a living in a hard city. Instead she only bowed – foolish, as the girl couldn't see – then turned and headed for the door.

As she started down the empty street, Ulrika found herself walking with a jaunty stride. Perhaps it was only Shanski's blood warming her and making her giddy, but she felt terribly noble and virtuous, and grinned at the thought of the singer sorting through her coins and finding her unexpected bounty among them. The gang-ster had stolen silver and copper, but Ulrika had replaced it with gold. She was like the hero from some hackneyed melodrama, defeating a moustache-twirling villain and saving a poor but virtuous maiden from ruin.

The thought sparked another, and her steps slowed as it grew in her mind. With sudden and perfect clarity she knew at last the answer to the questions that had been plaguing her since Chesnekov had told her the hordes weren't coming. All night long they had trod their tight measure in her head. What would she do? How would she live? Why should she bother to go on?

The blind girl had given Ulrika the answer. Her songs had reminded her of her father, a wise and noble lord who cared for and protected his peasants. The songs had also reawakened the Kislevite in her. She had been so long out of her native land, and had recently become so changed, that she had almost forgotten her heritage, and how much she loved her home. Now, thanks to the songs, she remembered, and this, combined with her vow to only prey on predators, had given birth to an idea of a way to live that she could live with, indeed be proud of.

She would stay here in Praag, and she would follow her father's noble example and protect the people of the city from monsters like Shanski. The hordes might not come, but she would still be able to lose herself in slaughter – and to kill without pricking her conscience – for Praag would provide her with an endless supply of villains to feed upon. It was a perfect solution.

She picked up her pace again, the burden of uncertainty that had weighed her down for so long lifting at last. It was good to have a plan. Now she could think about finding some place to stay, and settling herself into the fabric of the city.

She started across the street with renewed purpose, but then had to edge aside as three drunks weaved around a corner, talking animatedly amongst themselves.

'Did y'see him?' said the first. 'Throat cut neat as y'please, but no blood in him. Like an empty wine skin, he was.'

'An' Grigo says he saw a bat the size of a man fly up t'the roof of Danya the potter's place,' said the second.

'Wasna bat,' slurred the last. 'Wasa man. But flyin' like a bat. Thass what I heard.'

Ulrika turned up the collar of her heavy travelling cloak and hurried on, groaning to herself as, somewhere in the distance, a violin played a lilting tune. If she was going to protect the people of Praag, she was going to have to be more discreet about it, or they would run screaming to the watch to be protected from their protector.

AN HOUR LATER, with the eastern sky lightening from black to charcoal-grey, Ulrika picked her way through the demolished Novygrad, searching for a place to wait out the day. She had decided that, until she could get her bearings, the depths of the cordoned-off ruins would be the safest hiding place. People might be rebuilding on the fringes, but the areas closest to where the hordes had spilled through the collapsed city walls were not only smashed and burnt, but twisted as well by the dread powers unleashed there. Buildings of brick and stone had been melted to glassy black heaps, and ghosts and spirits were rumoured to drift amidst the piles, moaning and weeping and scaring the life from those who dared trespass on their territory.

Ulrika wasn't troubled by these rumours. In fact she welcomed them. If the people feared the ruins, they would shun them, and she would not be disturbed, except perhaps by ghosts – and she no longer feared ghosts.

On a street where strange purple vines pushed up through the black rubble of the buildings, Ulrika found a likely-looking place – a tenement with an intact ground floor, which meant – hopefully – no sunlight would leak down into the cellar. She stepped over its shattered doors, looking for a way down, and at the back, she found it, a narrow set of wooden stairs leading down, and partially collapsed.

Ulrika squatted down to examine the threshold. There were recent footprints in the dust, and the smell of shed blood came from below – not fresh, but not ancient either. She detected no pulse as she extended her senses, but nevertheless drew her rapier and dagger before starting down the stairs, and looked warily into the shadows.

The cellar was an earthen-floored hole, studded with rows of brick pillars that supported a barrel-vaulted ceiling, and at first she saw nothing that would explain the scent of blood. But as she moved further into the darkness, she saw, sticking out from behind a pillar, a hand and arm stretched on the ground. She stepped around the pillar on guard, and discovered a grisly scene. It appeared others had been taking advantage of the privacy of the ruins as well.

The hand and arm belonged to a girl, no more than seventeen, who lay naked and spread-eagled in the centre of a circle that appeared to have been gouged into the earthen floor with a stick. Ulrika grimaced as she saw that the girl's hands and feet had been pinned to the ground by heavy spikes, and that troughs had been dug under them to the gouged circle, so the blood from her wounds could flow into it, making a crimson moat around her. Strange symbols were carved into the victim's body, but Ulrika could see no fatal wound. Instead, it looked as if the girl had died of terror. Her face was frozen into a scream, eyes and mouth wide open, and her limbs rigid with tension.

Standing over her, Ulrika noticed a livid purple ring

bruising the flesh between the girl's breasts. It was about an inch in diameter, and looked like a love bite, except that it was perfectly circular and slightly raised. She couldn't imagine such a thing could have been the cause of death – it hadn't even broken the skin – but there was something eerie and unpleasant about it that made her not want to look at it any more.

She turned away, and saw a pile of clothes in one corner. She crossed to it. Girl's clothing, of course, but there was a lot of it – more than a girl would wear at once. Six dresses, all patched and poor, as well as shawls, bodices, caps and shoes, and a broken tin-whistle.

Ulrika snarled, angry, remembering the man in the alley who had asked if she had seen his daughter, and the soldiers in the White Boar, mourning the disappearance of a street singer. She was suddenly certain she knew what had happened to them. What vileness. She had been right before. She would never go hungry here.

She sighed, then started back to the steps. She could have stayed and slept there. She doubted the cultists would return during the day, and the corpse was nothing more than an empty vessel, but it was too pitiful. She would find somewhere else to rest.

AFTER SPENDING THE day hidden away from the sun inside a brick oven in the basement of a destroyed bakery, Ulrika woke and made her way back across the city, again passing the Sorcerers' Spire and crossing the Karlsbridge to the Academy District to return to the Blue Jug. And though the blind girl was there, and sang as beautifully as she had before, that was not why Ulrika had come.

The night before, Shanski had mentioned his boss – someone named Gaznayev – and Ulrika surmised that if this Gaznayev had learned that three of his thumbbreakers had been killed while at their appointed rounds, he would send someone to investigate. With luck, all she would have to do was wait and his toughs would come sniffing around. Then she could follow them back to his lair and kill him, destroying his protection racket at the root. She smiled, looking forward to the havoc she would wreak and the blood she would spill, and all without guilt or consequence.

She was dressed tonight in the black doublet and breeches she had stolen from Gabriella – patched since her misadventures with the roadwardens. She had also polished her boots and brushed out her good black cape. The dusty leathers and worn clothes she had collected from her various victims along the way had been a good disguise on the road, but here in Praag, they made her look like a refugee, and while that was a look that allowed one to vanish into a crowd, it kept one out of wealthier places, and was not the sort of thing a noble protector wore when she walked among her flock.

She knew this wasn't wise, that with her male clothing and her height and her short white hair she cut too memorable a figure, but having seen the fashions of Praag on parade the night before, she had decided she was safer dressing this way here than perhaps anywhere else in the world. What with nobles wearing bejewelled masks, boys flaunting rouge, girls flaunting corsets, students with elaborate facial hair and soldiers wearing ermine hats the size of pumpkins, she would only be one of a great crowd of memorable figures, just another oddity in a city of oddities – and hopefully no one would give her a second glance.

Just as she thought it, she felt eyes upon her. She turned, expecting to see some gangster sizing her up, or some watchman or dour chekist agent, but that was not the case. A young man with a rapier hilt showing beneath the grey robes of an art student sat slouched against the back wall, watching her from under a fall of lank black hair. His face was as sharp and pointed as a wolf's, and his dark-eyed gaze as cold and cruel, and he was most certainly a vampire.

CHAPTER TWELVE
THE CARGO

ULRIKA LOOKED AWAY, angry at the vampire for spying upon her, but angrier at herself. She had expected her exploits of the previous evening to have aroused the interest of the gangster whose men she had killed, and perhaps the watch, but it hadn't occurred to her the killings might awaken curiosity in other quarters as well. Fool! Of course they had. A corpse drained of blood, rumours of a man who flew like a bat. If the vampires of Praag were anything like the Lahmians of Nuln, these were the last sort of whispers they would want floating around, and the first they would investigate.

She should have been more discreet. She had let her blood rage run away with her again and she had exposed herself. Now they would come after her. They would try to control her as Gabriella had.

She closed her eyes, fighting for calm. Perhaps she could come to some sort of agreement with them. Perhaps, if she promised to be quieter in her feeding, they would let her be. Praag was a big city. Surely there was room enough for all of them.

With a grunt of resignation, she turned back, deter-mined to confront the vampire head-on and see what he had to say, but he was gone. His seat by the wall was empty. She looked around the room and checked the exits. He was nowhere to be seen. She sighed, annoyed. What was the use of cat and mouse? If they wanted to speak with her, then come out with it. If they wanted to kill her...

She paused at the thought. There might be an ambush waiting for her outside. Well, good. Her blood was up. If they wanted a fight she would welcome it. And when she defeated them, she could return to the life she had mapped out for herself, free from their interference.

She was just rising and stepping towards the door when she heard heavy boots entering the bar from the back. She turned. Four hard-looking men were swagger-ing in behind a fifth, a trim blond dandy with a velvet cap pulled low over one pale blue eye. The customers edged away from them, and the barman fumbled the mug he had in his hands, almost dropping it.

Ulrika cursed to herself. Her gangster quarry had arrived at the most inopportune time. Now what did she do?

The dandy leaned on the bar and smiled at the bar-man. 'Dobry vechyr, Basilovich. How's business?'

The barman took a step back. 'I paid Shanski last night, Kino. Everybody saw me.'

Kino waved a careless hand. 'Aye, aye. No worries there. It's only that some friends are saying Shanski stopped at the Jug just before he died. What do you know about that?'

The barman went pale. 'Nothing, Kino. Nothing. I promise you. He was alive when he left here. Ask any-body!'

Kino looked around the room, nodding. 'And anyone

follow him out? Or pick a fight with him while he was here?'

The barman shook his head. 'No one. I swear to you. But I heard Grigo down at the Muzhik's Toil saw something attack him, something that flew off into the night.'

Kino rolled his eyes. 'Aye, we talked to Grigo. He sounded like he'd been drinking his own stock.' With a sigh he crossed to the nearest table, then stepped up onto it and stamped his boot. 'Hoy!' he shouted, then turned towards the blind girl. 'Stop yer wailing, girly. I'm talking.'

The singer faltered then fell silent as everyone in the room turned their attention on Kino.

'You all know what happened last night. Well, my employer will pay good coin to know who did it. A whisper in my ear will get you a nice little purse.' He nodded around. 'Right, that's it. You know where to find me. Play on, girly.' He stepped down again, and the blind girl tentatively picked up where she had left off, while the room buzzed with whispers.

Kino shot a glare to the barman as he turned to go. 'Same goes for you, Basilovich. Money in your pocket if you think of anything, but if you're protecting somebody...' He made a throat-cutting motion, then turned it into a salute and strutted for the back door.

This time the barman did drop a mug.

Ulrika hesitated, looking from one door to the other. Once again it wouldn't do to follow her prey directly, but the lank-haired vampire might be waiting out front, and might try to keep her from following Kino. She shrugged and strode for it anyway, hand on the pommel of her rapier. Let him try. She'd send him back to his masters with his fangs stuffed down his throat.

But there was no dark figure waiting in the street. She looked up to the roofs and into the shadows but saw nothing. Had she been wrong? Had the black-haired youth been just a student after all? No time to worry about it now. She had prey to hunt. She hurried to the narrow passage she had taken the night before, then trotted down it to the alley that ran behind the Blue Jug.

Kino's voice came to her as she stopped at the corner. 'Somebody isn't talking,' he was saying. 'Somebody knows something, and I'm going to find out who.'

'What if it really was a vampire, Kino?' asked another voice.

'Have you ever heard of a vampire stealing purses?' asked Kino. 'It was some little gang trying to cover their tracks with butchery, you mark my words. Now, come on. Let's try Madam Olneshkaya's. She always hears everything.'

Ulrika shrank into the shadows and watched as Kino and his boys walked past and continued down the alley. After giving them a moment to get ahead, she slipped after them, silent as a cat. Her hunting instincts immediately pushed to the fore, and she had to restrain herself from loping ahead and tearing into them. Killing and feeding on the men would defeat her purpose. She was going to follow them back to their master. *Him* she would kill and feed on. The rest could be finished off later, at her leisure.

She glanced again at the roofs. Had she heard something just then? She saw nothing. It might have been a rat, or a pigeon fidgeting in its nest, but it probably wasn't. The lupine vampire was likely following her, just as she was following Kino. She growled under her breath. She would be ready if he made his move.

AFTER MORE THAN an hour spent going in and out of brothels, taverns, dog pits and kvas parlours, Kino and his men gave up their investigation and headed home. Ulrika was glad. Following them had been a strange mixture of boredom and anxiety – boredom because there was no challenge to it, and anxiety because she was certain she was being watched, possibly by more than one set of eyes, but she could never catch anyone spying on her. She almost wanted to turn and shout up to the rooftops, 'I know you're there! Come out and face me!' but she couldn't, or she might lose her link to Gaznayev.

Finally, Kino and his men approached a big dockside warehouse near where the River Lynsk flowed out of Praag through a gate in the city walls. A man in a heavy cloak waved them through the warehouse's door, then went back to rubbing his hands and stamping his feet and staring off into the night.

Ulrika crouched in the shadow of a furniture workshop across the street, sizing the place up. It was brick, and two storeys high, with big double doors for wagons to pull into, and the smaller door Kino had just now entered. There were shuttered windows above that – offices most likely – but the bulk of the place was windowless. The roof however, had louvred gables along its length for ventilation. They looked very inviting.

She circled around to the river and approached the warehouse from that side. Two more big doors opened directly to two stubby docks, and there was another guard, huddled in the lee of an empty wagon, smoking a pipe. When his back was turned, Ulrika ducked between the warehouse and the one next to it, then quickly scaled the brick wall to the roof and padded along it to the first gable.

Listening at the louvres she could hear the faint murmur of distant voices, and smell the scents of men and sharp foreign spices. She pulled at the louvre's frame, exerting her inhuman strength, and it squealed free. She paused, but no alarm was raised, so she poked her head in, then wrinkled her nose. The spice smell was overpowering.

The warehouse spread out below her, a vast dark space piled with barrels and crates and burlap sacks that her sensitive nose told her were full of pepper and cumin and coriander. At the far end, a crack of light showed under a closed door. She turned her head this way and that, looking for a way down. A network of rafters held up the roof, but the nearest was more than ten feet below her, and no wider than the length of her hand. Well, she could but try.

She wormed her way feet-first through the narrow window, getting her sword caught and scraping her hips on the splintered frame, but at last she dangled by her hands high above the dark floor, then looked down between her toes, sighting for the rafter. It was a little to the left. She swung back and forth until she had built up some momentum, then let go and dropped towards it.

She hit it perfectly, but with too much force. Her boots slipped and she had to scrabble ungracefully at a crossbeam to keep from falling onto the crates below. She listened again. Still no alarm.

With a sigh of relief she got to her feet and tiptoed across the rafters towards the lit door, but before she had crossed half the distance, something caught her ear and she paused, balanced like a tightrope walker. There were heart-fires and pulses to her right, where she hadn't expected any, and, very faint, the sound of weeping.

Ulrika looked towards the sound. In the back corner of the warehouse a towering fortress of crates had been erected. It looked almost solid, but from her high vantage she could see it was hollow in the centre. She changed her trajectory, bounding at an angle across the rafters, then creeping more cautiously as she neared the crates and looked down into their hollow centre.

In the middle was a tall, roofless animal pen, and in it huddled a score of half-naked young girls, all refugees

by the look of them. Ulrika wondered at first why they
didn't just climb over the top and escape, but a closer
look gave her the answer. Some slept, some wept, some
huddled together, shivering in the cold, but all were
bruised and starved and miserable. None would have
had the strength for such a feat.

A crimson rage welled up in Ulrika, and her claws dug
into the beam she crouched upon – the tales of disappearing young women, the girl sacrificed in the
abandoned cellar, and now these poor wretches. What
cruel fate awaited them? Were they to become prosti-
tutes? Would they be sold in some foreign port? Would
they be slaves?

She snarled. They would be none of these things.
They would be free – tonight. She turned and started
picking her way across to the lit door again. She hadn't
needed any further motivation to kill Gaznayev. Her
hunger and his criminality had been enough, but now
his death would be more than just fulfilling her vow.
This wasn't common villainy. This wasn't shaking down
shopkeepers for protection money and robbing blind
girls. This was barbarity, something the Chaos hordes
would do, and she wouldn't allow it to exist in her
domain. She would go through these villains like a
scythe through wheat until she reached Gaznayev, but
with him, she would take her time – and when she was
finished, he would give her the key to the cage.

Voices behind the door grew louder. Ulrika stopped.
A latch clacked and the door swung open. Two toughs
strode into the warehouse, one big and bull-necked, the
other scrawny and hunched.

'Wake those sluts,' said Bull-neck as he crossed
towards the first set of big doors. 'The buyer'll be here
any minute.'

'Aye, Lenk,' said Scrawny, and started through the
stacked barrels towards the fortress of crates.

Ulrika remained motionless as he walked beneath her and the big man pulled the bolts on the big doors and started to swing them open. The buyers were coming – the men who had paid the gangsters to collect the girls. Her mind churned. As much as she wanted to cut her bloody way to Gaznayev, he was only the middleman. Whatever horrors awaited the stolen girls, it was the men who were coming to get them who were behind it, and this might be Ulrika's only chance to discover who they were. Gaznayev could wait. She could come back to him later.

She turned on the rafter and watched Scrawny step to the wall of crates and open a door cleverly disguised as two stacked boxes. He disappeared into a tunnel through them and Ulrika heard a loud metallic banging.

'Wakey wakey, y'filthy whores!' Scrawny cried. 'On yer feet! Yer masters are coming soon!'

Ulrika padded back to the rafters above the crates and peered down at the cage. The man was circling it, rapping on the bars with the pommel of his dagger and leering at the girls inside as they cowered away from him.

'If only they'd waited another day,' he said. 'I weren't done sampling the merchandise.' He shrugged. 'Ah well. There's more where you lot came from.'

With a final bang on the bars he strolled back through the tunnel in the wall and shut the door behind him while the girls in the cage got slowly to their feet and collected their meagre belongings. Ulrika crouched above them, pondering. How best to follow them to their new masters? Then she had it. She would join them. She would drop down into the cage and… No. That wouldn't work – at least not dressed the way she was. But she could change that, if she was quick. All she needed was some way to carry her clothes with her.

She looked around. Stacked against the back wall of the warehouse was a pile of bulging burlap sacks. She skimmed across the rafters, then dropped down to them. They had a rich, spicy scent. She cut one open and out spilled a torrent of yellow turmeric. She upended the sack, dumping the powder out on top of the pile, then began stripping out of her cloak, doublet and boots and stuffing them in the sack.

Barefoot, with her breeches rolled up and hidden beneath the long billowing shirt she had stolen from Chesnekov, she hoped she would look the part of a kidnapped girl – perhaps if she kept her head down. But there was another problem. She doubted they would look twice if she carried the sack, but her rapier was another matter. She couldn't fit it in the sack, and she couldn't wear it.

The clatter of a horse and wagon came from outside. The buyers were here! She cursed. She would just have to hide the sword here and come back for it. She meant to come back for Gaznayev anyway. She would retrieve it then.

She leapt back up to the rafters, then ran across to the square of crates. At the big doors, Bull-neck and Scrawny were waving the wagon in as the driver backed the horses. Only seconds now. She laid her rapier along a beam, then dropped down to the crates with her sack. A few of the girls heard her and looked up. She waved them out of the way, then jumped down into the cage amongst them. There were a few shrieks and gasps, but most of the captives just stared dully at her with blank eyes, completely lost in their misery.

Ulrika looked around at the girls who had cried out, putting a finger to her lips, then did her best to mimic the lost ones, slumping her shoulders and hanging her head, her sack of clothes clutched forlornly to her chest. She wished she had some way to cover her hair, but there was no hope for it. If they noticed her, then she would kill them now, and find some way to hunt down the rest later.

The door in the crates opened, and Bull-neck and Scrawny led three cloaked and hooded men through the tunnel to the cage.

'There you are, sirs,' said Bull-neck, holding up a lantern. 'The week's catch. All as hale and hearty as you could wish.'

Ulrika raised her eyes just enough to peer at the three newcomers. She could not see their faces under their deep hoods. They were wearing thin black veils to hide their features. They were indeed, however, men. She could hear their hearts thudding in their chests.

The first of them took a leather purse from his sleeve and handed it to Bull-neck without a word, then gestured to Scrawny to open the cage. The little man gave a shiver as he turned, then unlocked the cage and swung open the door.

'File out, sluts,' he said, and banged on the cage with his key ring. 'Come on. Move.'

The girls shuffled forwards fearfully, and Ulrika went with them, keeping her head as low as she could. Her spine tingled as she passed between the hooded men, sure they would see she was not like the others and single her out, but they didn't seem to notice, and she followed the other captives through the tunnel in the wall of crates and out the other side.

Directly before the door was an entirely enclosed wagon – like a Strigany's caravan but without the colourful decoration – with a ramp leading up to an open door in the back. Some of the girls shied at the sight of it and held back, but two more hooded men prodded them forwards with sticks, and they crept timorously up the ramp and into the dark interior.

Ulrika crowded in with the rest, and by the time they

were all in and the door shut and locked, they were packed together as tight as toes in a pointed boot, and just as fragrant. The cramped box smelled of fear, faeces and death, and was as lightless as a coffin.

A moment later there came the crack of a whip, the wagon lurched and they were off. Ulrika wondered belatedly how far they would go. What if they were leaving the city? What if they were leaving the country? What if they were let out in daylight? She shrugged. She would face that dragon when she reached it. There was little she could do about it now.

Beside her, one of the captives began to weep, a tired hopeless sound. Ulrika put her arm around the girl, and tried not to think about the blood pulsing just beneath her skin.

AFTER ONLY A short while, the closed wagon slowed and made a tight turn, then started down a steep grade. All the girls in the box staggered and crushed together towards the front until it levelled off again and came to a stop. Muffled voices came from outside, then, with a rattle and a creak, the door swung open. The girls turned like flowers towards the sun, squinting in the dim firelight that filtered through the door.

Two hooded men placed the ramp, then beckoned the girls ahead. They trudged obediently forwards, and Ulrika followed, looking around at their surroundings. The wagon had stopped in one corner of a huge vaulted chamber full of looming shadows and smoke. A cold wind blew down from somewhere above, tearing at a fire in a nearby brazier which cast flickering light upon rows of giant brass vats and wooden kegs taller than a man. It was reflected also in a great hill of empty glass bottles piled in one corner that glittered like a thousand red eyes. The place reeked of fermented grain and strong liquor – a kvas distillery, it seemed, though long abandoned.

'This way, children,' said a hooded man, motioning with an empty kvas bottle he held in his hand. He led them to an arched alcove in the stone walls, within which had been set a door of iron bars.

From one cage to another, thought Ulrika.

The man swung the door open, then blew idly across the top of his bottle, making a hollow tooting sound as two other hooded men herded the girls into it. Ulrika allowed herself to be prodded in with the others, for she saw the bars were old and rusted, and would not hold her if she did not wish them to. First she wanted to see what their captors intended to do with them.

She did not have long to wait. The man with the bottle held back the last girl, then locked the rest in. The girl struggled as the two men grabbed her and led her across the room to an open space between the vats.

Ulrika pushed forwards to the bars and saw that a shallow circle had been carved in the hard earth of the cellar floor, and that its edges were black with dried blood.

CHAPTER THIRTEEN
SERVANTS OF SLAANESH

ULRIKA GRIPPED THE bars of the cage as, from all over the vaulted chamber, more hooded figures emerged from the shadows and gathered around the bloody circle. The design of it was just like that of the one she had found in the cellar of the abandoned tenement – the one with the sacrificed girl staked out in it. It seemed Gaznayev's gang was selling the girls to a murder cult.

The girl fought harder as she saw where the hooded men were leading her. 'What are you going to do?' she cried. 'Stop!'

The man with the bottle laughed. 'Stop? Just when we are about to give your worthless little life meaning?'

He motioned to the other men, then continued speaking as they stripped the girl of her clothes and a fourth man set candles around the perimeter of the circle and began lighting them.

'What would you have done with your span of years?' he asked. 'Shat out a litter of brats, lived in poverty, died in poverty? Your wretched life would have added nothing to the world. But now you will have greater purpose.

Now you will be part of something monumental!' He flipped the empty bottle in the air and caught it. 'When Mannslieb is next full, your soil will join the others in the great awakening that will begin the claiming of Praag by its rightful mistress!'

The two men dragged the now-naked girl into the centre of the circle as another man stepped forwards with a hammer and spikes. Ulrika had seen enough. She wrenched back sharply on one of the cage's iron bars. It squealed and bent, but didn't break.

The girls around her gasped and edged away from her, wide-eyed, while the cultists at the circle turned at the noise.

'What was that?' said the man with the bottle.

Ulrika pulled again, and this time the bar sheared in half, tearing her palm.

'What is she doing!' cried the man. 'Stop her!'

A handful of hooded forms trotted towards the cage, drawing clubs and daggers. Ulrika pulled at the lower half of the broken bar, trying to bend it down so she could slip through the gap. It snapped off at the base and she stumbled back with it in her hand. She grinned. Perfect.

The cultists slowed their steps, staring uneasily.

'Powers of darkness!' gasped one. 'How is she doing that?'

Ulrika eeled through the gap and rose to her full height before them, brandishing the iron bar. 'Let me show you the powers of darkness,' she said, and before they could react, she sprang among them, lashing out on all sides with her makeshift weapon.

Three died instantly, their skulls caved in and blood darkening the fabric of their hoods as they toppled to the ground. The other three darted in, stabbing for her stomach and swinging for her face. She kicked one man back, caught the wrist of the second as he slashed at her with a dagger, then whipped him into the third man. These last two went down on top of one another. Ulrika stabbed down and pierced them both through the chests with her iron bar, pinning them to the ground, then turned to face the last man.

He stood stock still, and though she could not see his face through the veil he wore under his hood, she could smell the fear oozing from his pores. She ripped the bloody bar from the bodies of his companions and advanced on him. He shrieked and fled – but not fast enough.

Ulrika caught him in two swift steps and bashed his head in from behind. His hood, as he fell, sagged and bulged like a sack full of wet meat.

The fight had taken all of twenty heartbeats, and as she turned towards the man with the bottle and his comrades at the circle, she could see they were as paralysed as her last victim had been. Ulrika looked back at the girls in the cage. They were frozen too, the whites of their eyes shining in the firelight as they stared at the bodies at her feet.

'Go!' she said. 'Return to your families.'

Most of the girls didn't move, but a few of the braver ones began to duck through the gap, and as they did, the more timid followed.

Ulrika turned back to the dozen cultists at the circle and started towards them, the iron bar held at her side.

The man with the bottle stepped back, pointing it with a shaking hand. 'Kill her! Don't let the sacrifices escape!'

His companions looked less than enthusiastic about the first part of his command, and instead split left and right to address the second, trying to get around her to the girls, who were breaking for the ramp. She let them go, and charged directly at the leader and the men who held the sacrifice. All three fled in different directions.

Ulrika pounced on the leader, then dragged him back to the circle, where the girl lay cowering on the ground beside the hammer and spikes that would have pinned her to it.

'Get away,' said Ulrika, nudging the girl with her toe, then shoved the man down in her place as she crawled off, weeping.

'You must not touch me!' the man cried, squirming as Ulrika picked up the hammer and a spike. 'Wait! What are you doing?'

'Saving you for a greater purpose,' said Ulrika, then knelt on his wrist and pounded the spike through the palm of his hand into the hard earth with a single strike.

He screamed and writhed as she stood and looked around the room. The other cultists had caught the escaped girls and were dragging them back towards the cage. She picked up her iron bar again and stalked towards them, growling low in her throat.

The men shouted as they saw her coming, and some released the girls and fled up the ramp. The rest clumped together and ran at her, weapons raised. Ulrika sprinted straight at these, then leapt over their heads, striking down with the bar.

She landed behind them, not turning to see if her blow had struck home, and charged up the ramp. The fleeing men turned at the sound of her steps, preparing to fight, but she leapt their heads too and got between them and the exit.

'Jackals,' she said, as they turned to face her. 'Preying on the weak. Now you will know what it is like to be prey.'

She sprang into the middle of them before they could move, whirling around with the iron bar and cracking skulls and snapping arms. A handful fell away, howling and clutching themselves, but the rest leapt in, screaming. She smashed a man with a hatchet in the neck, lifting him off his feet and sending him crashing into the wall of the ramp. Two more hacked at her legs with swords. She dodged one, but took a cut from the other, then ran him through.

More darted in, slashing and chopping. She pulled on the iron bar. It was stuck in the swordsman's ribs. A dagger gashed her back. A club smashed her shoulder. A sword grazed her arm.

Ulrika snarled, enraged, and shot out her fangs and claws as her vision turned crimson and black and a roaring filled her ears. The men around her gasped and cried out. She inhaled their fear and leapt at them, leaving the iron bar where it was. She didn't want a weapon now. It would only keep her at a distance from her victims.

Blood splashed the walls as she tore a man's throat out. Another stabbed at her and she ripped his arm off. Her claws found flesh wherever she turned, and she rended and tore in a red whirlwind, blind with fury, finding her victims by the hammering of their terrified hearts.

Then a deafening bang punched her ears, and a blow like a red-hot poker smashed her thigh and staggered her. She looked up, waking from her blood fugue as waves of searing pain radiated from the wound. The men she had vaulted were advancing up the ramp towards her. One had a smoking pistol in his hand, and was aiming a second.

Ulrika shrieked like a wildcat and bounded down at him. The second pistol cracked, but the ball whizzed past her and she tackled the man, smashing him through the others to slam him on his back at the base of the ramp. They skidded to a stop and she tore his throat out with her teeth.

The other men thundered down all around her, shouting at each other to attack. She looked up from her crouch, blood dripping off her chin, then launched herself at the nearest. Again the world became nothing but red and black flashes – frozen moments of glorious slaughter – a man falling, his veil and his face half-torn away, another man screaming and staring at the stumps of his fingers, a hooded head rolling away down the ramp.

Ulrika returned to herself some time later on her hands and knees at the base of the ramp, panting amidst the dead and dying, and deliciously happy. Rivulets of blood coursed down between the filthy cobbles from the men she had killed further up, and more dripped from her chin and nose. It was only as she stood and looked around at the carnage that shame chilled her contentment. There was a girl among the men, one of the abducted, as savaged as the others. There were bite-marks on her face.

Ulrika looked away, wincing and cursing. She felt no remorse for killing the cultists. They deserved worse than she had given them, and she hoped that, in death, they would find eternal torment at the hands of the cruel gods they had been foolish enough to worship in life. It was the way she had killed that repulsed her. She had once again lost control, once again broken her vow to herself, and once again paid for it in pain and self-loathing. Had she not been lost in scarlet abandon, she would not have taken the pistol ball in the leg, she would not have killed the girl, she would not now feel the crushing weight of guilt upon her shoulders.

She examined her gun wound. The ball had torn a ragged trench in her outer thigh, but had not remained. She didn't have to dig lead out of flesh again – a small comfort. With a groan she rose to her feet. Her once-white shirt was red and wet from neck to waist. Her hands were sticky with blood, and her hair was stiff with it. She sighed and limped into the vaulted chamber as, on the cold wind that blew down the ramp, the faint notes of a violin laughed in the distance.

The freed girls huddled in a terrified clump and backed away as she approached, looking more afraid of her than they had been of their captors. She didn't blame them.

'What are you waiting for?' she snarled as she passed them. 'Go! Run!'

They ran, stumbling up the ramp as she crossed to the leader of the ceremony, who lay panting and limp in the circle, his hand still spiked to the ground. At least she'd had the forethought to put him aside before her madness had consumed her. She could still question him.

He raised his hooded head as she approached, then struggled, only to shriek as he tugged on his pinned hand. 'Lord of Pleasure protect me!' he wailed. 'You are impossible. You can't–'

She knelt on his chest, cutting off his babble, then tore off his hood and veil. He was surprisingly ordinary – a balding, middle-aged man with the look of a prosperous shopkeeper. He stared up at her with wide eyes, sweating and grey with fear.

'Who are you?' he whimpered. 'What do you want?'

'Tell me of your mistress,' she said. 'She who means to claim Praag for her own. Who is she? What is this awakening you spoke of?'

The man shook his head. 'I will not speak. There is nothing you can do that will make me betray the cause.'

Ulrika smiled. 'Is that a challenge?' She pinned his free hand with her other knee, then caught up the hammer and another spike.

'No!' the man cried. 'No, no, please!'

'Then tell me,' she said.

'I cannot!' he wailed. 'I dare not!'

Ulrika put the spike to his wrist, and raised the hammer. The man shut his eyes, but kept his mouth clamped shut. She hesitated, but though he continued to cringe, he still said nothing. She cursed under her breath. He was willing to take the pain. He might be willing to die from it before he talked. She had no compunction against torture, if it worked, but the man seemed a true fanatic. Even in fear and pain he would not talk.

The twitch of the vein in his neck as he turned his head away drew her eye. Perhaps there was another way.

She put down the hammer and spike and stroked his throat. He blinked at the unexpected contact, and turned white-rimmed eyes to stare at her.

'What are you doing?' he bleated.

'I have been cruel to you,' she murmured, bending low over him. 'I have given you great pain, and I am sorry for it. Now I will sooth you.'

He shrieked as she opened her mouth and extended her fangs. 'No! What are you? Stop!'

She lowered her lips to his neck and bit into his flesh as gently as if she were kissing an infant. He spasmed and thrashed, but then, as she began to suck at the vein he froze like a rabbit, and after a minute, relaxed with a sigh. She had been afraid his blood would be tainted like that of the Norse marauder she had blooded during the attack on the caravan, but the cultist was apparently not so far gone as that. His blood tasted like any other man's. She closed her eyes as the sweet salt savour of it poured down her throat and filled her with soothing warmth, but she could not lose herself. She could not feed for the enjoyment of it. She took another pull, then drew away, licking her lips.

This time when he looked up at her, his eyes were heavy-lidded with desire. He reached his free hand up to her. It shook.

'Again,' he said. 'Again.'

'Answer me first,' she said. 'Your mistress?'

'I cannot,' he whined. 'I will never betray her.'

Her lips drifted back to his neck, brushing it lightly. She licked at the blood that welled from the wound. 'Never?'

He shivered with lust, but then shook his head. 'Never.'

'We shall see.' She drank again, deeper this time, and longer. His pawings got weaker the more she drew from him, and his moans became mere whispers.

She pulled away and looked at him again. His skin was pallid from lack of blood, and his lips blue. She turned his head and fixed him with her gaze.

'Your mistress?'

'I... I can't think.'

'Tell me,' she said, hoping she hadn't taken too much. He was barely conscious now. 'Tell me and I will give you more.'

His face twisted with confusion and fear. 'She... she is a champion of our god,' he murmured at last. 'A mighty warrior of the north, chosen to lead us to glory.'

This sounded unsettlingly like the warlord of whom Chesnekov had spoken – the thing, neither man nor woman, that hid in the nearby hills. 'And her plans for Praag?'

'We will open its gates to her... after – after the awakening,' he said, reaching towards her with a slack hand. 'She will be its queen, and we her consorts. Now, please...'

Ulrika frowned. Could a few lunatics in a basement truly conquer Praag from within? With outside help, perhaps. 'Where is she now?' she asked. 'And what is this awakening?'

The cultist shook his head. 'I don't know. I swear to you. Only the master knows. We... are not trusted with such things. Now, please, kiss me again. Please...'

'Who is the master?'

'I have never seen him,' moaned the man. 'He speaks

through… intermediaries. Please, you must not deny me.'

She nuzzled his neck. 'It is a terrible thing, is it not, to be a slave to pleasure? Tell me where I may find one of these intermediaries, and I will give you what you wish.'

He hesitated, then sobbed and looked away from her. 'I dare not,' he moaned. 'They will damn me. I will be condemned to eternal… torment.'

A thought came to her at this. She smiled at him. 'But I can save you from that. I can give you eternal pleasure. You could serve a different mistress.'

The man's eyes grew wide. 'You… you…?'

Ulrika nodded, holding his eyes like a snake mesmerising a mouse. 'You know what I am. You know what is within my power to grant. I would keep you at my side forever.'

The man swallowed, staring at her. 'Forever? You swear this?'

'On my father's grave,' she said.

The man hesitated, then closed his eyes. 'I know not his name, nor his face, but he lives on the Street of Jewellers, in apartments above the shop of Gurdjieff, the silversmith. Six long knocks is the signal. He will let you in. Now please… please,' he said, turning his head to show the wound in his neck. 'Give me what you promised.'

Ulrika bent low over him again, then whispered in his ear. 'My father was never buried. He was burned on a pyre.'

'What!' The man tried to turn his head, but she held it still with the heel of her hand, then tore his throat out with her teeth.

She rose to her feet as he clutched at his neck with his free hand, trying to press closed the gouting hole while he drowned in his own blood.

'May your gods give you the welcome you deserve,' she said.

She smiled as she walked back to the cage to collect the sack with her things in it. That was the way it should be done – calmly and neatly, without savagery. She had won the information she required, had hurt no one except her intended victim, had begun the healing of her leg with the blood she had taken from him and had maintained control at all times. This was the way she would be from now on.

In the cage, she tore off her soaking shirt, emptied the burlap sack and used it to mop the blood from herself, then threw it away and pulled on her doublet and cloak. She no doubt still looked a mess, but it would have to do. There was no time for primping.

A noise from the chamber as she tugged on her boots brought her head up. She hopped awkwardly to the bars on one foot and looked around. The shadow of a limping man was disappearing up the ramp.

Ulrika cursed. One of the cultists hadn't been as close to death as she had thought. Had he heard her talking to his leader? Did he know he had betrayed his superior? She stamped her heels down into her boots, then ducked through the gap in the cage and ran for the ramp.

The man heard her and limped faster, lurching through the open arch at the top of the ramp and into the night. Ulrika jogged after him, ripping the iron bar from the ribs of the corpse she had left it in on her way. She had the man's scent now. She could hear his pulse. He would not escape her.

She ran out into the yard of the demolished distillery and saw her prey stumbling towards a ruined gate. She started after him, then slowed as something incongruous caught her eye. There was a richly furnished black coach standing in the middle of the rubble, its driver watching her, its horses blowing steam in the cold night air.

'Stand where you are,' said a voice behind her.

Ulrika turned. A lean blonde woman in a long coat and fur hat was stepping out of the shadows of the distillery. She wore daggers tucked into a piratical red sash wrapped around her waist, and held a Kossar sabre in her hand.

The sound of the coach door opening made Ulrika turn again. Two women in fur cloaks and rich dresses of antique cut were stepping down from it. One was tall – nearly as tall as Ulrika – with a cold, proud face and the carriage of a queen, while the other was a tiny withered redhead, as dead-eyed as a porcelain doll. They glided between her and the gate, through which the fleeing cultist was just vanishing.

A dread foreboding prickled Ulrika's skin as she saw the women, but whoever they were, they would have to wait. The cultist came first. She made to dart between them, but the tall one caught her arm in an iron grip and held her back.

'Stop,' she said.

Ulrika wrenched free. 'Let me pass!'

The woman in the long coat stepped in and put the tip of her sabre to Ulrika's throat as the other two hemmed her in.

'Not yet,' said the tall one. 'We would speak to you first, *sister*.'

CHAPTER FOURTEEN
THE ANCIENT REGIME

Sister.

With that single word, Ulrika knew her suspicions had been correct. The shadows that had followed her all night had coalesced at last, revealing themselves to be Lahmians. She looked around for the male vampire who had watched her earlier, but he was nowhere to be seen. Was he their scout? Their dog? Their assassin?

'Let me go,' she said. 'I must stop that man.'

'You must do nothing until I allow it,' said the tall vampiress. She pointed at Ulrika with an ivory fan. 'Who are you? Of what bloodline? Why have you come to Praag?'

Ulrika didn't like her tone. 'What business is that of yours?'

The woman drew herself up. Close to, her face was a map of tiny dry wrinkles, covered, but not hidden, by thick white make-up. Her eyebrows were painted on. 'Everything that occurs in Praag is my business,' she said. 'I am Boyarina Evgena Boradin. I rule here by order of the Queen of the Silver Mountain, and all of the blood who abide here do so at my sufferance. I will have my answers, or Raiza will have your head.'

Ulrika flicked her eyes to the woman who held the sabre. She was a hard, hawk-nosed warrior, her lank blonde hair hanging from under her fur hat like a curtain. She looked more than capable of taking Ulrika's head off.

'But he's getting away,' Ulrika rasped.

'There are other mice,' said the little doll, giggling. 'One is not so important.' She too was wrinkled and painted, and Ulrika could see that her cascading mass of red hair was a wig which seemed too big for her head.

'You don't understand,' said Ulrika. 'He goes to warn his leaders of my coming. They will vanish. I will lose them!'

The ancient boyarina looked entirely unmoved. 'You are correct. I do not understand. You seem to be conducting some vendetta on my lands, and sowing slaughter at every turn without thought to consequence. We cannot have rumours of men drained of blood whispered in Praag. We cannot have tales of man-sized bats. You threaten our safety with these foolish antics. The chekist are already asking questions. Now speak. Who are you?'

Ulrika ground her teeth in frustration. 'My name is Ulrika Magdova Straghov, and I have come to Praag to defend it against the hordes of Chaos.'

The shrivelled redhead laughed. 'You are late for that.'

'Hush, Galiana,' said Boyarina Evgena, without looking away from Ulrika. 'And your bloodline?'

Ulrika hesitated. It didn't seem wise to mention her true parentage here. They were suspicious enough already. Telling them her sire had von Carstein blood would not ease their minds. 'My mistress was Gabriella von Nachthafen,' she said. 'A Lahmian like yourselves, but I serve no one now, and acknowledge no line.'

Galiana tittered at that. 'You haven't been dead a year yet, have you?'

'I know of your mistress,' said Evgena, frowning. 'She is in Nuln now, yes? There was trouble there. Were you the cause of it?'

Ulrika lifted her chin. 'I killed the cause of it. A mad Strigoi.'

'Then why did you flee?' asked Evgena.

'I did not flee!' barked Ulrika. 'I... I struck out on my own.' She glared at Evgena. 'Now, I have given you your answers. Will you let me pass?'

Evgena raised a painted eyebrow. 'Are you mad? Of course not. I cannot allow a vampire who has not sworn fealty to me to go free in my domain. You have three choices, girl. Accept me as your mistress, leave Praag immediately or be destroyed here and now. Which do you choose?'

Ulrika growled. She didn't want to kiss the hand of this dusty old crow, nor did she want to leave Praag. She wanted to strike out at them and run after the cultist, but armed with only a clumsy iron bar, she would not defeat them. These were not slow, frightened humans. She would probably not even escape the first thrust of the blonde swordswoman's sabre, the tip of which was still pressing against her throat. Her fists clenched angrily. It was just this sort of arrogant authority she had left Nuln to escape.

'I will not choose,' she said.

'Then I will choose for you,' said Evgena. She flicked her fan at the swordswoman, Raiza. 'Kill her.'

With the cold speed of an automaton, Raiza extended and thrust with the sabre. But Ulrika was not caught entirely off guard. Evgena's tone and gesture had given her a second's warning, and she threw herself back, twisting and falling, as the sabre's point shot forwards. The edge of the blade sliced into the side of her neck, but the point had missed her throat and veins.

She landed on her back, then rolled to her feet and raised her iron bar as blood ran down her neck and under her collar.

'Why can't you let me be!' she cried as Raiza came forwards warily, sabre in high guard. 'Why don't you fight a real enemy?'

The women did not answer, only moved to encircle her.

Ulrika snarled and backed towards the collapsed distillery, her fury rising. 'You say everything that occurs in Praag is your business,' she spat. 'You say it is your domain. Look in that cellar. A cult works under your noses to destroy the city, and you know nothing of it. You are more interested in making me toe your line than in defending your lands.'

'There are always cults,' said Evgena as she hemmed Ulrika in on her right. 'And they always work to destroy Praag. But in the two hundred years I have ruled here, they have never succeeded. They destroy themselves, or fight with other cults, or are rooted out by the priests or the Chekist. It is not our concern.'

'You do *not* rule here,' sneered Ulrika. She could sense the broken walls of the distillery looming behind her. 'A ruler cares for her subjects. Even a shepherdess protects her flock from the wolves before she has her mutton. You are nothing but parasites.'

Evgena and Galiana closed in on her from either side, their satin dresses rustling and their claws extending, as Raiza advanced on her front. Ulrika tensed. She could attack, but she would lose. The two ancients would hold her while Raiza chopped off her head. With a screech of rage, Ulrika flailed around wildly with her iron bar, then turned and bounded over the collapsed wall behind her.

She landed in a room that had once been an office.

Roof timbers buried the desk and chairs. She clambered over them and shot through the door on the far wall. Footsteps thudded behind her. She looked back. Raiza was leaping the desk in turn. Evgena and Galiana had not followed.

Ulrika pelted down a corridor with the swordswoman hot on her heels. She was fast, perhaps faster than Ulrika, and as focused as a hawk on the hunt. Ulrika toppled timbers and rubble behind her, but Raiza dodged it all, eyes never wavering from Ulrika's back.

Ulrika burst through a charred door and sprinted across an open area which still had half its roof. Great brick furnaces ran down one wall, with sand pits and wooden racks filled with dusty bottles and glassblowers' tools beside them.

Raiza gained ground in the uncluttered space, and Ulrika heard the whistling cut of her sabre at her back. She slashed behind her, aiming for Raiza's legs. The swordswoman chopped the iron bar in half, then gored Ulrika's shoulder. Ulrika cursed and pulled down a rack of bottles as she staggered on, hissing in pain. Raiza dodged the falling rack, but stepped on a rolling bottle and went down hard.

Ulrika didn't stop to fight. She vaulted up onto one of the old furnaces, then clawed to the hole in the roof and pulled herself onto the slates, her shoulder throbbing and bleeding. Raiza was already up again and climbing the furnace after her.

Ulrika turned and hurled the stub. It cracked Raiza in the head and she fell back to the floor. Ulrika pounded down the roof to the end of the building, pressing her wounded shoulder, then leapt an alley to the roof of a tenement and landed between two chimney pots. She scrambled up over the peak of the roof, only to find herself sliding towards a gaping hole on the other side.

With a wrenching twist, she threw herself to one side and skidded to a stop just to the left of the hole. She lifted her head and listened. She heard no pursuit, and took a second to check the shoulder wound Raiza had given her. It was deep, but already healing, thanks to the blood of the cultist she had fed from. She pressed it and hurried for the next peak. She couldn't stop. Raiza would recover, and she still had to beat the fleeing man to the address his leader had given her.

A thud behind her shook the roof. She turned. Raiza was in mid-leap, silhouetted against Mannslieb, sword high. Ulrika dived aside and scrambled away as the swordswoman landed and lunged. She wished now she hadn't thrown the iron bar. Even a stub of defence would have been better than nothing. She put a chimney between them, then glanced over her shoulder. The next roof was missing entirely, burned away, revealing scorched apartments below. She was backed against the drop.

She turned back as Raiza came around the chimney, then froze as something to the left caught her eye. A figure was watching from another roof – the vampire from the Blue Jug. He *was* in league with the Lahmians. But no, he just stood there, observing.

Raiza's sabre stabbed her in the ribs, striking bone. Ulrika gasped and fell back, flailing, through the burnt-away roof. A blackened rafter blurred past her. She grabbed for it and caught it. It snapped like a matchstick and she slammed to the charred floorboards of the ruined apartments, still holding a length of it. The planks creaked dangerously, and an interior wall, slumped against a splintered armoire like a drunk leaning on a friend, shifted ominously, shaking loose a rattle of plaster pebbles.

Raiza entered the room more gracefully, leaping down from roof to rafter to bed to floor, but her first step was almost her last. A blackened board gave way under her boot and she had to catch herself to keep from falling through.

An opening! Ulrika scrabbled up, slashing with the length of rafter, trying to disarm her. Raiza blocked easily and shot a riposte straight at Ulrika's heart.

Ulrika parried with her clumsy weapon, and the sabre blade slid past an inch from her ribs, cutting a white wedge in the burnt wood.

They leapt apart and went on guard, then circled, stepping carefully to avoid the holes and weak spots in the floor. Ulrika wished she had her rapier. The swordswoman was one of the finest fencers she had ever faced, and certainly the fastest. Facing her sword to sword, the fight could have been a joy, regardless of the consequences. Now it was only a frustration.

'You have a good arm,' Ulrika said, pushing a stray lock from her eyes. 'I regret not having a proper sword, so I might give you a challenge.'

'Accept the boyarina's offer,' Raiza said in a steel whisper, 'and we will duel every night.'

'I did not leave one mistress to crawl to another,' said Ulrika. 'I am my own mistr–'

Raiza sprang before Ulrika finished the sentence, stabbing forwards in a full lunge. Ulrika back-pedalled furiously, chopping at her blade with the length of timber, but the swordswoman dipped under and thrust. Ulrika threw herself back from the point, and landed heavily on the floor.

Raiza came on, sabre raised to slash. Ulrika pushed herself up, or tried to. Her left hand and arm broke through weakened planks and she slammed face-first on the floor. The sabre whistled over her head and she rolled, tearing her arm free of the hole and holding the blackened beam in front of her. Raiza knocked it from her hand and slashed again.

Ulrika crabbed back and her shoulders thudded into something heavy behind her. The armoire.

The armoire!

As Raiza thrust for her chest, Ulrika twisted aside and kicked at the base of the armoire, trying to upset it. It shifted and Raiza looked up, for the wall that was leaning on it shifted too, sending down a rain of debris.

Ulrika gave the armoire another kick. It started to topple forwards, and the wall followed it. Ulrika scrambled to the edge of the room as Raiza jumped back. The armoire and the wall slammed down an inch from the toes of her boots, missing her. Ulrika cursed. The woman was just too quick.

But the wall did not stop falling at the floor. It smashed through the rickety planks and took everything with it. The boards beneath Raiza's feet tilted like the deck of a listing ship and she slid down into the storey below in a shower of timbers, plaster and rubble.

Ulrika peered down into the hole, but could see nothing in the dense cloud of dust that rose from it. She hesitated, and almost called down to ask if Raiza was all right, then snorted at the thought. The woman had tried to kill her.

She turned and leapt up to the rafters, then climbed to the hole in the roof. Was the male vampire still there? She poked her head out and sighted around. She didn't see him. Nor did she see Boyarina Evgena or Galiana. Of course, they could all be lying in wait, but she would have to risk it. She couldn't give Raiza time to recover, and she still had to beat the cultist to his superiors.

She ran across the rooftops in the direction of the Merchant Quarter, cursing all vampires. Why couldn't they leave her alone? She meant them no harm. She wanted nothing to do with them at all. Must they be like wild dogs, fighting all who dared enter their territory? It wasn't until she smelled smoke on the wind and saw a bright yellow glow over the rooftops that she woke from her angry reverie to a sinking sense of dread.

Ulrika dropped down to the street and raced the last few blocks at a sprint. The smoke in the Street of Jewellers was thicker than fog, and people were running in all directions, shouting for ladders and buckets and water. She was certain what she would find, but her blood still boiled when she came around the last corner and saw it before her. The apartments above the shop of Gurdjieff the silversmith were burning like a torch. Indeed, the whole building and the buildings to either side were engulfed, and blackened bodies lay in the street where rescuers had dragged them, too late. A mournful violin played somewhere in the distance, a requiem for the dead, almost drowned out by the crackle of the flames.

Damn the Lahmians! Had they not stopped her, she would have run down that cultist within a block, then come here and caught the intermediary unawares. Instead he had been warned, and had covered his tracks in the crudest, most effective way possible. There would be no clues found in the apartments now. Her cursed sisters' unwanted interruption had cost her her best lead.

How was she to find the cult again? Should she return to the distillery? Should she watch the cellar where she had first found one of their victims? They might never return to those places. There had to be a quicker way.

Then she had it. She knew a man who took the cultists' money and dealt with them on a regular basis – Gaznayev, the gangster who procured their girls for them and held them at his warehouse. With a savage smile she turned from the fire and started for the river.

It was time to retrieve her sword.

CHAPTER FIFTEEN
RING OF FIRE

ULRIKA WAS AFRAID, as she approached Gaznayev's warehouse, that at this late hour the gangsters would have gone home to bed, and she would have to wait another day to confront them, but as she approached the front, she saw two men guarding the door to the offices, and another two making a circuit of the building, swords drawn and peering suspiciously into the shadows.

This made her pause. Something was amiss. The gangsters were stirred up. Did they know she was coming? How could they?

She slipped past the patrol and followed her earlier path up to the roof to the louvred vent, then stuck her head in and looked around. The warehouse was empty and quiet, but she could detect a faint constellation of heart-fires at the edge of her senses, in the direction of the offices. She dropped silently to the rafters and padded across to where she had left her sword. The relief that flooded her as she belted it around her waist was embarrassing. She had felt naked without it.

She tiptoed across the rafters until she was over the

door that led to the offices. She could sense pulses behind it, but the voices were coming through the wall directly beside her – a first-floor office? She edged along the beam to the wall and put her ear to it. More heart-fires here, seven or eight, all grouped close together, and a harsh voice trying to sound smooth.

'Friends,' it was saying. 'If you found the goods we provided not to your liking, I will gladly find you replacements for no charge. We aim to please, and–'

'Do you think I'm here for money, Gaznayev?' said another voice, this one dark and rich. 'You planted a damned cuckoo in our flight of doves, and I'll know the reason why.'

'Cuckoo?' wheezed a third voice. 'She was a bloody hawk! Fifteen of us she killed. Fifteen!'

Ulrika froze, her claws digging into the wall. They were talking about her. The men in the office were cultists, putting Gaznayev on the spot for including her in the shipment of girls.

'You can't hold us responsible for that,' Gaznayev was saying. 'I don't know nothing about it!'

Ulrika hopped down from the rafter and stalked eagerly to the door. By a stroke of luck, she had found her lost lead again. She would question the man with the dark voice about the leader of the cult. Perhaps he was the leader himself.

There were more murmurs behind the door. She listened.

'Easy, friends,' said a voice she recognised as that of the bull-necked gangster from earlier. 'Don't do anything foolish. The bosses are just talking, that's all.'

'Then you should lower your weapons as well,' said another voice.

Ulrika smiled. Tensions were rising among the minions as well as the masters. Good.

A shout came from above. 'None of that! None of that! Kino, stop him!'

A clash of blades and a rumble of boots and falling furniture followed, and was immediately echoed behind the door. Ulrika drew her rapier and dagger. Now was her time.

She wrenched open the door and darted through. Inside was a small office, with desks along one wall and flailing bodies in the centre. Bull-neck was bashing a cloaked man over the head with a boathook, while his scrawny companion was staggering back from two more, a dagger in his chest.

Ulrika sprang and ran Bull-neck through the throat before he knew she was there, then cut down the two cultists as they turned to face her. Scrawny writhed in pain on the floor. Ulrika raised her sword to him, then recalled his treatment of the girls in the cage and turned away. He didn't deserve a quick death.

The sounds of fighting from above ceased as she crept up the narrow steps. Only Gaznayev's voice continued, though it was so high and frightened it was hardly recognisable.

'I don't know!' he was shrieking. 'I don't know! They was all just girls! We took 'em from the usual places, I swear!'

Ulrika raised her head and looked though the railing at the top of the stairs. Another office, this one with a single large desk at the back wall, and dead men all over a mangy rug. Two were hooded cultists, but the rest were gangsters. Kino, the sly villain who had asked questions at the Blue Jug, lay with his sword slack in his hand and his eyes staring blankly over Ulrika's head, weird violet smoke curling from his half-open mouth.

Standing over the dead were five more cultists, cloaked and hooded, and in the middle of them, on his knees, a grizzled old tough in fine clothes, clawing at his throat, his face purple. The same violet smoke that drifted from Kino's mouth was thick in his, and had invaded his nostrils too. He was drowning in it.

'Let me go!' he gasped. 'You must... believe me!'

The cultist before him held up a clenched fist. He was as anonymous in his hooded cloak as the other four, but Ulrika's witch sight saw around him a shimmer that warped the air – a warlock.

She gathered herself to spring. She would need to strike swiftly, before he could turn his magics upon her, for she had no counters to them. But just as she was about to vault the rail, he turned and looked directly at her, his hands stretching wide and glowing with dread power.

'Come out!' he cried, as Gaznayev collapsed behind him. 'Show yourself!'

Ulrika snarled and cleared the rail in a single bound, leaping for him. Three of the cultists rushed to defend him, swords appearing from beneath their cloaks, while the fourth backed away, shrieking and pointing.

'It's her! It's her! The fiend from the cage!'

Ulrika hacked left and right, trying to bull through the cultists by main force, but these were of a different calibre to the men she had faced in the distillery, and did not give ground.

She snarled and disarmed the one in the middle, but before she could finish him, a snake of purple smoke weaved past him and forced itself into her nose and mouth, burning her throat with the taste of incense and black lotus. She fell back, coughing, but what would choke the living did nothing but annoy her. She did not breathe to live, only to speak. She recovered and killed the disarmed one, then drove back the other two.

'A vampire!' cried the warlock.

'Didn't I say?' shrilled the man who cowered behind him. 'Didn't I say?'

Ulrika disembowelled the left-hand swordsman with a

whirling slash and shouldered the other into a chair, but before she could impale him, the warlock cried a guttural word and she was suddenly paralysed with agonising ecstasy. Great pulses of excruciating pleasure snaked through her body, rippling down her arms and throbbing between her legs. She staggered back against Gaznayev's desk.

The last swordsman recovered and attacked, knocking Ulrika's rapier from her quivering hand and cutting deep into her hip. She grabbed the blade and held it tight, though it cut her palm, then stabbed her dagger at his throat. He caught her wrist and they struggled, each trying to break the other's grip. It was ridiculous. She should have had twice his strength, but the agony and ecstasy that coursed through her made her as weak as a child.

'I know not why you seek to destroy us, bloodsucker,' said the warlock, his left hand flickering with purple flames as he stepped beside the swordsman. 'But not even the aristocracy of the night will defeat the children of the god of pleasure. Our master will prevail. Our queen will conquer!'

The flames entwining his fingers blazed higher.

Ulrika knew what was coming, but couldn't stop it. She couldn't let go of the sword or break the cultist's grip.

The warlock raised his hand, the purple fire roaring, but just as he made to hurl it at her, the diamond-paned window behind him exploded inwards, and a figure in grey and black burst through feet-first to land in a crouch amongst the dead men as glass rained all around him.

The warlock whipped around in surprise. 'Another fiend!' he cried, then shot his flame at the intruder.

The man swirled his grey cloak in front of his face and caught the fire upon it, then flung it aside as it was consumed. The cultist swordsman ripped his blade from Ulrika's hand and charged him. Ulrika collapsed to the floor, still limp with excruciating ecstasy, and heard as

much as saw what followed – a roar of defiance, a shriek
of pain and the cultist hit the floor clutching his bleeding chest.

'Burn, vampire!' cried the warlock, thrusting out his
hands as the dark figure advanced on him.

The intruder dropped flat as billows of purple flame
shot over his head, setting the walls and furniture on fire.
He sprang up again and leapt for the warlock, but the
cultist retreated, spreading more fire, then fled for the
stairs.

'Brother, don't leave me!' screamed the last cultist,
who still cowered in one corner.

Ulrika heard a door slam below, and the receding
laughter of the warlock, quickly drowned out by the
roaring of the flames that devoured the room. The
intruder backed away from them, then knelt beside her
and turned her over. She squinted up, eyes burning. It
was the vampire from the Blue Jug, he who had watched
her from the rooftops as she fought Raiza.

'Can you stand?' he asked.

Ulrika nodded, then winced as he pulled her up. The
enervating ecstasy had faded now, but the pain from her
hip and hand was dizzying. She gripped the desk to
steady herself, then jerked away. It was on fire. The
flames were all around now. The walls, the rug, the stairs,
the ledgers on their shelves, all were burning, and the
heat beat at her like the pounding of heavy surf.

The vampire crossed to the remaining cultist, who was
curled on the floor, hacking and coughing from the
smoke, and hauled him up. The man shrieked and
fought him, but the vampire just slapped him and
shoved him at Ulrika.

'Feed,' he said.

She caught the cultist around the throat and pinned his
windmilling arms, then hesitated. 'But the fire–'

'You need strength,' snapped the vampire. 'Hurry.'

Ulrika tore the struggling cultist's hood and veil back, and bit hard into his neck, then moaned with relief. The vampire had been right. The pain of the hip wound receded and new strength flowed into her arms and legs as the cultist's blood spread through her body. Though she had fed well on the cultist in the ceremonial circle, fighting for her life against the Lahmians and resisting the warlock's spells had taken more out of her than she had realised. She pulled hard at the pumping vein.

'Enough,' said the vampire. 'We must go.'

Ulrika reluctantly lifted her lips from the cultist's neck and let him drop. The fire had crept even closer. She could hardly move without touching flame.

The vampire turned to the window. It was ringed with fire like the flaming hoop dogs jumped through in a Strigany circus.

'It is a drop to the street,' he said. 'Be prepared.' Then he sprinted through the flames and dived headlong through it into the night.

Next to the desk, Gaznayev woke screaming, his legs ablaze. 'Fire!' he cried inanely, beating at the flames. 'Save me! Help me!'

Ulrika ignored him and faced the window, then charged forwards and dived through the shard-toothed mouth of flames as the gangster bellowed and pleaded behind her. Cold air kissed her skin and the street shot up at her alarmingly. She tucked into a flip and landed in a perfect crouch beside her rescuer – then crashed forwards on her face, her hip screaming.

From somewhere in the distance, the dark voice of the warlock roared, 'They have escaped the fire! Kill them!'

Running footsteps echoed after the words. Her rescuer hauled her roughly to her feet and into the shadows of the next warehouse. There was an iron sewer grate there. She reached for it, ready to haul it up, but the vampire stopped her.

'No,' he said. 'They will know the sewers better than we do. To the roofs.'

Ulrika nodded, then climbed unsteadily up the wall of the warehouse behind him. He was already starting off across the angled slates as she pulled herself onto the roof. She groaned and followed, limping and hissing as she tried to match his leaps from building to building on her wounded leg.

At the peak of a high roof, she paused and took a last look back at the blazing warehouse. It hadn't worked out precisely as she had imagined it, but Ulrika had killed Gaznayev and put him out of business, just as she'd intended.

AFTER LEADING HER for a few more blocks, the lank-haired vampire stopped on the roof of a shop and looked out over the dark streets. Ulrika stumbled to a stop beside him, then sagged against a chimney, weary and blood-sick.

'We part here,' he said, and stepped to the edge. 'Farewell.'

'Wait!' called Ulrika. 'Stop.'

The vampire turned, his dark eyes cold. 'Yes?'

'You will at least allow me to thank you,' she said, pushing herself upright again. 'I owe you my life.'

The vampire stared at her for a long moment, his angular face unreadable, then spoke. 'Why do you bother with the affairs of men?'

Ulrika paused. It was an unexpected question. 'I... I have sworn to protect Praag. These daemon-worshippers threaten it. They plan some sort of "awakening" when Mannslieb is next full that will allow them to open the gates to a champion of–'

The vampire waved an impatient hand. 'As the Lahmian said, there are always cults, and they always have plans. Besides, you knew nothing of them at the start of the night. You were tailing common gangsters until you stumbled upon those caged women.'

Ulrika bridled. He had spied upon everything she had done. 'What business is it of yours what I do?' she said, her voice rising. 'How I live is my affair. I don't require approval from any of you!' She slouched sullenly against the chimney. 'Why don't you leave me alone?'

He eyed her again for a moment, then shrugged. 'I don't know. Pity, I suppose.'

Ulrika looked up, glaring. 'What?'

The vampire continued as if she hadn't spoken. 'I admit I was intrigued by you at first. You looked capable, and I have need of a capable hand. But after following you, I don't believe you would be an asset.'

Ulrika balled her fists. He was being deliberately insulting. 'What do you mean by that?'

He shrugged again. 'You are good with a blade, and you have luck, but in all else you are a disaster. You are obviously only recently turned. You show all the signs. You are unsubtle, unstable, sentimental, lacking in forethought and control, and divided in your loyalties. You love humans more than your own kind, and wish to live in two worlds at once.' He turned back to the edge. 'Perhaps I saved you so you would have a chance to learn. I don't know. But you should do it somewhere else.' He looked back over his shoulder. 'Go home, wherever that is. You aren't ready to leave the nest.'

And with that he leapt off the roof.

Ulrika snarled and lurched after him, slashing with her claws, but he had already landed on the street below and was running off into the night.

She could have chased after him, but her hip wound hurt too much, and so did her pride.

CHAPTER SIXTEEN
THE VENGEANCE OF KIRALY

ULRIKA RETURNED TO the basement of the abandoned bakery in the ruins, making doubly sure she wasn't followed, and climbed into her brick oven bed just as the sky began to lighten in the east, but sleep would not come. She was too angry.

The vampire's insults rang in her ears, and mocked her as she tried to refute them. She could see she might have been unsubtle in how she dealt with the cultists, but what about the rest of it? Was he right? Were her loyalties divided? Did she love humans more than her own kind? No. After tonight, she despised both equally. Both preyed upon the weak and powerless. Vampires took the blood of innocents, and gangsters and cultists took their freedom and their souls. She saw no difference between them.

And was protecting the victims of such predators really just sentimental foolishness? Was her wish to be a good shepherdess to Praag just idealistic nonsense brought on by a few sad songs and a moment's melancholy for the loss of her father? Perhaps, but

177

didn't it also serve a purpose? A Lahmian lived hidden within society, not outside it like other vampires. Therefore, maintaining the status quo was a matter of self-preservation. If society collapsed, what would all the Lahmians in their lovely little houses do then?

She groaned and rolled over in her brick bed. The Lahmians wouldn't even listen to her. Boyarina Evgena seemed a calcified tyrant, so concerned with defending her dominance she couldn't even allow Ulrika to exist. Why couldn't she leave her alone? With her father gone and his lands lost to the hordes, Praag was the only remaining place in the world Ulrika had feelings for. She wanted to make it her home. She couldn't let Evgena and her sisters drive her from it, any more than she could let the Slaaneshi cult destroy it.

The cult worried her. Though both Evgena and her mysterious rescuer had dismissed them as a toothless threat, Ulrika had felt their bite and was not so sure. Their organisation appeared far-reaching and well funded. They had manpower, money enough to hire gangsters to collect girls for them and powerful warlocks among their ranks, and if they succeeded, her city would be gone.

But how to track them down? They had swiftly and efficiently cut off and cauterised all leads. She was back to where she had begun.

She gnawed at the problem until her thoughts at last grew jumbled, and sleep drew her down into uneasy dreams, full of stealthy shadows and purple flames.

THE NEXT EVENING, as soon as the sun set, Ulrika, still unable to think of any other way forwards, returned to the cellar of the kvas distillery, looking for clues – and not having much luck. The bodies of the ceremony leader and his minions had been removed, as had any evidence of the sacrificial circle. The wagon that had brought the girls was gone too, and not a weapon nor a stitch of clothing had been left behind among the brass vats that lined the walls. Nor were there any books or notes or eldritch inscriptions to be found, just the smears and splashes and drying rivers of blood she had spilled in her frenzy the night before.

Still, there might yet be a trail. Her nose was as keen as a hunting cat's, and she had used it before to track her prey. The trouble here was there were too many scents, all mixed up together. They would be easier to pick apart in the yard.

She turned towards the ramp, then stopped and lowered her hand to her rapier. Someone, or something, was coming down it. She heard a heavy dragging sound – the slithering of a great snake? Some daemon conjured by the hated warlock? She extended her senses, but heard no pulse, nor felt the warm flicker of a heart-fire. Did daemons have hearts?

She hid behind a pillar and drew her blades. A long shadow stretched down the moonlit cobbles, extending like a slug as the dragging sound continued. Ulrika tensed to spring.

The slim silhouette of a man appeared at the base of the ramp, a man with a sword, but no heartbeat, dragging a dead man by the collar.

'You should be more cautious,' the swordsman said, letting the body drop. 'The Lahmians posted a swain to watch for your return.'

Ulrika grunted with anger and chagrin. It was her insulting rescuer. She stepped out from behind the pillar, but did not sheath her rapier and dagger. 'If you find me so pitiful, why do you follow me?'

He knelt and wiped his blade on the cloak of the dead man. 'I have reconsidered what you said about the cult,' he said. 'I fear they might be a threat to Praag after all, and I cannot allow that.'

'The fate of the city concerns you?' Ulrika curled her lip. 'I thought you did not bother with the affairs of men.'

'I care nothing for Praag,' said the vampire. 'But Mannslieb is next full in three nights. If these fools succeed in conquering the city by then – even if they fail, but still throw it into confusion – they may interfere with my vengeance.'

Ulrika raised an eyebrow. 'What vengeance is this?'

The vampire stood and sheathed his blade, then regarded her again for a long moment with cool grey eyes. 'As you despise your own kind so much, you may not understand this, but I have come to Praag to avenge the death of my blood father, Count Ottokar von Kohln, a great and noble prince of Sylvania who died at the hands of a false friend and betrayer.'

'I understand the love of a child for a parent,' said Ulrika stiffly. 'I loved my father more than I did my life.'

'You understand nothing,' said the vampire dismissively. 'Your true father was yours only by accident of birth. Mine chose me, and I chose him. He was more to me than any human father ever could have been. Indeed, he took me from my human father, and I thanked him for it.' He turned away suddenly, hiding his face from her. 'Now,' he said, after a long moment. 'He has been taken from me, and I will not rest until I kill his killer.'

Ulrika bristled at his arrogance, but his sudden emotion surprised and intrigued her. She had not expected it. 'Who is this killer?' she asked.

'A vampire named Konstantin Kiraly,' he said. 'He was my father's guest for centuries – his friend, we thought – until he revealed his true nature and killed him in his sleep.'

'Kiraly?' said Ulrika. 'A Kislevite then?'

The vampire nodded. 'Five hundred years ago Praag

and its environs were his domain, but then the Queen of the Silver Mountain sent a beautiful Lahmian to wrest it from him – the woman you know as Boyarina Evgena. For years she pretended to be his faithful consort, but then, during the Great War against Chaos, when he went with an army of swains to defend his properties in the hinterlands, she saw her opportunity, and cut off his head in his camp tent, making it look as if the marauders had done it. Only, Kiraly did not die.'

The vampire leaned against a pillar and continued. 'His head and body were taken away by some of his followers, and preserved in a coffin filled with blood. They took him to Sylvania and brought him to my father, who was wise in the ways of necromantic healing, and there he stayed for three hundred years, knitting slowly back together and regaining his strength as our guest, while his mind festered with thoughts of vengeance against the woman who had betrayed him. Now he has recovered, and comes north with the descendants of his followers to take that vengeance.'

'And you,' said Ulrika, 'come north to take vengeance on him.'

The vampire nodded. 'Aye.'

'Have you warned Boyarina Evgena of this Kiraly?'

The vampire laughed, sharp and cold. 'She feared *I* was here to kill her. She cast me out before I could speak.' He shook his head. 'If I can kill Kiraly before he kills her, I will. If not...' He shrugged. 'She is no kin of mine.'

Ulrika nodded. It sounded precisely how the boyarina would react. 'And this Kiraly is in Praag?'

'If he was, I would be hunting him, not the cultists,' said the vampire. 'No. He travels from Sylvania with all his followers, and they move only as fast as their baggage train. It was too risky to try him on the road, surrounded by his retinue and with no shelter to retreat to if things went badly, so I raced ahead. Here I will be able to separate him from his swains and lose myself in the maze of streets if I am overwhelmed.' He sighed. 'But only if Praag still stands when he arrives. If it falls to Chaos beforehand, he will fear to enter. Even if the cultists fail, but leave all in confusion, he may wait, as he has already waited two hundred years. I cannot wait. I do not have his patience. My blood father must be avenged! Therefore, these fools' plans must fail.'

'So, what do you want of me, then?' asked Ulrika.

'Information,' said the vampire. 'Who are these cultists? Where is their lair? What is their plan?'

Ulrika snorted. 'Would I be sniffing around down in this pit if I knew that? My last link to them burned to death in that warehouse. I know no more than you do.'

'That… is unfortunate,' he said. 'I had hoped to end this tonight.' He looked at her levelly for a moment, his eyes unblinking, then sighed and turned towards the ramp. 'I might have wished for a more seasoned hand, but time is of the essence, and it seems I must make do. Very well. You will assist me in finding the cult. Come. We will start immediately.'

Ulrika stared as he walked away from her, so shocked by his effrontery it took a moment for her rage to manifest. '*I* will assist *you*?' she sputtered at last. 'I'm damned if I will! I owe no fealty to you!'

The vampire turned on her, an eyebrow arched. 'Do you not? What did you say to me last night, after we escaped the fire? Do you recall?'

Ulrika stopped, then faltered, remembering. 'I… I said I owed you my life.'

'Do you deny it now?'

'I… No. I do not.'

The vampire nodded. 'You have the rudiments of honour, at least. The rest may come in time. What is your name?'

'Ulrika Magdova Straghov,' said Ulrika, bowing automatically.

'And your sire?'

'Boyar Ivan Petrovich Straghov, warden of the Troll Country marches.'

The vampire sighed. 'Your blood sire.'

Ulrika hesitated, then shrugged. A Sylvanian wouldn't care that she had a Sylvanian father. 'His name was Adolphus Krieger,' she said. 'And he was *not* more to me than any human father ever could have been. Indeed the swine killed my true father.'

'Krieger? The upstart?' The vampire curled his full lips. 'He who thought he would rule us all. I did not know he had made a get.'

'It was almost the last thing he did,' said Ulrika, grim. 'Before my companions killed him.'

The vampire smirked. 'Your companions did us all a favour.' He gave a formal bow, clicking his heels. 'Stefan von Kohln, of Castle von Kohln.' A dark look clouded his eyes. 'At least I was until Kiraly forced me from it.' He turned to the ramp again. 'Come. We have wasted enough of the night.'

Ulrika glared after him, still affronted by his arrogance. At the same time, if he wanted to stop the cultists, she could use all the help she could get, even if he thought she was helping him. With a sigh she sheathed her rapier and dagger and started up the ramp.

ULRIKA AND STEFAN did their best to follow the cultists' various scents, which led out of the distillery's yard and split up as they wound through the deserted streets of the ruined Novygrad, but the trails were too cold. As soon as they reached the more populated quarters they became overlaid with the smells and spoor of a day's traffic and vanished altogether. Five times they returned to the distillery and followed another trail, and five times the trail led to nothing.

'What about the sites of the fires?' Ulrika asked as they stopped, defeated, in the middle of the ruins. 'The jeweller's place and the warehouse?'

Stefan shook his head. 'The trail will be even more buried there. The bucket brigades, the gawkers and looters, the watch, all will have come and gone. We will never find the right scent among them.' He cursed. 'The villains have done an admirable job of disappearing.'

Ulrika nodded and sighed. 'Perhaps we can follow rumours of vanished girls.'

Stefan grunted with displeasure and turned away. 'There *must* be a quicker way. It is only three days until Mannslieb is full.' He frowned, then swung back to Ulrika, looking at her from under his long black locks. 'You say you are sworn to protect Praag. Was it your home, then, in life?'

Ulrika shook her head. 'I spent last autumn and winter here, during the siege, but it is not my home. I am from the northern oblast.'

'A pity,' he said. 'I had hoped you might know someone here with knowledge of this cult – rumours at least. There are always whispers, suspicions people dare not speak aloud.' He looked up at her. 'You have no former acquaintances that could be beguiled into telling what they knew? You don't know any chekist agents? Or perhaps some female friend? Women are always great collectors of gossip.'

Ulrika scowled at this casual slur, then put it aside and returned to the question. Who did she know here from before her death? Max Schreiber immediately came to mind, as well as her cousin Enrik, who was after all only the Duke of Praag himself, but she dismissed them as quickly as she thought of them. She had already decided she would never see Max again, and revealing herself to Enrik would be suicide. Besides, she doubted they knew anything. If they did, the cult would have already been destroyed.

'No,' she said at last. 'I have one or two old acquaintances here, but they would not be of use to you. Nothing but soldiers and foreigners.'

'Are you positive?' he asked.

Ulrika nodded, wishing she had a better answer for him. His idea was a good one. Finding someone with an ear to the ground made more sense then prowling the streets hoping to stumble upon the cultists by accident. But she really knew few people here, and no one who would know enough to make them worth turning over to Stefan's tender ministrations. She certainly didn't know any of Stefan's 'gossiping women'. She had never associated with the sort of ladies who whispered secrets to each other in parlours.

She paused, chuckling.

That wasn't precisely true. She had recently joined a sisterhood of such women – the Lahmians. Their entire empire was founded on the collection of secrets. They gained influence by learning them, and holding them over the heads of the powerful. They employed armies of seductresses, skilled at pillow talk, who won whispers from generals and lords and kings. They made slaves of men who then told them all that went on within the guildhalls and the court. If there were rumours to be heard, her 'sisters' would have heard them.

Ulrika smiled at Stefan. 'I know who to ask,' she said.

The vampire raised an eyebrow. 'Yes?'

'Boyarina Evgena Boradin. There will be no greater hoarder of secrets in Praag.'

Stefan's face went cold and still. 'Never,' he said.

'Why not?' Ulrika asked.

'I told you,' said Stefan. 'They attacked me when I went to them. They attacked you. You would get nothing from them but a dagger in the heart.'

'Perhaps not,' said Ulrika, thinking. 'The boyarina gave me three choices – swear fealty to her, leave Praag, or die. It is only when I refused the first two that she chose the third for me. If I was to return to her and agree to join her sisterhood, I think she would stay her hand.'

'And you believe she would then answer questions from you?' asked Stefan, sneering. 'You would be the lowest of her servants. She would tell you to know your place.'

'I will make answering my questions a condition of my agreeing to serve her,' said Ulrika, lifting her chin.

Stefan laughed. 'She will accept no conditions from you, girl. I certainly would not.'

'Then perhaps I can convince her the threat of the cult is real. If I go with head bowed, I might be able to buy myself a moment to plead my case.'

'You will buy yourself a swift death,' said Stefan. 'I will not allow it. You will not throw away the life you owe me so foolishly.'

'Have you a better plan?' Ulrika asked. 'A better source for rumour? As you said, we have three nights.'

Stefan turned away again, shaking his head, but after a moment he sighed. 'I will not come with you. And you would do well not to mention my name.'

CHAPTER SEVENTEEN
THE DRAGON'S DEN

ULRIKA GLANCED NERVOUSLY up at the dark windows and verdigrised domes of Boyarina Evgena's crumbling mansion as she climbed its cracked granite steps. It was the evening after the night of fruitless searching, and she wished now she hadn't argued so hard for this meeting, or that Stefan hadn't given in so quickly. He had almost convinced her to give it up. Had he made one more salvo of logic, her enthusiasm would have collapsed and she would have agreed to try something else. Now it was too late. She was committed. Stefan was waiting for her at the Blue Jug to hear how she had progressed – if she lived to tell.

She had spent much of the intervening day awake in the darkness of the bakery cellar, sewing the rips in her black doublet and breeches and brushing out the dried blood and dirt. She had polished her boots and her sword as well, and trimmed off the singed ends of her hair, entirely by feel, for she could of course not see herself in a mirror. She hoped she hadn't made a lopsided mess of it.

When the sun had at last dropped behind the western walls, she had dressed and followed the directions Stefan had given her to Evgena's mansion, a rambling sandstone pile lumping up like a baroque carbuncle out of a sprawling, overgrown garden. Now she stood before it.

Her hand hesitated as she reached for the rusted iron knocker in the centre of the heavy wooden door. Stefan had undoubtedly been right. She could expect to receive nothing from the Lahmians but the point of a blade. Raiza would be beyond that door – Raiza, upon whom she had dropped a wall when last they met. It would be a miracle if she was given even a second to speak, but there was no going back now.

Ulrika squared her shoulders and rapped three times with the knocker, then stepped back. Knowing Lahmians as she did, she was certain she was already being spied upon, so she did her best to look calm and demure, and kept her hands away from her weapons.

After a long wait the door opened, and an ermine-clad giant of a man with a great, square-cut white beard looked down at her. If she had seen him in other circumstances Ulrika would have mistaken him for the king of some eastern land, but he was apparently nothing but Evgena's majordomo.

'Yes?' he said, and there was more contempt in that single syllable than in all Stefan's casual insults combined.

'Ulrika Magdova Straghov to see Boyarina Evgena,' Ulrika said, bowing crisply. 'I have reconsidered her offer.'

'I shall enquire,' said the majordomo, and closed the door in her face.

Ulrika clenched her jaw at this rudeness, but maintained her calm, sure she was still being observed. Finally, after long enough that her knees had begun to ache from standing to attention, the door opened again and the mountain of dignity bowed her in.

Ulrika flinched as she stepped past him into the entry hall, for two huge black bears loomed on either side of the door, their massive paws raised and jaws agape. Fortunately, before she made any move to draw and defend herself, she saw they were stuffed and mounted on marble pedestals, lifelike masterworks of the taxidermist's art, though sadly bedecked by cobwebs about the ears and muzzles. She breathed a sigh of relief and grinned sheepishly to herself. That would have been embarrassing.

'Your sword,' said the majordomo, impassively.

Ulrika unbuckled her sword belt. She had expected this. Evgena would never let her into her presence armed. She handed the sword belt to the majordomo, and he put it in a small closet, then motioned her forwards.

'This way,' he said.

As Ulrika followed him across the dusty, cavernous hall, a hundred glittering eyes seemed to follow her, for the bears that flanked the door were not alone. In every corner, and on every wall, more cobweb-mantled animals crouched – silent wolves mounted on wooden bases, hawks and eagles frozen in the act of landing on gnarled branches, pouncing wild cats on top of decorative tables, even a wild boar, snarling and at bay beside an enormous Cathay vase.

And the zoo of trophies continued as they passed into a corridor – kites and owls and ospreys, their shoulders thick with dust, looking down upon her like a disapproving jury. The whole house seemed a menagerie of the dead, a tomb of the hunted. Ulrika swallowed, wondering if there was any special significance that they were all predators. There wasn't a deer or rabbit or pheasant among them. Had Evgena killed them all? If she had, it had been long ago. They looked as old and shabby as the house.

After a few more turns, and a dozen more frozen beasts, the massive majordomo opened a panelled door, then stepped in and bowed Ulrika in after him. The room was the colour of dried blood, with walls of faded crimson brocade, tall, thickly draped windows, heavy, dark-wood furniture and an enormous basalt fireplace that looked as if it hadn't seen a fire in five hundred years. There were no hunting trophies here, but the four men-at-arms in sober uniforms who stood at attention against the side walls looked as if they might have been stuffed, for all the expression they showed.

'Madam Magdova, mistress,' said the majordomo, bowing to the centre of the room.

'Thank you, Severin,' said Boyarina Evgena. 'You may retire.'

The vampiress sat ramrod-straight on a low divan, her piercing eyes staring unwaveringly at Ulrika as the majordomo bowed out and closed the door. She was dressed in an ancient dress of maroon velvet trimmed with sable, and thick coils of black hair were piled high on her cadaverous head. A closed fan was gripped in her right hand like a queen might hold her sceptre.

To her left, tiny Galiana curled like an alert cat in a high-backed overstuffed chair that threatened to swallow her whole. She wore black satin and a long black wig, and was pretending to read a book, but her eyes darted everywhere but the page. The family portrait was completed by the grim Raiza, looking entirely recovered from her burial under the wall of the collapsed tenement, who stood at Evgena's left shoulder in a long coat and high-collared black Kossar tunic embroidered with gold, one hand on the pommel of her sabre and her blonde hair pulled back in a severe queue. Of the three, only she looked untouched by time – a young hawk among decrepit crows.

'You save us the trouble of finding you, girl,' said Evgena. 'Now tell me why I should not order Raiza to kill you here and now, as she would dearly love to do.'

Ulrika pursed her lips. She had been given her opportunity to speak. She had better make it good. She bowed deeply before looking Evgena in the eye again.

'I have come to pledge myself to you, as I should have from the first,' she said. 'And also to warn you of a danger.'

The boyarina raised a disdainful painted eyebrow. 'Is this about the cults again? Are you going to lecture me once more about caring for my flock?'

'No,' said Ulrika. 'You were right. It was not my place to tell you how to treat those you live amongst. The warning is however about the cults, and your own safety.'

Evgena laughed like the rattling of dead leaves. 'Have I not told you they are no threat? I have seen a hundred cults rise and fall in my time here. They destroy themselves or the chekist burn them. They are no concern of ours.'

'But what if this cult is different?' asked Ulrika. 'I have fought them. They have powerful warlocks among them, and wealth and resources behind them. They have allied themselves with some Slaaneshi war queen from the Wastes, perhaps this Sirena Amberhair who I have heard lurks in the hills to the north, and they mean to cause an "awakening" that will allow them to turn Praag over to her on the night when Mannslieb is next full. That is three nights from now.'

'And in four nights we will all be waking in our beds as usual, because nothing will have happened,' said Evgena, gesturing with her fan. 'Now, let us talk of you swearing loyalty to me. This other subject begins to bore me.'

'Boyarina, please!' said Ulrika desperately. She dropped to one knee. 'For your own wellbeing, hear me out. I know you believe the cult's chances are slim, but what if they succeed? What if the city does fall to the hordes? What will happen to you? The servants of Chaos have no love for the lords of night. They will not spare you.'

'You try my patience, girl,' growled Evgena, but Ulrika kept talking.

'Where is the harm in making certain of the cult's demise?' she asked. 'What will you say to the Queen of the Silver Mountain if you are driven out of the city when you might have prevented its destruction with a night's work?'

The boyarina crossed her bony hands in her lap and sighed. 'You seem in earnest about our safety, child, so I shall explain. The harm lies in drawing attention to ourselves. Already you are the cause of rumours – men drained of blood, men torn apart, cellars full of bloody corpses. The whispers of "vampire" are in the air again.' She shook her head. 'Even in our own defence we cannot take our wars to the streets and risk being discovered by the Tzarina's agents. Instead, we must make our plays from the shadows, at second and third hand. Our attacks are a word in the right ear. Our battles are dances at court and banquets in the houses of the rich.'

Ulrika wondered when the boyarina had last attended a dance. Not in a hundred years, she wagered. She stood again. 'Then fight in your fashion, mistress,' she said. 'We – *I* have lost the trail of the cult, but I know they are well funded. They must have patrons among the ranks of the wealthy and noble-born. Can you not put a word in the right ear for *this*? Or perhaps you have already heard something. Is there no one at court or in town that is whispered about?'

Evgena glared at her, saying nothing, but beside her, Galiana looked up from under her heavy wig.

'Surely we can do this much, sister,' she said. 'We can at least see if there is a threat to be concerned about.'

'No,' said Evgena. 'Even to ask about the cults is to draw suspicion that one is a cultist oneself.' She laughed, sharp and angry. 'What comedy that would be – to be accused of daemon-worship and discovered as vampires.'

'But, sister,' pressed Galiana, 'there are some we could ask who would not dare speak against us. If we were to–'

'Enough, beloved,' said Evgena, and Galiana stopped speaking immediately.

There was a tense silence while Evgena stared at Ulrika unblinkingly. Ulrika didn't dare speak again. Any more pleading would only anger the boyarina into obstinacy – if it hadn't already.

Finally Evgena snapped open her fan, then slapped it shut again. 'Leave us, girl,' she said. 'Severin will take you to the library. We will make our pleasure known to you there.'

Ulrika blinked, taken aback, then bowed as one of the men-at-arms crossed and opened the door to the corridor.

'Thank you, mistress,' she said, and turned and stepped out, hope rising within her. She had thought she was about to be thrown out on her ear. Perhaps her gambit had worked after all.

The immense majordomo waited for her in the hall. 'This way,' he said, and led her deeper into the bowels of the huge, silent house.

* * *

ULRIKA PACED THE library for what seemed an hour, waiting under the frozen scrutiny of a pack of white-furred winter foxes who prowled the tops of the dust-furred bookshelves. She looked at the spines of books in a dozen different languages, and occasionally pulled one out and flipped through the brittle pages, but she was too anxious to read. Were the boyarina and her sisters discussing the merits of her request, or were they discussing how best to kill her? Would they come through the door with open arms, or armed with wooden stakes?

In the end, it was neither. They came unarmed, but hardly welcoming.

Boyarina Evgena entered and glided noiselessly to the centre of the room with her men-at-arms behind her and Raiza and Galiana ranked to either side.

'We have made a decision,' she said.

Ulrika bowed. 'I am eager to hear it.'

'Raiza believes you care nothing for us,' said Evgena. 'And that you mean to use us only to further your human-loving foolishness.'

Ulrika struggled to kept her face still. It was unnervingly close to the truth.

'But Galiana believes your motive doesn't matter,' Evgena continued. 'Whether you act in our interest or your own, the threat, if it exists, affects us all.' She clenched her jaw. 'In the end, I agreed.'

Ulrika bowed again, letting out a long-held breath. 'Thank you, mistress!'

Evgena waved her fan. 'Thank Galiana, if you must thank anyone. She was your advocate. Now, hear me.'

Ulrika came to attention again. 'Mistress.'

'We have consulted with each other and our swains, asking after rumour and innuendo at court and in the city, and have thought of a man who might be what you seek.'

Ulrika blinked, stunned. 'This is more than I had hoped, mistress. What is his name? I will go to him.'

'You will not,' said Evgena sharply. 'Not alone, at any rate. I know what happens to men who you "go to". They end up in dead in alleys.'

Ulrika prickled with annoyance, and almost protested, but instead just hung her head. An outburst here might ruin everything.

'Raiza will go with you,' said Evgena. 'And teach you something of spycraft.'

Ulrika fought to hide her alarm. 'Er, thank you, mistress. I am honoured at the company.'

Galiana tittered. 'Are you, now?'

'But first,' said Evgena, raising her fan, 'we must reach an understanding.'

Ulrika straightened. 'Y-yes, mistress.'

Evgena crossed to a table and sat, maintaining her perfect posture, but did not offer a seat to Ulrika. Raiza and Galiana took up positions at her shoulders, then she spoke. 'You said you were here to swear fealty to me.'

'I – I did.'

'As I mentioned,' the boyarina continued, 'Raiza thinks this was only a ruse, so that you might say your piece, and I am inclined to agree with her.'

Ulrika opened her mouth to protest, but Evgena stopped her with a flick of her fan.

'There is no need,' she said. 'For regardless of your intent, I have decided to hold you to your words. I accept your offer of service. You will make your pledge to me, or you will not leave here alive.'

Ulrika darted glances around at them all. Evgena looked smug. Galiana's button eyes glittered with amusement. Raiza was as unreadable as ever. Ulrika swallowed. Before, filled with noble thoughts of defending Praag, she had been ready to make the pledge, but now that it came to it, she was feeling less sanguine. What was she agreeing to? To serve Evgena until death? For a vampire, that was a long time. She might be trapped in this musty mausoleum for a hundred years, or a thousand!

'Tell me what vow you wish me to make,' she said.

'You will accept me as your mistress, and vow to serve me until such time as I free you from my service,' said Evgena, and Ulrika could tell she had said it many times before. 'You will protect me from harm and work to further my interests in all things. You will cause no harm to come to me by your actions or inaction, nor will you make intrigues against myself or any in my service, or against any of my allies. You will obey my orders above all others save those of our Queen. Do you so vow?'

The words, 'Until such time as I free you from my service,' rang loud in Ulrika's ears. It was as bad as she had thought. 'And… and what do I get in return for my service?' she asked.

Evgena sneered. 'Besides your life?'

'Besides that, yes.'

'In return,' Evgena sighed, 'you will never lack for blood to drink, nor shelter from the sun. You will live in comfort and share in the spoils of my conquests. You will rise as I rise, and fall as I fall. Is that fair enough?'

Ulrika's fists clenched at her sides. This was not a step she wanted to take, but she could not see a way out of it. She nodded at last. 'It is. I accept these terms. I vow to serve you as you ask.'

Evgena at last let a smile curl her wrinkled lips. 'Very good,' she said. 'You are smart enough to surrender when cornered. It remains to be seen if you are honourable enough to stay true to a vow made under duress. We shall have to watch you.'

Ulrika drew herself up. 'I am a boyar's daughter. I do not break vows.'

Evgena raised an eyebrow. 'Strange. I have never met a

boyar who did not.' She waved aside Ulrika's outraged retort with her fan. 'No matter. No matter. If your fears about this cult are true, we have no time for japes. Now, the ceremony.'

She motioned to Galiana, who took from her satin robe a shallow gold bowl and a small curved knife with Nehekharan hieroglyphics etched into the blade, and set them on the table before her. Ulrika watched in alarm as the boyarina stood and picked up the knife, then held it up and began muttering over it in a language she didn't understand.

'What is this?' Ulrika asked. 'Is my word not enough? I never did this with Countess Gabriella.'

Evgena stopped her invocation and lowered the knife, annoyed. 'She was your blood mother. There was no need. You are bound to her by birth. We share no direct kinship.'

'This will bind my will to yours, then?' Ulrika didn't like that idea at all.

'You will not be my mindless slave,' said Evgena, 'if that is what you fear. No oath would be necessary then, would it? It is only a symbolic joining of blood. It will make you part of our family. I will be your mother.' She lifted the knife again. 'Shall I continue?'

Ulrika shuddered. The boyarina's explanation wasn't making her any more eager to participate, but there seemed nothing for it. There was no backing out now.

She nodded. 'Please.'

Evgena raised the knife again and resumed her invocation, closing her eyes as the strange words slipped from her lips like hissing serpents. Despite her assurance that it was all mere symbolism, Ulrika felt the hairs rise on the back of her neck as the chant continued. There were suddenly other presences in the room, unseen but watching, as if called to witness the oath, and the knife shone with reflected moonlight, though there were no windows in the room.

Finally, the chant stopped and Evgena drew the blade across the palm of her left hand, then clenched it over the golden bowl. She was so desiccated and gaunt Ulrika wondered if she would bleed at all. She did. The blood dripped from the jutting bones of her wrist into the bowl until some fifty drops had been shed, then Evgena lifted her hand and the blood ceased to flow as if there had never been a cut. She held out the knife to Ulrika.

'Repeat after me,' she said. 'Then cut your palm and bleed into the bowl.'

Ulrika hesitated, then took the knife. It felt like she was taking a piece of ice. It was freezing cold, and stung her fingers. She gripped it and laid the edge against her palm.

'Neferata, Queen of the Night, whose blood is my own,' said Evgena.

'Neferata, Queen of the Night, whose blood is my own,' repeated Ulrika.

'In your name and by your law,' continued Evgena, 'I pledge myself to your servant, Boyarina Evgena Boradin, and accept her ever after as my mother, whom I shall serve faithfully and obey in all things as a daughter should.'

The words stuck in Ulrika's throat, and she had to push them out by main force. 'In your name and by your law, I – I pledge myself to your servant, Boyarina Evgena Boradin, and accept her ever after as my mother, whom I shall serve faithfully and obey in all things as a daughter should.'

Evgena nodded gravely. 'Now cut,' she said.

Ulrika drew the freezing blade across her palm and felt a wave of dizziness that had nothing to do with pain. It felt as if the blade was taking more from her than blood. She swallowed thickly, then held her fist over the bowl and squeezed her hand. Blood ran from the cut into the vessel and mixed with Evgena's.

Evgena, Galiana and Raiza watched intently for a full minute as the level of blood in the bowl rose, then Evgena raised her hand.

'Enough,' she said.

Ulrika withdrew her fist and set down the knife as Evgena picked up the bowl with both hands and lifted it to her lips. She looked Ulrika directly in the eye.

'Daughter, in the name of the Queen of the Silver Mountain, I accept thee. Our blood is one,' she said, then drank.

After a few sips, she held out the bowl. Ulrika took it in both hands, then did as she had done, holding it to her lips and looking directly at Evgena.

'Mother,' she said. 'In the name of the Queen of the Silver Mountain, I accept thee. Our blood is one.'

She tipped the bowl and finished the blood. It was nothing like drinking directly from the vein. There was no pulse of life behind it, yet there was something there, some emotion that entered her as the blood spread through her. Not exactly affection for Evgena, nor loyalty born of respect, but attachment, precisely the same sort of attachment one felt for family, no matter how little one cared for them. It was a breakable bond, thought Ulrika, but not one that could be severed without consequence.

Evgena took the bowl and the knife and handed them back to Galiana, then returned her gaze to Ulrika.

'Welcome to the family, daughter,' she said. 'We are pleased you are one of us.'

'Thank you, mistress,' said Ulrika, bowing. 'I am honoured.'

Evgena snorted at that, shattering the solemn mood, and turned away from the table without another glance at Ulrika. It was as if the ceremony had been no more out of the ordinary to her than washing her hands.

'Now, go with Raiza to the address I have given her,' she said over her shoulder, 'and see what there is to be seen. I will listen with interest to her report of your conduct when you return.'

Ulrika stiffened at the boyarina's condescending tone, but only bowed to her back, regretting her vow already.

CHAPTER EIGHTEEN
THE GOAT AND THE WOLF

'SISTER,' SAID ULRIKA hesitantly. 'I… I want to apologise for what happened when first we met. I hope you are not still angry with me.'

Raiza didn't look around. 'Your resourcefulness is to be admired,' she said. 'I bear no grudge. Now be silent.'

Ulrika grunted and turned back to the window. So much for a warm welcome to the family.

She and Raiza were perched like gargoyles on either side of a round window over the front door of the mansion of the man Evgena had sent them to spy upon. His name was Romo Yeshenko, a furrier grown more wealthy than the nobles to whom he sold his wares. According to Evgena, he owned large mink and ermine farms outside the city, and employed an army of freelance hunters and trappers who brought him the pelts of fox, bear, elk and rabbit, which he then turned into coats, cloaks, rugs and ruffs for the wealthy and discriminating.

He was known as a gracious host and a generous philanthropist, who gave money to widows and orphans and hosted yearly charity banquets at his enormous mansion. But there were other, stranger rumours whispered about him as well. It was said he liked to dress up in a suit made of goat hide – complete with horns, hooves, long ears and chin beard – and have his wife stalk him through his house while dressed as a wolf – complete with sharp white teeth. It was also said that one of his maids had died from a broken back in a 'kitchen accident', and that once a butler had been sent to the madhouse gibbering of 'stains in the rug' after gouging out his own eyes.

These and similar tales were what had made Evgena think Yeshenko might know something of the cult of the pleasure god. It was therefore somewhat of a disappointment when Ulrika and Raiza reached his mansion to find that it was a typical Praag manor, and the man himself a balding, middle-aged burgher with a well-upholstered belly and rich, but conservatively cut clothes.

Only the glitter of his wife's eyes, and the venom in her tongue as the couple prepared to go out for the evening, promised any sort of cruel passions. She was a contrast to Romo in every way – a decade younger, voluptuous and sullenly beautiful in green velvet and a fox stole, and as harsh a harridan as any Ulrika had ever heard.

'We've missed the beginning, I'm sure of it,' she snipped as a maid and a footman helped them on with their fur coats. 'And all because you must have a second helping. Don't you think you've had too many second helpings, darling? You have as many chins as I have fingers.'

'I'm sorry, Dolshiniva my love,' Romo mumbled in a soft voice as he struggled to find the sleeve of his coat. 'It was a long day. I was hungry.'

Dolshiniva snorted. 'You're always hungry. Now, don't dawdle. The coach is waiting.'

With a long-suffering sigh, Romo at last got his arm

through his sleeve and shuffled out the door after Dol-shiniva, who sashayed to the coach with a saunter that would have made a courtesan blush.

'I can see him as a goat,' whispered Ulrika to Raiza as the couple got into the coach. 'Albeit a fat one, and she as a wolf, but he doesn't look the sort to join a cult.'

Raiza didn't answer, only watched the coach pull away, then rose and ran along the rail of a balcony to the side of the house, leapt down to the wall that surrounded the property, and from there to the street. Ulrika glared after her, then followed. Raiza had so far remained as cold and silent as she had been when they were enemies, only speaking when absolutely necessary. Ulrika was therefore taking malicious pleasure in forcing her into conversation at every opportunity.

'Why follow them?' she asked, falling in beside Raiza as she started down the street after the coach. 'Why don't we search the house instead? It looks like they're only going visiting.'

'Searching might reveal they are cultists,' said Raiza, unclenching her jaw reluctantly. 'But they would never be fool enough to write down their masters' names. If we follow them, they might speak them.'

Ulrika wanted to find fault in the swordswoman's logic, just to make her argue more, but she couldn't. She gave up and paced beside her as they tailed the coach.

ROMO AND HIS wife did indeed go visiting, and not far from home. After only a few blocks, their coach turned in at the gate of another mansion, this one even larger than theirs, and blazing with lamplight from every window. A throng of coaches choked the circular drive, and footmen ran hither and thither, handing down elaborately dressed ladies and gentlemen and bowing them towards the arched front door.

As their quarry stepped out of their coach and joined

the crowd, Ulrika looked up at the mansion, seeking a way in. The windows in the top-floor rooms at the back of the mansion were not lit, and all the columns and mad filigree that decorated the walls would make for an easy climb.

'Around the side and up?' she asked Raiza.

The swordswoman shook her head without looking away from Romo and his wife. 'No need. We are dressed well enough. Only...' She frowned and turned to Ulrika. 'Have you a mask?'

'A mask? No. Should I?'

Raiza nodded over her shoulder. 'There is no surer way to blend in.'

Ulrika looked back to the drive. It was true, fully half the men and women who were flocking to the mansion's door were wearing masks, from simple opera masks to wild papier-mâché creations that looked like things seen in a nightmare.

'I see,' she said. 'And where can I get one?' Raiza looked past her down the street that ran beside the mansion. It was lined with coaches and carriages, all waiting for their owners to call for them. The horses stamped and shifted, blinkered, while the coachmen gathered at the front of the line, chatting and smoking pipes and rubbing their hands in the cold.

Raiza pushed past Ulrika and strolled down the line of coaches. Ulrika followed, wondering what she was up to.

Once out of sight of the coachmen, Raiza began stepping up onto the running boards of the coaches and carriages and looking inside. At the fifth one, an open rig, she reached over the door and plucked something from the seat.

'Put it on,' she said, handing Ulrika a mask.

Ulrika looked at the thing as Raiza pulled another from her long coat and began to tie it on. The stolen mask was pink, with lace edges, and baby-blue ribbons. 'Lovely,' she said dryly.

'Beggars can't be choosers,' said the swordswoman. 'Now come.'

Ulrika growled and followed, tying on the mask. She noticed that Raiza's was black and simple, and gave her an air of mystery. She could only imagine what *her* mask gave her an air of.

THE GUARDS AT the gate let Ulrika and Raiza pass without a second glance, and they jostled in with the other merry-makers as they went up the steps and through the front door.

Inside was noise and glittering confusion. Men and women stood in the entry hall, all talking at the tops of their voices as footmen wandered through the crowd filling glasses with wine. Romo Yeshenko and his wife were not in sight.

'Go that way,' said Raiza, pointing to a room on the left. 'If you find them, stay near them. I will find you. If I find them, you find me.'

'Aye,' said Ulrika, and edged towards the door as Raiza started in the other direction. More people crowded the left-hand room, swarming around a huge centre table piled high with pastries and meats and fruit, and stuffing their faces like pigs at a trough. Ulrika's mind flashed to the starving refugees who filled the streets, and felt her chest tightening with anger. Who were the true vampires of Praag?

In a further room, men and women played cards at little round tables, and gold coins were changing hands to a chorus of curses and shrieks of laughter. Beyond that was a ballroom, where young couples swirled around the floor as a woodwind quartet puffed vigorously away at a Bretonnian gavotte and older couples watched from the walls.

Ulrika finally spotted Dolshiniva Yeshenko's shapely green velvet rump in the next room, a darkened conservatory where a play of some sort was being performed. She stood with Romo behind a group of seated watchers who surrounded an improvised proscenium where painted players trumpeted their lines. Ulrika sidled close as Dolshiniva whispered in her husband's ear. Was she speaking of the cult?

'You see, toad?' she hissed. 'Had we arrived sooner, we would be sitting.'

'I'm sorry, my love,' said Romo dully. 'I'll eat more quickly next time.' He took a big gulp of wine from the glass he held in his hand and sighed heavily.

'And don't drink so,' Dolshiniva snapped. 'You're making a spectacle of yourself.'

Ulrika rolled her eyes. Hardly the dark plottings of secret cultists. Nonetheless, she dutifully positioned herself behind them and pretended to watch the stage, all the while keeping an ear out for their sweet nothings.

The play was an old saga of the Gospodar people, about how Miska, the Khan Queen, drove the Ungol tribesmen from the settlement that was to become Praag, and made it the greatest city of the north. It was full of blood and sword-waving and stirring speeches, and a statuesque woman in very few clothes playing Miska. Ulrika didn't think her much of an actress, but her other assets held the men in the audience riveted.

'Are you looking at her?' hissed Dolshiniva in Romo's ear. 'Do you think she's more attractive than me?'

'Of course not, dearest,' said Romo mournfully. 'You are all I could ever want.'

A few moments later Raiza appeared at Ulrika's elbow.

'Nothing of interest yet,' said Ulrika. 'Unless you care for low comedy.'

Raiza nodded gravely, and together they watched the

play. It ended at last after a battle scene which consisted of six men with wooden swords doing some sort of dance, Miska taking the rest of her clothes off and impaling the chief of the Ungols, and declaring that forever and anon Praag would be the bastion of the north.

The audience applauded rapturously, with many shouts of 'Hear hear!' and 'Praag will never fall!'

Ulrika thought Romo and Dolshiniva might move on to another room, as some of the other attendees were, but before anyone got far, a compere in a doublet that glittered with glass beads skipped out to the front of the stage.

'Lords and ladies!' he called. 'Thank you for your kind attention! Our next history will start in a very few minutes – a tale of ghosts and murder in fabled Albion, but while we change the scene, a musical aperitif!' He turned and gestured grandly to the curtain. 'I give you the pride of the Academy, Valtarin the Magnificent!'

There was fresh applause at this, and a buzz of anticipation, and a few people who had turned away now turned back – Romo and Dolshiniva among them. Ulrika looked with interest to the curtain, remembering the name from the conversation of the music students the night she had listened to the blind singer.

A thin figure of medium height backed through the curtain, already playing a skirling, slithering glissando on his violin, then turned and strode out to centre stage. He held on a shivering high note and fixed the audience with a baleful eye, then, with elbow flying, he plunged into the melody of the song – a wild fling from the eastern oblast that started the audience clapping in time.

He was a handsome young man, in an intense, starving-poet sort of way, with high cheekbones and a mop of sandy hair that he constantly flung back out of his eyes. His fingers were long and as thin as the rest of him, and danced over the fretboard like spider legs as he played fast, fluid and impossibly complicated melodies. Ulrika could hear the pulses of those around her throbbing with excitement at the display, and it stirred her as well. Thoughts of passion and bloodshed welled up within her as the notes soared and charged and attacked.

But after he finished the first song and moved on to a mournful old ballad, Ulrika found herself beginning to agree with the student who had claimed Valtarin had no soul. Though he played the sad song with precision, it did not move her. His music seemed to have no difficulty enflaming anger and lust, but didn't appear capable of tugging at the heart or inspiring melancholy the way the voice and playing of the blind girl had done. He put on a great show, there was no denying it, and she could certainly see why girls fluttered at him, but he fluttered nothing in her.

'They're moving,' said Raiza.

Ulrika turned, embarrassed to have been so distracted. Valtarin certainly held the attention, but apparently not for Romo and Dolshiniva, who were edging through the crowd who had flooded into the room to hear the violinist.

Ulrika and Raiza started after them, murmuring pardons with every step, then followed them at a distance to a door that led out to a lavish garden lit by strings of hanging lanterns. It appeared the hearty Praag elite were willing to carry their merry-making even into the chilly spring night, for there was more dancing here, with a lively ensemble playing reels and jigs on a stage carved from blocks of ice to resemble the gates of Praag, with an ice statue of Duke Enrik presiding over all with upraised sword.

Romo and Dolshiniva circumnavigated the dancing at a leisurely pace, bowing to their betters and chatting to acquaintances along the way, and Ulrika and Raiza followed behind at a slow saunter, though Ulrika was beginning to wonder why.

'This is fruitless,' she said. 'They're nothing but rich climbers. Nothing is going to happen here. The boyarina must have got it wrong.'

Raiza didn't respond, only continued to trail them like an implacable shadow. Ulrika sighed, thinking that if Evgena had ordered the swordswoman to watch paint dry she would have done it with exactly the same unwavering obedience.

And then, something did happen.

Romo and Dolshiniva had stopped at a low wall near a set of steps that led down to the wilder parts of the garden, and were watching the dancers moving through their parts. But then, as if out of mere idle curiosity, they turned to look out over the grounds, and a few moments later, still apparently led by nothing more than whim, they went down the stairs and began strolling through the trees.

'They are leaving,' said Raiza.

Ulrika stared, then laughed. 'Ha! What a trick. They arrive here, make their presence known, then leave for some other rendezvous without anyone noticing, and later return to the party the same way. Who can say they ever left? A perfect alibi.'

Raiza nodded, and they crept cautiously down into the lower garden, then sprinted on tiptoes across the open ground as Romo and Dolshiniva disappeared behind a screen of shrubbery. Ulrika and Raiza paused there, listening, then pushed quietly into the undergrowth.

On the far side of the bushes, they saw their quarry standing at a small door in the garden wall. Romo had a ring of keys, and sorted through them as Dolshiniva waited impatiently at his elbow.

'You might have had it out before we got here, fool,'

she hissed. 'What are you playing at?'

'My apologies, beloved,' said Romo. 'I didn't want to appear suspicious. Ah, here it is.' He stuck the key in the lock and pushed open the door.

Dolshiniva elbowed ahead of him. 'Finally,' she said. 'Now hurry. We're late.'

Romo sighed and followed, then closed the door behind him. Ulrika heard the key turn in the lock as she ran with Raiza to the wall. They sprang upon it as silent as cats and looked down into the narrow service alley behind it. Romo and Dolshiniva were hurrying down it as fast as Romo's bulk would allow, which, if Dolshiniva's imprecations were to be believed, was not nearly fast enough.

Ulrika and Raiza padded along the top of the wall and saw a closed coach pull up at the end of the alley.

'That isn't their coach,' said Ulrika.

'It wouldn't be,' said Raiza.

As the couple reached it, the coach's door swung open and they climbed up. The coachman geed the horses almost before they were fully in, and the coach rolled off down the street.

Without a word or a look back, Raiza jumped down from the wall and followed.

Ulrika growled under her breath, then leapt after her. 'You're right, sister,' she said. 'We should follow them. Thank you for asking.'

roze, keeping her body exactly where it was,
led for cries or alarms. Nothing. She let out a

ggling,' Raiza continued. 'You are not quite the
retend.'

rowled at the jibe, then inched forwards at a
e until she heard Raiza grunt behind her.
ou're through.'

rew her legs up carefully, then stood and
kling on her sword as Raiza rose to a crouch
ne foot forwards. Her arm was shaking now,
ready-pale face was ashen. She ducked and
und her own fist like someone slipping
curtain while holding a heavy-laden tray.
ne,' said Ulrika as the swordswoman stepped
ap and slowly drew her arm back to let the
closed behind her. 'Now do you have an
ver way to climb a sheer wall?'

get me there,' said Raiza, nodding wearily.
l get you there. Lace your hands and put your
wall.'

ised a sceptical eyebrow, then did as she was
was very little room between the temple wall
n of shimmer that surrounded it. If she threw
ad angle, she would break it and the cultists
w they were there. On the other hand, that
n the sneaking was done and the fighting
n, and Ulrika was beginning to long for a

ped back as close to the shimmer as she
set herself as Ulrika dropped into a deep,
t.

dded. Raiza took two quick steps forwards,
in the stirrup of Ulrika's hands and sprang
aved with all her might.

CHAPTER NINETEEN
THE BLACK DAGGER

KEEPING THE COACH in sight was not difficult. Ulrika and Raiza were swift, and it was slow, moving through the city at an unobtrusive trot and taking a circuitous route to the Merchant Quarter, then doubling back to burrow into the winding, debris-strewn streets at the edges of the demolished Novygrad.

It wound past beggars' hovels and through encampments of refugees before coming to a stop at last in an alley behind what had once been a temple of Salyak, but was now a dilapidated wreck, slumping between two high tenements with half its façade sloughed into the street. Ulrika and Raiza watched from the shadow of a gutted tavern as Dolshiniva and Romo and another man stepped from the coach and crossed to the back of the temple. They were cloaked and hooded now, like the cultists Ulrika had faced before, but there was no disguising Romo's bulk or Dolshiniva's curves. A door opened as they approached the temple, and they went in, while their coach rattled down the alley and away.

Ulrika started forwards, but Raiza stopped her and

nodded towards the roof of the temple. There was a man there, crouching at the corner and watching all approaches.

'He is easily dealt with,' said Ulrika, as they moved out of his line of sight.

'He will *not* be dealt with,' said Raiza. 'It is not enough to spy on these fools. They must never know we were here.'

Ulrika bridled at her tone, but nodded. She was right. 'Very well.'

They darted into the lee of the tenement and flattened themselves against the wall, then sidestepped along it until they reached the narrow gap between it and the temple. Raiza looked around the corner, then slipped into it with Ulrika following. They looked up. A row of shattered windows pierced the temple wall about three body lengths above the ground, but the wall below them was of smooth, unbroken stone.

'Difficult,' said Raiza, rubbing her chin.

'Not at all,' said Ulrika. She pointed to the wall of the tenement, all crumbling brick and warped timber. 'We can climb there until we are opposite the windows, then leap the gap.'

'Aye,' said Raiza. 'But for that.'

She pointed between the two buildings, and for a moment Ulrika thought she was indicating something at the far end of the alley, but then, using her witch sight, she saw a nearly invisible shimmer of purple only a few feet from her face. It curved out from the temple wall like a soap bubble, and cut the alley in two – a magical ward of some kind. She cursed. She was sure she would have noticed it if she had been on her own, but she was trying so hard to impress Raiza that she was distracting herself.

'Have you a way to pierce it?' she asked.

Raiza shot out her hand and pulled back her sleeve to

reveal her sinewy left wrist
bracelet that appeared to b
ment, folded into overlapp
over in a script Ulrika did n

'A gift of Mistress Evgena,
said Raiza. She turned tow
and slowly extended her ha
does not break their flow.'

Ulrika watched as Raiza i
transparent skin of the ward
the purple swirls began to
candle smoke struck by an
around it. Raiza stopped and
descence slowly drew furthe
trembled with effort, and U
set and hard.

After a moment, a ripple-e
as a halfling, but narrowing
formed in the bubble. Raiza
one knee, so that the widest
the plane of the ground.

'Crawl through,' she said, t
not touch the sides.'

Ulrika crouched forward
beside Raiza, then paused.
ward. There was very litt
swordswoman without bur
the surface of the ward.

She unbuckled her sword
gap ahead of her, hissing
pened. She got down on all
almost flat. Her shoulders
wavering sides. She drew th
elbow-walked slowly forwa
a time.

'Your hips!' rasped Raiza.

Ulrika
then liste
breath.

'Less w
boy you

Ulrika
snail's p

'Good

Ulrika
began b
and slid
and her
edged
through

'Well
from th
ward fle
equally

'You
'Then I
back to

Ulrika
told. Th
and the
Raiza a
would
would
could
fight.

Raiza
dared,
braced

'Reac
Ulrik
put her
as Ulri

She craned her neck as the swordswoman shot straight up, skimming past the stone surface of the wall. For a second Ulrika thought she hadn't thrown her high enough, but at the top of her arc, Raiza shot out a hand and caught the sill of one of the windows by her finger-tips, then pulled herself up.

After some manoeuvring, the swordswoman turned in the window and began unwrapping the red sash she wore wound about her waist. When she was done, she tied one end around her sabre's brass scabbard, then braced it sideways in the narrow window so the tip and hilt caught on the edges, and threw down the rest of the sash.

The fringed end stopped a few feet higher than Ulrika could reach. She backed up like Raiza had, then ran at the wall, leapt, kicked and caught the sash in two hands. Her shoulders jarred against the wall as she flopped against it, but her grip held, as did the sash. She got her legs under her and walked up the wall to the window, where Raiza handed her in and put a finger to her lips.

Ulrika nodded. Flickering purple lights and voices raised in invocation came through the ruined room's missing door. Whatever was going on, they were close to it. She waited while Raiza belted on her sabre and retied her sash, then crept with her across the room, which seemed to have been the office of some Salyak administrator before the siege, and peered out the door.

Beyond it was a pillared gallery that overlooked a large, high-roofed room. The room was not the temple Ulrika had been expecting, but the remains of a hospital ward. The cots had been shoved to the walls, leaving a wide space in which more than two score people in cloaks and hoods stood in a loose ring, chanting and facing inwards, their hands stretching forwards.

Ulrika rose a little so she could see over their heads, but she already knew what she would find. A circle of blood was painted on the floor in the middle of them, and within it lay a terrified girl, her naked flesh covered in strange calligraphy and her hands and ankles impaled by iron spikes that had been driven down through the flagstones. Six purple-flamed candles flickered around her, and a tall, crook-backed cultist stood at her head, leading the others in the cacophonous chant. Ulrika growled as she saw that the girl was not the first to die that night. A pile of naked bodies lay beside the circle, all bleeding from the palms and feet.

Her eye flicked back to the leader as he raised an empty glass bottle over his head, shaking it in time with the chant. Ulrika frowned. The cultist at the kvas distillery had carried a bottle too. She had thought he had just toyed with it unconsciously, but now she wondered. Had it some meaning?

As the chorused voices of the cultists crescendoed, Crook-back stretched out his arms and turned the bottle upside down over the girl. She shrieked and bucked as if she had been stabbed, and then, to Ulrika's horror, her torso began to lift off the ground like a tent in a high wind. Unfortunately, also like a tent, she was pegged at four corners, and though her body rose, the spikes tore cruelly at her hands and feet.

Ulrika growled and stepped forwards, her hand dropping to the hilt of her rapier, but Raiza caught her arm.

'We are here to discover their leaders,' she said, 'not interfere.'

'But they're killing her!' Ulrika whispered.

Raiza only looked at her. 'You are far too human,' she said.

Ulrika jerked away from her. 'And you are far too cold!' She started forwards again. Behind her, the swordswoman half-drew her sabre.

'Will your vow to the boyarina break at the first testing?'

Ulrika stopped, her fists clenched. Had Raiza only threatened violence, she might still have gone forwards, but a vow made was stronger than steel, and cut deeper when broken. She cursed and stepped back, her jaw clenched.

'It will not break,' she said.

Raiza nodded and sheathed her sword. They returned their attention to the ceremony.

The crook-backed cultist was lowering the bottle towards the wailing girl as his followers shrieked their chant, and the unnatural updraft that lifted the victim off the ground was growing stronger, threatening to rip her hands and feet from the spikes. A strange white glow was pulling out of her body, stretching and fighting like a snail being pulled from its shell.

Then, so suddenly Ulrika almost missed it, the bottle jerked down of its own accord, tearing from the leader's hands, and the open mouth of it struck the girl square on the sternum with a crack like a pistol shot, then stuck there. The girl screamed, a high bloodcurdling shriek, and the white glow ripped free of her body and was sucked into the bottle.

With a cry of triumph, the bent cultist corked it and held it high between his two hands as the staked girl flopped to the ground, dead and shrunken. The cultists cheered, basking in the white glow that pulsed inside the bottle.

Ulrika turned away, shaking, her mind flashing back to the girl she had found in the cellar in the ruins. There had been a bruised purple circle on her breast she had not known the cause of. Now she did.

'They must all die,' she said.

From below came a ringing voice. 'Seven souls tonight, devoted!'

Ulrika looked back. It was the crook-backed cultist, speaking as he slipped the glowing bottle into a leather sack that already contained a handful of others.

'Seven souls nearer to the hour of awakening,' he continued. 'The hour when all your dreams will be fulfilled. And tomorrow night, the last great hurdle to victory shall be cleared. The master's most trusted acolytes will steal the Viol of Fieromonte from its hiding place, and the fall of Praag will be assured! All hail the master and the coming of the queen!'

Raiza inclined her head towards the crooked man as the cultists repeated the invocation.

'We follow him,' she said.

Ulrika nodded.

Crook-back held up his hands for silence. 'But,' he said, dropping to an ominous whisper, 'we humble ones still have much to do to prepare for her coming, and we are beset by dangers on all sides. Only last night, our brothers in the Novygrad were attacked by a fiend who deprived us of a score of souls. What its intent was, none can say, but we cannot allow it to prevail.'

Ulrika smiled as the cultists muttered anxiously. She was tempted to reveal herself just to watch them flee in terror.

The crooked man thrust out a hand. 'But do not fear, friends,' he cried. 'The master protects us all. Not even the undying can stand before him. Still, you must be vigilant, and report any stirrings in the shadows so he may deal with them. Have I your word on it?'

The cultists murmured their assent.

'Very good.' He turned and looked at them all in turn. 'Now, hear me. Those lost sacrifices must be made up. We have many bottles yet to fill, and only days to do it. I call upon you to redouble your efforts. There are girls everywhere in this city. Reap them in the name of the master and for the glory of the queen.'

'All hail the master!' intoned the crowd. 'All praise the coming of the queen!'

Ulrika growled under her breath. More dead girls. She would not allow it.

'Bring these chosen at the appointed time,' said the crook-backed man. 'You will be informed of the next meeting place in the usual way. Now, go. Be vigilant and fruitful, and may the blessings of the Lord of Desire inspire you!'

'We shall do the will of the Lord of Desire,' murmured the crowd, bowing low, then turned away from the circle and started filtering towards the various exits.

Ulrika and Raiza paid them no mind. They focused entirely on the bent cultist, watching as he slung the sack of bottled souls over his hunched shoulder and started towards the temple door. Two hulking cultists fell in behind him, then stepped out the door to check the street. When they gave the all-clear, he started forwards again, then paused on the threshold and waved his hand.

A tension Ulrika hadn't realised was pressing at her chest and eardrums suddenly released, and the air seemed to thin.

'He has lowered the wards,' said Raiza, then turned. 'Now to the rooftops.'

Ulrika followed her to the office window and stepped up onto the sill. The walls above it were not smooth like those below. Crumbling brick and decorative pilasters made easy handholds. Ulrika expanded her senses as they climbed, searching for the man who had been watching from above, but his heart-fire was descending through the building, and the roof was empty when Ulrika and Raiza pulled themselves onto it.

They padded quickly to the other edge and looked down. The crook-backed cultist and his guards were leading three horses from a ruined building opposite the temple. The crooked man slung his pack over the saddle-bow and they mounted and started off west towards the river.

Ulrika and Raiza loped after them, leaping from roof to roof with the Sorcerers' Spire silhouetted in the distance by the two moons that rose behind it. Ulrika smiled as she ran and the night wind kissed her face. The bliss of unfettered movement, of having the grace she had once only dreamed of, filled her, and she nearly forgot why they followed the men, only revelled in the doing of it. She shot a look at Raiza as she ran beside her. The swordswoman's face was as grim and emotionless as ever. Ulrika's smile faded. Was this what awaited her down the road of her eternity – the loss of all joy? Would she too someday become as cold and unfeeling as a machine?

The cultist and his guards veered their horses into a northbound street. Raiza and Ulrika changed course to follow, but as they leapt a narrow alley, Ulrika saw something moving out of the corner of her eye and turned her head. A figure in cultist's robes was bounding after them over the roofs, moving as swiftly as they were, and hurled something in Raiza's direction.

'Look out!' Ulrika cried.

Her words had the wrong effect. The swordswoman slowed and turned to see what was the matter, and ended up directly in the path of the spinning object. Ulrika thrust out a desperate hand and shoved her, sending her windmilling aside, and the thing struck Raiza's wrist instead of her heart. It was a dagger-sized shard of onyx.

Raiza shrieked in a voice Ulrika would not have expected to come from her, and crashed to the roof, clutching at her arm.

'So fall all who seek our destruction!' screeched the cultist, then turned and ran away across the roofs.

Ulrika sprang instinctively after him, snarling and drawing her sword, but to her shock, he increased the distance between them. It was impossible a normal man could be so fast and strong. His leaps were longer and stronger than hers. He was getting away!

'Face me, coward!' she cried, but he did not slow.

She sprinted gamely after him as he pulled ahead of her, sailing over streets and clearing chimneys with feet to spare, but then he disappeared over a high, steep-roofed tenement, and when she reached the peak and looked around, he was gone. She ran to each of the edges, looking down into the streets and alleys and extending her senses to search for his heart-fire, but she couldn't feel it. He was already out of range.

With a curse, Ulrika turned and ran back the way she had come, retracing her steps as a giddy violin played a wild tune somewhere far in the distance, barely audible over the sounds of the city.

'I lost him,' she said as she leapt onto the roof where she had left Raiza.

The swordswoman didn't look up. She was slumped against a chimney with her sleeve pushed back to reveal her left wrist, and she was staring at it. Ulrika stared too, her heart constricting. Raiza's hand and forearm were withered and shrunken. The muscle that should have covered her bones was nearly gone, and her skin hung loose from them like wet tissue. She could hardly contract her fingers.

'Ursun's teeth!' said Ulrika. 'What happened?'

'Only a scratch,' Raiza whispered dully. 'Only a scratch…'

She trailed away and looked at the onyx shard that lay beside her. Ulrika swallowed. The thing had been black before, she was sure of it. Now it pulsed red at its core.

'What is it?' she asked, kneeling.

Raiza shook her head. 'I know not. But it is worse than silver. It… it took a part of me – part of my essence. Had it struck my heart–' She shuddered and looked up at Ulrika. 'You saved my life. I will not forget.'

Ulrika reached out to help her up. 'Come. I will see you home.'

Raiza accepted her arm and stood, but shook her head. 'I will return on my own. Go after the hunchback. Follow him to their destination if you can. We must win something from this night.' She stooped and picked up the sharp shard of onyx with her right hand. She moved like an old woman. 'I will speak to the boyarina of this cult.' She glanced at her withered wrist. 'I believe I can convince her now of its danger. Now hurry.'

Ulrika saluted. 'I'll find him,' she said, then turned and leapt to the next roof.

BUT SHE DIDN'T find the crook-backed man. In the time it had taken her to chase the assassin and return to Raiza, he and his men had vanished. She searched all the neighbouring streets and alleys from the rooftops, then dropped down to the ground and tried to follow them by scent. For a few blocks that worked, but then the trail led to the Grand Parade and was drowned in the smells of all the other horses, carts and people who had passed and were still passing along it.

She considered for a moment returning to Evgena immediately to tell her she had lost the men, but she was reluctant to face the chastisement – particularly if it influenced the boyarina's decision about whether to fight the cult. Besides, she had promised to meet Stefan at the Blue Jug to tell him how things had gone, and it was getting late. Maybe he would have news of the cult – something she could bring to Evgena tomorrow night.

She shook her head as she trotted past the Sorcerers' Spire towards the Academy District. She had left Nuln for Praag because she hadn't wanted to serve any master, and somehow she had ended up, not three days after arriving, beholden to two. How had it happened?

* * *

THE BLUE JUG was shuttered for the night when she reached it, but Stefan was still there, waiting in the shadowed doorway.

'So, the sisters didn't kill you,' he said, raising his head as she approached.

'No,' she said. 'They listened, and agreed to help. We spent the night trailing the cultists then... lost them again.'

'Tell me,' he said, then stepped out and beckoned her to walk with him.

Ulrika paced alongside him, telling him about meeting Evgena and agreeing to take her pledge as they walked through the district's deserted streets. He gave her a sharp look when she told him of drinking the mixed blood from the golden bowl.

'It would have been wiser of you not to have done that.'

'I feared as much,' said Ulrika. 'But she told me it would not make me her slave. My mind would still be my own. Did she lie?'

'No,' he said. 'But neither did she tell you the whole truth. You still have your own will. You could still betray her if you wished, but she will know it when she looks at you. She will be able to read your emotions, no matter how hard you try to hide them.'

A knot of unease twisted Ulrika's guts. As much as she disliked the vow, and how Evgena had cornered her into taking it, she had no intention of harming her. Indeed, she was trying to help her, trying to save her city from the cult, but at the same time, she had already begun to think about finding a way to escape her service sometime in the future. Would that count as betrayal? Would Evgena see it in her eyes, or did she know it already?

She put that aside and continued her story, telling Stefan about going with Raiza to spy on Romo Yeshenko and his wife at the meeting of the cult. He listened without comment until she told him of the cultist with the black onyx dagger. Then he turned to her, his grey eyes glittering and hard.

'What did this knife look like?' he asked. 'Describe it!'

Ulrika blinked at his vehemence. 'It – it was hardly a knife,' she said. 'It was nothing but a length of onyx, jagged and black. Only, when it struck Raiza's arm, it withered it horribly, and afterwards seemed to glow red from within.'

Stefan's face went cold and stiff. 'It withered only her arm?'

'Aye,' said Ulrika with a shiver. 'But had it struck her heart–'

'She is lucky it didn't,' said Stefan. 'It is one of the Blood Shards. They belonged to my master until Konstantin Kiraly killed him and stole them.' He turned away from her, staring off into the night. 'My nemesis has arrived, and has begun his revenge against the Lahmians.'

CHAPTER TWENTY
THE FENCING LESSON

'What is a Blood Shard?' Ulrika asked.

'A terrible weapon,' said Stefan. 'There are six. My master was a collector of arcane objects, and the Blood Shards were some of his favourites. They are prisons. They suck out the soul of anyone they kill, and trap it, fully conscious, within their crystalline structure, where it can be subjected to whatever magical tortures the owner of the shard wishes to inflict upon it, for eternity.'

Ulrika shivered. What an awful fate.

'Even vampires are not immune,' continued Stefan. 'Some may debate if a vampire has a soul, but he certainly has a consciousness, and it too can be trapped within a Blood Shard. That… that is what happened to my master. Kiraly killed him with a shard and imprisoned him within it.' His hand dropped to the hilt of his sword. 'When I have killed Kiraly, I will seek to find some way to free him, though I have been told it is impossible.'

'That is a terrible thing,' said Ulrika. 'I hope you find some way.'

Stefan waved that away. 'Never mind. What of Kiraly? Did you fight him?'

'You think the cultist… you think it was him?' Ulrika stammered.

'It can have been no one else.'

Ulrika blinked. No wonder she had sensed no heart-fire. He had none. 'I… I lost him,' she said. 'He was too fast. I'm sorry.'

'Did you see which way he went?' said Stefan through his teeth.

'He was running east into the Novygrad when he vanished,' she said. 'But he could be anywhere now.'

Stefan turned immediately east. 'I must find him,' he said, and strode off down the empty street.

Ulrika hurried after him. If what he said was true, then this Kiraly was Boyarina Evgena's enemy too. 'Wait,' she called. 'I'll help you.'

'If you wish,' said Stefan, not looking back. 'But he is mine alone when we find him. You will not interfere.'

'Of course,' said Ulrika.

They jogged on towards the Karlsbridge and the east side.

STEFAN SEARCHED THE deserted ruins of the Novygrad like a man possessed, practically sprinting from shattered building to shattered building, and roaring Kiraly's name in the streets. He tore down doors and kicked through broken floors to explore collapsed basements. He scattered sleeping squatters and mutants, and questioned cowering refugees about seeing suspicious strangers or finding corpses drained of blood. None had heard anything.

Ulrika followed Stefan with some trepidation, afraid that, in his madness, he would bring the watch or chekist agents down upon them, or worse, the roof of some precarious tenement. His fervour was terrifying, and somewhat frustrating, to see. If he could have put as much effort into finding the cultists, they might have defeated them by now.

And what if he found Kiraly? Stefan's only interest in stopping the cult was to be certain Praag still stood when the vampire arrived. If Stefan killed him, he would cease to care. He would take the Blood Shards and return to Sylvania. Of course, now that she had joined the Lahmians, perhaps his help was unnecessary. But despite sharing blood with Evgena, she didn't trust her strange sisters. Their fear of betrayal seemed stronger than their fear of the cult, and she worried the slightest misstep or stray thought on her part would have them coming for her head again.

A cold hand clutched her heart as a thought came to her. Was she making that misstep now? Should she be helping Stefan search for Kiraly, or should she be running back to warn Evgena he was coming to kill her? What if he had already attacked the Lahmians' house? It would be Ulrika's fault if Evgena wasn't prepared. She already felt to a certain extent complicit in the attack on Raiza. Kiraly had obviously been watching Evgena's house. If Ulrika hadn't asked the Lahmians for help against the cultists, Raiza would not have left the house to investigate and put herself in danger. Ulrika had unwittingly drawn her out so Kiraly could attack her.

'Stefan,' she said as she followed him down the stairs of a tenement they had just searched. 'I must go back to the Lahmians immediately.'

'Go, then,' said Stefan, distracted, and kicked through the front door into the street.

Ulrika strode out after him, then stopped as she saw a bright pink glow in the sky over the eastern walls of the city. It had become dawn while they were inside. There was no way she could make it back to Evgena's mansion before the sun rose. Now she wouldn't be able to warn the boyarina until nightfall. Unless...

Could she take the sewers? Aye, but she would have to come up to the streets to approach the house, and it would be full daylight by then. She would burn to a crisp on Evgena's front steps. She cursed. There seemed no way. Of course, the sun would stop Kiraly as well – unless he had already attacked. Ulrika sighed. There was nothing for it. She would have to wait out the day, then race to the mansion as soon as the sun went down again, and pray she wasn't too late.

She looked around. Stefan hadn't seemed to notice the dawn. He was kicking in the boarded up-windows of the burned-out shop next door.

'Stefan,' said Ulrika.

He didn't seem to hear her.

'Stefan!'

He turned, his eyes mad and bright. 'What? What is it? Have you found him?'

'Dawn is coming,' she said. 'We must take shelter.'

'Damn the dawn!' he snapped. 'I must find Kiraly!'

Ulrika raised an eyebrow. 'The dawn will damn you,' she said. 'But go on if you wish. I'm going to retire.'

Stefan snarled. 'I don't care what you do! I–' He caught himself and ran a hand through his lank hair. 'No, no. You are right. We must stop. We must.'

'I have a place nearby,' said Ulrika. 'It isn't anything, but it is secure. You could–' She stuttered as she realised what she was saying, but it was too late to draw it back. 'You could stay if you like.'

Stefan bowed politely. 'If it isn't too much trouble.'

'Of course not,' said Ulrika, thinking it might well be. 'This way.'

She led him through the ruins towards the bakery, wondering if she had made a mistake revealing her hiding place to a man who was almost a complete stranger. Well, she could always find a new place, couldn't she?

ULRIKA SHRUGGED, EMBARRASSED, as she led Stefan down into the cellar of the bakery. It had none of the comforts of home. There was no furniture except for piles of rubble, dusty bakery tables and the oven in which she slept, and no place to wash. Nor had she collected any blankets or pillows. She had been sleeping with her head resting on her pack.

Stefan seemed unperturbed. 'It is better than where I have been staying,' he said, and promptly began to dust off one of the bakery tables to make a bed for himself. 'I have been too preoccupied to think much about lodging.'

Ulrika hesitated, then indicated the oven. 'You can join me, if you like. No light gets in.'

He looked at her with a half-smile, then bowed. 'You are kind to offer, but I will not intrude. Thank you.'

Ulrika nodded, not certain if she was disappointed or relieved. She sat down in the rubble and began taking off her boots. 'I must go back to the Lahmians tonight. I must tell them I failed to follow the cultists. And Evgena must be warned that Kiraly is after her. Perhaps they will help us hunt him.'

Stefan laughed. 'Help *us*? Ha! You they may help, but if they learn I am with you, they will hunt *me*.'

'But, surely,' said Ulrika, 'when they learn the true threat–'

'You are young,' he said. 'You have much to learn. The Lahmians think of anyone who is not Lahmian as a true threat. My intentions matter not. My actions matter not. Only my blood matters, and they despise it.' He shrugged. 'It would be in all our interests if we who face these common enemies fought them together, but it will not happen. They will not accept me.'

'But why not?' Ulrika growled. 'Our enemies are strong. The cultists nearly burned us alive, and this Kiraly nearly killed Raiza. We would all be safer allied. We would be able to share what we know of these villains and present them a united front.'

'You think logically,' said Stefan. 'It is not a Lahmian trait.'

'Then I will make it one,' said Ulrika, standing, one boot off. 'I will go to them and – No, *we* will go to them. We will tell them of Kiraly and the Blood Shards, and–'

'You're mad, girl,' laughed Stefan, cutting her off. 'I won't go anywhere near them. They'll kill me.'

'But you just said it was the right thing to do!' Ulrika protested.

'It may be right,' said Stefan, 'but it is also fatal.' He sighed and shook his head. 'I apologise. It is honourable of you to want to be above-board with your mistress, but she is too closed-minded to listen to reason. If I went into her lair, I would not come out again.'

Ulrika cursed and turned away, but then an idea came to her and she spun back. 'What if I brought them to you?'

Stefan frowned. 'What do you mean?'

Ulrika smiled. 'We shall do it in stages, so they get used to the idea. I will go to them alone, and tell them of you – that you have knowledge of Kiraly which will help them defend against him. If they accept that, I will bring them to speak to you, on neutral ground, where you may withdraw if they attempt to attack. Once they hear you out, I'm certain they will welcome you.'

Stefan shook his head. 'You are naïve if you think that,' he said. 'But…'

Ulrika looked at him hopefully. 'But?'

'But it might still be worth a try,' he continued at last. 'If they refuse, we have lost nothing. If they try treachery, I can escape, and we will know their disposition.' He looked at Ulrika. 'My only fear is for you. Evgena may be angry at you for speaking with me, and may seek to punish you or banish you.'

'I'll take the risk,' said Ulrika. 'If she can truly see into my heart, then she will know it was done with good intent. We cannot continue to fight two threats separately. Will... will you do it?'

Stefan hesitated, then nodded. 'I will do it. Let us meet... let us meet at the kvas distillery. We all know the place, and–' he smirked. 'And there are many escape routes if all goes wrong.'

'Yes. Excellent,' said Ulrika. 'This is good. We will be stronger for it.'

She sat down again and started pulling off her other boot, feeling greatly relieved. Not only would joining forces make them all safer, it would end her need to keep Stefan a secret from Evgena. All would be right tonight, and they could turn their attention to fighting their enemies, instead of each other.

'Ulrika,' said Stefan.

She looked up.

He smiled at her – the first true smile of their acquaintance. 'I... I want to thank you. This is not a step I would have made on my own. You have courage. I will try to emulate it.'

'Th-thank you,' she stammered, smiling in return. She struggled for something else to say, then found she had been holding his gaze too long. She broke it suddenly, and there was an awkward silence. Neither of them seemed to know where to look.

At last Stefan turned and lay down on the bakery table. 'Sleep well,' he said, then rolled on his side to face the wall.

She looked at his back for a moment, then finished pulling off her other boot. 'Goodnight.'

She climbed into the bakery oven and curled up

inside it. The stone surface seemed more uncomfortable than it had on other nights.

ULRIKA SMILED WRYLY to herself as she reached for the knocker on Evgena's front door. Once again she was coming to the boyarina with a proposal that was sure to anger her, and might indeed spur her to cast Ulrika out, but she felt less nervous about it this time. Joining forces with Stefan was the right thing to do. Ulrika knew it in her heart, and if Evgena disowned her for suggesting it, then Ulrika could part company with the old shrew and her sisters with a clean conscience.

Still, she didn't want it to go that way. The twin threats of Kiraly and the cults were too great. The help of the Lahmians would be vital to defeating them. She must succeed here. There was no other option. She squared her shoulders and knocked on the door.

The wait was much shorter this time, and when Severin opened the door and looked down at her over his broad, square beard, his, 'Yes?' was not nearly as full of contempt as before.

'Ulrika Magdova Straghov, returning to report to Boyarina Evgena,' she said.

The massive majordomo bowed her in and she entered, stepping once again between the shadows of the two gigantic bears that guarded the door. The dust-hooded eyes of all the other trophies glittered at her in the darkness of the entryway.

'The boyarina is dressing,' said Severin. 'If you would care to wait in the parlour.'

'Thank you,' said Ulrika, then paused. 'Ah, is Mistress Raiza awake?'

'She is in the ballroom,' said Severin. 'You wish to see her?'

'Please.'

'This way.'

Ulrika followed him through the hushed house, pleased he hadn't asked for her sword this time – another improvement over the last time she had visited. He led her again through cobwebbed corridors lined with stuffed birds and beasts to a set of panelled double doors, behind which she heard a long-forgotten swishing and thudding and cracking. He pushed them open, then bowed into the room.

'Mistress Ulrika, mistress,' he said.

Raiza's steel whisper came from within. 'Show her in.'

Severin turned and bowed to Ulrika. She stepped in and, just as she had expected, found Raiza, in white shirt and tan breeches, engaged with a fencing dummy, which had been set up at one end of the long, heavy-beamed room. Ulrika smiled. She had guessed it from the sounds, which she remembered from her days training with her father's Kossars – the swish and thwack of wooden sword on leather, the shuffle and thud of boots as they stamped and lunged.

Raiza was belabouring the dummy with her usual lightning precision, beating aside the wooden pole that stuck from its chest and thrusting home, only to thrust a second time before the dummy had stopped rocking from the first.

'Mistress, I am relieved,' said Ulrika stepping forwards with a smile. 'You are recovered.'

Raiza gave the dummy a final stab in the throat, then turned and bowed. 'Only partially,' she said, and held up her left arm. It ended in a stump just below the elbow.

Ulrika stared, aghast. Raiza's movements as she fenced had been so smooth she hadn't noticed. 'Mistress, I... Forgive me. I didn't–'

'Do not apologise,' said Raiza. 'But for you, it would be all of me that was missing. As I said before, I will not forget.'

Ulrika looked down, embarrassed. 'So, it did not heal? It will not grow back?'

Raiza shook her head. 'Boyarina Evgena is a skilled sorceress and healer, and tried everything in her power to restore it, but could not. The black knife is a fell weapon.'

'It is,' said Ulrika. 'I have learned more of it, and have returned to warn Boyarina Evgena of it and the man who wielded it.'

'Then you should wait to speak of it until she comes,' said Raiza. She turned to the wall and leaned her wooden practice sword against it, then picked up her sabre and tucked it under her truncated left arm. 'Until then, will you fence? I am learning to adjust my balance to my new... condition.'

'I would be honoured,' said Ulrika.

She undid the points of her doublet and shrugged it off, then unbuckled her sword belt and drew her rapier as Raiza unsheathed her sabre and let her scabbard fall to the ground. They crossed to the middle of the ball-room, saluted each other and went on guard.

Raiza raised an eyebrow. 'An Imperial stance and a Tilean sword. Are you not from the northern marches?'

Ulrika grinned. 'Aye, but I practised for a time with a skilled swordsman of the Empire, and adopted some southern techniques.'

'Very good,' said Raiza. 'We shall see if they avail you.'

And with that she lunged forwards, aiming straight for Ulrika's heart. Ulrika dropped her hand and turned the thrust on her hilt, then returned it, aiming for Raiza's throat. Raiza's sabre knocked her point aside and slashed back at her shoulder. Ulrika leapt back, unable to avoid the attack in any other way.

The loss of a hand seemed to have in no way impaired the swordswoman's abilities. She was just as fast and agile as before, her blade as hard to catch as flickering lightning. No sooner had Ulrika parried it, than it struck somewhere else.

Then Ulrika saw a weakness – a tendency for Raiza to block too wide to her right side, leaving her middle momentarily open. Ulrika attacked her three times in quick succession, each time leading her arm a little more to the right, then a fourth time, a dip under her blade to disengage, and a second thrust straight for her belly.

Raiza's knuckle guard smashed down on her hilt like a hammer and Ulrika found the tip of her sabre pressed hard against her sternum. She froze. She had been caught, and would have been impaled if Raiza had followed through.

'A trap,' she said. 'I'm embarrassed to have fallen for it.'

'Do not be,' said Raiza. 'You only fell for it because you are an excellent blade. A lesser sword would not have seen the bait, and therefore would not have taken it.'

'Then I will have to strive beyond excellence,' said Ulrika as they stepped apart. 'For I would wish to know the bait for what it was next time.'

The swordswoman smiled. 'I have many years of tricks in my head,' she said. 'And you will have ample time to learn them.'

'I look forward to it.'

They reset, but then Ulrika lowered her rapier. It was rare to meet another woman who fought, and she was curious. 'Forgive me,' she said. 'But how did you come to the sword, and… and to the boyarina?'

Raiza's jaw clenched, and Ulrika was afraid she had pushed the swordswoman's new friendliness too far, but after a moment she spoke.

'I came to the sword as you did,' she said. 'By way of family. My brothers rode in a rota, as did my husband.

When the hordes came the last time, they took my farm, and my daughters, and in the end my husband too. When my brothers brought his horse and his armour back to our village, I put on the armour and mounted the horse and rode with them to war.'

'The last time?' asked Ulrika. 'This past winter?'

Raiza shook her head. 'Two hundred years ago, during the Great War against Chaos. We fought here in Praag, at the Gate of Gargoyles, and then through the streets, when Magnus and the Tzar retook the city. It was then that I met Mistress Evgena.' A frown creased her forehead. 'She and her men were defending her house – a different house at the time – from pillagers, and my brothers and I came to her rescue. All… all were killed but me, and I was dying. She gave me the dark kiss. I have been with her since.'

Ulrika nodded, but she was surprised at the end of the story. She had not seen anything like compassion in Evgena. 'The boyarina was moved by your sacrifice?' she asked.

Raiza snorted. 'She saw a serviceable sword on the street, and picked it up. That is all.'

Ulrika looked at her. 'You don't like her?'

'She is perfectly fair,' Raiza said, evenly. 'What else can one ask from a mistress?' She raised her sabre into guard. 'Shall we go again?'

Ulrika made a salute, but as she readied herself, there were footsteps in the hall and the doors opened. She and Raiza lowered their blades as Evgena and Galiana entered, their long dresses hissing on the floor. They were followed by a handful of men-at-arms.

Ulrika bowed low. 'Mistress. Sister.'

They did not return the courtesy.

'You did not return last night,' said Evgena, eyeing her levelly. 'We were concerned for your safety.'

Concerned I had abandoned my vow, more like,

thought Ulrika. Well you will see in my heart that I haven't. 'I apologise, mistress,' she said aloud. 'My hunt for your enemies left me far from here at sunrise. I was forced to find shelter elsewhere.'

'And was your hunting fruitful? Did you follow the cultist Raiza told me of to his lair?'

'Mistress, I did not,' said Ulrika. 'By the time I set off for him, he had vanished.'

Evgena's eyes flared. 'So, you lost the monster who cost Raiza her hand, and also fumbled the lead with which we provided you. Most impressive. Have you *anything* to show for your night's endeavours?'

Ulrika suppressed an angry response. 'Yes, mistress, I have. I have learned the identity of the man who attacked Mistress Raiza, and the nature of the weapon that hurt her.'

The boyarina's rigid face softened a little. 'This is good news,' she said. 'Come to the drawing room. We are to hear from some of our spies now, but we will hear you first.'

Ulrika bowed, then slipped into her doublet and strapped on her sword belt and followed the others through the house to the room with the dried-blood walls and the cold hearth. There, Evgena took her seat on the divan, while Galiana curled in her chair, and Raiza stood at the boyarina's shoulder, just as she had the night before. Ulrika wondered if anything about this ritual had changed in two hundred years.

'Speak, then,' said Evgena, when Ulrika had taken her place before her. 'Who is this cultist who wields such powerful weapons?'

'The weapons are called Blood Shards, mistress,' said Ulrika. 'And there are five more. They are soul prisons. They suck the essence from their victims and hold it within them for eternity. Had Raiza taken a worse wound from it, she… she would have been consumed.'

Galiana shivered and Raiza's face grew more grim than usual. Evgena's remained cold and composed.

'And the cultist?' she asked.

'He is not a cultist, mistress,' said Ulrika. 'It was only a disguise. He is someone from your past. A vampire.'

'Don't be coy with me, girl.' snapped Evgena. 'Who?'

'His name is Konstantin Kiraly,' said Ulrika. 'And he has come north to take revenge on you for–'

Evgena cut her off with a dry laugh. 'Who has been telling you this nonsense? Kiraly is long dead. I killed him myself. I cut off his head.'

'I was told he was taken to Sylvania and… and brought back to life.'

Evgena scowled. 'Told by whom? Who knows of Kiraly?'

Ulrika hesitated. She had reached the point of no return. If she couldn't convince Evgena that Stefan's story was true, and that he was no threat to her, she would likely be thrown out on her ear, or worse. Not for the first time, she wished she had Countess Gabriella's gift for persuasion. She swallowed.

'It was a vampire named Stefan von Kohln who told me, mistress,' she said. 'He seeks vengeance on Kiraly for the death of his blood father. He wishes to ally with you – to combine forces to defeat Kiraly and the cultists.'

Evgena's lined brow furrowed. She turned to Galiana. 'Stefan von Kohln. Is that the name of the Sylvanian pup who came sniffing around here recently?'

'It is,' said Galiana. Her bright black eyes glittered suspiciously at Ulrika.

'He did come to you recently, mistress,' said Ulrika. 'You turned him away without allowing him to speak.'

Evgena curled her lip. 'Turned him away? Raiza would have killed him had he not run so fast. And now you tell me this assassin is your confidant?'

'He is no assassin, mistress,' said Ulrika. 'Your enemies

are his enemies. He too hunts the cult, and he has sworn to kill Kiraly, who has sworn to kill you. You should fight on the same side.'

Evgena's eyes blazed, her hands gripping the arms of the divan. 'You are either a dupe or an assassin yourself. I am not sure which is more dangerous. Either way, you have broken your vow to protect me by consorting with this Sylvanian, and will pay the price.'

'Mistress, I have not!' said Ulrika, her voice rising in spite of herself. 'You *know* I have not. I have done all that I have done with the best of intentions. I am trying to protect you.'

'Then you are a dupe, as I said,' sniffed Evgena. 'And are too much a fool to live.'

'Please, mistress,' Ulrika begged. 'Will you not consider even for a moment that Stefan's story is true? Kiraly lives! Raiza and I have faced him! Can you deny the loss of her hand?'

'Oh, I am certain you faced someone,' said Evgena. 'And I am certain I know who it was – and so do you.'

The thought froze Ulrika. Could it be true? Could it have been Stefan hidden behind the cultist's mask? It didn't seem possible. She had seen his face when he learned of the Blood Shards. He had been aghast. He had gone mad. He had torn the Novygrad apart looking for Kiraly. Could it all have been a trick? Well, yes, it could, but to what end? She couldn't see a reason for it.

'I don't believe it, mistress,' she said. 'Stefan has wanted nothing to do with you from the beginning. It was I who suggested enlisting your help in fighting the cult, and he who rejected the idea. It was I who insisted we must all join forces. If he had wanted to use me to get to you, wouldn't he have *begged* me to do these things?'

Her words fell into a cold, hard silence. All three of the Lahmians were looking at her now with hard, dangerous eyes.

'From the beginning?' said Evgena in a voice like ice. 'Precisely how long have you known this von Kohln?'

Ulrika's skin prickled with dread. Her tongue had betrayed her. 'I…'

'How long?' snapped Evgena.

'Since… since the night you found me at the kvas distillery,' Ulrika said, hesitantly. 'He helped me fight the cultists.'

Evgena's eyes bored holes into Ulrika. 'So, you admit you knew him before you came to us. Indeed the two of you discussed allying with us, and yet, when you swore your oath to me, you hid this from me. Why?'

'I… I…'

'Enough!' cried Evgena. 'I will hear no more lies. You are no dupe! You are a Sylvanian spy! A foresworn traitor to your own bloodline! You and your von Carstein master have come to kill me and my daughters!' She sneered. 'Well, von Kohln will have to do his own dirty work from now on.' She flicked her fan towards Raiza and her men-at-arms. 'Kill her.'

CHAPTER TWENTY-ONE
THE VIOL OF FIEROMONTE

RAIZA AND THE men drew their swords and moved in as Ulrika stepped back and put her hand on her hilt.

'Please, mistress,' said Ulrika. 'I swear I have not conspired against you. Can you not see it in me? Did I not push Raiza aside when the Blood Shard was thrown?' She turned to Raiza. 'Sister, tell her!'

The swordswoman looked uncertainly at Evgena. 'She did, mistress,' she said. 'It would have been my heart.'

'Can you say she wasn't trying to push you *into* its path?' said Evgena, then waved her fan dismissively. 'It matters not. Spy or dupe, she made oath to us under false pretences. She must die.'

'Yes, mistress,' said Raiza and started towards Ulrika with the others.

Ulrika drew her rapier and backed away as they surrounded her and Evgena began some sort of incantation. If she stood and fought she would die. Either Evgena's sorcery or Raiza's blade would kill her while she was engaged with the rest. With a shout, she spun and leapt at the two men between her and the door, slashing at them as Raiza and the others bounded forwards.

Ulrika cut down both men and sent one crashing into Raiza's path. The swordswoman jumped him, raising her sabre, but Ulrika threw open the door and caught her edgewise on it, then slammed it shut behind her as Raiza staggered back. Heavy thuds shook the panelling. Ulrika laughed wildly, surprised she had made it out of the room, then turned and ran down the corridor towards the entry hall. Could it be this easy? Just a few more paces and she was free!

Something shrieked in her ear and clawed her face, wings flapping and beating her. She ducked away instinctively, then caught it and dashed it against the wall. It was a hawk, but she had felt no pulse beneath her fingers.

Another bird attacked her, and a third, tearing her flesh with their claws and beaks. She looked around wildly as she slashed at them. More were coming, diving down from their perches on the walls. Ulrika stared. The hunting trophies – they weren't stuffed, they were undead!

Raiza and the men burst from Evgena's drawing room and raced towards her. Ulrika ducked through the storm of birds, throwing her cloak over her head, and bolted into the entry hall, then skidded to a terrified stop.

The two giant bears on either side of the door were lumbering down from their pedestals and loping towards her across the floor. Glass-eyed wolves were padding from the side rooms, trailing cobwebs. The wild boar knocked the Cathay vase to the floor and charged her, its sharp hooves skittering on the marble tiles. The whole house had come alive.

Ulrika knocked more birds of prey from the air, then darted for the stairs and vaulted the banister, inches ahead of the boar. Severin the majordomo thundered down from above, roaring and swinging an immense curved sword of eastern design. She ducked it, then grabbed him by the belt and hurled him down the stairs behind her, flattening a pair of wolves.

The great bears mauled him as they climbed over him towards her. She ran up to the first-floor gallery, flailing at the birds that screeched around her head, and sprinted to the nearest door. Locked. She tried another. Also locked. A wolf leapt at her throat as she tried a third. She hacked its head off in a spray of dust and twisted the latch. Again locked. The bears shouldered into the narrow corridor side by side, and advanced on her, growling.

Ulrika backed to a fourth door, her rapier out in front of her, and felt behind her for the latch. Before she found it, Raiza leapt over the bears and landed before them, on guard.

Ulrika's fingers touched the handle and twisted. It turned. She let out a sigh of relief. 'I'm sorry, sister,' she said. 'I'm not ready for another lesson.'

She backed through the door as Raiza darted forwards, and slammed it in her face, then leaned hard against it, fumbling with the lock and feeling the swordswoman's implacable strength pressing at the other side. Finally the bolt shot home and she backed away, then turned, afraid she might have locked herself in a room with more undead animals.

There were none. She was in a conservatory of some kind, with leaded glass walls on two sides and flowering trees that reached up to the arched glass ceiling. A sunroom was a strange room to find in the house of a vampire, but from the look and smell of the unsavoury plants that grew from the pots and urns that cluttered the room, Ulrika guessed Evgena must use them in her necromancy.

A heavy clawing shook the door. The bears. They

would tear through it in short order. She stepped to the glass wall and looked for a door. There was none. No matter. She picked up a potted succulent in her off hand, but just as she made to throw it at the glass wall, it smashed in from outside.

Ulrika stepped back as shards spun past her and Raiza crashed through the hole, her handless arm shielding her face. Ulrika threw the plant and charged in behind it, but Raiza blocked both pot and sword and returned to faultless guard.

Ulrika clenched her teeth. She would have to fight her after all. 'Very well, teacher,' she said. 'If you insist.'

But as she edged forwards, Raiza lowered her sabre.

'Cut me,' she said.

Ulrika frowned. 'What?'

'Cut me and go,' Raiza whispered, and looked over Ulrika's shoulder to the door, which was beginning to splinter under the bears' attacks. 'We haven't much time.' She turned her right shoulder to Ulrika. 'I will say you bested me. Now hurry. Make it deep.'

Ulrika hesitated. 'Are you certain?'

'Yes! Hurry!'

Ulrika nodded, then raised her rapier and hacked Raiza in the shoulder, cutting through cloth and flesh and hitting bone. Raiza staggered aside and fell against a table full of potted plants, grimacing and hunching in pain.

'Good,' she said through her teeth. 'Now hurry.'

Ulrika stepped past her to the hole in the glass wall, then turned. 'Thank you,' she said.

'I told you I would not forget,' said Raiza, clutching her wounded arm. 'But my debt is cleared now. I will not disobey my mistress again.'

Ulrika swallowed, caught off guard by sudden emotion, then saluted Raiza with her sword, ducked out through the hole and leapt to the garden below.

As she raced through the grounds towards the street she heard the smashing of a door and Evgena's angry cry.

'Where has she gone? How did she get past you?'

She ran on.

ULRIKA WALKED INTO the yard of the kvas distillery and looked around. Stefan was not to be seen.

'Stefan!' she called, turning in a circle. 'Come out. They are not coming.'

There was no response. She frowned. Her hand dropped to her hilt. Had he left? Had he given up? Had something happened?

'So,' came Stefan's voice from behind her. 'They would rather lock themselves away than confront the dangers that face them?'

She turned.

He stood on the broken wall of the distillery, a sardonic grimace twisting his face. 'I expected as much.'

'It isn't that,' she said, as he jumped down and crossed to her. 'I... I blundered.' She hung her head. 'I let slip that I had allied with you before I pledged myself to them, and Evgena cast me out for treachery. She ordered me killed.'

Stefan's jaw clenched, and a flash of anger flared in his eyes, but he let out a breath and it passed. He lifted her chin and looked at her scratched face. 'You fought your way out, I see. Did you kill any of them?'

Ulrika turned from him, pulling her chin from his fingers. 'Raiza let me go. She said she owed me for saving her from Kiraly. She made me cut her so it would look like we'd fought.'

'Most noble of her,' said Stefan gravely. 'But I cannot say the same for Evgena. She is a fool to do this. She makes war on her allies when enemies abound.' He sighed. 'And it leaves us to fight Kiraly and the cultists alone. We are back where we began.'

Ulrika nodded, but did not speak, nor did she look at him. His mention of Kiraly had returned Evgena's words to her. She had been turning them over in her head since she left the Lahmian mansion, not wanting to believe them, but not able to dismiss them either.

'Is something wrong?' Stefan asked.

Ulrika raised her eyes and looked at him. 'Evgena did not believe Kiraly lived. She said she thought *you* were the cultist who threw the Blood Shard – that you had come here to kill her.'

Stefan stared, then sighed and shook his head. 'I admit I have been tempted. She is a bad leader – a cloistered fool too long set in her ways. But no, I am not Kiraly. I am not here to kill her, though...' He chuckled darkly. 'Though, after this I would willingly use her as bait to draw him out.'

Ulrika frowned. What he said sounded plausible, but it also sounded like the sort of thing a cunning villain would say to draw suspicion from himself, and Stefan was undoubtedly cunning. She just couldn't tell if he was a villain.

'If you ask for proof that I don't want to kill her,' he continued as she remained silent. 'I'm afraid I have none. It is notoriously hard to prove a negative.'

Ulrika nodded, still thinking. She could ask him to turn out his pockets for the Blood Shards, but it would prove nothing if he didn't have them. He could have hidden them anywhere. She could ask him for his word, but a villain would give his word without hesitating. All she had to go on was what she knew of him already.

Of her acquaintances in Praag so far, only he and Raiza had treated her well. Raiza had honoured her debt, and Stefan had saved her life and helped her against the cult, and both had been at least civil, if not friendly. Evgena, on the other hand, had tried to kill her from the start, had openly mistrusted her even as she accepted her vow of service, and had attacked her after welcoming her into her house.

So, in the final tally, she couldn't be certain Stefan wasn't out to kill Evgena, but if he was, she couldn't blame him. She was beginning to feel the same way herself.

She raised her head and looked at him. 'I think,' she said slowly, 'that I don't care. If you are with me against the cult, then I will ask no more. If you tell me there is no Kiraly, and that it is you who seeks to kill Evgena, it will not prejudice me against you.'

Stefan laughed. 'To thine own self be true,' he said with a wolfish smile. 'I believe you are at last becoming a vampire.'

She shrugged, uncomfortable. 'I am only thinking of Praag.'

'Precisely,' said Stefan, then sighed. 'Unfortunately, there is indeed a Kiraly, and I must still kill him, but...' He paused, then turned back to her, coming to a decision. 'But I begin to fear I will not be able to do so before your cultists intend to strike, and I am afraid of what madness will follow if they succeed – even if they fail. Kiraly may retreat. I may lose him. I could be killed before I found him. Anything could happen, and so I think I must put aside my hunt for him and help you first.' He turned and looked at her. 'Tell me again what leads you have. I'm afraid I didn't listen further once you told me of Kiraly last night.'

'There was little else,' said Ulrika. 'When I chased Kiraly, I lost the man who led the sacrifice and couldn't find him again.' She frowned. 'But now that I think of it, he did let something slip during the ceremony. He said the cult would be stealing something tonight called the Viol of Fieromonte, and that the success of their venture depended on it. If we could stop them, or steal it first, we might end their threat in a single stroke.'

'The Vial of Fieromonte?' Stefan asked. 'I don't know it.'

'The *viol*, I think,' said Ulrika. 'As in violin.'

Stefan raised an eyebrow. 'Their success relies upon a fiddle? Did he say where it was?'

'No,' said Ulrika. 'Only that it was in a hiding place.'

'That is little enough to go on,' said Stefan. 'It might be anywhere. It might not even be in the city.'

'Aye,' agreed Ulrika, glum, then looked up, brightening. 'Ah, I know! The goat and the wolf.'

'Who?' asked Stefan.

'The cultists who Raiza and I followed to the sacrifice,' said Ulrika. 'They may know where it is.'

'Ah,' said Stefan. 'What strange names they have.'

Ulrika laughed and turned towards the street. 'Not as strange as their habits. Come, I'll take you to their house.'

BUT WHEN ULRIKA and Stefan reached the Yeshenko mansion it was surrounded by the city watch, and priests of Ursun and Dazh circled the grounds, chanting invocations and prayers. Other men, dressed in dark civilian clothes, went in and out of the house carrying out books and papers and trunks – the Ice Queen's chekist agents, no doubt, Ulrika thought.

'This does not bode well,' said Stefan.

'No,' agreed Ulrika, looking around at the rest of the street.

Yeshenko's wealthy neighbours peered from behind the curtains of their mansions, but their servants were less circumspect. They huddled in little groups outside several houses, watching the proceedings and whispering amongst themselves.

Ulrika stepped away from Stefan and sidled up to a trio of scullery maids who were standing outside the gate of the house opposite.

'What's all the fuss, devotchkas?' she asked. 'What happened to the Yeshenkos?'

'Oh, we shouldn't say,' said a round dark-haired maid. "T'ain't nice to gossip.'

'Were they arrested then?' Ulrika asked.

'Oh no!' said a thin blonde girl. 'Murdered! And in the Novygrad of all places!'

'The Novygrad?' said Ulrika, feigning shock, though in truth it was shocking enough. She hadn't heard or seen any signs of trouble at the temple of Salyak when she and Raiza had left it to follow the crooked man. Had there been some fight after they left? 'What were they doing there?'

The three maids looked at each other, fearful.

'Wicked things,' said the third, finally. She was another brunette, but square and sturdy. 'That's what Yuri the groom says. The watch found 'em dead in a coach near some place where they was makin' black magic.'

'Filthy daemon-worshippers,' hissed the round girl.

Ulrika frowned. 'Dead in a coach,' she murmured, then louder. 'But why did anyone think they were connected to the black magic?'

'They was wearing weird robes and masks,' said the skinny blonde. 'Leastwise the husband was, and the wife had strange marks on her body, under her clothes.'

'Always thought she was a witch,' said the squarish girl peevishly. 'The way she steered him around. Like she had him by the wedding tackle.'

Ulrika edged away again as the girls began to tear into Madam Yeshenko's character, or lack thereof, and returned to Stefan.

'Dead,' she said. 'And discovered as cultists.'

'How did it happen?' asked Stefan.

'They were found murdered in a coach. Romo was

wearing his cult cloak and mask but… Dolshiniva was not.'

'You think that significant?' he asked.

'It makes me wonder where Konstantin Kiraly got his disguise,' she said.

Stefan nodded. 'That would explain it.' He sighed and looked back at the Yeshenko mansion. 'It seems we will learn nothing of the violin here, then,' he said.

Ulrika sighed. 'Aye, and they could already be stealing it. I'm afraid we've lost our chance.'

'Perhaps,' said Stefan. His brow furrowed in thought. 'But I will not give up yet. Surely someone in this musical city must know of the thing.'

Ulrika smiled. 'You're right.' She turned towards the east and the Academy District. 'And I know just where to start asking. Follow me.'

It wasn't until they had passed the Sorcerers' Spire and were halfway across the Karlsbridge that Ulrika realised she was growing hungry again.

ULRIKA AND STEFAN visited five instrument shops before they found anyone who had heard of the Viol of Fieromonte. The fifth was the workshop of one Yarok Gurina, a white-haired maker of violins, cellos, balalaikas and mandolins. He was a big barrel of a man, who looked like he should be shoeing horses rather than making delicate instruments, and Ulrika had to keep herself from licking her lips at the smell of his strong, vigorous blood. She would have to feed soon, but not yet. They had to find the violin first.

'Aye, lady,' Yarok rasped, looking up from pressing a piece of thin veneer to a violin-shaped frame as his stoop-shouldered young apprentice tightened a clamp to hold it in place. 'Sure I've heard of it. The daemon's box, they used to call it. An ill thing to speak of, for them of a superstitious nature.'

Ulrika exchanged a quick glance with Stefan, who remained in the shadows, looking at the beautiful instruments mounted on the walls of the shop, then turned back to Yarok.

'Do you know where it is?' she asked.

Yarok cackled. 'It's nowhere! It never was,' he said. 'A fairy tale, a legend, a – Seva, you cloth-headed dolt!' he cried suddenly, and swatted his apprentice on the ear. 'You've split the veneer with your tightening! Do you know how much that wood costs?' He shoved the boy away, and pointed him towards the back. 'Go cut another piece, and mind it has no knots or scars.'

The boy scurried off, dodging more blows, pausing only to blink, slack-mouthed, at Ulrika before vanishing in the back.

Yarok sighed and threw the broken strip of wood aside. 'Sorry, m'lady,' he said. 'The boy's moon-eyed for beauty. Happens every time a lovely girl comes in the shop.'

'I'm flattered,' said Ulrika, trying to mimic the sultry Lahmian tone Countess Gabriella murmured so easily. 'But you said the Fieromonte never existed?'

'Well now,' said Yarok, leaning back on his bench, and fishing a pipe from his belt pouch. 'I've read it did, and I've read it didn't. But even if it did, no one's seen or heard it for ages.'

'Tell me of it,' said Ulrika, trying not to sound too eager. 'Where did you read this?'

Yarok filled the pipe, and then lit it from a brand he took from a little stove at his elbow. He puffed it to life, then blew out a cloud of smoke. 'It was when I was a student at the Music Academy, forty years ago,' he said. 'I found mention of it in an old book in the library there. Said the viol was made by a mad Tilean named Fieromonte sometime before the Great War against Chaos. Supposedly he wanted to make the most beautiful, sweetest-sounding violin in the world, and sold his soul to a daemon to do it.' He laughed. 'According to the book, it worked. People would break down in tears to hear it play. It's said a woman killed herself when it was played at her husband's funeral, and there's another tale of an entire company of winged lancers dancing themselves to death at a ball.' He waved his pipe dismissively. 'All rubbish. There were more books that said it was just a story. A myth of music-makers.'

'What was supposed to have happened to it?' Ulrika asked.

'Lost in the war, mayhap?' said Yarok, shrugging. 'I can't exactly recall, but whatever it was, it was a tall tale like all the rest.'

'No doubt,' said Ulrika. 'Still, it's an interesting story. Do you recall the name of the book you read of it in?'

Yarok frowned and sipped at his pipe, then blew out more smoke. 'What was the name? It was one of my favourites then. Full of wild stories and strange pictures. Read it when I should have been studying more reliable histories. Ah! *The Memoirs of Kappelmeister Barshai.* He was court composer to Tzar Alexis. Mad as a hare, old Barshai, and you should have heard some of the things the old Tzar got up to before the war. We all think of him as the great hero, but he was quite the lad. Once–'

Ulrika cut him off with a bow. 'Thank you very much for your time, Master Yarok,' she said, 'but I'm afraid I must go. You have been a great help.'

Yarok looked displeased to be cut off just as he was getting started, but he raised his pipe politely to her nonetheless. 'A pleasure, lady,' he said. 'Any time.'

Ulrika turned and strode out the door with Stefan as Yarok's voice followed them down the street. 'Seva, you clot! Where's that veneer? Name of the Bear, where's that cack-handed idiot got to?'

CHAPTER TWENTY-TWO
MUSIC OF THE NIGHT

'I SHALL HAVE to feed soon,' said Ulrika, chewing her lip as she and Stefan hurried towards the Music Academy.

'So, feed,' said Stefan. He swept a hand around at the few students who threaded through the streets. 'We may need our strength later.'

Ulrika hesitated, embarrassed. 'I... I am a bit choosy,' she said. 'It may take some time to find someone suitable.'

Stefan raised an eyebrow. 'What, do you require the blood of virgins, or royalty? You drank readily enough in the midst of the fire.'

'I prefer villains,' said Ulrika. 'I do not like those who prey on the innocent, and I do not wish to be one myself.'

'Ah,' said Stefan. 'The babe's disease. Many vampires in their first year suffer from it. It will pass.'

'I don't see how time will change my ideals,' said Ulrika, stiff.

'It is inevitable,' said Stefan. 'You still feel connection to your human past. Your friends still live. The events of your life still affect the present. But in twenty years, or thirty, when those you know are all dead, and when all that happened before your rebirth has passed into history, you will see your attachment to humanity is an illusion. We share their form and language, but we are a species apart.'

'I acknowledge that,' said Ulrika. 'But that doesn't give us the right to prey indiscriminately upon them. It is only a minor inconvenience to avoid the innocent.'

'Their innocence is another illusion,' said Stefan. 'Do you think even the kindest, most open-minded of them would lift a finger to defend you if they learned your true nature?' He laughed darkly. 'They would take up torch and rowan stake like all the rest, and would not spare the time to question you as to the moral superiority of your feeding habits.'

'What they would or wouldn't do doesn't matter,' said Ulrika obstinately. 'My sense of honour is born within myself, not in what others do or think. I refuse to act like a monster because they think me one.'

Stefan smiled indulgently. 'Very high-minded of you,' he said. 'I applaud you for your adherence to your principles. I only hope you don't expect me to follow you on this narrow path.'

Ulrika frowned. The question hadn't occurred to her before. If she refused to allow the opinions of others to influence what she thought was right and wrong, but then expected others to change *their* ways to match *her* morals, that would make her a hypocrite. And yet she had vowed to prey on the predators of humanity. If Stefan was one such, did that mean she must prey on him? Must she stop him from killing innocents? Must she somehow convince him of the rightness of her way of thinking? Or should she make an exception for him because they fought on the same side against the cultists? 'You must of course follow your own path,' she said slowly. 'I can only hope you see some wisdom in mine.'

'Wisdom? No,' said Stefan. 'Idealism, disgust with your own kind, denial of your nature – those I see. But I see no great wisdom in it.'

'Is there not wisdom in protecting the society from which you feed?' asked Ulrika. 'You protect Praag now so you can have your vengeance on Kiraly. Is that not the whole of your life in miniature? Do you not need the human world to be stable so that you may pursue your goals, whatever they are? You must keep the peasants of your castle safe and productive so that they continue to pay you rent and allow you to live in the manner to which you are accustomed. You need the Empire to remain strong to keep the northern hordes from overrunning your lands. Would you rather be fighting for your existence at all times?'

'There is indeed wisdom in that,' said Stefan. 'But I fail to see how taking the blood of an occasional milkmaid here, or an honest burgher there, threatens the stability of this human bulwark.'

'I... well,' Ulrika stuttered. 'Bandits and murderers and cultists threaten the fabric of society, yes? So, removing them strengthens it, and... and...'

'Rationalisations,' said Stefan. 'I think your true reason is that the thought of harming the poor helpless little things repulses you, and so you look for reasonable-sounding arguments to bolster your sentimentality.'

Ulrika pursed her lips, struggling for a counter-argument. Was Stefan right? Was she only acting like a little farm girl who didn't want to see her favourite calf killed because it was so soft and sweet? She wanted to believe there was more to her conviction than that, but she was finding it hard to articulate it.

'Here we are,' said Stefan.

Ulrika looked up. The gates of the Music Academy were before them – two ornate stone columns topped with gargoyles playing flutes and trumpets, rising among the trees of the wooded northern fringes of the Magnus Gardens. She looked on them with a touch of relief. Their debate would have to be postponed, and she could use the time to find a better answer to Stefan's question.

If only she wasn't so hungry.

They stepped through the gates and into a strange, glittering world. It seemed as if the madness that had twisted Praag had struck most forcefully here, but also whimsically. The buildings of the Academy were weird, oddly angled edifices, spired and turreted and banded with glittering tiles of blue and red and orange. Minarets sprouted from their roofs like jewelled mushrooms, and statue-bedecked fountains dotted the grounds, all portraying various mythical heroes, each contorted and straining, their hands clawing the air and their faces grimacing as if caught in the throes of some terrible passion.

But as bright as the buildings were on the outside, they were dark on the inside, and the college seemed nearly as deserted as the streets that surrounded it. Only a few students shuffled across the quadrangles, and for an academy of music, it was eerily silent.

Ulrika wondered where they had all gone, but a moment later, a statue told her the answer. It stood outside the concert hall, a winged woman with a sword in her hand, and its limbs were so covered in black ribbons it appeared furred like a bear. Ulrika stretched out one of the ribbons as she passed it. There was writing on it in white ink, *Andre Verbitsky – Clarinet – Slain at the battle of Zvenlev, may Father Ursun receive him.*

They were all like that – cellists, flautists, harpsichordists, timpanists, who had set down their

was intoxicating. Ulrika was beginning to regret not agreeing to kill them as Stefan had suggested.

'Searching for knowledge,' she said, as calmly as she could. 'And you?'

'But... but th' library ish closed,' Valtarin said. 'You aren't allowed here.'

'Nor are you, I'll wager,' said Ulrika, then smirked and looked at the girl. 'Certainly not for the reason you've come. So we would both be in trouble if our trespasses were discovered, yes?'

Valtarin looked from her to Stefan to the girl, weighing the situation. 'I... I...'

Ulrika cut him off. 'Do know how to find a book in these catalogues?'

Valtarin blinked, apparently surprised at the question, then shook his shaggy head. 'Only Gorbenko knows. He made a mesh of 'em jusht so he could keep his job. No one can find anything without him any more.'

Stefan's hand dropped casually to the hilt of his rapier. Ulrika stepped down from the desk to keep Valtarin's eyes on her.

'Then perhaps you have direct knowledge of what we seek,' she said.

Valtarin's eyes followed her as she crossed to one of the tables and leaned against it. The girl picked herself up off the floor and clung to Valtarin's arm.

'I represent a collector of fine musical instruments,' Ulrika said, taking her purse from her belt and opening it. 'A nobleman of Sigmar's Empire who is seeking a rare, legendary instrument that perhaps you've heard of.' She took out five gold coins and laid them one at a time on the table. 'The Viol of Fieromonte.'

Valtarin's eyes went wide at the name and he stumbled back, almost upsetting the girl again. His heart hammered even harder.

Ulrika exchanged a glance with Stefan, who was stepping down to circle around behind Valtarin. Such a strong reaction. Could it be the boy knew something of the theft?

'I see you've heard of it,' Ulrika said, advancing on him. 'Do you have some interest in it too?'

'What?' said Valtarin, looking nervously from her to Stefan. 'No! I don't think it even exists any more. It is just an unlucky name, a musician's curse. It is bad luck to hear it, and worse to speak it.'

'I think it is more to you than that,' said Ulrika. 'You are sweating, sir. Why?'

The boy backed away from her, eyes rolling. 'I... I... Why don't you madmen leave us alone!' he cried. 'Nobody here knows where your cursed violin is!'

Ulrika stopped and looked to Stefan again, then turned back to Valtarin. 'There have been others here?' she asked. 'Inquiring after the Fieromonte?'

He nodded, his eyes still wide with fright. 'I... I didn't see them myself,' he said. 'But I heard. They scared old Daska near to death.'

'How long ago was this?' asked Stefan. 'Who were they?'

'I don't know,' said Valtarin. 'I only heard that they came sneaking around a few weeks ago, saying they wanted to buy it, like you. And they didn't like it when nobody could tell them where it was.'

'Well, we are not so rough,' said Ulrika, pushing the coins towards the quivering young man. 'If you were able to tell me where it was, or where in this place I might find knowledge of it, these coins would be yours. We were seeking a book called *The Memoirs of Kappelmeister Barshai*.'

Valtarin looked at the gold, then up at the three floors of books. He shook his head. 'I don't know where that is. I've never...'

Ulrika sighed and reached for the coins, while Stefan reached for his sword.

'Wait!' said Valtarin, edging away from Stefan. 'Wait! I wasn't finished. I was going to say, I've never heard of it, but I know someone else who might know. I... I'm sure he would.'

Over Valtarin's shoulder, Stefan shook his head, clearly impatient to return to their search. Ulrika ignored him.

'Who is this person?' she asked the boy.

'My old tutor, Maestro Padurowski,' he said. 'He knows everything about violins. If the Fiero–, er, the instrument, still exists, he could surely tell you where it was.'

'Where is he now?' asked Ulrika.

'He will be in his offices,' said Valtarin. 'Working on his arrangements for the duke's victory concert.'

'And did these others speak to him?' asked Stefan.

Valtarin shook his head. 'I don't know. I don't think so. It was tutor Daska they saw. He didn't come out of his apartments for a week, after.'

'Can you bring us to this Padurowski then?' Ulrika pressed. 'The coins will be yours.'

Valtarin hesitated, looking towards Stefan. 'Will you hurt him?'

'We are not like the others,' said Ulrika. 'We will pay him, just as we are paying you.'

The boy nodded at last. 'Come with me.'

He turned to the entry hall and beckoned them to follow. Stefan shot Ulrika a disapproving look as she scooped up the coins, and they fell in with him. She shrugged.

From behind them came a plaintive, drunken whine. 'But, Valtarin, I thought you were going to show me Astanilovich's bed.'

* * *

MAESTRO PADUROWSKI'S OFFICES were in an unassuming faculty building on the edge of the campus, a cramped hive of tiny suites that smelled of dust, wood polish and decaying paper. Valtarin knocked on a door at the back of the second storey and a brisk voice called, 'Come!'

The young man pushed open the door and bowed, and Ulrika saw over his mop of hair a narrow room lined with paper-filled shelves and lit by a lamp set on top of a pile of folios. A man was hunched at a desk, wild white hair hiding his face as he scrawled rapidly with a goose-quill pen across a large sheet of music-ruled paper.

'Is that my dinner, Luba?' he said without looking up. 'Just put it on the chair, will you?'

'It is I, maestro,' said Valtarin, bowing again. 'Valtarin.'

Maestro Padurowski raised his head and flipped back a great mane of white hair, beaming. 'Valtarin, my boy! How nice!' He had a long, lined face, all nose and chin, with a high forehead and white eyebrows that would have shamed a magister.

'I've brought some people to see you, maestro,' said Valtarin, stepping in. 'They want to ask you some questions.'

Padurowski scowled. 'No time for that, my boy,' he said, waving his quill and flicking ink everywhere. 'We are rehearsing tomorrow and I haven't transcribed the brass parts yet. Later, later. Next week.'

'I can pay you for your time, maestro,' said Ulrika.

Padurowski shook his head and bowed to his work again. 'You can't pay me enough to save my neck if I disappoint the duke at his concert. Go, go.'

'It will only take a few minutes,' said Ulrika. 'And I will pay you a gold Reikmark for each of them.'

The maestro raised his head again, his eyes glittering. 'A Reikmark for each minute? Even the duke doesn't pay so well.' He put down his pen and sat back. 'Ask your questions.'

Ulrika put a coin on the desk. 'I represent a collector of musical instruments who seeks a famed violin known as the Viol of Fieromonte. Your student said you might know where it was.'

'I told them that others came asking about it before, maestro,' blurted out Valtarin. 'I told them they questioned tutor Daska and got angry when he didn't know!'

Padurowski made a face. 'And I don't know why there is suddenly all this interest in an old legend.'

'A legend?' asked Ulrika. 'You mean it doesn't exist?'

The maestro smiled wryly. 'It seems I will not win many gold coins,' he said, 'for the answer is short. It did, but does no longer. It was burned just after the Great War against Chaos. The tale goes that it had become possessed by a daemon when the hordes took the city, and afterwards it had the power to drive men mad. The duke at the time ordered it burnt at the stake, as if it were a witch.' He laughed. 'I know not if it was truly possessed. Perhaps so. But I do know it was burned, and its ashes scattered to the four winds. A great shame. For it was said to have the purest tone in all the world.'

Ulrika sighed. It couldn't be true, not if the cultists had staked so much upon it, but Padurowski obviously thought it was, and there seemed little point in pressing him further. She laid two more gold coins on the desk beside the first. 'Thank you for your time, maestro. I will inform my patron of this.'

'I am sorry not to have been able to give you news more to your liking,' said Padurowski. 'But I thank you. I have never won coins so easily before.'

Ulrika handed Valtarin the five coins she had promised him, and she and Stefan made their way down the narrow stairs of the faculty building and back into the Academy grounds.

* * *

'I DON'T UNDERSTAND,' said Ulrika as they stepped through the Music Academy's gates and started aimlessly through the streets of the student quarter, empty but for a dispirited-looking watch patrol. 'How can the cultists be after a violin that was burned two hundred years ago?'

'Padurowski must know less than he thinks he does,' said Stefan. 'Perhaps the story of the burning was planted at the time in order to hide the true fate of the violin.'

Ulrika nodded. 'But if so, where is it?'

She paced on, trying to think of places within the city where an instrument could be hidden. Her hunger was making it hard to think. She had suppressed it during their interview with Padurowski, but now it was growing again, nagging at her like an insistent child. She forced it down and returned to the question.

There were treasure vaults in the duke's palace, of course, and Praag had many private collectors of unusual objects. Or perhaps the violin was hidden at the Opera House or the Music Academy itself, but in which of those places, or a hundred others should they begin their search? The cult meant to steal it tonight, and if they couldn't stop them, they would use it in two nights, when Mannslieb was next full–

A new thought blasted all others from her head. The Opera House? The full moon? Ursun's teeth, she had it!

She caught Stefan's arm. 'I know what they're going to do! I know how they intend to use the violin!'

'How?' said Stefan.

'Duke Enrik's victory concert!' she said. 'It takes place on the night when Mannslieb is full.'

Stefan frowned. 'Aye, but–'

Ulrika cut him off. 'The tales say the violin drives men mad when it is played, yes? The cultists are going to play it before the duke and all the nobles and generals and guild masters of Praag and turn them into raving lunatics! That is how they intend to bring down Praag – by destroying its leaders.'

Stefan's footsteps slowed. 'I... I... By my master, I believe you could be right. This... this is a grave danger, graver than I previously thought. It must be stopped.'

'Aye,' said Ulrika. 'But, how–?'

A movement in the corner of her eye caught her attention. As she turned, a figure ducked back into an alley. She looked away again as if she had seen nothing.

'We have picked up a tail,' she said.

Stefan nodded, keeping his eyes forwards. 'Where?'

'In the alley behind us,' said Ulrika.

'Let us speak with him, then,' said Stefan.

As one, they turned and strode swiftly to the alley.

The man in the alley gaped as they approached him and began to back away. Ulrika frowned. She had seen those sloped shoulders and that slack-lipped mouth before. Then she had it – the instrument-maker's apprentice. Had he followed them since they visited the shop? That was embarrassing.

The apprentice turned to flee as they closed in. Ulrika leapt over his head and landed in front of him, drawing her rapier. He skidded to a stop and looked back, eyes wide with terror. Stefan approached him from behind, also drawing. The boy pulled a dagger from his belt with a trembling hand.

'Put it away, apprentice,' said Ulrika, stepping towards him. 'We only want to speak–'

'For the coming of the queen!' screeched the apprentice, then plunged the knife into his neck and tore it across.

Ulrika and Stefan sprang forwards and caught his arms, but they were too late. The boy was sagging to his knees, a torrent of blood pumping from his gaping throat and the light dying in his eyes.

'Damn him!' snarled Ulrika, shoving him down. 'Damn him!'

'Don't damn him,' snapped Stefan. 'Drain him, quickly!'

Ulrika started, annoyed, then dropped to her knees and closed her mouth over the gushing wound. So hungry, but in her frustration she had pushed away what she needed most. She sucked in the boy's blood, trying to catch it before it all spilled on the ground.

Her eyes closed in pleasure, but as the sweet song of blood throbbed in her ears, the faint trill of a violin joined it, playing a discordant, laughing counterpoint to her rapture that caught at her like a barbed thorn and held her head above the flood of red warmth, nagging at her. It seemed there was always a violin playing somewhere in Praag, sometimes plaintive, sometimes laughing, and always carried to her by a trick of the wind. Was it the *same* violin? And if so, who played it, and why did she always seem to hear it at times of great distress or horror?

Ulrika's head jerked up from the apprentice's neck, an impossible idea coming to her. She looked up at Stefan, her mouth dripping blood. 'Do you hear that song?'

Stefan cocked his ear. 'Aye,' he said. 'A fiddler, somewhere.'

Ulrika wiped her mouth on the boy's sleeve and stood. 'Have you heard it before?'

Stefan frowned, thinking. 'Aye,' he said at last. 'Now that you mention it, I have. Always in the distance, and always just a snatch.'

'Yes,' said Ulrika, excitement growing in her chest. 'It has been the same for me. I have always ignored it. There is so much music in Praag now. It just seemed another part of the symphony. But... but it is *everywhere*, though only when something terrible has happened. I heard it after I killed Gaznayev's thugs, and when I slaughtered the cultists in the distillery, and when the Blood Shard wounded Raiza.'

'Are you certain?' asked Stefan.

Ulrika shook her head. 'I don't know. Perhaps it is only my imagination. Do you remember when you–?'

They both paused as the song died again, fading away as if the wind had changed.

Stefan frowned, thinking. 'I heard it when the Lahmians chased me from their house, and again just before I came to your aid in the gangsters' warehouse. Other times too, I think. Sometimes it sounded like a voice. Sometimes like a violin.'

'Not *a* violin!' said Ulrika with sudden conviction. '*The* violin! The Fieromonte!'

Stefan scowled. 'That is quite a leap,' he said. 'The music could be anything. It could be a different instrument each time. It could be mere coincidence.'

'I know it,' said Ulrika. 'But what else have we to go on? These damned cultists cover their tracks at every turn.'

'What about the instrument-maker?' asked Stefan. 'Perhaps he sent this fool after us.'

Ulrika shook her head. 'Would he have given us the title of the book if he were a cultist? Would he have told us where to find it?'

'We never found it,' countered Stefan. 'It could have all been a lie.'

'To what purpose?' asked Ulrika. 'Would it not have made more sense to send us away empty-handed and try to follow us to our homes? Or attack us in the street?'

Stefan sighed. 'Very well, but how are we to make use of a note on the wind? There's no following it. I have heard it in every quarter of the city.'

Ulrika bit her lip. He was right. Knowing the haunting melody came from the Fieromonte didn't suddenly give them the ability to find it. Or did it? She looked up.

'What direction was the tune coming from just now?' she asked.

Stefan paused, then pointed east. 'That way.'

Ulrika nodded. That was as she remembered too. 'And when you first heard it? At Evgena's house?'

Stefan rolled his eyes. 'Do you expect me to remember that? Can you remember? In any of the instances?'

Ulrika tried to think back. She had heard the violin at Max's house, when she had discovered him with that woman, but all she could remember was her rage. What about the other times? She had heard it after killing the thugs who had stolen from the blind singer. That had been in the student quarter, as now, and it had come from... from the east – yes – just as now. But when she had chased Kiraly across the rooftops after he had thrown the Blood Shard at Raiza, that had been on the fringes of the Novygrad, in the eastern half of the city, and the melody had come from the west.

'North,' said Stefan abruptly. 'When I heard it outside Gaznayev's warehouse, it was coming from the north. I remember looking that way.'

Ulrika pursed her lips. 'So in the west we hear it from the east. In the east we hear it from the west. In the south, we hear it from the north.'

'That would put it in the centre of the city,' said Stefan. 'Somewhere near–'

'The Sorcerers' Spire,' breathed Ulrika. 'The old Tzar's College of Magic!'

Stefan frowned. 'Another leap,' he said, then shrugged. 'But what else have we?' He turned and started towards the street.

CHAPTER TWENTY-THREE
THE SPIRE

ULRIKA AND STEFAN looked upon the Sorcerers' Spire from the roof of the building nearest to it, which wasn't very near at all. The spire sat at the intersection of the Grand Parade, Praag's main avenue, and the River Lynsk, and was surrounded by a wide empty space, as if the rest of the city was edging away from it. A high stone wall with no door or gate had been built around its base, though whether to keep the public out, or lock something in, Ulrika didn't know.

From within this barricade, the tower rose like a shattered mast. Even ruined, it stood three times as tall as the tallest of the nearby tenements, its jagged top tearing holes in the low mist that swirled perpetually around it. The lower reaches showed little damage, the red walls straight and true, the buttresses and balconies unbroken, but further up, the stone was scarred and twisted in terrible ways, signs of the deadly energies unleashed when it had exploded. There, the stone grew mottled and crumbling, and gaping black holes yawned in it. Near the top, a section seemed to have melted, the walls folding down on top of each other as if they were made of wet clay, and the pinnacle was just a ragged blackened stump, like the severed wrist of a man who had been holding a bomb when it went off.

'I do not see or sense anyone,' said Ulrika.

'Nor do I,' said Stefan. 'Either we have beaten them to it, or they have already taken the violin.'

'Or it isn't here after all,' said Ulrika.

'Let us go see,' said Stefan.

They swung down the front of the building, then jogged across the wide bare plaza to the wall that surrounded the tower. Ulrika looked around to see that they were not observed, then started up it. It was crudely made, and did not lack for holds. A row of spikes ran along its top, but she and Stefan stepped between them and clambered down into the narrow, rubble-filled space between it and the tower.

Ulrika sighted up the tower, frowning. Its walls, at least near the base, were much smoother that those of the barricade, and all the windows in the lower storeys had been bricked up. Climbing might be difficult.

Stefan started around the base, looking for a way in. She followed him. On the far side they found the old entrance, a grand, arched opening with stone dragons winding around its columns and the head of a bear growling from the keystone. It was also bricked shut – but not entirely. Near the ground in one corner, a hole had been smashed through the bricks.

Ulrika cursed as they ran to it. 'They've got here before us!'

Stefan shook his head. 'If they did, it was years before. Look.'

Ulrika peered closer. It was true, the litter of bricks that surrounded the hole was caked in dust. It had been made long ago, and the dust was undisturbed.

'Bold thieves of ages past,' said Stefan.

'My thanks to them for breaking the trail,' said Ulrika and squatted down to poke her head through the hole.

Inside was a grand entry chamber rising more than three storeys to an arched basalt ceiling inlaid with constellations of bronze stars, planets and moons. Below these false heavens, towering, crumbling statues of men and women in mages' robes looked down from alcoves set in the walls, their granite hands holding wands, staffs, astrolabes and scales. The statues' postures were straight and noble, but their stone faces were leering masks of depravity and corruption, tongues sticking out, eyes bulging, pig snouts instead of noses and horns jutting from their foreheads. Surely the sculptors had not carved them that way. She shivered, unnerved, and returned to her survey of the room.

In its centre, a weird double-helix stairway, as delicate as if it had been built by the elves of Ulthuan, rose towards the ceiling from a hill of rubble like a pair of snakes curving around each other, and beyond it, dark doors gaped in the far wall. Some seemed to lead to further rooms, while one opened to a stairway leading down. She pushed her senses out and up and down, searching for heart-fires and pulses hidden in the storeys above and the cellars below, but felt nothing. The place seemed as empty as a tomb.

She squirmed through the hole to the dusty floor and stood, looking around and brushing herself down as Stefan pushed through behind her.

'Shall we work our way down, or up?' she asked.

Before Stefan could answer, a sound froze them – a sad, haunting melody drifting down from above, played on a violin.

'Up, it seems,' said Stefan, and started for the double set of spiral stairs.

Ulrika shivered, then followed. It sounded like the thing was calling to them. Beckoning them on.

The twin staircases corkscrewed towards the ceiling, but weren't quite true. They leaned against each other like drunk lovers, neither reaching all the way to the hole in the ceiling through which they had once gone. There was a gap roughly three times Ulrika's height between the tops and the broken sections that stuck down from the hole, and Ulrika could see that the bases of both stairways had broken too. She swallowed. There was nothing holding the intertwined stairs up but each other. They were not connected at either the base or the top.

'Perhaps we should try to scale the exterior after all,' she said.

'They have stood like this for two hundred years,' said Stefan. 'Our paltry weight should make no difference.'

He started up the left-hand stair with confidence. Ulrika waited a moment, ready to spring away if it all came crashing down, then followed. Their feet puffed up huge clouds of dust with every step, but the stairs did not shift or sway.

After two revolutions, they reached the break, and again found signs of earlier explorers. Ropes and pulleys spanned the vertical gap like the work of a giant spider, and a scattering of tools littered the surface of the last crumbling stair.

Stefan stepped to the edge and tugged hard on a rope. A mist of dust shivered from it as it snapped tight, but it held. He put his weight on it, then climbed hand over hand to the stairs that screwed down out of the ceiling. Ulrika held the bottom of the rope for him, then, when he had pulled himself onto the bottom step, she climbed after him, her skin prickling only a little as she swung out over the long drop. Stefan caught her arm at the top and helped her up onto the hanging steps. The distant violin congratulated them on their efforts with a lilting phrase, then faded away again.

The tune set Ulrika's teeth on edge. 'It wants to be free,' she said.

Stefan nodded, and they drew their rapiers and started curving up through the opening in the ceiling into the chimney of the stairwell. After a full turn they came to a landing that connected to a circular gallery lined with doors. Through these, they could see wood-panelled lecture halls with ranks of benches and lecterns and slates with strange symbols chalked on them. Skeletons in decayed scholars' robes choked the door of one of the rooms, as if the students had died while all trying to get out of the room at once.

After another half-turn they found another skeleton lying on the stair, head down and face down, as if the man had fallen while running down from above. He held a bar of gold in his skeletal hands. Ulrika winced as she saw that his finger bones were gold too, indeed, all the bones in his hand had turned to gold, and the gilding continued up to his wrists. There were paper-thin flakes of gold leaf all around his hands, as if his skin had turned to gold too. She and Stefan stepped around him and continued on.

A moment later she sensed someone standing at the balustrade on the next level, and looked up, going on guard. No one was there, but as soon as she looked away, she could sense them again, and others too, moving about. She looked at Stefan.

'Ghosts,' he said. 'Or echoes of times past.'

The further up they went, the stranger things became – statues whose eyes wept fresh blood, weird whisperings that burbled lascivious impossibilities in Ulrika's ears, terrified shrieking from empty rooms, a room where the sun shone brightly through the narrow windows, though all the other rooms were bathed in moonlight.

Nor was all the strangeness tangible. Emotions blew through the tower like gusts of wind, enveloping Ulrika and Stefan briefly in clouds of hate, lust, giddiness or unbearable sorrow, and these winds grew stronger the higher they climbed. Ulrika alternately wanted to weep, or laugh, or attack Stefan, though whether to tear his clothes off or tear his throat out changed by the moment. It was all she could do not to be dragged into the highs and lows of these false feelings, and she held herself clenched with the effort of resisting.

They passed a spot where the stone of the stairs was so hot the soles of their boots smoked and they could not touch the banisters, and another floor where everything – the walls, furniture, wall sconces and people – had turned to glass – a scene of terror and flight frozen in crystalline perfection for centuries. Glass scholars were caught fleeing and looking over their shoulders, as if from an explosion. An older woman shielded a younger woman in her arms. A young apprentice ran, his arms overladen with books. Most were fused to the floor where their feet touched, but a few had snapped from this base and lay in scattered pieces where they had fallen. The violin played again as Ulrika and Stefan passed these unfortunates, and sympathetic vibrations in the glass made it seem as if they were screaming.

A few floors later, the stairs were choked with a dense thicket of gnarled black vines that bore red leaves and fat purple fruit. The vines spilled from the rooms and onto the galleries and spanned the drop between the two spirals. Ulrika and Stefan looked for a way around them, but they filled the whole shaft. There seemed no choice but to crawl through.

With Stefan at her side, Ulrika pushed through the fleshy leaves and pulled herself up onto a vine. She grimaced. Its bark was slick and oily and smelled of mildew. It was hard to maintain her grip. Then a rustling sound brought her head up. Stefan looked around too. The red leaves rattled, then fell silent.

'What was that?' asked Ulrika.

'Rats?' said Stefan.

They went on, climbing from vine to vine, and burrowing deeper into the thicket. Ulrika paused as she saw a skeleton a few feet below her, fallen between two vines, and then another hanging a little further on. They wore the ragged remains of black clothes, and had ropes and tools slung about them.

'The ancient thieves?'

Stefan nodded. 'But what killed them?'

The rustling sound came again, and Ulrika looked around as something moved in the corner of her eye. She turned. It was one of the vine's bulbous purple fruit, rearing up on its stalk like a snake.

The moment she looked at it, it split like a seedpod and darted straight at her eyes, extending a stamen like a barbed bone needle. She shrieked, and only her inhuman reflexes allowed her to catch the stem before it impaled her pupil with its spike. Another stabbed her arm, the fleshy lips of the pod closing around the spike and sucking at the wound. She tore away from it, howling, and it took a patch of skin with it as it recoiled. Beside her, Stefan was cursing and thrashing as well, and more gaping pods were darting out from the leaves on all sides, stabbing with their stamens.

'On! On!' Stefan shouted. 'Keep moving! Cover your face!'

Ulrika flailed about her, swatting the things back, then pulled her cloak over her head and stuffed part of it in her mouth to keep it tight as she scrambled on, blind and clutching for the next vine.

The pods attacked her from every direction as she went, stabbing her in the arms and legs and back and making her scream and twitch, and from the curses and grunts beside her she knew Stefan was similarly infested. A vision for how it had been for the thieves flashed through her mind. Without the speed of a vampire, they must have been blinded instantly, and then torn apart by the sucking pods as they fought desperately to make their way out of the vines. A horrible death.

Ulrika and Stefan were more fortunate. Indeed, to Ulrika's relief, but also her confusion, after the initial attacks, the pods bit less and less. They continued to writhe and batter her, but struck less frequently with their spikes, though they seemed angrier and angrier. Finally, Ulrika's hand touched stone instead of slippery vine, and she crawled out from the thicket onto the steps. Stefan dragged himself out behind her, and they crawled away from it up the steps, as the pods strained at the end of the stalks behind them.

'Vile vegetable!' snarled Stefan, sinking down to the steps and massaging his wounds once they were safely out of their reach.

Ulrika collapsed beside him, doing the same. Her hands and wrists were covered in lacerations and angry red punctures. 'I believe we are fortunate we do not live,' she said.

'Why is that?' asked Stefan, pulling a broken stamen from his leg.

'They didn't seem to care for our taste.'

'I hope they die from it,' said Stefan.

Ulrika smiled wryly. 'I wonder if it was necessary that we come here. The violin seems well guarded. Could any living men make it through these obstacles?'

'They are cultists,' said Stefan. 'They will have magic.'

Ulrika's smile faded. He was right. The cult might have no difficulty at all. She sighed. 'On we go, then.'

They stood and continued up the stairs, but after only two more full turns, they came to an obstruction that seemed entirely impassable. As Ulrika had noted when they had been observing the spire from a distance, part of it seemed to have melted. They had reached that part now. The walls of the stairwell and the tower had folded like they were made of hot wax, the storeys sinking down and flattening one on top of the other, and sealing off the way up in a closed throat of bulging, buckled walls.

Ulrika stepped up to the weird drooping ceiling and touched it. It was hard granite. Whatever force had melted it was gone now and the stone had reverted to its natural state.

Stefan sighed. 'This may be the end,' he said. 'Not even a warlock will get through that.'

'No,' said Ulrika. 'But a vampire might get around it.'

He looked at her curiously, and she beckoned him to follow, then returned to the landing they had just passed. The rooms of this storey seemed to have been the personal apartments of the mages who had lived there, for there were beds and tables and writing desks in them. There were also human silhouettes burned into the walls and floors, like shadows cast by a bright sun.

Ulrika crossed to a tall, shattered window, poked her head out and looked up. Unlike the smooth walls at the base, the stone here was pitted and crumbling, with plenty of handholds, while above, where the tower had melted, it was wrinkled and bulging and even more worn, like the skin of a snake, half-shredded.

'It is practically a ladder,' she said, then climbed out and began her ascent as Stefan stepped out and followed behind her.

But as they reached the level of the melted walls, the climb got more difficult. The stone hummed with trapped energy and made her fingers tingle and twitch, while weird winds with human screams battered her and tried to pull her off the tower. Then, out of nowhere, a man fell towards her, flailing and shrieking.

She flinched, and had to scrabble with her claws to regain her grip, but he fell through her, as insubstantial as the air. More men fell as she continued on, and flashes of noise and blinding light began to explode all around her, only to vanish again instantly.

In the flashes she could see horrible winged creatures circling the tower, belching fire and black bile, while robed warlocks hovered on floating purple discs and blasted it with arcane bolts. Sorcerous defenders fought back with blasts of their own, burning the warlocks out of the sky with fire, and crusting the wings of the abominations with ice so they fell, though there were always more to replace them.

It seemed to Ulrika she was climbing through a storm of trapped time, where the events of the spire's destruction played out for ever. Fire and black energy billowed around her, burning her flesh without seeming to damage it, while the wall beneath her hands was alternately straight and true, then molten and shifting, then warped and cold and unmoving. More than once she grabbed at holds and nearly fell when her hand discovered they weren't really there. After that, she closed her eyes and climbed only by feel. Still she was buffeted by noises and winds and memories not her own, but eventually these grew less frequent and the currents and sounds abated.

She opened her eyes again and saw she had climbed above the melted section to an area where the stone was black and cracked, and the char came off on her hands and clothes. There was a window above her and to the left, and she crabbed carefully up and over to it, and at last pulled herself in, her arms trembling with fatigue, then turned and helped Stefan in as well. When they were both safe, they stood, brushing soot from their clothes and hands, and looked around.

The room was a high-ceilinged, wedge-shaped quarter of the tower, with a small door to the stairwell in the far wall, and large, arched and columned doors on either side, leading to other quarter sections. It looked as if it had once been some sort of treasure room, for there were chests and coffers and strange objects all around, all destroyed. The chests were blackened piles of tinder, and the things they had contained nothing but unrecognisable lumps. Suits of armour were heaps of shining slag, the jewels that had encrusted them cracked and clouded. A collapsed shelf spilled charred book covers whose pages had all burned away. Rivulets of silver and gold ran across the flagstone floor from cracked coffers. An obelisk from ancient Nehekhara lay black and shattered in one corner.

Ulrika squatted and picked up a cracked jewel. 'If the fires destroyed this, how has the violin survived?'

Stefan shook his head and started for the door in the right-hand wall. Ulrika stood and followed. The next room was the same as the first, a black ruin filled with charred treasures. They crossed it to the next. The third room was also a field of wreckage, except for a massive stone vault built into the interior wall.

'That is how,' said Stefan.

They crossed to it, picking their way through the mess. It rose to the ceiling, and though its walls were as black with soot as the rest of the room, they were whole, as was its metal-banded door and all its hinges and locks and fittings. From within it, the violin called to them, a pitiful, pleading melody.

Ulrika stared, amazed. 'The battle warped stone and made it burn like wood, and yet this survived?'

Stefan stepped forwards and wiped the soot from the lock plate, revealing a band of squat, angular runes running around it.

'Dwarf work,' he said. 'My master had such a vault to protect his treasures. It was no guard, however, against Kiraly's treachery,' he added bitterly.

Ulrika pulled on the door's sturdy handle. It didn't budge. She kicked at the door. It was as solid as it appeared, and felt as if it were feet thick. She walked around it and looked at the sides. They were whole and solid.

She shook her head. 'If all the power of Chaos couldn't open it, I doubt we will find a way.'

Stefan turned towards the door. 'We have only checked three sides yet,' he said. 'We may have better luck with the top, bottom or back.'

But they didn't. When they went out to the circular gallery that surrounded the stairwell, and against which the back of the vault butted, it was whole, and trips to the storeys above and below the vault revealed the same for the top and bottom. In a place where nothing had remained untouched by magic, the dwarf walls alone had survived intact.

Ulrika sighed as they returned to the vault room and stood in front of its heavy door. 'I was right earlier. We needn't have come. No one will breach this vault. Not even a warlock. The cultists' plan, whatever it is, will fail.'

'You are likely correct,' said Stefan, his brow knitted. 'Still, it would be best to be sure.'

'But how can we be?' asked Ulrika. 'The only way to be certain is to take the violin ourselves and destroy it.'

'That would be the most certain way, yes,' said Stefan. 'But seeing the cultists thwarted by the vault would be a great reassurance too.'

Ulrika raised an eyebrow. 'Wait here and watch them fail, you mean?'

'Exactly.'

'Very good,' said Ulrika. 'And afterwards they will be trapped here with us. We can question them in peace.'

Stefan smirked. '*Now* you sound like a vampire.'

* * *

THEY FOUND THE perfect place to wait and watch atop the columns that flanked one of the doors to the other rooms. These were crested with blackened, broken statues of double-headed Kislevite eagles, each taller than a man, and crouched behind them, Ulrika and Stefan were well hidden, yet still had a good view of the vault.

For an hour nothing happened, and Ulrika began to worry the sun would rise before the cultists came, and they would have to spend the day hidden within the spire, but then a sudden skirling of the violin brought her head up. Stefan looked up too.

Ulrika strained her hearing and her senses. There were faint voices from outside the tower and far below, and on the furthest edge of her perception, human pulses.

After a moment, a rich voice rose above the others. 'You will experience some strange sensations as we rise, brothers. Close your eyes and ignore them. They are echoes of the past, nothing more.'

There were murmurs of assent, and then all fell silent.

Ulrika exchanged a glance with Stefan. She recognised the voice. 'The warlock from Gaznayev's,' she whispered. 'The one who tried to burn us.'

'Excellent,' said Stefan. 'I have wanted to meet him again.'

They edged forwards, looking down towards the windows. She could sense three heart-fires coming closer, rising up the outside of the spire. A moment later came stifled shouts and grunts.

'Steady!' hissed the warlock's voice. 'Ignore them!'

Ulrika's jaw clenched, hoping the men would lose themselves in the violent illusions of the mind-storm and fall to their deaths, but, disappointingly, she heard no further screams.

Then faint shadows touched the sill of one of the windows. Ulrika and Stefan crouched lower, trying to see better. Ulrika frowned. The men seemed to have scaled the wall very quickly. Even she and Stefan had taken longer.

The shadows loomed closer, and, as Ulrika and Stefan stared, three men in the veiled hoods and cloaks of the cult floated through the window hand in hand, surrounded by a nimbus of violet energy, and settled gently to the floor. The warlock in the middle was perfectly calm, as if flying was as natural as walking to him, but the other two men breathed sighs of relief to be on solid ground again.

'On your guard,' said the warlock, pointing to where Ulrika and Stefan's footprints showed bright against the soot-blackened floor. 'The interlopers are here. Search the place.'

CHAPTER TWENTY-FOUR
THE HANDMAIDEN OF THE QUEEN

THE TWO GUARDS looked around uneasily.

'Can you not use your sight, brother?' asked one.

'Here?' The warlock laughed. 'I can barely see reality for all the illusion that swirls around this place. My sight is useless. Go. And use the blades we made for you. If they are the ones who attacked before, you will need them.'

Ulrika and Stefan exchanged a glance at that, then watched as the men drew long swords and began to look through the burnt clutter that filled the room. The blades of the weapons gleamed with the sheen of silver. They looked as if they had been dipped in the stuff. The cultists had come prepared to face them.

While his men searched – one walking right under Ulrika and Stefan into the next room – the warlock stepped to the vault and began murmuring and moving his hands in complicated patterns. Despite what he had said about his sight being useless, Ulrika was sure he was trying to determine what was in the vault and what warded it. She wondered what powerful magic he would use to open it. It would have to be a great spell indeed.

After a while the two men returned.

'We did not see them, brother,' said one.

'We checked the floor above and the floor below,' said the other. 'They have been there, but they are not there now.'

The warlock nodded. 'Very well. Perhaps they gave up. Even for such as they, the vault would be impregnable. Be vigilant regardless, but first, you will do what you are here to do. Have you the hag's hand, Brother Song?'

The man nodded and took a bundle from a pouch at his waist. He unwrapped it. It was a withered hand.

The warlock stepped back. 'Do not let it touch the floor or walls or anything else here – myself included,' he said. 'Only the hand of one who draws their magic from the coloured winds may open the lock, and it must be untainted by any hint of Chaos.'

'Yes, brother,' said the man, holding the hand gingerly.

'And you, Brother Lyric,' said the warlock, turning to the other man. 'Have you the key?'

'Yes, brother.' He drew a large key from his doublet and held it up.

'Good,' said the warlock. 'Now, fix them together as I showed you.'

The two men stepped together and positioned the key in the severed hand as if it were holding it, then bound it in place using tarred cord.

'Is it firm?' asked the warlock.

'It is, brother,' said Brother Song, testing it.

'Then open the door,' said the warlock. 'But be on your guard. I know not what lies within. You must protect me.'

'With our lives, brother,' said the men in unison.

Brother Song stepped to the door, holding the severed hand by the stump, while Brother Lyric stood on guard behind him and the warlock prepared a spell. Ulrika shook her head at the simplicity of it. She had imagined great magics being wielded. It hadn't occurred to her the cultists might somehow have obtained the key.

Brother Song slipped the key in the lock, and tried to turn it. It did not move, for the fingers that held it were slack, and despite the cord, did not hold the key tightly. Frustrated, Brother Song reached forwards to clamp them tighter, but the warlock cried out behind him.

'No!' he said. 'It must be by her hand alone. If your fingers touch the key while it is in the lock, it will not open.'

Brother Song grunted, annoyed, and tried again, pressing the hand against the lock and twisting. Had it been a human-made lock, the trick might not have worked at all, but dwarf locks, while immovable if the wrong key was used, were known for their smooth action, and finally, with the fingers of the hag's hand twisted in a position that would have broken them in life, the key turned in the lock and there was a rumble of great counterweights moving and bolts drawing back.

'Excellent,' whispered the warlock, rubbing his hands. 'Now step back and be on your guard. I will take over from here.'

Brother Song did as he was told, tossing aside the severed hand and key and readying his sword as the warlock stepped forwards and heaved on the handle. For a moment the door did not move, but then slowly, it began to glide open and a wild burst of violin music skittered out and danced about like a gleeful child freed from school.

Ulrika looked to Stefan, wide-eyed with shock. He motioned her to come to him. She shot a look at the two guards. Their eyes were fixed on the interior of the vault as the warlock stepped into it. She shifted across the arch.

'When he has it,' said Stefan, 'we kill them. Him first, then the other two.'

'Him?' Ulrika asked. 'But they have silver.'

'And he has fire, remember?' said Stefan.

Ulrika nodded and stepped back across the arch behind her eagle. She and Stefan drew their swords and daggers, then climbed up until they were crouched upon the eagles' shoulders. Stefan raised his hand.

'At last!' came the warlock's voice from the vault. 'And unmarked by flame or decay. Splendid!'

The guards stepped back as he strode out, holding an oblong, gold-hinged mahogany case in his arms as if it were a baby.

Stefan dropped his hand, and like twin shadows, he and Ulrika leapt silently from the stone eagles and landed running, only a few paces from the three cultists.

The two guards hadn't even heard them when Ulrika and Stefan shoved past them, and the warlock was just turning when they struck. Stefan ran him through the heart. Ulrika thrust her rapier into his surprised mouth, punching it out through the back of his skull and killing him instantly. It seemed too brief a death for one who had nearly murdered her with fire, but there was nothing for it.

They whipped their blades from his body and turned to face the two guards as he collapsed to the floor behind them, the violin case spilling from his grasp.

The guards charged in, slashing feverishly with their silvered long swords. Ulrika stepped back, parrying warily. Her man was a good blade, but no match for her – except for the silver. Without it, she would have dared a quick thrust and finished the fight as swiftly as possible, but one unlucky cut from his sword and it would be she who was finished.

The cultist laughed. 'Aye, fiend! We know your weakness!'

He pressed in, slashing for her extended arm, but her hesitance had made him overconfident, and he left himself exposed. She bound his sword to the side with her dagger, then ran him through the heart with her rapier as he tried to retreat. Stefan dispatched his man at the same moment, ducking a wild slash and running him through the neck.

Ulrika let out a sigh of relief, then frowned. 'We neglected to question them.'

Stefan shrugged. 'With the violin in our possession, there is no need. Their plan is foiled.'

Ulrika turned to where the mahogany violin case lay on the floor beside the dead warlock. It was covered in runic wards and seals, all apparently designed to imprison the violin, but despite them, the thing radiated eldritch power like a black sun, making her skin itch. 'Let us destroy it here and now,' she said, raising her rapier. 'I can feel its vile influence through the box.'

'No!' said Stefan. 'If it is truly possessed by a daemon, we would be in mortal danger. Smashing it might release it, and it could kill us both.'

Ulrika looked at the case again, uneasy now. 'But then what is to be done with it? If it remains whole, the cult will try to get it again.'

Stefan frowned. 'It is a pity Boyarina Evgena has added you to her blacklist. She is a great practitioner of the arts, I have heard, and would likely know a way to destroy it safely.' He grunted angrily. 'Well, we will find some way, but now is not the time to think on it. We will have to take it with us and decide later.'

'Very well,' said Ulrika.

Her head swam as she reached for the case, and an almost uncontrollable urge to open it and take out the violin came over her. It begged her for release, promising her the fulfilment of all her desires, the vanquishing of all her enemies, the love of all whom she held dear.

All she had to do was free it from its prison. She fought down the urge with difficulty, then slipped the case into a leather pack the dead warlock wore looped through his belt. Her spine shuddered as she slung the pack on her back. She could feel a burning that wasn't heat sinking into her skin.

'Let's go,' she said. 'Quickly. I want to be rid of it as soon as possible.'

Stefan nodded and they stepped onto the windowsill. Stefan started down immediately, but Ulrika stared to the east. The sky above the mountains was light grey. Dawn was coming. They would have to move swiftly if they were to make it back to the safety of her bakery basement before the sun rose. Ulrika steadied herself, then began to descend, forcing herself to move at a measured, moderate pace.

As they reached the band of twisted stone, she braced, waiting for the visions and disorientation, but strangely, though they came, they were weaker, and did not overwhelm her. She didn't need to close her eyes in order to find handholds this time. Was it because she had experienced the storm before? Was she used to it now? Had the warlock somehow damped them?

Then she knew the cause. The violin was doing it. It wanted to escape, and was helping her get to the ground by suppressing the visions. The thought made her shiver. Was she doing the right thing taking it with her, or was it manipulating her mind? How could she know if she was in control of herself or if it was pulling her strings?

They descended below the melted area and entered the spire again through a window. Ulrika worried about the vines and the bloodthirsty purple fruit, and wondered if they would have to return to the outside of the tower to avoid them, but when they reached the thicket, it was withered and dead, and all the pods lay motionless on the stairs, nothing more than little dried husks.

'As I predicted,' said Stefan as they ducked through the desiccated vines. 'The warlock has cleared the way for us.'

Ulrika was suddenly very glad they had killed him before he was able to utter his spell.

From there on they hurried down the stairs almost at a run, passing without pausing at the strange scenes they had stared at on the way up. Then, just as they rounded the last turn before descending into the vaulted entry hall, Stefan jolted to a sudden stop. Ulrika stopped too, catching herself on the banister.

'What is it?' she asked.

'Heartbeats,' he said. 'Below us.'

Ulrika extended her senses and felt them too. A dozen or so, at rest at the bottom of the stairs. 'More cultists.'

They crept silently down the stairs until they descended through the roof of the great chamber, then stopped at the wide gap where the stairs had broken away, and peered over the edge into the murk below. In the light of a few lanterns, a group of cultists in cloaks and masks waited amongst the rubble. Some paced, some sat, some murmured together.

One of the pacers turned to a man who reclined on the stairs, quietly reading a book. 'What takes so long? Where are they?'

The man with the book spoke without looking up. 'The climb is difficult and the vault may take some time to open, brother. Be patient.'

Ulrika's lips curled. She knew this voice too. It was the crook-backed sorcerer she and Raiza had observed leading the ceremony in the temple of Salyak – the man who had trapped the innocent girl's soul in a bottle.

Another cultist looked up at the pacer and laughed. 'Do you fear this place, little one? When the queen

comes, it will be a shrine!' The voice was harsh and foreign, and sounded like two people talking at once.

Stefan pointed to the hole in the bricked-up front
door and whispered in her ear. 'If we can cross this gap
silently, we can descend low enough that we will be able
to gain the hole in the door before they can react.'

Ulrika looked at him, disappointed. 'But the crooked
man is here. The one who got away from me before.'

Stefan eyed her levelly. 'Do you want vengeance, or do
you want to save Praag?'

Ulrika hung her head. 'You are right. Forgive me.'

Stefan shrugged, then, with infinite care, he took up
one of the ropes that dangled from the broken banister
and lowered himself over the edge of the last step.
Ulrika selected another rope and did the same, slipping
slowly down it hand under hand so she did not make it
creak with her swaying.

At last her feet touched the top step and she planted
them with care, making sure not to nudge any of the
tools still scattered there. Stefan landed with equal
silence beside her, and together they began to tiptoe
down the curving stair towards the oblivious cultists.

It was then that the violin decided to play a tune.

Ulrika froze with shock as the cultists sprang to their
feet and looked up towards the wild melody. Stefan
glared at the pack on her back.

'Treacherous thing!' he hissed. 'Down! Quickly!'

He pounded down the stairs and Ulrika sprinted after
him, the violin shrieking its fevered song in her ears as
it slapped against her spine.

'Stop them!' cried the leader. 'They have the
Fieromonte!'

The cultists swarmed up the stairs, drawing swords
and daggers and howling barbaric battle cries as the violin sawed out a wild dance. Ulrika and Stefan met them
two-thirds of the way down the spiral – and cut through

them like so much chaff, their rapiers and daggers lick-ing like lightning among them, blocking clumsy strikes and impaling chests, necks and groins.

But as they broke through them, three more – one small and two huge – charged up to block their way. Ulrika and Stefan attacked them negligently, but these cultists were different, and slashed back at them with unnatural speed and strength – and silver. One of the giants wielded a huge silvered axe that nearly knocked Ulrika's rapier from her hand. The little one whirled two silvered long-knives, and Ulrika had to lurch back as one flashed an inch from her eyes. Beside her, Stefan barely dodged the second giant's axe – identical to that of the first.

'Defilers!' snarled the smaller cultist, raising a voice like two voices over the wail of the still-screaming vio-lin. 'Give us the vessel!'

Higher up the stairs, the cultists Ulrika and Stefan had pricked in passing were recovering and edging down towards them.

'Across!' called Stefan.

He kicked back one of the giants and vaulted from their staircase to the other. Ulrika laughed and did the same, fanning back her attackers and bounding across the gap to the second spiral as they slashed futilely after her.

The weight of the violin case slapped against her back and made her stumble as she landed. Stefan steadied her, and they turned to descend, but before they took a step, the little cultist and the two giants landed in front of them, blocking their way. Ulrika gaped as she went on guard. What manner of men could make such a leap?

'Do you think your night-born strength will save you?' shrilled the little one in its strange double voice. 'We are stronger! We are blessed!'

And with that, the three cultists ripped off their cloaks
and flung them aside, revealing themselves to be entirely
naked, and not entirely human. Ulrika recoiled, repulsed.
Stefan grunted a curse.

The little one was a woman, red-haired and sun-
bronzed, with twisting Norse tattoos all over her wiry,
slim-hipped body. She was brutally attractive, with sultry
eyes that looked out from under snakelike dreadlocks, but
she was repellent as well, for the mouth on her face was
not the only one she bore. A fat goitre grew from her neck,
as if she were birthing a second head, and a drooling
mouth distended from it and licked its plump lips with a
long pink tongue.

Her monolithic companions were just as disturbing, for
though they were identical twins – hard-muscled, barbar-
ically beautiful giants with braided blond hair and blue
eyes – one was emphatically male, while the other was
abundantly female, and the skin of both gleamed with
the hard white lustre of porcelain.

'Foolish corpses!' said the little woman from her
mouths. 'You stand before Jodis the Unsated, hand-
maiden to Sirena Amberhair, she who will soon be Queen
of Praag. In her name, I shall be your doom. In her name,
I shall–'

'Get on with it,' sneered Ulrika, and lunged at her while
she was still in mid-sentence.

If the woman was caught off guard she didn't show it.
She parried Ulrika's stroke with ease and pressed back, her
long-knives blurring, as her companions charged Stefan,
chopping with their axes and ululating like banshees.
Ulrika could not stand against Jodis's attack – it was too
fast, and she feared the silver too much. Just one touch of
those knives could cripple her. She backed away, parrying
and dodging, looking for a hole in the shining web the
Norsewoman wove around herself while the violin
shrilled and sawed in her ears. If only it would shut up.

Beside her, Stefan too was backing up. His sword was striking the twin giants repeatedly, but it only chimed off them as if they were made of marble, and each time, their silvered axes sliced perilously close to his head and neck.

Beyond their fights, the remaining cultists were stumbling down the other stairway and coming for the one she and Stefan had leapt to. They would be surrounded again in moments, and couldn't hope to survive it.

Ulrika blocked Jodis's blades, but the mutant woman kicked her in the chest with a bare foot and she crashed against the banister, jamming the violin case painfully into her spine and making the instrument howl with anger. As she stopped herself from pitching headlong over the rail, Ulrika saw the crook-backed sorcerer staring up at the fight from the floor below and waiting, shimmering purple energy wreathing his hands.

Jodis attacked again and Ulrika ducked away, an idea forming – a way to remove at least one threat. She blocked the Norsewoman's blades again, knocking them to the sides. Jodis took the bait and kicked her in the stomach as she had before. Ulrika threw herself back and deliberately flipped backwards over the banister, dropping right towards the crooked man.

He dived aside with a cry, the energy in his hands dissipating in his surprise. Ulrika twisted in mid-air and landed in a crouch, then sprang instantly at him, aiming her rapier at his heart, but the unaccustomed weight of the violin case threw her off and she ran him through the guts instead. He shrieked and collapsed in the rubble, clutching his torn middle.

Ulrika rose to finish him off, but Jodis dropped down and blocked her way. Behind her, three lesser cultists were racing to join her.

'Cease your struggles, puppet,' the Norsewoman laughed, with both her mouths. 'Don't you see that Slaanesh pulls your strings?'

Ulrika lunged at her, hoping to kill her before her help arrived, but the violin case again threw her off balance, and Jodis's silver blades turned the attack. Ulrika cursed, frustrated, as the violin laughed and the three cultists swarmed in. Damn the violin. It was hitting her and bumping her arms with every move, and its constant shrilling melody was making it hard to concentrate.

Ulrika killed a cultist, then glanced up at the stairs, drawn by a horrible squeal echoing from above. The male giant was reeling back, crashing through a mob of lesser cultists, his silver axe buried in his beautiful face, as his female twin lashed out at Stefan with berserk fury.

Jodis came at Ulrika again, long-knives flashing. Ulrika parried the left blade, but the violin case knocked her dagger arm out of position and the second knife slid across the back of her wrist. Ulrika jumped back, hissing, as sickening pain shot up her arm to her shoulder. The silvered knife had made only the shallowest of cuts, but already the skin around the scratch was peeling back and blackening.

Ulrika's dagger fell from her fingers and the world swam around her. She fought not to faint, backing and lashing wildly with her rapier to keep Jodis and the last cultists at bay. The violin laughed in her ears, its weight tugging at her, making her stumble. She couldn't fight like this! With a curse, she shrugged the straps of the pack off her shoulders and tossed it and the violin aside, then went on guard again, holding her throbbing wrist behind her.

'Now,' Ulrika growled. 'Now I will kill you.'

She lunged, stabbing savagely, and Jodis fell back, barely turning the rapier's point aside in time. Ulrika feinted at her, then slashed to the side and cut down the last two cultists before following up with another thrust at Jodis. The Norsewoman retreated in confusion, dancing away from Ulrika's questing point and grunting with effort. Ulrika grinned. Now she was fighting like she should! Without the weight of the violin and its incessant yammering, she was light as air, she could think. She would end this in seconds.

But in the next instant, Jodis recovered her composure, and was suddenly blocking all her attacks with ease. She laughed as she forced Ulrika back. 'Did I not say Slaanesh pulled your strings?'

Ulrika didn't know what she meant until, out of the corner of her eye, she saw the crook-backed sorcerer limping quickly towards the door, her pack clutched to his bleeding stomach.

From over the sounds of battle above she heard Stefan curse. 'Fool of a girl! What have you done?'

Ulrika's guts shrivelled. What mad impulse had made her throw aside the violin? What had she been thinking? But it hadn't been her, had it? The violin had made a dupe of her, just as she'd feared.

With a snarl of rage she dodged around Jodis, trying to catch the hunchback before he reached the door, but the Norsewoman skipped back, staying in front of her and slashing with her knives.

'What?' she laughed with both mouths. 'Will you take back what you have given?'

A cry of pain shrilled from above and Stefan blurred down the stairs, racing after the sorcerer as the female twin toppled over the banister behind him.

Jodis looked towards him, crying out. 'No! Stop!'

Ulrika took advantage of the Norsewoman's distraction and stabbed her through the ribs, then shouldered her down and ran for the sorcerer as well. Daylight shone through the hole at the base of the door. They had to stop him before he got out or they wouldn't be able to follow.

The crooked man yelped as he saw them converging

on him, then raised his free hand. It coruscated with shimmering power. Ulrika and Stefan sprinted faster, hoping to strike before he attacked, but when he released the boiling energy, it wasn't at them, but at the door.

A near-invisible eruption of power smashed like a fist into the bricks that walled it up, and they burst outwards in a thunderous explosion of dust and rubble.

Ulrika and Stefan back-pedalled desperately as the sorcerer ran out of the tower and morning sunlight stabbed into the darkness like a blazing spear-tip, but Ulrika couldn't stop in time and sprawled into the searing shaft, throwing out her hands and dropping her sword as she slammed to the sunlit floor. The skin of her knuckles blistered and smoked. Her face felt as if it were on fire.

CHAPTER TWENTY-FIVE
RED PASSION

ULRIKA SCREAMED AND rolled as the fiery rays lanced her body. A firm hand pulled her into the shadows. She looked up through eyes half-blind with agony. Stefan stood above her, apparently unhurt.

'Cover up,' he said. 'Quickly. We must go.'

'G-go? But–'

'I cannot fight them all! Hurry!'

Ulrika looked past him and saw Jodis standing and starting towards them, blood streaming down her naked torso from where Ulrika had stabbed through the ribs. The giant female was also still alive, rising from the rubble at the base of the stairs with strange wounds all over her body that looked like star-shaped cracks in thick glass. Behind them, a few cultists lurched forwards too.

'What's wrong, corpses?' laughed Jodis. 'Why don't you run?'

Dizzy with pain, Ulrika fumbled gloves from her belt and hissed as she pulled them on over her blistered fingers. The Norsewomen and the cultists were spreading out to surround them. She threw her cape over her throbbing head, then looked up. Stefan had pulled up the hood of his scholar's cloak, but was otherwise unprotected.

'But what about you?' she asked. 'You will burn.'

Stefan pulled her roughly to her feet. 'I will not. Now come,' he said, then dragged her towards the door.

Ulrika stumbled after him, cringing and pulling her cape tight as the sun pressed on her shoulders like hot bricks and the reflected light from the floor stabbed her eyes. Behind them, Jodis cried out in surprise and anger, and Ulrika heard the swift slap of bare feet on stone.

There was a metallic scrape and Stefan pressed Ulrika's rapier into her hand as they ran on, down the steps and into the narrow area between the tower and the outer wall. 'You will have to climb while I–' he began, then stopped and laughed. 'No. They have pierced the wall. Good. Hurry.'

Ulrika weaved after him, one hand in front of her, as he led her along the outer wall. The footsteps behind them were gaining. Suddenly, Stefan whipped her ahead of him, and there was a clash of steel from behind.

'Out! Out!' he shouted.

Ulrika tripped over rubble on the ground and fell against the wall. There was a break in it. She stumbled through into the street. Another clang of swords and a shriek of anger and Stefan's hand pulled at her arm again, laughing and leading her away from the spire.

'They thought to trap us with the sun,' he said. 'But they are trapped now. They cannot follow naked into the streets of Praag bearing mouths where they shouldn't and skin that cracks like glass.'

'I don't understand how you can walk in the sun,' Ulrika said. 'How does it not hurt you?'

'It hurts,' he said. 'But it does not burn, not

immediately. And I do not understand it either. I was born with it, that's all. Now, hurry. We must get you home.'

'But the violin,' said Ulrika. 'The sorcerer.'

'He is long gone,' said Stefan. 'And we are too weak to fight him. We will have to try again tonight.'

Ulrika hung her head. 'I am sorry for throwing off the violin. I... I think–'

'It worked upon your mind,' said Stefan. 'I know. You will know to defend against it next time. Now come. We must find a grate to the sewers.'

They hurried on, searching frantically as the sun beat at Ulrika through her clothes like a flaming club. It amazed her that Stefan could bear it. She could hardly stand beneath it, even fully covered. What a wonder to be able to walk abroad during the day. Such a gift removed almost all the curse of being a vampire. One could move in normal human society. One could ride during the day, and travel in an open coach. One could turn the witch hunters' suspicions with a single noon meeting.

A block on, Stefan found a grate just inside the mouth of an alley. He kicked away the beggars that slept on it, then hauled it up and helped her in before following and closing it over his head. Ulrika groaned with relief and she lowered herself unsteadily down the iron ladder to the brick tunnel below. The pain of her burns did not abate, but at least she wasn't cooking them any more.

THE SEWERS, IT quickly became apparent, were not an ideal way to travel in Praag, particularly when one was almost too weak to walk, let alone run or fight. They smelled abominably, and were slick with slime and thick with rats. All those things were to be expected, of course, but there were other, more sinister residents as well. Strange hunched figures moved through the channels in

packs, splashing away into the shadows at the sound of
Ulrika and Stefan's approaching footsteps. Eerie hooting
and whistling echoed all around them, and they saw
occasional campfires far down branching tunnels,
throwing distorted shadows on the arched walls.

More dangerous than these shy horrors were the companies of Kossar infantry who marched through the
maze in single file, spears at the ready, with silent scouts
prowling to the fore, hunting the creatures who hid
there. More than once, Ulrika and Stefan had to duck
back into a side tunnel and wait for them to pass, and
once they were forced to edge around a full-scale battle
between the soldiers and men in rags, all with extra
arms or legs, or heads with horns, or too many eyes or
mouths where their stomachs should be.

Ulrika wondered, as they hurried away from the
screams and clash of steel, if these horrors had always
been here, or if the Chaos magic Arek Daemonclaw's
sorcerers had focused on the city during the siege had
birthed them.

As THEY FOLLOWED the sewer into the Novygrad, the
tunnels soon became too populated to navigate, and
they were forced to return to the surface. There were
just too many mutants huddled in the shadows, and
in their own territory, they were no longer so shy.

Ulrika cringed, wilting, as she and Stefan climbed
back out onto the ruined streets and the sun struck her
again like a hammer. It was full daylight now, and the
ten blocks to her hideout in the abandoned bakery
were utter torture. By the end, she was so weak Stefan
had to carry her. Her entire body throbbed as if it were
on fire, and her arms and legs felt like they were made
of paper and twigs, but her hunger nearly drowned
out all of those things. She needed to feed desperately.
The fighting and the burns and the sun's leeching heat

had sapped all the strength she had taken from the apprentice's blood, and it felt as if she would crumble to dust if she could not have more.

Stefan laid her on the baking table by the oven and unwrapped her cape, then hissed in sympathy as he saw her blistered skin. His skin was unmarked, but as red as a boiled lobster, and his hands shook as he tucked her pack under her head for a pillow.

'Wait here,' he said. 'I will bring us sustenance.'

Ulrika could do nothing but nod and lie back, staring at the brick ceiling as he hurried away. She could not sleep, or relax. She shivered like a plucked wire, and blinding jolts of pain shot through her body with every twitch. She had been burned by the sun before, but that had been the merest touch of the flaming brush compared to this. The backs of both her hands looked like milk on the boil, bubbling with hideous, pus-filled translucent blisters. She probed her face. It was the same. And under that bright pain was the dull sick throb of the wound Jodis had given her with the silver knife. The cut on her wrist was as black and brittle at the edges as burnt paper.

After an interminable time, in which she drifted in and out of waking dreams where women in gowns made of cobwebs clawed at her with hands like hawks' talons, and where a faceless man in cultist's robes cut open her veins with a shard of onyx that pulsed red at the centre, she woke to footsteps and voices above her.

'I don't take no damaged goods,' a rough-voiced man was saying. 'Only the youngest, most beautiful girls.'

'I assure you,' came Stefan's voice, 'she is so beautiful I wish I didn't have to part with her, but in these hard times, one needs money more than beauty, eh?'

Ulrika frowned as the man with the harsh voice laughed. She didn't understand what was happening.

'Don't I know it,' said the man. 'Right, then, where is she?'

'Just down here,' said Stefan. 'In the cellar.'

There was a pause at that. 'The cellar? This ain't some trick? You ain't got some mates down there, waitin' to jump me?'

'Of course not,' said Stefan smoothly. 'Here. You may hold my sword if you wish.'

'Nah,' said the hoarse voice. 'Nah. It's fine. Can't be too careful though, you know?'

'Indeed,' said Stefan. 'Now let me light a lamp and we shall go down.'

Ulrika raised herself up on one elbow and drew her sword as she heard the scritching of a flint. Was Stefan going to sell her? Why? Where did this betrayal come from?

Yellow light blossomed in the arch that led to the stairs, and steps creaked down them. Stefan entered the room with a gaudily dressed bravo behind him. The man lifted his lantern, squinting into the darkness and revealing curling moustaches and a wide, feathered hat, which he wore over a black bandana, like an Estalian bandit.

'Where is she?' he asked.

'There on the table,' said Stefan. 'Waiting for you.'

The man turned towards the table, then recoiled, gagging. 'Her face! What happened to her face?'

'Oh, that will heal,' said Stefan. 'She only needs a good meal.'

And with that, he tore the lantern from the man's hand and shoved him towards Ulrika.

Ulrika threw aside her sword and caught the man's arms as he screamed, her fears allayed. Stefan hadn't betrayed her. Indeed, he seemed to have gone out of his way to pick a victim she would approve of – a predator of the worst kind. It would be a pleasure to drain him.

The slaver thrashed and tried to get away, but as weak

as she was, she was stronger than he. She pulled him close, knocking off his hat and gagging on the stink of cheap scent and pomade, then sank her teeth into his neck.

Cooling relief flooded through her body as the blood spilled down her throat and his struggles weakened. Her dry tissues swelled and smoothed and the pain of her burns and the cut from the silver knife began to lessen. The deep-sea pulse of the slaver's pumping heart countered the throbbing of her head and enveloped her in soothing salt waves. Her eyes closed and she clung to him like a lover, wrapping her arms and legs around him and pulling him down on the table.

Too soon, a gentle hand rocked her shoulder.

'Enough,' said Stefan's distant voice. 'Enough. I too am hungry.'

Ulrika batted at the hand. 'Leave me be!'

Stefan caught her wrist. 'Enough,' he said again. 'You will be sick.'

Ulrika glared at him for a moment, unable to understand the words, but then reason returned to her and she let the man go. 'I'm sorry,' she said.

'No need to apologise,' said Stefan, pulling the man from her. 'Your need is great, but there will be more later.'

He bit the man precisely where Ulrika had, and she watched, fascinated, as the man's hands struggled feebly, then ringed Stefan's waist and clung to him. It shouldn't have shocked her that a male victim should feel pleasure from the bite of a vampire of the same sex – had not poor Imma, the maid at Herr Aldrich's house, pledged undying love to Ulrika after she had fed upon her? Nevertheless it did, but at the same time it was somehow arousing. Stefan was strangely gentle with the man, supporting him and stroking him as he drank, and not pulling or tearing at his neck.

When he had finished, and the man hung limp in his

arms, Stefan carried him to another table and laid him on it, folding his hands over his chest. Stefan's eyes, when he turned back to Ulrika, were glassy and heavy-lidded.

'We will take care of him later,' he said, stepping to her with a smile. 'But first we must take care of you.'

Ulrika frowned. 'What do you mean?'

He reached out and turned over her hand. The blisters had shrunk, but they were still there, and still painful, and the black cut of the silver knife was still dark, and had not entirely closed.

'You are not fully healed,' he said. 'And you have lost much strength. It would take many victims and many days to return you to the height of your powers, and we haven't time for that, but there is another way.'

Ulrika drew back as he looked into her eyes. 'What other way?'

'I have strength to spare,' he said, and turned his head to expose his neck. 'I would share it with you.'

Ulrika blinked, shocked. 'You want me to… to feed on you?'

He raised an eyebrow. 'Surely you have heard of this before.'

'Y-yes,' she said. 'But I was told it was… lovemaking.'

He smiled again. 'It can be. But it also heals and imparts strength. Do you want to face those northern daemon-lovers again while weak and sick?'

She shook her head, remembering Jodis's flashing long-knives, but still she hesitated. 'Does it not also bind one to the other? Make them loyal to each other? Like the blood I shared with Boyarina Evgena?'

'It forms a bond,' he said, nodding. 'And stronger than that of blood drunk from a bowl. We will be as brother and sister. You will find it hard to turn against me, and I will find it hard to turn against you.'

Ulrika frowned. Was that what she wanted? Stefan had been cold at first, but he had come to be a good companion to her. Did she want him to be more than that? It would certainly be advantageous to make it harder for him to betray her, but what if she became besotted with him and couldn't turn against him if she needed to?

'I will not press you,' he said. 'If you wish to remain in pain that is your prerogative.' He leaned in to her and turned his head again. 'I merely make the offer. The decision is yours.'

Ulrika looked at his strong, slim neck, and the thick blue vein that ran beneath the alabaster skin. There was a pulse there, borrowed from the man from whom he had drunk, but slower and stronger than any human pulse. She could smell the blood through the skin, clean and pure, and without the human stinks of sweat and perfume and illness that so often masked it. Though she had just fed, she found she was hungry again, desperately hungry. Her burned skin begged for relief. Her depleted veins begged to be filled. Her heart begged as well. It too wished to be filled.

Slowly, like a blade drawn by a lodestone, her lips drew closer to Stefan's neck, then kissed it. He trembled but stood still, hands at his sides. The pulse beat slow and heavy under her lips, like the pounding of a galley master's drum, and just as insistent.

She could resist no longer. Her fangs extended and she bit, remembering at the last moment to be gentle, and then drank. Stefan grunted and steadied himself against her, and she held him in her arms. His blood was richer than any she had ever taken from a living man. Its power flowed through her like lava, not just warming her, but enflaming her. It was as if it had been distilled, cleansed of all impurities and made into an elixir of strength.

Her head whirled as emotion coursed through her, though whether it was hers or Stefan's, carried along on the blood, she didn't know. Great joys, titanic sorrows and all-encompassing rages brought her to the verge of tears in turn. With each sip she felt she was learning more of Stefan's heart, his loyalty to his father, his hatred for his father's enemies, his affection for her, his loneliness, his lust.

At last she could take no more. It was too rich, too overwhelming. She shuddered and slumped back on the table, gasping and looking up at him. His eyes were closed.

'It was… it was…' she said.

'It was, indeed,' he said, opening his eyes with difficulty and giving her an unfathomable look. 'You… you are strong in your drinking, sister. You could pull the heart from a man.'

Ulrika's eyes widened in alarm. 'I'm sorry,' she said. 'I haven't–?'

He touched her cheek and shook his head. 'Do not apologise. It was a gift I am blessed to have received.'

She smiled sleepily. 'It is you who has given me a gift,' she said, holding up her hands. They were healed. Even the cut from the silver knife was only a thin black scar. 'I have never felt stronger. Thank you.'

Stefan took the proffered hand. 'No thanks are necessary,' he murmured, kissing it. 'But, I too have wounds. If you would allow…?'

Ulrika hesitated at this further step. It was when one was fed upon that one lost one's will, but how could she refuse Stefan after he had given so freely of himself? She pulled him down beside her and turned her head. 'Take what you will.'

Stefan encircled her in his arms and lowered his lips to her neck. She shivered as he kissed her, both aroused and vaguely unsettled. The last person to drink from her had been Adolphus Krieger, the vile predator who had made her what she had become, and the feel of Stefan's lips on her throat reminded her of her blood father's soft manipulations, of the way he had toyed with her and pretended she had a choice in what he did to her. Was Stefan the same, as Evgena had suggested? Was he tricking her in some way? To some unfathomable end?

She almost pushed him away as doubts crept into her heart, but memories of Krieger's kiss, of the pleasure it had given her, began to push them aside. It had been a pleasure that, to her shame, she had found herself begging for when he denied her it. Her hands remained where they were and she lay still, tensing as Stefan's sharp teeth dragged across her skin, then sighing and clutching him tight as they pierced her flesh with a delicious shock of pain and found her vein.

She closed her eyes as he began to draw blood from her with gentle pressure. This was a different sort of pleasure than taking blood. That was the pleasure of hunger sated and strength returned. This was the pleasure of control lost and the drifting, sleepy rapture of tension released. The dark memories of Krieger faded away, to be eclipsed by rosy dreams of flying, of gliding with Stefan like dragons in a sky of blood. He was leading her, drawing her on in his wake, and she was happy to follow, to let him choose the path, to give herself up to his will and let him do with her as he pleased. If he wished to drink his fill and let her die, so be it. She would die in bliss, floating towards his warm red sun until it consumed her in its molten core.

She groaned in dismay when he raised his head and the kiss ended. It felt as if a cord between them had been cut, and she was suddenly cold and alone. She cupped the back of his neck and pulled him back down again, but he resisted.

'I dare not,' he said. 'Lest I weaken you too much.'

'Then let me take more from you,' she said. 'And you can take it again.'

She pulled his mouth to hers and bit his lips and

tongue, drawing blood and sucking greedily. He bit back. They clawed at one another, tearing away each other's clothes and writhing against one another.

From the few things Gabriella had told Ulrika about love between vampires, she had thought it would be nothing more than the exchange of blood, but now she discovered that was not the truth. They were animals, after all, beasts, who must learn to control their savage natures or they would tear their victims limb from limb. Their love was just as animal as their feeding – pain and pleasure in equal measure, biting and kissing, clawing and caressing, wounds that healed as soon as they were made, and bare skin made slippery with blood and tongues.

She had never experienced anything like it before. Not during the rough galloping of horse soldiers, nor the fights with Felix that became romps and then fights again, nor the shameful, sensual surrender to Krieger. This was wilder than any of those, the pleasure stronger and more enduring, the play more give and take. There was a danger to it that only made it more exhilarating. Either of them could take too much and kill the other. It felt as if they were rolling on the edge of a precipice, daring each other to fall to their deaths.

Finally, after a time without time, they lay together, sated and exhausted, naked in each other's arms. Ulrika rested her head on Stefan's strong, smooth chest, utterly at peace. This was what she had been looking for. This was the thing that had been missing. This was why she had felt trapped among the Lahmians, and condemned to her eternal life – because she had no one to share it with. This was how being a vampire was meant to feel. Now she was on the right path. Now she knew what she wanted.

Stefan shifted and stroked her hair. 'This,' he murmured sleepily. 'This is right.'

Ulrika caught his hand and kissed it. 'Yes,' she said. 'This is right.'

CHAPTER TWENTY-SIX
THE VANISHED

Ulrika and Stefan woke at dusk to the sounds of shifting and shuffling and found that the slaver was crawling weakly for the stairs, trying to make his escape. They stopped him at the door, dragging him back and sharing the last of his blood, then broke his neck, threw his corpse in another room, and dressed to go out.

There was an awkwardness between them as they went about these mundane, earthly tasks. What had seemed so perfect and certain in the midst of the morning's afterglow now gave Ulrika pause, and she thought she saw the same wariness in Stefan's eyes. Neither seemed to want to broach the subject of what had been said, however, and for a moment it made conversation stilted and strange.

Fortunately, the urgency of their quest gave them safe things to talk about, and soon they were discussing what to do next. They were on their own now, cast out by the Lahmians, and with only this last night before the concert to find and stop the cult and destroy the violin.

'Once again,' said Stefan, pacing the cellar room, 'we have lost their trail. We know not where or who they are. I fear we will have no choice but to go to the concert and wait for them to strike.'

'That may be too late,' said Ulrika. 'If only we could–' She cut off as an idea struck her. 'Ha!'

'Yes?' said Stefan.

Ulrika sat forwards, smiling. 'The simplest way to foil the cultists' plan is to call off the concert. We don't dare go to the authorities ourselves.' *She* certainly didn't, Ulrika thought. If she tried to reach her cousin, Duke Enrik, there would be all sorts of awkward questions, and most likely a wooden stake at the end of them. 'But Padurowski, Valtarin's tutor, is to be the conductor. If we told him of the cult's plans, perhaps he could warn the duke or someone at the Opera House.'

Stefan frowned. 'Would he believe us? He was certain the violin was destroyed. And if he does, would the authorities believe *him*?'

'With the duke's life at stake, could they dare risk *not* believing him?' asked Ulrika. 'The hole in the wall that guards the Sorcerers' Spire must have been discovered by now, as well as the bodies of the cultists inside the entry chamber. The duke's protectors and the chekist must have an inkling something is in the wind. A word passed through Padurowski might frighten them enough to cancel the concert. And if not, we will continue our search.'

Stefan nodded slowly. 'Do you think it would be worth trying to convince Boyarina Evgena to help again? She may have more influence at court than a lowly conductor.'

Ulrika snarled. 'Evgena thinks I am your dupe. She thinks we want to kill her. I don't want anything to do with her any more.'

'Nor do I,' said Stefan. 'But if she can save Praag…'

'She is too worried about bloodlines and betrayals to be concerned with the fate of the city,' said Ulrika bitterly.

'She will turn from defending herself against us to find it has burned down behind her.'

'Very well,' sighed Stefan. 'Then let us go see the maestro.'

STEFAN WAS QUIET and withdrawn as they hurried through the shattered nighttime streets of the Novygrad and then across the teeming Merchant Quarter. He hardly seemed to watch where he went, just weaved, head down, through the jostling crowds of soldiers, beggars and drunks, until, just as they stepped onto the Karlsbridge, he looked up, frowning thoughtfully.

'You should rule in her stead,' he said.

'What?' said Ulrika.

He turned to her. 'You are right about Evgena. She is a fool, a mummified dowager too long shut up in the mausoleum of her house. You should rule in her stead.'

Ulrika laughed. 'Me? I don't want to rule. And I'm done with the Lahmians.'

'Damn the Lahmians!' said Stefan. 'Why do you need their consent? You could be queen here, on your own.'

Ulrika shook her head. 'They would come after me. The Queen of the Silver Mountain would hear of it and I would be killed.'

'Aye, aye, I know, but–' He cursed, then suddenly took her hand and looked her in the eye. 'This morning. What I said. I meant it. This is right, what we share, and I don't want it to end.' He stopped walking in the middle of the bridge and swept his hand to encompass the whole of the city, its lights mirrored and glittering in the waters of the Lynsk. 'Praag could be our home. We–'

He cut off, smiling wryly, his grey eyes glinting. 'Foolish though they are, I find myself strangely attracted to your silly idealistic notions of good stewardship, and preying only on predators. Think what Praag could be like if we ruled it. Think what we could do.'

Ulrika blinked, staggered, as a vision, a perfect gleaming future, rose up complete before her at his words. Praag, whole and healed, as it hadn't been for two centuries – a place where the people lived without fear, and cultists and gangsters and slavers feared to tread – and hidden at the centre of it, herself and Stefan, living in easy luxury in Evgena's mansion, the secret saviours behind it all. It was an intoxicating dream, and for a moment she nearly lost herself in it, but then she drew back.

'You weave a tempting tale,' she said at last. 'But it is impossible. Despite the fact she has driven me out, I still owe fealty to Evgena. I couldn't usurp her. And the Queen would never allow it. I… I don't want what we share to end either, but… it can't be like that.'

He nodded sadly. 'No. No, I suppose not. But…' He looked up at her again. 'But, you'd be with me, whatever happens?'

Ulrika hesitated. What she felt for him was strong, but again eternity reared its head. Was she ready to pledge herself to him for so long? She swallowed. 'Let me… let me give you my answer when this business is finished. It may be we won't live past it.'

Stefan frowned, but then inclined his head. 'Very well, m'lady,' he said. 'You give me incentive to survive.'

They turned and continued across the bridge, once again in silence.

ULRIKA STOLE GLANCES at Stefan as they twisted through the student quarter towards the Music Academy. He looked so grim that, more than once, she nearly spoke up and told him she was ready to give her answer, but each time she held off. She wasn't ready. She had made too many vows recently, and had too often regretted them immediately afterwards. She would be certain before she did it again.

There were more students than usual in the quarter

tonight, all talking to each other in hushed voices. Some of the girls with them were weeping. But it was only after Ulrika had passed half a dozen gatherings that a name, repeated and repeated, broke through the din of her own thoughts – 'Valtarin.'

She slowed her steps and listened closer as she and Stefan passed another cluster.

'Gone,' said a young man with a cello on his back. 'Vanished. Foul play, they say.'

'I don't believe it,' laughed a bearded companion. 'He's probably drunk somewhere.'

'Maybe some girl killed him,' said another. 'Out of jealousy.'

Ulrika spun the cello player around. 'What is this?' she asked. 'What's happened to Valtarin?'

The young man glared to be manhandled so, but his urge to gossip won over his outrage. 'He vanished from his rooms last night,' he said. 'At least that's what I heard. His landlord heard him go up with a girl, as usual. Then in the morning he was gone, and the girl was weeping and carrying on, saying he went to answer the door and never came back to bed.'

'Ha!' said the bearded boy. 'He found the girl was uglier in the morning than she had been the night before and slipped out. I've done it before.'

Cello shook his head. 'He hasn't been seen all day. He was to play at the Kossar's Return tonight, and he didn't show.'

'Then he's drunk in a kvas parlour somewhere,' said the bearded one. 'Like so many times before.'

'I hope so,' said Cello.

'So do I,' said Ulrika, and let the young man go. But as she turned back to Stefan she shook her head. 'But I fear it isn't so.'

'Aye,' said Stefan. 'It makes me wonder. All those souls the cult collects. Do they feed them to the violin? And are they feeding it the souls of musicians now?'

Ulrika shrugged, then stopped in her tracks. If that were true, then… Suddenly she turned and ran down a side street, beckoning Stefan to follow.

'What's the matter?' he asked as he caught up to her. 'Where are you going?'

'I have to check on someone,' she said.

ULRIKA STOPPED IN the door of the Blue Jug and stared, her guts sinking. A girl was singing and playing the balalaika on the stage, but it was the wrong girl, a brassy blonde singing dirty songs.

Ulrika crossed to the bar and waved down the barkeep. 'The blind girl,' she said. 'Does she not sing tonight?'

'She was meant to,' said the barkeep. 'But she didn't come in. I sent Misha around to her place to see if she were asleep or something, but she wasn't there.'

Ulrika groaned. 'Is there any other place she might be?' she asked.

The barkeep shook his head. 'She's blind. She don't go nowhere. Has a little friend who brings her food, and walks her here and back. That's all she does.'

Ulrika closed her eyes. 'Thank you,' she said at last, then turned away.

Stefan was waiting for her at the door. 'Bad news?'

'She has been taken,' Ulrika said, her voice dead and cold. 'They will pay.'

She strode out into the street and started again towards the Music Academy. She would give Padurowski the warning, but whether or not the concert was cancelled, she would still hunt down the cult. This was no longer for Praag, no longer for some noble idea of protecting the weak. This was for vengeance.

* * *

ULRIKA AND STEFAN banged on the door of Maestro Padurowski's offices on the second floor of the musty faculty building. There was no answer. Ulrika looked up and down the narrow hall, looking for signs that any other faculty were still in their offices, but all the doors were closed, and no light shone from beneath them.

'We must find out where he lives,' she said.

'Perhaps he's at the Opera House,' said Stefan, 'rehearsing.'

They started back down the cramped wooden stairs, and found a stooped old lady in a headscarf looking up at them suspiciously from the bottom step.

'What you want?' she said. 'You are not students.'

'We're looking for Maestro Padurowski,' said Ulrika. 'Do you know where he is?'

'Gone,' said the old lady.

'Yes,' said Ulrika. 'I am aware of that. Do you know where?'

'He didn't come today,' said the old woman.

Ulrika clenched her jaw, struggling for patience. 'So he is at home?'

The old lady shook her head. 'The duke's men said no. They went there to take him to the opera, then came here.' Her eyes narrowed. 'What you want with the professor? Do you know where is?'

'If I knew where he was, I wouldn't be asking, would I?' snapped Ulrika.

She and Stefan pushed past the old woman and crossed to the door. She followed them with her eyes as they stepped out into the Academy grounds, muttering under her breath.

Ulrika sighed as they started across the campus. 'I fear you are right,' she said. 'These disappearances must be in preparation for tomorrow night. The cult will kill the blind girl and Valtarin and the professor in some ritual. If only we could find–'

She stopped short as she heard someone whistling in the distance – a wild, haunting melody, and very familiar. 'The song!' she said, looking around. A fog had risen while they had been looking for Padurowski, and the grounds of the Academy were thick with it, the trees and buildings looming out of it like towering ghosts. She could see nothing.

Stefan listened too, his eyes growing hard. 'The Fieromonte played that song.'

'Forget I spoke,' said Ulrika, smiling wolfishly. 'The cult seems to have come to us.'

'How courteous of them,' said Stefan.

They stalked across the quadrangle in the direction of the whistling, but as they neared the fountain in the centre, another whistle repeated the melody off to their right. They turned towards the new sound, drawing their swords and going on guard. A third whistle came from behind the faculty building, then a fourth far to the left. Still they could see nothing. The fog and the shrubs and trees that dotted the Academy grounds hid everything, though Ulrika could detect heart-fires on the perimeter of her perceptions. There were dozens of them.

'Surrounded,' said Stefan, growling.

The whistling stopped, as suddenly as it had begun, and the night was utterly silent. Ulrika and Stefan turned in a slow circle, staring all around. Nothing moved. Nothing stirred. Ulrika didn't like it.

'What are you waiting for!' she shouted. 'Come out and fight!'

A sharp snapping came from all sides, and a dozen black shafts darted out of the mist. Ulrika and Stefan dodged and batted them from the air with their rapiers. Crossbow bolts. One passed so close that the fletching brushed Ulrika's left ear. Stefan snatched another out of the air.

'Silver-tipped,' he said, looking at it. 'Naturally.'

Ulrika turned in a circle, snarling and spreading her arms. 'Face me, you cowards! Steel to steel!'

Another volley of bolts shot towards her, but Stefan tackled her and they zipped harmlessly overhead.

'We can't win here,' he hissed. 'We must fall back.'

'But we'll lose them again.'

'We won't,' he said. 'We'll draw them off and take them when they spread out to find us. Come on!'

Ulrika saw the sense of that. She rolled up with him and ran in the direction of the street, on the far side of the lecture halls. A rain of bolts whistled after them, but they dodged and weaved and the missiles shot past. Three cultists rose from the bushes before them, waving swords. Ulrika and Stefan cut them down without slowing.

As they sprinted on, Ulrika saw more than a score of hooded silhouettes coursing through the grounds after them, crossbows and swords in their hands. Most were falling back, unable to match their speed, but a few paced them, as swift as greyhounds.

'They're separating,' said Stefan. 'Just a little further.'

Ulrika nodded. They burst from the trees and clattered onto the cobbled street. There was an alley opposite, a darker grey in the grey of the fog. They ran for it, the swiftest of the cultists close behind.

'Now we must lose them,' said Stefan as they splashed through the alley muck. 'Then double back as they split up to search.'

Ulrika grinned. 'You've done this before.'

'An old trick with vampire hunters,' said Stefan. 'They think they have you, and you have them.'

They led the cultists a twisting chase through the back alleys and mews of the student quarter, leaping fences and dodging around heaps of garbage, then finally Stefan stopped at the back of a stone carver's shop and listened. Their pursuers' footsteps echoed to them out of the fog, a block or so behind.

'Now!' he said. 'Up to the roofs. We will watch them pass from there.'

He motioned for Ulrika to start up before him. She jumped and caught a jutting beam end, then spidered up the wall of the workshop. Stefan started up after her, but just as she was pulling herself onto the roof, he grunted and slipped, then toppled back into the alley.

Ulrika turned and saw him lying in the mud below her, writhing in pain. 'Stefan!'

He did not reply. Her chest constricted with fear. She clambered swiftly back down to kneel beside him. Their pursuers' footsteps were getting closer.

'Stefan,' she whispered. 'What's wrong?'

He jerked something from the back of his leg – a silver-tipped bolt. It was running with blood. Ulrika swore. She hadn't even heard the shot.

'Help me up,' he said, wincing.

Ulrika took his arm and lifted him to his feet, looking nervously for the shooter. She saw nothing in the fog. Stefan's knees buckled and he fell against her.

'On!' he rasped, motioning to a nearby corner. 'I can't climb!'

Ulrika threw Stefan's arm over her shoulder and helped him around the corner, trying to look at his leg. The wound was hidden by the cloth of his breeches, but they were drenched with blood.

'Don't slow down,' he hissed. 'Hurry.'

Ulrika ran on, hauling Stefan along. The sounds of pursuit were all around them now and he was hissing with every step.

'It's no good,' he said, lurching beside her. 'They will follow the trail of my blood. We will not escape them.'

'Just keep going,' said Ulrika.

She pulled him into a yard and around the side of a

tenement. She could hear the cultists coming into the alley behind them as they hurried towards the front.

'Yes,' he said, nodding. 'Keep going. But not together. We must part ways. They will follow my blood and you can get away. I will see if I can catch one and speak to him.'

'But–' said Ulrika.

He cut her off with an impatient hand. 'We two cannot fight these daemon-lovers alone, this night proves it. You must go back to the Lahmians and get them to help you. It is your only hope of defeating the cult.'

'But they'll kill me,' said Ulrika.

They ran across a side street to another alley, Ulrika practically carrying Stefan in her arms. A fence blocked the far end.

'Tell them I'm dead,' he said, leaning against the wall as she tore a plank from the fence.

Ulrika looked back at him. 'What?'

'Tell them I died fighting the cultists,' he said. 'That I died defending you.' He laughed. It sounded like he was being strangled. 'Tell them you are no longer my "dupe".'

'But you're not going to die!' said Ulrika.

'Not if I can help it,' said Stefan. 'But it might be better if they thought I had. The Lahmians have the connections to stop the concert, and a web of spies to find the cult again if I fail here, but, because of me, they won't help you. So, it is best if I vanish. Now, take to the roofs. I'll draw these fools off.'

'You can't,' she protested. 'You're hurt. You can barely walk.'

'A wolf is at his most dangerous when cornered. I will meet you at the bakery and give you what information I have learned. Now go.'

'No,' she said, and turned towards the footsteps that were echoing nearer behind them. How could she go?

How could she leave him when she had just found him – when she had only just discovered what they could have together? What if this was the last time she ever saw him?

'No,' she said. 'I'll fight by your side.'

Stefan snarled. 'Fool! You will win no vengeance against these madmen if you die here! You must live to foil their plans and destroy them.' He shoved her. 'Go!'

Ulrika clenched her fists, not wanting to bow to his logic. Finally she cursed, then grabbed and kissed him, biting his lips angrily, before pushing him away and glaring at him.

'Yes,' she said. 'My answer is yes.'

Then she fled up the wall as the sound of footsteps grew loud in all directions.

CHAPTER TWENTY-SEVEN
THE ENEMY OF MY ENEMY

IT WAS NOT Severin who answered Evgena's door this time, but Raiza, and she held her sabre drawn and ready. Ulrika was startled to see that the swordswoman's left arm now ended in a jointed steel gauntlet.

'I told you I would not spare you again,' she said.

Ulrika raised her hands. 'Tell the boyarina that Stefan von Kohln is dead,' she said. 'And that I continue to uphold my vow to her.'

Raiza didn't seem to hear. 'Draw your blade,' she said evenly. 'I would not kill you unarmed.'

'Sister, please,' said Ulrika. 'You saw the cultists at their work. You know their threat is real. I have learned their plan now, but alone I can't stop them. Boyarina Evgena is my best hope. Please–'

'Draw your blade,' Raiza repeated.

Ulrika dropped her hands to her rapier, but instead of drawing, she unbuckled her sword belt and threw it at Raiza's feet, then spread her hands. 'Would I come here to certain death if I wasn't sincere? You may do what you like with me, only hear me first. I beg you.'

Raiza looked from her to the rapier, then toed it into the entry hall. 'Wait here,' she said, then used the tip of her sabre to close the door.

Ulrika let her shoulders relax. She was at least not dead, though from Raiza's impassive expression she couldn't tell if the swordswoman was going to plead her case or gather reinforcements.

She looked over her shoulder into the foggy night and shivered. Somewhere out there, Stefan was fighting the cultists, wounded and alone. She tried to shake the image of him falling to the ground with a silver-tipped crossbow bolt in his back, but she could not. She knew he had insisted she leave him, but if he truly died, she would never forgive herself. Not even vengeance on the cult would free her of that.

Her mind returned to the golden future Stefan had conjured for her – together forever, ruling Praag. She wanted it so deeply she ached. And, really, Praag was the least of it. She would give up that if only she could be with Stefan and live as they wished for the rest of time. Of course they would have to survive the cult, and Kiraly, and then there was the small matter of having pledged her eternity to Evgena, but perhaps if she protected her from those threats and abided by her vow, the boyarina would reward her with her release.

Ulrika sighed. Aye, perhaps, but nothing Evgena had done so far gave her any reason to hope. Ursun's teeth, why had she made that vow? How could she have allowed herself to be trapped in Evgena's stifling embrace for all time when true happiness was within her grasp?

The door opened and Raiza held it with her steel hand, her sabre still at the ready.

'She will see you,' she said. 'But know you are unlikely to live long if you enter here.'

Ulrika swallowed, glancing to either side of the door,

where the massive bears had resumed their pedestals, then nodded. 'I will take the chance.'

Raiza bowed Ulrika in, then led her again through the dusty, trophy-crowded halls. Ulrika noticed that many of the perches and stands were now empty. She smiled to herself. A few less to deal with if she did have to fight her way out again.

The boyarina waited in the drawing room with the red walls and the cold fireplace as she had before, sitting stiff and upright on her divan with bright-eyed Galiana in a chair beside her. Raiza left Ulrika standing before her and resumed her usual position at Evgena's shoulder, her sword still drawn. Men-at-arms stood around the walls, also with drawn steel.

'He is dead?' Evgena asked, without preamble. 'You are sure of it?'

Ulrika shook her head. 'I cannot be sure, mistress, but I cannot imagine how he would have survived.'

The boyarina's posture grew even more rigid. 'What do you mean? If you have entered my house under false pretences you will die for it.'

'I mean I left him defending my escape against the cultists,' said Ulrika, wishing she was certain it was a lie. 'He was wounded, surrounded and outnumbered.'

'And so you have come to finish his work and kill me?' sneered Evgena.

'He did *not* come to Praag to kill you, mistress,' she said, clenching her jaw. 'He came to stop the vampire who means to try, as I told you before. And though you have given me great provocation, *I* am not here to kill you either, nor have I broken my vow to you, or ever intend to. I come to ask again the only thing I have ever asked of you. Help me defeat the cult that threatens your city and yourselves.'

Evgena folded her hands in her lap. 'Raiza said you have learned their plan? What is it?'

Ulrika bowed and began. 'Thank you, mistress. The cult have acquired a relic of great power, a violin called the Viol of Fieromonte. It is possessed by a daemon, and has the power to drive men mad when played. The cult intends–'

Evgena laughed. 'A violin? Your all-powerful cult threatens Praag with a violin? Will we all die from bleeding ears?'

'I have felt its power myself, mistress,' Ulrika said. 'Von Kohln and I took it from the cult as they attempted to steal it from the Sorcerers' Spire. The daemon within it muddled my mind and tricked me into letting go of it, and the cultists escaped with it. I fear it is fully capable of doing what they expect it to do.'

'And that is?' asked Evgena.

'I believe they intend to play it at the duke's victory concert, using it to turn the duke and all the most important people in Praag – every noble, general, priest and ice witch – into murderous lunatics. In the confusion that will follow, the cult will open the gates to their queen, Sirena Amberhair, a champion of Chaos who hides in the hills with her horde. She will take Praag unopposed.'

The boyarina sneered, and looked as if she was going to dismiss the story, but then her expression faltered and she paused. 'I… I remember this violin. A passing wonder from just after the Great War against Chaos. Belarski's White Eagles, the bravest company of winged lancers in that age, were all executed after they went on a rampage while dancing to its tune.'

'I remember too,' said Galiana. 'They butchered their own wives and children, saying they were daemons in disguise. But the violin was burned at the stake, if I recall – a diverting spectacle for the duke's court.'

'If a violin was burned,' said Ulrika, 'it was not the Fieromonte. It still exists.'

Evgena was silent, thinking.

Raiza coughed politely. 'Emil spoke this morning of hearing of a disturbance at the Sorcerers' Spire last night. Agents of the chekist investigated. The bodies of cultists were found.'

'And Maestro Padurowski, who was to conduct the orchestra, has gone missing,' added Galiana. 'My maid told me of it. It was the talk of the markets today.'

Evgena continued silent for a long moment, then opened her fan and fluttered it, agitated. 'This plot might succeed,' she said. 'It is madness, but it might succeed.'

'It might unless you do something to stop it, mistress,' said Ulrika.

Evgena shot an angry glance at her. Ulrika thought she saw fear in it. 'What? What would you have me do?'

'The concert must be cancelled,' said Ulrika. 'You have spies at court. If you told someone the duke's life was in danger if he appeared at it, they would not allow it to continue. Once that is done, we must find these cultists, destroy the violin and send the daemon back to the Realm of Chaos.'

Evgena laughed. 'Child, you are mad!' She snapped her fan closed. 'Banishing daemons? Drawing the attention of the Tzarina's agents? I don't know which is more dangerous, but I'm not about to do either.'

Ulrika finally lost patience. 'Are you not a Lahmian? Are you not a mistress of secrets and manipulations? I do not ask you to do any of this yourself, but through your minions and blood-swains, as you would normally do.'

Galiana and Raiza were looking at Evgena as if they wanted to urge her to action as well, but were afraid to speak. The boyarina stood abruptly and stalked to the empty fireplace, her every move tense and stiff.

'Even that is not without risk,' she said at last. 'It is one thing to send a gift to the duke through an intermediary and suggest that one man is more qualified for the job of captain of the watch than another. It is quite another thing to ask that intermediary to whisper that the duke's life is in danger. People who say such things are brought to the chekist interrogation rooms and questioned, and will be asked their sources, and no amount of blood-born loyalty will keep an intermediary's mouth shut when the irons glow red.'

She slapped her fan against her skirts. 'I have taken such risks before, when the alternative was ruin, but this…'

'Ruin is precisely what the alternative is, mistress!' said Ulrika. 'I know you fear risk. You have grown comfortable here. You don't wish to endanger your position, but do you not see that the risk in doing nothing is greater than the risk of helping?'

'I don't know,' said Evgena, tearing the paper of the fan with her claws. 'I don't know. Perhaps the wisest course is to retire to Kislev for a time. Our sisters there would welcome us until all had resolved itself.'

Anger boiled up in Ulrika's breast. For all her cold dignity and superior tone, Boyarina Evgena was a coward, too afraid of taking action to defend herself. 'Mistress,' she said, through clenched teeth. 'I do not believe the Queen of the Silver Mountain would look well upon retreat or–'

Evgena gasped and looked around, and Ulrika broke off, thinking she had spoken too bluntly, but the boyarina was staring past her to the door.

'They are here!' she said, then cried out an arcane phrase and slashed a pattern in the air with her hands.

Galiana stood, her doll eyes wide. 'Who is here, sister?'

'How many?' asked Raiza.

A cacophony of screeching and flapping and roaring erupted behind the hallway door, followed by the frightened cries of men and the thud and crash of battle.

Evgena stabbed her fan at Ulrika. 'Little fool, you have led them to us!' she hissed. 'You have dragged us into your idiotic war!'

'Mistress, I didn't,' said Ulrika. 'I–'

Evgena turned to her men. 'Go! Out! Guard the door!'

The men-at-arms ran to the corridor door and out. As they opened it, the sounds of battle grew louder, and with them, a familiar voice rising in incantation – the crooked sorcerer. The shrieks of the undead animals changed from rage to pain as he sang his spell, and the cries of the cultists became cheers, then Evgena's men slammed the door and all was muffled again.

'They are strong,' growled the boyarina, then beckoned to Galiana. 'Come, sister.'

Galiana hurried to her, gashing open her palms with her claws as she went. Evgena did the same, and they joined hands, blood mingling as they touched wound to wound. They closed their eyes and began to murmur together as red swirls of mist formed around them and blurred their outlines.

Angry cries and heavy blows came from just outside the corridor door. It sounded as if Evgena's men were dying in the defence of it.

'With me, sister,' said Raiza, striding swiftly to the door.

'You took my blades,' said Ulrika.

Raiza pointed with her metal hand. 'The window bench.'

Ulrika ran across the room, an icy coil of dread writhing in her guts. How were cultists here? Had she led them? Was Stefan dead? He would never have let them pass him while he lived. Her heart blazed with fury and guilt. She should not have left him. She had killed him!

She lifted the seat of a built-in bench in the window.

Inside were her sword belt, rapier and dagger, resting on pillows and furs. She snatched them up and ran back, belting them on as she went.

The door burst in, ripping off its hinges, and Evgena's guards fell backwards into the room, wounded, dying and dead, as the naked white giantess from the Sorcerers' Spire strode in, her silvered axe flashing in the firelight. A mob of cultists roiled behind her, fighting a screeching flock of undead hawks and kites. More raptors shrieked around the giantess's head and shoulders, but their claws could do nothing to her glassy, gleaming skin.

Raiza thrust for her heart, but her sabre was no more effective than the birds' talons. The giantess swiped with her axe. Raiza dodged, stumbling over a fallen guard. Ulrika charged in, shouting and slashing, and succeeded in getting the woman's attention, but her attack was as futile as the others.

She danced back from the axe, eyes darting around for something heavy enough to shatter the mutant woman's slick white carapace. A marble statue of some ancient Khemri goddess stood on a pedestal next to a side table. Ulrika grabbed its cat-faced head and swung it like a club. In life she would have needed both arms to lift the thing. Now it felt hardly heavier than her sword.

The giantess parried with her axe, striking splinters from the sculpture, but before she could follow through, a red shimmer passed through the air like a spreading ripple in a pool of blood, and as it touched her, she began to choke and clutch at her throat, eyes bulging. Blood frothed at her lips and she doubled up – and she wasn't the only one. The ripple swept across the cultists on the corridor, and they choked too – Evgena and Galiana's blood-sorcery at work. Ulrika was not slow to take advantage. She swung again at the gasping giantess. The statue snapped in half as it shattered the porcelain skin of her back and crushed her ribs. She howled in agony and swung wildly at Ulrika, vomiting blood.

Raiza buried her sabre deep in the splintered fissure of the wound. The giantess gasped and crumpled to the ground, dead at last. Ulrika leapt her massive body and waded into the cultists in the corridor, with Raiza and the remaining men-at-arms falling in behind her. It was a slaughter, for the cultists were all choking and spewing blood, and still harassed by the hawks that clawed at their heads.

But just as Ulrika began to think they had won, a tremendous silent concussion struck her chest and tore through her mind, staggering her. It felt as if she had been hit by an ocean wave and slammed into a rocky shore. Raiza staggered too, and in the drawing room, Evgena and Galiana cried out in unison, clutching their heads and crashing to their knees. The red shimmer of their magic vanished, and all the hawks dropped to the floor, stiff and motionless, all at once.

'Mistress!' cried Raiza, stumbling to Evgena. 'Are you hurt?'

Before she reached her, something big and black smashed through one of the room's high windows, taking the curtains with it, and bounced across the rug to the fireplace, trailing dust. It was a bear's head, the severed neck desiccated and bloodless.

As Ulrika turned the stare at the thing, a figure leapt into the broken window and crouched there, laughing with two voices. It was Jodis, the lithe, dreadlocked Norse mutant with the fat-mouthed goitre growing from her neck, naked and painted for war, her silvered long-knives at the ready.

Here they are, brothers!' she called over her shoulder. 'This is the heart of the nest.'

'Hold the door!' Ulrika barked at Evgena's guards, then turned and ran at Jodis, howling with rage.

Ulrika started for her, snarling, but then, from the corridor, she heard more cultists thundering through the house. She cursed and shoved Evgena's three remaining men-at-arms into the hall, shouting 'Hold the door!', then ran at Jodis, howling with rage.

The Norsewoman jumped down to meet her, while behind her, a dozen hulking, bare-chested marauders crashed through the rest of the windows, swords and torches in their hands.

Ulrika lunged low, trying to tear open Jodis's naked belly, but the silvered knives turned the thrust and darted for Ulrika's neck. Ulrika parried with her dagger, barely in time.

'So, the sun didn't kill you,' Jodis said from both her mouths. 'Good. I want the pleasure for myself.'

'Then you should have come alone.'

She backed away, blocking on all fronts as Jodis and her wild men pressed forwards. She was too weakened from the sorcerous attack that had hurt Evgena and killed her pets to fight so many superior opponents. She felt faint and limp and hollow. A marauder swung a black long sword at her. She twisted aside, knowing she wasn't going to be able to avoid it, but at the last second, Raiza appeared beside her and beat it away, clawing the marauder's eyes with her metal hand.

'Thank you, sister,' Ulrika breathed, and focused again on Jodis.

Raiza fought on silently, angling to keep the Norsewoman and her men from reaching Evgena and Galiana. Ulrika did the same, but it was impossible. They were only two swords. They couldn't hold back so many.

But then help came from behind. Weird wisps of red floated towards the marauders like spiderwebs on a breeze. Jodis and her men stumbled and shrieked as the strands tangled around their arms and heads, burning their flesh with each silky touch. Ulrika and Raiza took advantage, and cut down three men in an instant, then pressed Jodis back.

Ulrika dared a glance around. Evgena remained slumped, half-conscious, on the divan – the sorcerous concussion seemed to have struck her hardest – but Galiana hunched over her, her red wig askew and her thin arms outstretched. Red smoke came from her fingertips, then coalesced into drifting strands. At the door, Evgena's men-at-arms fought more cultists in the corridor. They were holding. If Evgena recovered, they might all have a chance.

Then a movement over Jodis's head brought Ulrika's eyes up. A man in the hood and cloak of a cultist hunched in one of the shattered windows, something black glinting in his hand. He was raising it to throw.

'Sisters!' she called. 'Look out! Kiraly!'

Raiza looked up as Kiraly threw the onyx shard straight at Evgena. With a roar, the swordswoman leapt, forgetting her opponents, and swatted the thing out of the air with her metal hand, sending it skittering across the floor as Kiraly drew a second shard.

Jodis took advantage of Raiza's distraction and stabbed her in the ribs with a silvered dagger. The swordswoman stumbled, gasping, just as Kiraly hurled the second shard.

Raiza dived to knock it down too, but her wound made her clumsy, and instead she fell into its path. The black shard thudded into her chest, heart-deep. She shrieked and fell to the ground, clutching at it, and shrivelling into a slack-skinned skeleton before Ulrika's eyes.

CHAPTER TWENTY-EIGHT
THE TELLTALE WOUND

THE ENTIRE ROOM, vampire, cultist and marauder alike, froze for an eye-blink at Raiza's bloodcurdling scream and her hideous transformation.

Ulrika snapped from her paralysis first, fuelled by fury. Kiraly had killed the most honourable of the Lahmians of Praag, the only one Ulrika would have called friend. She hacked at Jodis, gashing her head and knocking her flat, then shoved through the marauders towards Kiraly, sword high.

'Murderer!' she roared.

The masked vampire whipped a third black shard from under his cloak, but then hesitated, as if weighing different targets, and in that instant, Ulrika slashed at him, her blade biting deep into his wrist. With a bellow of pain, he fell backwards out of the window, and Ulrika leapt up to the sill, making to spring out after him.

'No, sister! Protect your mistress!'

Ulrika looked back. Little Galiana was dragging Evgena towards the fireplace as the marauders fought

335

through her web of burning red threads to follow. Jodis lay where she had fallen, blood pouring from her head.

'Guard our retreat!' called Galiana.

Ulrika hesitated. Her soul howled for vengeance upon Kiraly, but she had vowed to defend Evgena with her life. She cursed and sprang back into the room, charging the backs of the marauders who were closing in on her mistresses. Vengeance would have to come later.

The Norsemen scattered as her rapier gashed their shoulders and necks, and Raiza was revealed, withered, lying where they had stood, her chest caved in around the now red-glowing shard that stuck from it. Ulrika couldn't leave her. She caught her up and put her over her shoulder – she was as light and brittle as a sheaf of dried corn – then flailed her blade around at the marauders and stumbled through to Galiana and Evgena.

'What now?' she asked, lowering Raiza to the floor and turning to fight as the Norsemen closed back in around them.

'The fireplace hides a stair,' said Galiana, guiding Evgena towards it. 'Hold them while I get the boyarina through it.'

'Aye, sister,' said Ulrika, slashing madly in every direction

Galiana whispered a short phrase and, with a rumble of hidden counterweights, the fireplace began to rotate. But before it had turned even a hand's-breadth, Evgena's men-at-arms, still doggedly defending the door to the corridor, staggered back, moaning and clutching themselves as if in ecstasy. The cultists surged forward, cutting them down and pouring into the room as, behind them, a tall, crook-backed figure in a purple robe limped in from the corridor, guarded by a hulking, paint-striped champion.

Ulrika cursed and redoubled her defence as the

cultists joined the circle of marauders and attacked her while the crooked sorcerer raised his arms and began to chant.

'Hurry, sister,' she croaked.

The fireplace finished turning, revealing a narrow door, but before Galiana could help Evgena to it, snakes of purple energy exploded from the sorcerer's hooded forehead, slipping around the marauders to lance straight at Ulrika and the Lahmians.

Galiana shrieked and swept her tiny hands in a broad arc, creating a lens of rippling air. The snakes punched through it without slowing, but came out pale violet shadows. Still they were enough.

Ulrika staggered back from the cultists and marauders as a tendril pierced her, and serpents of pain slithered through her guts, biting her from inside. Her foes pressed in. She could not hold them back. The pain was crippling.

'Get her in,' she rasped, flailing weakly at them. 'Go!'

'I cannot and hold the shield at the same time,' hissed Galiana.

A figure in black and grey reeled into the room, looking around wildly, his rapier drawn. Ulrika stared. It was Stefan. He was covered in wounds and blood and alley muck, but he was alive. Alive!

'Stefan!' Ulrika called. 'The sorcerer!'

Stefan seemed to take in the situation in an instant, and charged, slashing for the crook-backed sorcerer's neck with his blood-smeared rapier.

The sorcerer's champion spun as he came, and turned the cut with his sword, but only just. The rapier chopped through the meat of the sorcerer's shoulder instead, and he staggered, yelping with surprise and pain.

Immediately the purple tendrils dissolved into nothing, and the serpents in Ulrika's guts stopped biting. She slashed at the ring of cultists and marauders with renewed strength.

'Now, sister!' she cried. 'Go! Stefan! To me! Hurry!'

Ulrika heard Galiana start dragging Evgena away as, through the blurring limbs of her attackers, she saw Stefan run unsteadily for her, the painted champion thundering after him. The mob parted before Stefan's flashing blade and he crashed through to her, then faced out beside her and thrust the champion through the neck. He had a wound on his wrist that showed bone, and one on his forehead that made his face a crimson mask.

'I'm sorry,' he gasped as he helped her fight the rest. 'I… failed to draw them away.'

'Never mind,' she said. 'You're here. You're alive.'

'It is not enough. I–' His words died as he saw Raiza's shrivelled body at their feet. 'Kiraly,' he breathed. 'Kiraly was here?'

'Yes,' said Ulrika, impaling a cultist. 'He–' A grating rumble made her turn her head. 'Mistress?'

Galiana and Evgena were no longer behind her, and the fireplace was rotating slowly closed, its hidden door narrowing.

'Treacherous bitch!' Ulrika snarled, then grabbed Stefan's arm. 'Back! Quickly! Through the door!'

Stefan looked around, then jumped back from his opponents and darted in. Ulrika took a last swipe all around, then caught Raiza's body by the collar and dragged her through the closing gap as the marauders and cultists surged forwards.

The door boomed shut just as Raiza's toes cleared it. Ulrika let go of her and turned, sword raised. Galiana stood at the head of a cramped spiral stair at the back of the tiny stone chamber they were in, staring down at Stefan while a red nimbus of energy brightened around her fingers. Her wig had come off entirely, lying like a dead spaniel at her feet and revealing her shrunken, wispy-haired head.

'Don't!' Ulrika cried. 'Will you attack the man who saved you?'

'It was you he saved,' whispered Boyarina Evgena. She was struggling to her feet behind Galiana, and raised her head with difficulty. Her already-lined face was now shrivelled and skeletal, and her voice was like the wind from a dry cave. 'You led those madmen here hoping they would do your work for you, and got caught in your own trap.'

'Mistress, it isn't so,' Ulrika pleaded. 'If we were conspiring against you, why wouldn't we attack you now?'

'Ulrika is right, boyarina,' said Stefan. 'You are both weakened. Nothing would stop us from killing you here if we wished to.'

'Except our backs are not turned,' sneered Evgena.

Ulrika was going to reply when something clutched her ankle. She looked down. Raiza was gripping her with a withered hand, her parchment lips moving and her eyes shifting, agitated, in their sunken sockets.

'Raiza,' gasped Ulrika, kneeling down beside her. It seemed impossible the swordswoman was still alive. 'Raiza, what is it?'

'Fe... dor,' Raiza murmured.

Ulrika leaned in closer as the others gathered around. 'What do you say? I don't understand.'

'My... husband,' whispered Raiza. 'Where is my... husband?'

Ulrika opened her mouth, but said nothing. She had no idea what to say.

Evgena knelt down on the other side of the swordswoman and put a hand on her arm. 'He is dead, beloved,' she said, and Ulrika had never heard her voice so warm and kind. 'But you had vengeance on his killers, as I promised you would. They are all dead by your hand. Now you may rest.'

Raiza stared blankly at her for a long moment, then let her head sink back. 'Yes,' she said. 'Rest.'

As the life faded from the swordswoman's eyes, Evgena reached out and pulled the Blood Shard from her sunken chest. It pulsed red like a beating heart.

'And now,' she said, 'I will have vengeance on your killer.' And with that, she lurched forwards, stabbing at Stefan with the shard.

Stefan dodged back, cursing, barely in time, and Evgena stumbled weakly after him, slashing wildly.

'No, mistress!' cried Ulrika, and caught her wrist.

Evgena struggled in her grasp, but she had no strength. She could not break free. 'Unhand me!'

'Mistress,' Ulrika said. 'He saved us! He could have stood by and let the sorcerer destroy us, but he put his own life in danger and defended us! Is that not proof enough that he means us no harm?'

'He is von Carstein,' Evgena snarled. 'No proof is enough.'

A heavy thudding vibrated the walls of the little room. They all turned. The cultists were trying to break through the fireplace.

Evgena glared at the wall. 'They shall die too. All of them. No one attacks me in my own home and lives.'

Galiana took Evgena's arm. 'Sister, we cannot stay here. Let us finish this argument at the safe house.'

'He will not come there,' said Evgena, turning her eyes back to Stefan. 'I will have no spies there.'

'I do not trust him either, mistress,' said Galiana, raising her voice over the hammer-falls that boomed through the wall. 'But the girl is right. He had ample opportunity to strike, and did not. He may have some ulterior motive, but if so, it does not seem to involve our immediate harm. These cultists are a greater threat. They mean to bring down the whole of Praag, and we

will need all the tools at our disposal to stop them –
even von Kohln.' She picked up her wig and settled it on
her wizened head. 'Let us fight them together. We can
resume our own war afterwards.'

Stefan bowed to Galiana. 'I am in full agreement, mistress.'

Evgena sneered. 'Of course you are.'

Another hammer-strike shook the room, and dust
and pebbles rained down on her from the ceiling. She
bared her fangs at the noise, then sighed and turned
cold eyes on Stefan and Ulrika. 'You will be watched,'
she said, then motioned them to precede her down the
spiral stair.

Stefan hesitated, then bowed stiffly and limped past
her. Ulrika picked up Raiza's corpse and joined him.

As the two vampiresses fell in behind, Evgena held up
the pulsing Blood Shard. 'And remember what is at your
back.'

THE SPIRAL STAIRCASE twisted down many storeys below
ground until it opened into a network of ancient low
tunnels that Ulrika, who had spent time in Karak
Kadrin, was certain was dwarf work. They were not sewers or culverts, but whatever their original purpose, they
were in surprisingly good shape – dry and sound,
though dusty and filled with rats and scuttling insects.
Ulrika was afraid that, like the sewers she and Stefan
had traversed before, they would also be filled with
mutants and soldiers fighting underground skirmishes,
but they were not. There weren't even any signs of previous occupants – no old fires, no heaps of trash or
bones, no markings on the walls. The tunnels were as
silent and undisturbed as an unlooted tomb.

At last they stopped at a blank wall. Evgena said a
short phrase and a section scraped open, revealing
another spiral stair. The house at the top of the stair was

more modest than Evgena's mansion, but still a large and comfortable place, with a small staff of servants and men-at-arms who showed no surprise whatsoever at their mistresses' sudden appearance from behind a bookcase in the library.

Evgena fed immediately and without preamble upon one of the maids, then turned to her guests, wiping her mouth on a linen handkerchief, her face and form returned to their usual gauntness. She spoke first to Stefan, holding up the Blood Shard.

'Raiza's essence is trapped within this thing?' she asked.

'Yes, boyarina,' said Stefan, inclining his head.

'Can she be freed? Can she be returned to her body?'

'I hope so,' said Stefan. 'For Kiraly holds my master's essence in another. But I have been told it is impossible.'

Evgena nodded, then motioned to Ulrika. 'Leave her body here. I will keep it and the knife until I can learn more.'

Ulrika bowed and laid Raiza's body on a library table as Evgena turned next to Galiana.

'Sister,' she said. 'Send word to our friends and agents. We will work the day through to cancel the concert and get a warning to the duke.'

'Yes, mistress,' said Galiana, curtseying.

'Once we are certain Praag is safe, we can hunt down and destroy the cult, but until then...' Evgena smiled at Ulrika and Stefan darkly. 'I think it best if we kept our *allies* safely out of harm's way.' She waved her fan at her men-at-arms. 'Lock them in the cellar.'

'Mistress!' cried Ulrika sharply. 'You insult us! I have sworn allegiance to you. Stefan has saved your life. What more must we do to win your trust?'

Evgena stared hard at them for a moment, then turned and laid the Blood Shard on Raiza's chest. 'I can think of only one way,' she said. 'Follow my dear daughter's example, and die in my defence.'

THE CELLAR WAS just that, a wine cellar that had lost its original purpose when the Lahmians had moved in, as they did not drink wine. Great dry wine barrels lined one wall, and empty wine racks had been pushed up against the other. The space they had once taken up was now used for storage, and there were crates and trunks and stacks of paintings and furniture covered in sheets piled up all around.

It might not have been the dank cell Ulrika had feared it would be, but its walls were still yard-thick stone, and the door was sturdy, iron-bound oak. It was still a prison. They were not free to leave.

As the men-at-arms had locked them in, Ulrika had managed to beg from them some water to clean themselves with, and Stefan had found a pair of hardbacked chairs to sit upon amongst the draped armoires and sidetables, but other than that, there were no amenities, and they had not been allowed to feed. Evgena apparently didn't want them strong while she was still weak.

Ulrika had cleaned herself and her clothes as best she could, but was too restless to avail herself of the chairs. Instead she paced by the short stair that led up to the door, her mind churning, while Stefan took his turn with the water on the far side of the room.

Evgena's treatment of them was intolerable. They had acted in her best interests from the start, and still she treated them like assassins. Certainly, Ulrika had had ulterior motives for swearing loyalty to her, but since then she had not broken her vow, and had always worked to protect her.

Or had she?

Certainly she hadn't done it maliciously, but she could not deny she had somehow led the cult to

Evgena's doorstep and caused the slaughter of her guards and pets, and the fate worse than death of poor Raiza.

Ulrika closed her eyes as the grisly scene played out in her mind again. Why had it been Raiza who had died? The swordswoman had been a grim companion, but loyal and honourable, and unexpectedly kind beneath the stone façade she showed the world. A lifetime of servitude to Evgena might have been bearable with Raiza to fence with. Now, with her dead, Ulrika wondered if she could stand a week of it.

How had the cult followed her? It didn't seem possible. She had heard no footsteps. She had sensed no heart-fires. And could even Jodis have kept up with her as she leapt from roof to roof? Then she knew the answer. Kiraly! He had been among them, and had led them to Evgena's, and he would not have had to follow Ulrika. Surely he must have known the way to the house of the woman he had travelled a thousand miles to kill.

Selfish relief flooded Ulrika. It hadn't been her! She wasn't responsible for Raiza's death. She wasn't responsible for the attack on the house at all. Of course, she would never convince Evgena of that, but at least she knew it herself.

The splashing of water on the other side of the room turned her thoughts to Stefan, and she saw him once again stumbling into Evgena's drawing room, covered in blood and terribly hurt. The silver-tipped arrow in the leg had been only the first of his wounds. How he must have fought to keep the cultists from following her.

A sudden thought shook her. Ursun's teeth! Had he fought Kiraly? In the whirl of battle and what followed there had been no time to ask. She hadn't even thought of it. Had he failed to hold back the cultists because

Kiraly had driven him off? No wonder he was wounded so.

The pile of trunks and furniture was between her and Stefan. She started around it. Poor Stefan, to fight such a desperate battle while still in pain from the silver-tipped arrow. And he would still be in pain. He would still be in agony. She knew that from bitter experience. The bite of silver would not fade quickly. Not without blood to heal it, and Evgena had given them no blood. But Stefan had showed her another way to heal wounds. She stepped forwards, desire rising within her.

After all he had done, after doing his best to defend Evgena against the cult and Kiraly and receiving nothing but scorn and suspicion in return, he deserved more than wash water and imprisonment. Ulrika would heal him and soothe him, and in the giving, be soothed and healed herself. The pleasure would ease her sorrow at Raiza's death and her anger at Evgena's mistrust. She would lose herself in it and, for a while at least, all would be well.

Padding softly, she stepped around the corner of the stacked furniture. Stefan stood facing away from her, naked, as he scrubbed his forearms over a drain in the floor. She stopped, admiring the trim lines of his back, and the lean strength of his long legs. Despite his wounds, he was as beautiful as a hunting cat. Perhaps they even added to his beauty, giving him an air of danger and experience. Well, she should savour them while she could, for after she and Stefan had exchanged blood, they would be gone. Even the wound from the silver-tipped crossbow bolt on the back of his leg would be nothing more than–

Ulrika paused, frowning.

There was indeed a wound on Stefan's leg, red and deep and crusted with scabs, but that wasn't right.

She looked at her wrist, where Jodis had cut her with

her silvered long-knife. Even days later, and after drinking Stefan's powerful blood, the edges of the scar were still black – black, not red.

CHAPTER TWENTY-NINE
A VOW IS BROKEN

ULRIKA STARED AGAIN at the angry red wound on Stefan's leg. How had the edges not blackened and peeled back as hers had? It didn't seem possible. Was this another strange gift he had, like the ability to walk in the sun, or…?

Her mind sped back to their flight from the cultists. Stefan had sent her up the wall before him. He had fallen when she was looking the other way. She had not heard the twang of a shot. She had not seen the wound, only blood and a hole in his breeches. But the bolt – he had held a silver-tipped crossbow bolt. Surely–?

Her mind turned back further. He had caught a bolt – snatched it out of the air – when the cultists had first sprung their ambush by the fountain at the Music Academy. Her stomach sank with dread. He had faked the wound. But why?

Her theory that it had been Kiraly who had led the cultists to Evgena washed away, replaced by another. It had been Stefan. He had separated himself from her so he could guide them to the house without her knowing.

But then, where had Kiraly come from? Had he been with the cultists the whole time? Or had he been watching Evgena's mansion and only struck when the opportunity presented itself?

Or...

The two theories came together, like drawings on glass that only made a whole picture when laid on top of each other. Ulrika extended her fangs and claws, and took another step towards Stefan's back.

'Kiraly.'

Stefan turned, drying his hands on his ruined shirt. 'What about him–?' He paused as he saw her claws. 'What's wrong?'

'Your leg wound has betrayed you,' said Ulrika, continuing to advance. 'You were not wounded by silver. You sent me on to Evgena's alone so you could bring the cultists down on her. You are the cultist with the Blood Shards. You killed Raiza.'

Stefan stepped back, knocking over the pitcher of water. 'Ulrika, wait. You jump to conclusions.'

'No more lies!' Ulrika snarled. 'Evgena was right! You are everything she said you were. I am a fool!'

'You are not,' said Stefan. 'Listen to me. I can explain.'

'What is there to explain? Your own flesh bears witness against you!'

Stefan backed around the two chairs, putting them between them. 'Please, Ulrika. Listen. You are right – in part, at least. I did trick you with the silvered bolt, and I did lead the cultists to Evgena's house, but not for the reason you think. I did it to help you.'

Ulrika snorted, the ridiculousness of the claim bringing her up short. 'You speak nonsense. How was attacking Evgena to help anything?'

Stefan passed a hand over his face. 'It – it didn't go as I planned.'

Ulrika sneered. 'You mean some of us survived?'

'No, that's not what I mean,' Stefan snapped. 'Just listen, and I will explain.'

Ulrika glared at him, then folded her arms and waited.

Stefan watched her warily for a moment, as if afraid she might still attack, then sank into one of the chairs and looked up at her, sighing. 'You see, I knew that, alone, we two could not defeat the cult. They were too strong. There were too many of them. We needed the Lahmians' help. But I also knew that no argument you put forwards would stir Evgena to action. She would only hide and hope someone else saved Praag for her. She needed a goad. She needed to be attacked personally. Only then would her pride force her to retaliate.'

Ulrika stared at him. 'But... but...'

'I didn't tell you,' said Stefan, cutting her off, 'because I knew you wouldn't agree. You... you are too honourable. You had taken Evgena's oath. You would not knowingly have allowed harm to come to her or her household, even to save her from a worse fate.' He spread his hands. 'I have taken no oath, so I did what you could not.'

Ulrika stepped back, her mind whirling. His plan made a mad kind of sense – for he was right. Before the attack, Evgena had been contemplating retreating to Kislev rather than facing the cultists, and Ulrika doubted anything she could have said would have convinced her to do otherwise. And he had also been correct about her. She would not have let him go through with the plan, even if she had agreed with it, for she would not break her oath.

But...

'But you didn't just goad her!' she cried. 'You cut off her right arm! You killed Raiza! You brought Kiraly and the hunchbacked warlock down on us! We all nearly died!'

Stefan closed his eyes and hung his head. 'I know. I know, and I am sorry for it. I did not count Kiraly into the equation, nor the warlock. I don't know where they came from, and I tried to stop them when they appeared. I didn't want any of the Lahmians to die. I thought they would destroy the cultists easily. I… I was a fool. I should have found another way.'

Ulrika stared at him, unable to decide if she believed him, and if she believed him, if she forgave him. She wanted to, desperately. She had given her answer. She had told him she would be with him for all time. But it all seemed so thin, so cobbled together. His story fit everything she knew, but there was no way to prove any of it. Her more damning version of events could also be true. Except… except he hadn't killed Evgena when he had the chance.

A faint flame of hope flickered to life in her breast at the thought. Even if the rest of it sounded like a lie, that was still true. If Stefan was Kiraly, wouldn't he have sprung on Evgena when she was at her weakest? He could have killed all of them in the little room behind the fireplace, but he hadn't. He hadn't – and that was the proof.

Ulrika sighed and sat down heavily in the other chair. 'When Evgena hears of this, it will confirm everything she thinks of you.'

Stefan looked up, eyes wide. 'Don't be a fool. She mustn't know.'

Ulrika frowned unhappily at him. 'Stefan, I vowed not to conspire against her. I must tell her what I know.'

'You can't,' he said. 'Tell her after the cult is stopped, if you must, but not now. Please, Ulrika, I don't say this because I fear her. I say it because, as underhanded and disastrous as it was, my plan succeeded. Evgena hates the cult now. She works to stop them as we speak. If you tell her of it, what will happen? She will cry conspiracy again and turn all her fury upon me. The cult will be forgotten. Will you make Raiza's death pointless? Do you want everything we have just gone through to be for nothing?'

Ulrika blinked as what he said sank in. He was right. Evgena would go mad if she learned he had brought the cult down upon her. She would claim it was all a trick to kill her. There was no help for it. Though it went against her vow, for the safety of Praag – and Evgena's safety as well – Ulrika would have to keep silent.

'Very well,' she said at last. 'I will not speak.'

'Again, I am sorry,' he said, lowering his head. 'I have abused your trust and strained your honour. I will not ask forgiveness, for what I did should not be forgiven. I only hope we succeed in the end because of it, and you have an opportunity to avenge yourself on Kiraly for Raiza's death.'

Ulrika looked at him. 'I thought you had reserved that for yourself.'

Stefan nodded, curt, then turned away. 'He had hurt no one but me before. That is no longer true.'

She swallowed. It was a great gesture. 'You are generous,' she said.

He shrugged. 'As long as he is dead and my master's essence recovered, I am content.'

Ulrika looked at his profile, sharp and sad and lost in thought, then trailed her eyes down the rest of his body, and the wounds which had not yet healed.

She took his hand. 'I… I came in here to offer you… healing,' she said. 'I see you still need it.'

He raised an eyebrow. 'You would share blood with me, now? Knowing what I have done?'

Ulrika licked her lips. The hunger within her howled that she would share blood with him even if he were Kiraly himself, but she only said, 'You must be strong and ready for the battle ahead.'

'Aye,' said Stefan, smiling. 'And you as well.'

She pulled him to her, and turned her neck. 'Drink, and be strong.'

ULRIKA WOKE TO the turning of a key in a lock. She raised her head blearily. She was lying naked next to Stefan on the cellar floor. The flagstones were spattered with dried blood, as were she and Stefan.

At the top of the stone stairs, the heavy oak door was swinging open, and lantern glow spilled in from the corridor. Boyarina Evgena's tall frame ducked into the cellar, followed by Galiana's shorter one, and then four men-at-arms behind them. One held a lamp as they started down the stairs.

Ulrika shook Stefan. He grunted and looked around, then cursed and sat up. Ulrika did the same, fumbling for her bloody shirt to cover herself.

The boyarina seemed to have regained her strength, but Ulrika thought her shoulders had lost much of their proud bearing. She looked sad and tired as she approached them, and barely raised an eyebrow to find them lying together.

'You,' she said, looking down at them. 'You have ruined us.'

Ulrika and Stefan exchanged a glance. Did she already know Stefan had led the cultists to her house?

'What do you mean, mistress?' asked Ulrika.

'You dragged us into your little war and now we are done. We will have to begin again from scratch.'

'I don't understand,' said Ulrika.

Evgena sighed deeply. 'The battle fought at our house did not go unnoticed. The watch came. The chekist came. Things were found that could not be explained.' She waved her fan with a limp hand. 'The state of my pets might have been dismissed as vandalism, but there were other things – grimoires and artefacts of mine no one without witch sight could have found, and yet they were strewn about the house for anyone to discover.' She smiled bitterly. 'We sought to stymie the cult. They have stymied us.'

'So, you were not able to warn anyone?' asked Stefan. 'The concert goes on, then?'

Evgena's eyes blazed at him. 'Have you not listened? I have been branded a witch! There is a warrant for my arrest! I can do nothing. I can stop nothing. None of my associates dare speak to me, even through intermediaries. Ha! I have no intermediaries any more! My web is cut!' She groaned. 'I will have to retrench – new faces, new names, new houses. It will be decades before I am in a position to influence the court again.'

Ulrika stared at her, guilt gnawing at her insides. It was what had happened to Gabriella and the Lahmians of Nuln all over again. They too had been ruined and forced to start anew, but where, in Nuln, it had been the mad Strigoi, Murnau, that had brought about the Lahmians' destruction, here it had been her. She and Stefan had involved Evgena, Galiana and Raiza in a conflict they wanted nothing to do with, and it had shattered their lives irreparably.

She rose to one knee and bowed her head. 'Forgive me, mistress. I wish now I could take it all back. I should never have asked you for help in this. It was all done with the best of intentions, but–'

Evgena laughed, harsh, cutting her off. 'Was it? By the Queen, then I would hate to see what you might have done had you set out to ruin me!' She turned away, and all the fire went out of her again, as if it had never been. She looked as old and broken as a Nehekharan ruin. 'Get dressed. We leave for Kislev within the hour.'

Ulrika's head snapped up. 'You – you're leaving? But what about your vengeance on the cult? You swore to hunt them down and kill them.'

'And I will,' said Evgena. 'When we are strong again we will return. In ten years, perhaps. Or twenty.'

Ulrika stood. 'Mistress, you can't leave. You must fight them now or there will be no Praag to return to. We must go to the opera and stop the cultists ourselves.'

'Yes,' said Stefan, standing as well. 'Yes, we must.'

Galiana laughed, then stifled it with a hand.

Evgena looked at them as if they had grown horns and hooves. 'You're mad. Go to the opera? And then what? Do you suggest we brawl with these daemon-lovers? In public? Did I not say there was a warrant for my arrest?' She snapped open her fan then slapped it shut again. 'No no no. We must vanish. We must regroup, rebuild.'

'Mistress,' said Ulrika, stepping to her. 'How will you rebuild when Praag has fallen? Will you seek influence in the court of Sirena Amberhair? Will you become a follower of Slaanesh?' She raised her chin, glaring. 'If we do not stop them tonight, you will have no position to reclaim. Praag will be gone. The Lahmians will have no power and no eyes in the north. Will our Queen thank you for that?'

'You dare tell me my duty?' snarled Evgena.

'I tell you nothing,' said Ulrika. 'I only show you what will happen if you fail in it.'

Evgena hissed and struck her across the cheek with her fan. Ulrika stepped back and went on guard, shooting out her claws and growling, but the boyarina had turned away and was sobbing against the wall, her head in her arms.

'Sister!' said Galiana, and went to her, stroking her.

Evgena shrugged her off and remained turned away from them, her back shaking and her fists clenched. Then, after a long silent moment when no one dared speak or move, she lifted her head and straightened her shoulders, and turned back to them, her face white, and cold as snow.

'Come upstairs,' she said. 'We will find you clothes and masks suitable for the opera.'

Ulrika blinked, then stepped forwards, making to speak, but the boyarina held up her hand.

'You are not forgiven for bringing this crisis upon us,' she said. 'But as you have thrust it in my lap, and as all now depends on me, I will not falter. But do not expect my goodwill when all is done.'

And with that, she turned on her heel and led them all upstairs.

CHAPTER THIRTY
THE CONCERT

An hour later, with night falling, Ulrika, Stefan, Galiana and Evgena left the safe house – a modest townhouse in a quiet cul-de-sac in the Merchant Quarter – and travelled in chilly silence within a black coach through the Noble Quarter to Windlass Square, Praag's greatest plaza, upon the southern edge of which sat the duke's palace, and upon its east flank, the Opera House.

Ulrika and Stefan were dressed now in the height of Praag fashion – Ulrika in doublet and breeches of dark green and black with a cloak to match, and her cropped white hair hidden beneath a Kossar's fur hat, and Stefan in deep blue and white with a short cloak that draped over one shoulder. To complete their costumes, Evgena had given them masks. Ulrika was certain there was some petty spite behind her selections, for she had chosen for Stefan the traditional black, full-faced mask of comedy, and for Ulrika, comedy's ancient counterpart, tragedy, complete with a diamond tear, and lugubrious, down-turned mouth.

Evgena and Galiana had dressed up as well, Evgena in

a forest-green gown with black trim to match Ulrika's colours, and Galiana in midnight-blue over white silk to match Stefan, though *their* masks were beautiful, glittering works of art, plumed with iridescent feathers, rather than ugly jokes. In addition to these disguises, the boyarina and her sister had donned new wigs, chestnut-brown waves for Evgena, and a spill of blonde curls for Galiana – but the true transformations were those of the women themselves.

Through darkest Lahmian magic, the boyarina had cast an illusion of youth and beauty upon them that was stunning to behold. Evgena, who had looked like a skinned and mummified cat since Ulrika had first met her, now appeared to be a dignified beauty of perhaps forty years, with an imposing bosom and alluring eyes, while Galiana, who had seemed a wizened doll with a wig too big for her head, now looked a fresh-faced young girl, with pink cheeks and plump, parted lips. It made Ulrika wonder when they had given up the effort to maintain the illusion, and why. It also made her wonder if she had ever seen Countess Gabriella's true face.

WINDLASS SQUARE WAS a jostling confusion of coaches and carriages when they arrived, all debouching beautifully clad men and women who drifted in slow, swirling clusters across it like jewelled leaves stirred by a lazy wind. At the edges of the square, a wall of guardsmen held back crowds of hollow-cheeked refugees and beggars, who watched the glittering creatures within in glassy-eyed wonder, as if the masked and painted things were specimens from some strange zoo.

On the south side of the square, the palace, underlit by a thousand lanterns, loomed like some bizarre red and gold rock formation, with crenellated walls and towering onion-domed spires covered in mosaics of garnet cabochon and hammered leaf. The Opera House was hardly more sedate, with a baroque façade of blue and red tile, marble statues and a turreted roof of verdigrised copper – and amongst this ornate decor, the scars it had received in the Great War against Chaos. Repairs had not been made, for Praag was proud of its war-torn history, and shattered columns and black-edged pockmarks showed the prosaic brick behind the beauty of the fantastical walls and roof.

In the midst of this madness, Ulrika alighted from Evgena's coach with the boyarina on her arm, and Galiana and Stefan following likewise linked, to stride through the laughing hordes.

Men in rich clothes or military uniform paraded by, wearing hats and capes made from the fur of fox and bear and snow cat. Women flirted in ermine-trimmed bodices of every colour, and layered, petticoated dresses that swept the ground. And both sexes wore masks of all varieties, from simple dominos that covered only the eyes, to wild, leather and lacquer creations that hid the whole face behind stylised depictions of gods and heroes, animals and birds, daemons and monsters. Even the most august and noble ministers and members of the priesthood had got into the spirit of the night, and wore bright colours and shining baubles as well as their chains and sigils of office.

Just as they reached the marble steps that led to the Opera House's forecourt, a liveried page with a bugle stepped out and blew the tantara signalling that everyone should come and take their seats. There followed a great migration towards the doors, and Evgena, Ulrika, Stefan and Galiana joined the crush. All around them as they inched forwards was the buzz of conversation – the usual gossip of who wore what and who accompanied whom, but intermingled with that, Ulrika began to hear a familiar name, and listened closer.

'Padurowski? Truly?'

'But someone said Padurowski was dead.'

'No, he's back.'

'Where has he been? No one could find him, not even the chekist.'

'The hospital, I heard. Under the care of the Daughters of Salyak.'

'Probably had a case of the nerves. I know I would, if I had to perform before the duke.'

Ulrika exchanged a look with Stefan as the surmises continued. They had thought the maestro kidnapped or killed by the cultists. Had he escaped their grasp? Had he been hiding instead? Or recovering from wounds?

'Does this mean Valtarin wasn't kidnapped either?' murmured Stefan.

Ulrika shrugged, but then a thought came to her. The blind singer – was there hope for her too?

They reached the gilded doors at last and Evgena stepped forwards boldly. Ulrika feared they would be asked for an invitation, but after a dazzling smile and a show of cleavage from the boyarina, the usher bowed them through without a word – poleaxed by Lahmia's most powerful magic.

Once inside, Evgena led them immediately upstairs to a private box – not her own, for she feared it might be watched, but that of a courtier she knew was sick and would not be attending – and sat in one of the luxurious seats.

'Be silent,' she said. 'I must look for them.'

She closed her eyes and folded her hands in her lap. Galiana sat beside her and did the same. Ulrika left them to it. Her own witch sight was so poor it wasn't worth her time to try. Instead, she stepped with Stefan to the rail, and looked out at the interior of the Opera House through the eyeholes of her mask.

Below, the lesser attendees made a crazy quilt of

colour as they took their seats in the stalls, while their betters laughed and talked amongst themselves in the three tiers of private boxes that rose above them, supported by gilded columns decorated with sculptures of grotesque gargoyles with the bodies of violins, horns and drums, all playing instruments made of human bones.

The stage at the front of the theatre was hidden by enormous tasselled curtains of burgundy, emblazoned with the crest of Praag as well as the coats of arms of the duke and other patrons. The elaborate proscenium continued the motif of music, madness and death, portraying the siege of Praag with sculpted daemons climbing up the columns to the left of the stage, and the brave defenders of the city climbing up those to the right. They met at last in a titanic battle that came to a climax high above centre stage where Magnus the Pious swung a golden hammer at the head of Asavar Kul as skull-faced minstrels looked on, lutes and harps in their hands.

As Ulrika was taking in all these details, a flood of applause started in the stalls, then spread up into the boxes. She looked around. The people below were standing and turning to look up at the central box at the back of the theatre, and all the people in the private boxes were doing the same.

Ulrika followed their gaze and saw the slim, elegant figure of her cousin Enrik, the Duke of Praag, entering his box and stepping forwards to acknowledge their acclamation. He was dressed head to toe in brilliant white, from his fur cap to his ermine half-cape, to his doublet and breeches which glittered with a frost of diamonds, to his cavalry boots, which had quite obviously never been anywhere near a horse.

He saluted the room and bowed graciously, then motioned to his guests, a glittering assemblage of generals, ministers, priests and ice witches, to take their seats. When they had done so, he took his own, a silver throne, crowned with the head of a pure-white snow bear, the pelt and paws of which hung down over the arms of the chair. Ulrika smiled to herself. Some called her cousin mad, but he had ruled admirably during the recent siege, and always knew how to put on a good show.

A moment later, Evgena opened her eyes. 'They hide themselves well,' she said, sighing. 'As they would have to, with so many priests and witches in attendance. If I was not certain they were here, I might never have found them. As it is, I can only surmise their presence indirectly.'

'How so?' asked Ulrika.

'There is an area somewhere behind or below the stage,' she said, 'that deflects my gaze almost without me knowing it is being deflected. When I try to look there, I find myself thinking I have already done so, and pass it by.' She laughed. 'Had I only looked once, I would never have given it a second thought. But since I was determined to find something, I finally noticed the compulsion to look away. It is very sophisticated magic, and very powerful. I hope we are enough to best it.'

She stood, and turned to Galiana, who stood as well. 'Stay here, sister, and watch the audience. There may be cultists among them. Watch the winds and be ready to act if anyone begins to gather them.'

Galiana curtseyed. 'Yes, sister.'

Evgena started to the door, beckoning to Ulrika and Stefan. 'Come. Let us find these daemon-lovers. I am prepared now. This time it will be I who strikes first.'

EVGENA AGAIN USED the mighty magics of eyelashes and smile and cleavage to draw away the guard who watched the door that led backstage so Ulrika and Stefan could slip in behind him. The boyarina joined them a moment later, smirking.

'I have sent him for the watch,' she said, 'saying I saw Boyarina Evgena Boradin, who is under suspicion of witchcraft, sneaking into her private box.'

Ulrika smiled as they hurried up a dimly lit stair. The boyarina seemed to have warmed to her work, now that she had begun it. It was proof of something Ulrika had learned many many battles ago, that anticipation is a hundred times worse than action.

The steps ended at the wings of the stage, and they looked around. A rickety stair rose into the cavernous darkness above the stage, and nearby, stagehands stood at a line of tied-off ropes and pulleys, waiting. In the centre, behind the closed curtain, musicians in simple black surcoats sat in rings of seats around a podium and tuned their instruments while a stage manager with an open ledger in one hand eyed them anxiously.

'Ready now, gentlemen?' he asked. 'It is time. It is time.'

There was a general grunt of assent.

'Excellent, excellent,' said the stage manager. 'Then we begin.' And with a soft whistle and wave of his hands, he trotted towards the far side of the stage.

'There is nothing here,' said Evgena, and turned towards a door in the side wall as the stagehands began to haul on the ropes and the curtains began to open. 'We must go further in.'

Applause spilled through the parting curtains, and then redoubled as a tall, white-maned figure strode towards the podium. Ulrika looked back as the others went through the door. It was Maestro Padurowski, in a long lilac jacket and knee breeches, beaming cheerfully and waving his baton.

At centre stage, he bowed to the audience. 'My lord duke, ladies and gentlemen, I am deeply touched at the outpouring of concern for my safety, but as you see, all is well, and we need dwell on it no further. Tonight is a celebration of our beloved duke and his brave generals, of our divine Tzarina, and of the countless men and women who united to defeat the terrible horde that threatened us this winter past. And so, without further ado, we begin. For Praag! For Kislev!'

And with that, he turned and raised his baton to the orchestra. Ulrika turned and followed the others out into a dim corridor as the musicians thundered into a stirring rendition of 'Gryphons of the North'.

The music followed them as they wound through a maze of tight corridors and stairways. Doors opened into property rooms and rehearsal rooms, and rooms full of machinery Ulrika did not understand. Stefan pulled aside a curtain to find a closet full of halberds made of wood and papier-mâché. Another was hung with fierce horned helmets made of tin. Evgena opened a door into a high room where scaffolding was set up before a canvas two storeys high and forty paces wide, upon which was an unfinished painting of what looked like an elven garden in far Ulthuan.

Hurrying on with the others, Ulrika passed a descending stair with a door at the bottom that looked as if it went under the stage, but she dismissed it. Nothing would be happening down there.

Five paces on, she stopped. 'Mistress,' she whispered, pointing back. 'That stair. I have the idea we shouldn't check it.'

Evgena turned on her, frowning. 'Of course we shouldn't. Nothing could possibly–' She paused. 'Ah. I see.' She shook her head in admiration. 'Even knowing, I still missed it.'

'Well spotted,' said Stefan.

'Yes,' said Evgena, then turned to continue down the hall. 'Now come, we have other places to check.'

'Mistress!'

Evgena turned again, her eyes widening. 'By the Queen!' She started for the stair, taking measured steps and giving it her full concentration. 'My thoughts roll off the ward like water off wax.'

Ulrika and Stefan followed her down, and with every step, Ulrika's mind told her she had already checked behind the door, or that she could sense nothing there, or that she had something more important to do elsewhere. Beside her, Stefan was grinding his teeth, and she knew he must be affected too.

At last they reached the door. Ulrika could still feel no magical energy behind it, and the rousing strains of 'Praag Ever Rises' were all she could hear through it, with the exception, strangely, of glass shattering, over and over again.

Evgena stopped, holding up a hand. 'There are other wards here as well,' she said.

Ulrika focused her witch sight and at last made out a faint purple sheen shimmering a few feet in front of the door. Evgena drew back her velvet sleeve to reveal the same sort of paper bracelet Raiza had used to pass through the wards that had protected the ceremony in the temple of Salyak. She stepped forwards, murmuring and clenching her fist.

Ulrika watched, preparing to wait for a narrow hole to develop in the ward, but the oily skin boiled away from the bracelet instantly, and much further than it had when Raiza had done the trick. Soon there was a hole in it taller and wider than the narrow stairwell they stood in.

Evgena motioned Ulrika and Stefan forwards, her jaw set. They drew their rapiers and daggers and stepped through the hole to the door. Ulrika turned the latch. It was locked. She twisted harder and it snapped with a muffled crack. She waited, listening for any alarm, but heard nothing over the sounds of the orchestra above.

Pulling her mask down to her neck so she could see better, she opened the door a crack and peered in. The music got louder, as did the strange shattering sound, and through a confusion of beams and pillars and odd contraptions made of gears, pulleys and rope, Ulrika saw men in purple robes kneeling in a half-circle, chanting and throwing things she could not quite make out.

She slid through with Stefan and Evgena behind her and looked around. The understage was a high, dark space, cluttered with ladders and wooden stairways leading up to narrow catwalks. Bits of scenery were stacked against the walls, and big crates, over-stuffed with wooden swords, prop shields, papier-mâché crowns and the banners of long-dead tzars were tucked under stairs that ringed an open area in the centre.

As she inched further in, the scent of freshly shed blood found her nose and she looked down. Two stage-hands lay just inside the door, their throats cut. She stepped over them and crept through the forest of wooden pillars with Stefan and Evgena following, until a large rough hole in the stone floor blocked their way. It was freshly dug, and went far down into the moist, dark earth. A pile of picks and shovels lay beside it, as well as a mound of pulled-up flagstones.

'Up from the sewers,' murmured Stefan.

Ulrika nodded and edged around the hole.

The open area beyond it was dominated by a large hollow wheel, like the water wheel of a mill, with two men standing inside it. The contraption was attached by ropes to a square platform in the very centre of the space, and upon the platform stood a cultist, cloaked and hooded like all the rest, who held aloft a violin that could only be the Fieromonte.

CHAPTER THIRTY-ONE
THE SONG OF THE DAMNED

THE SCENE SEEMED to Ulrika a strange mockery of that which was occurring on the stage above. The man who held up the violin stood in the same position as Padurowski at his podium, while two score cultists knelt in a half-circle before him like the musicians in their chairs. But while the orchestra played music, the cultists were doing something far stranger and more disturbing.

A squat stone brazier sat on the floor before the platform, a purple fire blazing within it, and as Ulrika, Stefan and Evgena watched, the kneeling cultists picked up corked bottles they had lined up before them, and threw them at the brazier in time with their chant. One after another, the bottles smashed on its stone lip and clouds of translucent mist billowed from them, making the purple flames leap higher and releasing curls of white smoke.

As it drifted up towards the Fieromonte, the smoke turned in the air, as if pulled towards the flue of a chimney, and was sucked into its sound holes while the violin moaned and keened.

'The souls,' whispered Ulrika, clenching her fists. 'The souls of the sacrificed girls.'

'They are feeding it,' murmured Evgena. 'Bribing it for the great task they wish it to perform.'

'Praag Ever Rises' came to its crashing conclusion above them just as the last bottle was thrown, and Padurowski's voice filtered through the boards of the stage.

'Now we will play for you a song to honour the wardens of the marches,' he said, 'who so bravely guard our northern border. This is a traditional song of that land – an old ballad called "While I Reap and Sow"'.

A hunched figure rose from the first row of cultists and beckoned to men at the far side of the room. 'Quick!' he whispered. 'The last victim!'

Ulrika recognised the man instantly. It was the crook-backed sorcerer, he who had nearly destroyed them all with his magics at Evgena's mansion. Evgena recognised him too. She growled and began to move her hands in complicated patterns.

The first strains of the ballad wafted through the air as two cultists dragged a woman to the brazier. Ulrika choked. It was the blind girl from the Blue Jug. Her hands were bound, and she hunched in abject terror between her captors.

The crooked sorcerer stepped to her and shook her. 'Sing!' he barked. 'Sing the song!'

The girl cowered back, mewling in fright.

He put a dagger to her throat. 'Sing, curse you!'

The girl sobbed again, but then, haltingly, began to sing in time with the orchestra. With her first words, Ulrika recognised the song. She had sung it that first night in Praag – the ballad of the girl who waits when her lover goes off to war. Ulrika hadn't known it from the title, or from Padurowski's syrupy arrangement, but now she did.

Her chest constricted as she listened, for, as terrified as the blind girl was, she could not help singing well, and the song, so sweet and sad and full of memories of home, was like a lance of sunlight burning straight into Ulrika's heart. She couldn't imagine why these degenerates would want to hear something so pure and good, but then she saw the reason.

White wisps of vapour, almost invisible, were coming from the girl's mouth with each note – a translucent mist that mixed with the smoke from the brazier and drifted up to be inhaled, just as the essences of the sacrificed girls had been, into the sound holes of the Fieromonte.

'No,' Ulrika rasped, and started forwards. 'No!'

Evgena broke off her incantation and tried to grab her. 'Idiot girl! What are you doing?'

Stefan did the same. 'Ulrika, wait!'

Ulrika writhed away from them both. 'They're taking her voice!'

She charged out of the shadows, launching herself straight at the crooked sorcerer. The man looked up, letting go of the singer and falling back as the rest of the cultists cried out and started to their feet. He threw up his arms as Ulrika slashed at his face, and her rapier stopped in mid-air as if it had struck a wall. He smiled cruelly, and began to twist his hands in arcane gestures, but a bolt of sizzling black energy shot from Evgena's hiding place and tore through him. He crashed to the floor, twitching and shrieking as crackling arcs danced over his skin.

Ulrika stepped forwards to finish him, but the cultists surged in at her, pulling knives from their robes. She turned to face them and found Stefan at her shoulder, his teeth bared.

'That was one way to do it,' he growled.

Together they stabbed and kicked at the howling mob, puncturing throats and guts and groins while trying to reach the cultists who held the singer, but before they could get close, a glint of silver flickered in the corner of Ulrika's eye and she ducked aside, an inch ahead of a long knife that slashed for her face.

She spun, on guard. It was Jodis, naked again, and lunging with her second knife. Ulrika skipped back, ending back to back with Stefan as four of Jodis's hulking marauders elbowed through the robed cultists to surround them.

'You keep running from us, corpses,' the Norsewoman said with both her mouths, then turned and barked at the cultists and the men who led the blind singer. 'You, leave these and kill the witch! You two, get her up! Him too! Out of reach!'

Ulrika lunged, trying to kill the Norsewoman while her attention was divided, but the marauders inervened, hacking at her and Stefan from all sides while the cultists backed away and crept warily towards Evgena.

Within the marauders' circle of slashing steel, Ulrika could only watch helplessly while the two men heaved the blind singer onto the platform next to the cultist who held the Fieromonte, then waved at the men inside the wheel.

'Up!' cried one. 'Up!'

The wheelmen began to walk forwards, turning the spool from within, and with a creaking of ropes and timbers, the platform rose. The singer lay unmoving upon it, still singing, her soul being torn from her mouth by the violin, word by word and note by note.

'A voice to pierce the heart of all who hear it, eh?' sneered Jodis as she flicked her blades at Ulrika's legs. 'And deliver to them our lord's sweet venom like a snake's hollow fang.'

Ulrika drove the Norsewoman back toward the platform in a flurry of steel, and Stefan moved with her, protecting her back and flanks, but they weren't moving fast enough. The platform was almost to the roof.

'Mistress!' Ulrika cried. 'Stop them! Stop the wheel!'

Evgena had her hands full holding back the throng of cultists that with a wall of shimmering red, but she did her best, shooting a blast of crackling energy towards the wheelmen. But before the bolt reached them, a violet mist formed around them, absorbing it. Ulrika looked past Jodis and saw the crooked sorcerer lurching unsteadily to his feet, violet energy dancing around his hands.

'You will not spoil our surprise,' he hissed, and sent an eruption of purple snakes towards Evgena.

Above the battle, the old folk song came to an end, and the blind singer's voice trailed off in a hideous rattle as the applause of the crowd echoed through the stage floor. Ulrika glanced up and saw a last breath of white vapour leave her mouth to be sucked into the violin, then the cultist that held the instrument kicked her off the platform.

Ulrika jumped back, pulling Stefan out of the way, and the singer's falling body flattened the marauder to their left, then slid to the floor. The look of uncomprehending horror on her beautiful face made Ulrika want to tear Jodis apart with her bare hands. She sprang at the Norsewoman, her rapier and dagger blurring.

As Jodis blocked and parried, Padurowski's voice rang out from above.

'And now, lords and ladies,' he cried, 'a special treat for you all! A solo performance by the pride of the Academy, the most talented musician of his age, playing a song that hasn't been performed in Praag for two hundred years!'

Ulrika glanced up from her fight as the cultist on the platform whipped off his robes and threw them aside. It was Valtarin! He flipped back his mop of hair, tucked the Fieromonte under his chin and began to play a wild melody as a trap in the stage opened and the platform lifted him through it. The Opera House burst into spontaneous applause at his ascension, and began to clap along to the lilting tune.

Ulrika knew the song. She had been hearing it on the wind since she came to Praag. She cursed as all became clear. How could she have been so blind? How could she not have seen that Valtarin and Padurowski were cultists? They had played her like a fool!

Jodis laughed from both her mouths and jumped back, spreading her arms in triumph. 'You see, corpse? You've failed. Already they dance to Slaanesh's–'

Ulrika lunged, and impaled the Norsewoman through the heart with her rapier. Jodis stared at the wound, then crumpled to the floor, the mouth that grew from her goitre shrieking while her true mouth gurgled and spewed blood.

'You talk too much, *corpse*,' said Ulrika, then whipped her blade from her ribs and backed to Stefan, who was still fighting the other marauders. 'We have to get to the stage.'

'Aye,' he said, and together they drove them back towards the door to the stairs.

'Brothers! Stop them!' rasped the crooked man.

He was locked in his duel with Evgena, and could not move. Nor could Evgena. Tentacles of purple energy emanating from Crook-back's hooded forehead writhed around her, trying to penetrate the shimmering red-tinged sphere she had formed around herself.

Obeying the sorcerer, the cultists turned from the boyarina to block Ulrika and Stefan's escape.. Frantic, Ulrika impaled one marauder with her rapier, then stabbed the last in the neck with her dagger while he was engaged with Stefan, and they ran for the door with the cultists hot at their heels.

'Go on,' said Stefan, pushing her forwards and turning in the doorway to face the mob. 'I'll hold them here.'

Ulrika staggered into the stairs, blinking back at him. 'But–'

'There's no time to fight them every step of the way,' he snapped as the first wave reached him. 'Go. This was your war from the beginning. It should be you who ends it!'

Ulrika hesitated for the briefest of seconds, then ran up the steps. She would much rather have had Stefan at her side, but he was right. There was no time. She raced through the maze of corridors, putting on her mask of tragedy again as she went. It wouldn't do for her cousin the duke to recognise her in her stage debut.

THE SCENE BEFORE her as she burst into the wings appeared so normal she almost questioned her senses. What could be threatening about a soloist playing a violin while a kindly-looking conductor led an orchestra in accompaniment and the audience swayed and clapped along? But a closer look at the crowd revealed the truth. Their eyes were glazed and wild, like merry drunkards in the last giddy stage before collapse, and they clapped and sang along like automatons, all in precisely the same time.

Some, Ulrika saw, were struggling against it – sweat beading on their foreheads as they tried to resist the call of the melody. An old general clenched his teeth and balled his fists as his head bobbed. A priest of Dazh murmured furiously under his breath but could not keep his hands from moving. They knew something was wrong, but they had been caught in the insidious spell before they could summon the will to resist.

Ulrika too, found it hard to fight the pull of the song. As she ran towards the stage, the rhythm was so insistent it tripped her, and the melody, though jaunty and mischievous, had a poignant melancholy that nearly brought her to tears. That must be the blind girl. The voice of her soul, mixed with the soaring shimmer of the violin, was doing just what Jodis had said it would, opening a passage to the hearts of the audience and allowing the poisoned song to enter and corrupt them.

A blistering rage welled up in Ulrika and weakened the grip the music had on her. To use something so pure to do something so foul was despicable. She charged onto the stage, raising her rapier.

The audience gasped and Padurowski turned, then cried to Valtarin, but neither could stop performing, or the spell would be broken. Hope surged in Ulrika as she rushed closer. All she had to do was cut the violinist and the song would stop, but with only five strides between them, he turned, glaring, and played an improvised jig over Padurowski's accompaniment, practically flinging the notes at her. Ulrika staggered as the full force of the violin's power struck her, then began to dance, jerking and capering like a marionette on a string, all control ripped from her.

The audience roared with laughter and clapped all the louder. They thought she was part of the show. And why shouldn't they? Ulrika must look a comic figure with her mask of tragedy and her foolish dancing. She tried to fight it, but she could not make her legs stop skipping and kicking. The harder she tried, the more the violin's will bore down on her, making her jerk and flail.

But what if she gave in?

She let the music take her, surrendered to the rhythm and danced towards Valtarin, slashing gracefully in time to the music. His eyes widened in alarm and he stepped back. She grinned. It was working, like tacking into the wind instead of sailing directly into it. She pirouetted again, and came within a foot of him with her blade.

But as she jigged closer, Padurowski leapt in front of

her, his lilac coat flapping, and went on guard with his conductor's baton, grinning and mugging to the audience.

'You see, my lords!' he cried. 'How music and culture are the best weapons against savagery and barbarism?'

The audience cheered its approval at this as Ulrika thrust at him. If he wanted to die to protect Valtarin, so be it. His death might shock the crowd from their poisoned euphoria.

But as her blade shot towards Padurowski's heart, he parried with his baton, and the strength of the block nearly shivered the sword from her hand. Ulrika gaped. How could it be? She should have chopped the slim wand in half.

Padurowski laughed. 'Lord Slaanesh has been generous with his gifts,' he whispered. 'The vigour of youth, and a weapon of power with which to do his will.'

He lunged with the baton, and Ulrika, still stunned and dancing to Valtarin's tune, did not move in time. It struck her on the thigh, only a glancing blow, but it cut through cloth and muscle.

She cried out in pain and stumbled in her jig as the crowd roared. The world flickered around her, and for a brief second, she saw a different Padurowski in the place of the old man she thought she faced. He was still lanky and white-haired, but his face was unseamed and beautiful, and his frame strong and true – and in his hand was not a conductor's baton, but a dagger like a needle – a long stiletto blade that shimmered with unearthly power.

'Play on, Valtarin!' cried this different Padurowski. 'I shall take her measure as we tread the measure.'

Then the vision was gone and the world snapped back around her. Padurowski giggled and flicked the baton at her neck, but she had seen its true form now, and parried it as she would a sword. There was a clash of steel, and her rapier was knocked back, a gouge in its edge, but she had turned the thing.

Padurowski cursed and came in again, his cheerful expression slipping, but again she countered, for he was no fencer.

'It is a shame your lord did not gift you with the skill to match your weapon,' she sneered.

'It will be enough, parasite,' he growled, and slashed furiously.

Ulrika looked to the audience as she danced and circled with him, hoping someone had noticed that they fought now in earnest, but the faces she saw were more lost than before, their glee now bestial, their eyes glittering as much with hate as with cheer.

'Kill her! Kill her!' they chanted in time to Valtarin's playing, and rose from their seats to sway and dance.

Ulrika groaned. If she didn't stop it soon, the song would consume them completely, but she could still not turn towards the violinist, could still not stop herself from her mad capering. Then it came to her. She must do as she had before. She must go with the current.

She backed from Padurowski, turning so she retreated towards Valtarin.

The conductor's eyes gleamed, his grin returning. 'You see? You weaken, while I grow only stronger!'

He lunged in, thrusting towards her heart with the fell dagger. Ulrika staggered back towards Valtarin, flailing behind her with her rapier as if for balance, then smashed it down across the bridge of the Fieromonte.

The result was catastrophic. As her blade snapped its catgut strings and cracked its wooden body, the violin shrieked like a hundred hurricanes and exploded in a ball of purple-white light, hurling Valtarin and Ulrika and Padurowski through the air and knocking the musicians of the orchestra from their chairs. The audience, so recently laughing and dancing, now screamed and shielded their eyes.

Ulrika stared from where she had crashed at the left side of the stage as, from out of the white light, rose a towering, translucent figure more beautiful than any being she had ever seen – no matter that it seemed to have no single shape or face, but shifted constantly from one to another. It howled in the soaring voice of the violin, then turned its golden, ever-changing eyes towards Valtarin and Padurowski.

'Where are the fools that promised us the souls of an entire city?'

CHAPTER THIRTY-TWO
UNMASKED

ULRIKA'S MIND REBELLED at the sight of the daemon, and the urge to join the people in the audience who were shrieking and trampling each other as they tried to escape its presence was almost overwhelming. But at the same time as it filled her mind with terror, the ever-changing being rooted her to the spot with its beauty and charisma. She could feel her skin tingling in its aura as if she were bathing in acid, and felt powerful forces pulling at her flesh, as if trying to warp her in their own image.

Fortunately, something within her, perhaps the dark power that animated her dead body, seemed to fight against this transformative imperative. Others were not so lucky. All around her, the musicians of Padurowski's orchestra were writhing and mutating before her eyes. A horn player's head sprouted a dozen fleshy, gaping stoma that blared like trumpets, while a cellist had become one with his instrument, his body melting into the wooden shape of the cello, and his hands curling up like scrollwork tuning heads. Others simply exploded into shapeless masses of tentacles and mouths, flopping about on the boards like drowning fish.

Many in the audience were similarly affected. The whole of the first three rows were splitting out of their fancy clothes as tentacles and new limbs and screeching heads sprouted from their bodies. Many more, though apparently untouched by mutation, had their sanity ripped away by the advent of the daemon, and gibbered and clawed at themselves in their horror, gouging out their own eyes, savaging their companions and leaping from the private boxes to die broken on the seat backs below.

In the midst of this madness, Valtarin abased himself before the beautiful daemon, pressing his face against the boards. 'Forgive us, lord!' he said. 'We… we… we…'

The daemon pounced upon him, and Ulrika expected to see the violinist torn limb from limb, but instead the being's insubstantial body sank into him like a ghost slipping back into its grave, and the boy began to scream and glow.

Ulrika crabbed back as Valtarin rose, reforming before her eyes, growing taller and stronger and more beautiful, like a lascivious saint carved from white marble. Gleaming trumpet mouths grew from his spine like a dragon's ridge of plates, and wings made of fanned organ pipes hung in the air above his shoulders.

Padurowski shuffled towards the daemon on his knees, arms wide. 'Lord, please! The souls of the city are still yours! You have only to sing and they will beg you to take them!'

The daemon stretched out an alabaster hand and a swarm of piano wires sprouted from it and stretched towards the maestro, wrapping around his limbs and neck and torso like the creepers of a vine, to lift him off the stage. 'And we will start with you,' chorussed the daemon, 'who thought to use us and lock us away again.'

Padurowski's eyes went wide as he squirmed in mid-air, dropping his dagger. 'No, lord! Never!'

'Will you lie to one who knows your darkest desires?' The daemon's laugh sounded like a drunken orchestra. 'Your soul is as open to us as a wound.'

And with that, Padurowski flew apart as the piano wires constricted and diced him into a rain of blood and bone shards and red gobbets that spattered Ulrika and the stage in all directions. Only a shrivelled wisp of white vapour remained, glowing within a cage of dripping red wire.

The daemon raised the cage to its face, drawing the vapour to it, then closed its eyes and inhaled it.

With the beautiful horror distracted, Ulrika at last found the will to stand, and backed away, hoping to escape while it was distracted. She had never been more afraid in life or death. The daemon was more powerful than anything she had ever faced, and she knew she could do nothing to it.

But before she got halfway to the side of the stage, its eyes snapped open and it looked directly at her, freezing her in her tracks.

'Our rescuer,' it purred, 'who freed us both from the tower and the vile, four-stringed prison that held us for too long. We are greatly obliged to you and would reward you.' It smiled. 'Yes, for this service, we shall keep you with us. We have never had an immortal lover before, one who could heal from any caress. There are so many things we have wanted to try.'

Ulrika stumbled back as it stepped towards her, its organ-pipe wings fanning majestically, then saw Padurowski's dagger lying on the stage behind it. She dived under the daemon's grasp and came up with the dagger, then spun and stabbed it in the back. It was like stabbing a lightning bolt. She flew back, thrown by the shock, and crashed to the stage, her hand smoking

where it clutched the dagger. The blade had trans-
formed into a long wet tongue that curled around her
wrist, licking her.

'Foolish girl,' said the daemon, drifting towards her.
'Would we give a servant anything that could harm us?'
It stretched out its hand and piano wires again burst
from it and wrapped her in an imprisoning embrace.
'Still,' it said, lifting her, 'you must be punished for the
attempt. What are the limits of your regeneration, we
wonder?'

Ulrika screamed as she felt the wires slowly sinking
deeper into her flesh. She writhed in mid-air, but there
was nothing to gain purchase upon. The pain increased.
Blood welled up as the wires sawed into her neck and
wrists. She held out her hands to plead for mercy she
knew would never come, but before she could speak, a
beam of golden light lanced across the auditorium and
struck the daemon in the chest, followed by a howling,
unnatural wind that blasted it with daggers of ice, pushing it back through the chairs and the mutated
musicians as the proscenium's velvet curtains whipped
and snapped around it.

The alabaster being stumbled and bellowed under the
dual assault, and Ulrika thudded to the stage, gasping in
relief, as the piano wires whipped away from her. She
looked up. The daemon, cringing within the shrieking
sphere of light and whirling ice, was turning towards the
seats, roaring like a thousand trumpets, and searching
for its attackers. Then a second beam of light, brighter
than the first, struck it from another angle, knocking it
sideways.

Ulrika shielded her eyes and looked out from the
stage. Through the glare of the attacks, she could half-
see a priest of Dazh standing in the duke's private box,
invoking his god, while coruscating streams of ice and
gold poured from another box at the daemon.

The daemon's angry roaring turned into a song, baroque and discordant and painful to the ear. It sang a violet aura into existence and it blazed around its body, throbbing in time to the melody and pushing back the ice and the golden light. It trilled like a soprano and purple tendrils of power snaked back along the bolts that struck at it, dampening them and reaching for the casters.

One touched the priest of Dazh, and he shrivelled like a raisin and died. His light died with him, and the daemon's tendrils grew stronger, but before they could touch its other tormentors, more magical and priestly attacks began to strike it from all over the Opera House, and it fell back again, its outlines wavering.

It had been Padurowski's intention to use the violin to destroy the minds of every magister, witch and priest in Praag, and consequently, they were here, and now that the violin's spell had been broken, they were angry, and fighting back with all the power at their disposal.

Ulrika tried to crawl away from the great seething nexus of energy that battered the daemon and threw around the chairs and instruments and bodies of the poor, distorted musicians like they were in the centre of a whirlwind, but she couldn't move. It was all she could do to dig her claws into the stage and hold on.

Finally, the daemon could take no more. It staggered back, its organ-pipe wings falling apart and its song becoming a mere howl again. Its purple aura flickered and faded and its questing tendrils withered.

'We will return,' it moaned, glaring out at its persecutors. 'And all Praag will sing their souls to us.'

And with a thunderclap of scintillating violet light, it crumpled to the stage, shrinking and curling in on itself until it was just Valtarin who lay there, shivering and staring with eyes turned purple and gold and opaque.

Ulrika looked up and blinked around, dizzy and

nauseous and pins-and-needles from head to toe. She felt as if she had been trapped inside a giant bell while ogres rang it, but seemed otherwise whole. She was one of the lucky ones. The aftermath of the battle was horrible to behold. The bodies of the mad and mutated were strewn all over the stage and the seats, and the wailing of the survivors curdled the air. Even the stage itself had been changed. The gilded figures that climbed both sides of the proscenium had become twisted, tentacled parodies of themselves, with gleaming purple gems for eyes. It would take many priests many months to purify the Opera House and make it fit to be used again.

After a long moment where she could do nothing but stare at the devastation, Ulrika recovered enough to push herself to her feet and stumble for the wings, desperate to get away before the guards regrouped and stormed the stage.

Valtarin looked up as she shuffled past him, but stared beyond her, unfocused. 'Who's there?' he asked, holding out his hands. 'Oh, gods, I can't see. I can't see. How can I play if I can't see?'

'Ask the girl you killed,' Ulrika snarled, and stumbled on. She could have killed him, but it seemed more fitting to leave him to his life. She wished him joy of it.

She had almost reached the curtains when a voice called to her from the back of the theatre. 'Stay, friend!' it said. 'I would speak with you.'

Ulrika looked up. Duke Enrik was stepping to the front of his private box as the rest of his guests cowered warily behind him.

'Praag owes you a great debt tonight, sir,' said Enrik. 'And I would know your name.'

'Yes,' said another voice. 'Show us your face, friend, that we may thank you.'

Ulrika turned and saw a magister in rich saffron robes

looking down at her from another box. A jolt of shock ran up her spine as she saw that it was Max Schreiber. She was suddenly certain it had been him that had first attacked the daemon, blasting it with his purifying golden light. She stepped back, unsteady. The meeting she had both longed for and dreaded had finally come to pass. A wild impulse to do as he asked struck her with irresistible force. His expression when he saw her face would be worth all the trouble that was sure to follow.

She raised her hand to her mask, grinning beneath it, but before she could lift it off, a beautiful woman in ice blue and white stepped out from behind Max and joined him at the balustrade – the ice witch, his lover.

Ulrika's mad glee died. She supposed she owed the witch her life, for she and Max had jolted the daemon into dropping her with their combined attack, but she still hated her.

Ulrika let go of the mask and instead saluted the duke, then turned and jabbed two fingers up in Max's direction before staggering quickly into the wings, laughing at the look of shock and confusion on the magister's solemn face.

ULRIKA LIMPED DOWN the stairs into the understage and looked around, tugging her mask to her neck again. The place was loud with muffled hubbub from the stage above – it sounded as if the duke's entire personal guard was trooping around upon it, and orders were flying back and forth – but all was quiet below, and but for the dead and dying, empty. She ran forwards and saw the bodies of Jodis and the crook-backed sorcerer lying near the platform, but no sign of Stefan or Evgena. Panic gripped her.

'Stefan?' she called, searching the bodies. 'Boyarina?'

A noise from the hole in the floor made her turn. Evgena was climbing from it with Stefan following behind.

'What happened?' Ulrika asked as they came forwards.

'They tried to flee,' said Evgena, smiling and brushing the dirt from her dresses. 'None escaped.'

'And Valtarin and Padurowski?' asked Stefan, pulling off his short cloak and wrapping it around his hand. 'They are dead?'

Ulrika nodded. 'Dead and worse than dead, and the violin and the daemon within it destroyed. The cult is finished.'

Evgena let out a sigh of relief.

Stefan did too. 'At last. Then I am finally free to finish my work.'

And before they could ask him what he meant, he picked up one of Jodis's silvered long-knives with the hand he had wrapped in his cloak, and plunged it between Evgena's shoulder-blades.

Ulrika stared, frozen with shock, as the boyarina screamed and clawed at her back and the veins in her neck began to turn black beneath her pale skin.

'What... what are you doing?' cried Ulrika. 'I don't understand!'

'Only my duty,' said Stefan, and carefully picked up the second silver knife. 'Killing Boyarina Evgena Boradin and her brood.'

Evgena turned on him, reaching out a shaking hand and opening her mouth, but before she could do more than gargle, Stefan hacked off her head with the second knife and she dropped to the floor. Her head rolled to Ulrika's feet. There was no blood. The edge of the terrible silver-struck wound was as black as burnt wood.

Ulrika looked from Evgena's lifeless stare to Stefan's glittering eyes. 'Y-you *are* Kiraly!' she said. 'You *did* come here for vengeance!'

He dropped the silver knife with a hiss of distaste. 'Not vengeance,' he said. 'Duty. And Kiraly is two hundred years dead. I only used his name to try to lure out the boyarina.'

Ulrika shook her head, trying to stop it churning. Nothing made sense. 'This can't be! You spared her! That is why I trusted you. You had a chance to kill her when we fled her mansion and you did not!'

'Aye,' he said thoughtfully. 'A difficult decision. When I led the cultists to the house, I expected Evgena to destroy them, freeing me to kill her, but slaying Raiza was a mistake I shouldn't have made. I realised immediately the fight would go the other way, and I could not allow that. Praag is to be mine. I am to claim it in my master's name. I could not let these dupes of Chaos steal it out from under me.' He looked down at Evgena's head. 'I was forced to let the Lahmians live until they helped me defeat the cult. Now they have.'

Ulrika went on guard at last. 'And now you mean to kill me.'

Stefan's face fell. 'No, beloved. Not at all. I meant what I said. We will rule Praag together. We will live here forever.'

'What?' cried Ulrika. 'You expect me to believe that? The moment I turn my back, I will die like all the others.'

Stefan's eyes flashed. 'I have lied in many things,' he said. 'But not in that. We have shared blood. We have a bond.'

'And you broke it, here, with this!' said Ulrika, pointing at Evgena's corpse. 'Blood of eagles! You think I could love you now?'

'I don't understand you!' Stefan snapped. 'You despised her! You said before you didn't care if I killed her!'

'I – it doesn't matter if I despised her,' said Ulrika. 'You said you weren't here to kill her. You lied to me. You–'

She cut off as memories came back to her – a hundred

little things Stefan had said, seemingly insignificant at the time, but now so clear. It had been his comment about gossiping women that had turned her mind to asking the Lahmians about the cult, thereby drawing Raiza out where he could attack her. It had been he who had put the idea of a meeting on neutral ground into her mind. Ha! If Evgena had agreed to it, she and Raiza and Galiana would have been dead that very night!

'You used me to get to them!' she said. 'You used what I felt for you! Ursun's teeth! I handed them to you!' She raised her blade and advanced on him. 'I had no love for Evgena, but I am no one's cat's-paw. I will die before I allow you to succeed through me.'

Stefan's grey eyes grew cold, and he knelt to pick up the silvered knife again with his wrapped hand. 'Your answer was yes,' he said in a voice like ice. 'Do you not remember? You said you would be with me, no matter what happened. You have broken your word.'

Ulrika sprang, trying to run him through before he grabbed the knife, but he turned her blade with his rapier and scooped it up, then rolled and came up slashing with it.

She snarled and scrambled back from the shining edge. 'I said those things to a man I trusted,' she said. 'You are not he.'

Stefan lunged, gashing her arm with his rapier as she parried the knife. She fell back and crashed into a crate full of prop swords and shields.

'Perhaps you should fight with those,' said Stefan, sneering. 'They are false as well.'

Footsteps clicked on the stairs, and Galiana's voice whispered into the room.

'Sister? Ulrika?'

Stefan turned his head, alarmed, and Ulrika hacked at his wrapped left hand. The silvered knife bounced across the floor as her blade cut him to the bone. He staggered back, cursing. She thrust for his neck, but he ducked under her blade and stumbled past her to fall amongst the wooden swords.

'Galiana! Here!' called Ulrika, lunging again. He knocked the thrust aside with his rapier, then grabbed a prop sword from the pile and stabbed wildly. Ulrika's block was too late, and the dull wooden point punched through her abdomen and ripped upwards to wedge between the ribs of her back.

She froze, transfixed with agony. It hurt like no sword cut she had ever taken. It was more like the pain of falling in the river – like the wood had impaled not just her body, but her essence. Now she knew why the stake was the preferred weapon of the vampire hunter. It was poison to her kind.

'I… I'm sorry,' said Stefan, stepping back.

She toppled to the side, unable to move a muscle. Had the sword pierced her heart? She could not tell. Her whole body screamed. There was no distinguishing one part from the other.

From across the room came a gasp of surprise. Through her dimming eyes, Ulrika saw Galiana staring from the doorway.

'What have you done?' she cried, then saw Evgena's headless corpse. 'Mistress!' she shrieked, and ran to her, falling to her knees.

Stefan picked up the silvered knife Ulrika had knocked from his hand, then started cautiously towards Galiana, cupping it. 'Ulrika killed her,' he said. 'I tried to stop her, but was not in time. She was a Sylvanian assassin, sent to destroy your sisterhood from within.'

Galiana looked up from staring at Evgena, seeming to hear him for the first time. '*She* was the assassin?' she asked. 'Not you?'

'I swear it, mistress,' he said, edging closer. 'She meant to kill you all and rule in your place.'

Galiana stood, backing away from him warily and extending her claws. 'Is that so? But then who killed Sister Raiza?'

'She had an accomplice,' said Stefan smoothly, still advancing. 'And he remains at large. But worry not, I will protect you. We will rule Praag together.'

Footsteps and the rattle of scabbards came from the stairway.

'Down there, you four,' barked a voice. 'We'll search further on.'

Stefan froze, but Galiana's eyes lit up.

'Gentles!' she cried, running for the stairs. 'Gentles, help me! This way! There are cultists!'

Stefan tensed like he meant to spring after her, but boots were thundering down the steps. He would not reach her in time. 'Lahmian cow!' he rasped. 'You will not live to see another sunset!'

He glanced back at Ulrika, raising the silvered dagger, but men were pouring into the room. With a curse he leapt to the hole in the floor and vanished from sight.

Ulrika's head sagged to her chest as Galiana fell into the arms of the first man through the door, a soldier in the uniform of the duke's private guard. 'Praise Ursun you arrived, sirs!' she sobbed. 'I fear they meant to sacrifice me! Quick! They have fled through that hole!'

The last thing Ulrika saw as her vision faded entirely, was the soldiers looking around with wide eyes at the bodies of Evgena and the dead and dying cultists as they ran for the hole, and her last thought before her consciousness faded was that Stefan's threat had not been idle. He could walk by day, and he knew where Evgena's safe house was.

He was going to kill the last Lahmian of Praag in her sleep.

CHAPTER THIRTY-THREE
GIRDED AGAINST THE DAY

ULRIKA JOLTED AWAKE as something wet splashed her in the face. At first she thought it was water, but then it burned her eyes and made her gag. She coughed, then gasped in pain, for it felt as if she had been run through the guts. The agony was indescribable. She forced her eyes open, blinking away the burning liquid, then grunted as she looked down at herself. She *had* been run through the guts. A wooden sword stuck from her belly, and the liquid, it smelled like lamp oil. Why would anyone throw lamp oil on her?

She turned her eyes left and right, then froze in horror. She lay among robed and hooded and mutated bodies – some still moaning – which were piled upon a mound of timber, and soldiers were walking around and around, soaking the whole assemblage with oil while a crowd of richly clad onlookers watched. It seemed the authorities were preparing to burn the cultists of Slaanesh and the victims of the daemon, and she was on the pyre.

In a paroxysm of panic, she tried to thrash her way off

the mound, but her limbs would not answer her. They did nothing more than twitch. She stared down at the silly wooden sword that impaled her. It might not have pierced her heart, but it had somehow paralysed her. She could not move. Not an inch.

She looked around again. She was in the centre of Windlass Square, with the duke's palace ablaze with light off to the south, and soldiers still bringing bodies out of the Opera House and throwing them on the pile. She had a little time, then, but what did time matter if she couldn't move? It would only give her leisure to anticipate her burning. She shivered in fear. She could imagine no worse death.

A pair of soldiers was coming her way, dragging a cultist by the legs. She licked her lips. A chance! She would use her Lahmian wiles on them. She would trick them into removing the sword.

The men threw the cultist down beside her, then turned away as he groaned and mumbled incoherently.

'Sirs,' she whispered, then tried again, louder. 'Sirs! I beg you! A small mercy!'

The soldiers looked around, scowling. They did not look the merciful sort. She smiled, trying to look sultry.

'Sirs, please,' she murmured as they slouched closer. 'I would not burn alive. Pull out the sword, so I may bleed to death before the flames find me.'

The soldiers looked at each other and laughed. The first kicked her in the face. The second spat on her.

'You want mercy, daemon-lover?' he asked. 'I'll give you mercy!'

He grabbed the wooden sword and twisted it in her guts. Ulrika cried out in agony, but he wasn't done. He ripped it out of her and beat her with it, smashing her head and shoulders and arms until it splintered and snapped.

'There's your mercy, you traitorous bitch!' he cried,

then flung the broken sword at her and turned away, laughing, with his mate.

Ulrika sagged forwards, groaning, her head throbbing and blood running down into her eyes. She lifted her hand to wipe it away, then stopped. She could lift her hand! She grinned to herself through bloody teeth. She might have failed at Lahmian wiles, and taken a beating for it, but the men had pulled the sword out nonetheless.

Still, she was much too weak to run away. She doubted she could even crawl, and there were hundreds of people between her and freedom. She needed strength.

She looked to the cultist the soldiers had thrown down beside her. She had heard him moan. He still lived. With a wary glance around, she caught him by the collar and pulled him on top of her. He mumbled wordlessly and his head slumped against her chest. She pulled back his hood and removed the black veil he wore over his face, then tipped up his chin and sank her fangs into his neck. He twitched and grunted, but was too broken to pull away.

She drank deeply, moaning with relief, and willing the blood to mend the torn tissues of her middle. She knew it would take more than one feeding to heal such a wound, but as long as she gained enough strength to run, she would take care of the rest later.

From nearby came a sergeant's hoarse bellow, and more soldiers came forwards, these armed with torches and halberds. She lay still, hiding under her victim's bulk, as two shoved their brands into the pile a few paces on either side of her. Immediately flames leapt up and she heard the screams of the not yet dead.

The soldiers backed away again, watching the flames, and she resumed her feeding. She had to heal as much as possible before her attempt. The cultist's blood flowed again into her veins, warming them and spreading strength to the muscles of her arms and legs, but the flames were roasting her face now. There was no more time.

She shoved the man aside and looked around. The crowd stood fifteen paces back, with the soldiers in a ring just in front of them. The Opera House was directly before her, and the darkest part of the square to her right. That was where she would go.

She rolled away from the pyre, hoping the eyes of the crowd would be watching the flames. There was no outcry, so she rolled again, then pressed up onto her hands and knees. The wound in her gut grabbed her and made her arms tremble, but she fought through it and started to crawl.

'Hoy!' came a woman's voice. 'One of them's escaping!'

Ulrika looked up. Three soldiers were coming towards her, halberds lowered. She fought the urge to run, and stayed down, crawling like she could barely move.

They spread out as they approached her, pulling back to stab her from three sides. With a shriek, she leapt up and dashed between them, though her belly felt like it was tearing asunder. They cried out and thrust at her, but she was already past them and sprinting for the hole they had left in their line.

The other soldiers converged towards her, and the crowd, filled with patriotic spirit, closed ranks to stop her. Ulrika sprang at them, snarling and shooting out her claws and fangs, and they fell back screaming. She broke through them with the soldiers after her, and sprinted for a gap between two buildings at the edge of the square. A thrown halberd skittered under her feet and almost tripped her, but she ran on, clutching her stomach.

She ran into the gap and collapsed against one of the

buildings, heaving up a throatful of blood and bile that spattered her legs. It had been too much too soon. Her whole body shook with pain and fatigue.

Footsteps thudded behind her. They were coming. She looked up the side of the building. It was cut stone, loosely mortared. She grabbed for the first handhold and pulled herself up, groaning, then climbed on, closing her eyes against the pain.

The boots boomed below her.

'There she is!'

'Bring her down!'

'Call for a gun!'

Another halberd glanced off the stone beside her. She flinched, but climbed on as rocks and cobbles struck all around her. A few yards further and she felt the lip of the roof. She pulled herself onto it and lay there, gasping.

'Into the building!'

'We'll go up through the roof!'

Ulrika moaned and pulled herself up, then staggered, doubled over, across the flat roof. There was a gap on the far side. She gathered her strength and leapt it, then crashed down on the slanted slates of the building beyond. The world dimmed as pain blossomed inside her. She was going to black out. They would find her.

She lifted her spinning head. There was an ornamental cupola at the peak of the roof, little more than a dovecote with an onion-dome on top. She crawled for it. Tiny arched windows lined the base. Were they large enough?

She caught the sill of one and pulled her head and one shoulder in. A score of pigeons squeaked and battered her face with their wings as they fled. She shielded her eyes, then pushed in. It was tight, and her ribs and guts screamed as they pressed against the frame, but at last she squirmed through and dropped to the wooden floor within. It was inches thick with pigeon droppings and she covered her nose and mouth to keep from gagging.

From outside came the echoes of men's voices. They were on the other roof now. Had they seen her? Had they seen the pigeons? She tried to draw her sword so she could fight them when they came, but her limbs were too weak. She hurt too much. She couldn't move. Her head fell back, thudding on the filthy boards, and blackness overwhelmed her once again.

ULRIKA WOKE WITH a cry as something touched her shoulder. She jerked away, reaching for her sword, and a pigeon flapped away from her, spooking the rest of the flock. She rolled, groaning, as they clattered from the cupola again, and clutched her aching abdomen. How long had she been out?

She looked out the little windows. It was still night, but only barely. The sky to the east was lightening. It would be morning soon.

Morning?

Panic clutched her as memory returned. Stefan had threatened to kill Galiana before sunset today. Ulrika had to stop him – kill him. But as she rose, her wound tore at her from the inside and she flopped back, hissing and grunting with pain.

How was she to do it? It seemed impossible. Wounded as she was, and with no more than an hour of night left, she would never find him in time, and wouldn't be strong enough to fight him if she did. But perhaps speed wasn't so important. Perhaps it would be better to let him kill Galiana and find him afterwards. She had no particular love for the woman, nor enough loyalty to the Lahmian sisterhood to want to defend it at the cost of her life. She could hunt him later, at her leisure.

But she couldn't. She might not care about the

Lahmians, but she had made a vow to protect them, and she had failed in that vow when she had brought Stefan amongst them. Through her, he had killed Evgena. Through her, he had imprisoned the soul of Raiza, the only one of the Praag sisters Ulrika would have been honoured to call friend. Through her, his plan was one last step away from succeeding. She would not allow him to take that step, though it cost her her life. Vengeance after the fact would be not be nearly as sweet as spoiling his game.

She rose again, determined, and squeezed out of the cupola, clenching her teeth against the pain, but as she crawled down the slant of the roof, she stopped again. It was all very well saying she would stop Stefan, but she needed a plan.

She had to go to Evgena's safe house, that much was certain. No matter where Stefan hid, that was where he would go in the end. But before that, she had to feed again, and finding a victim would take time. The sun would be up before she reached the house. And what if Galiana didn't let her in? She couldn't wait in the street for Stefan to come. She would burn to death.

Ulrika growled and lowered her head. It was impossible. Time and the sun were against her. Everything was in Stefan's favour.

The mask of tragedy that still dangled around her neck mocked her with its down-turned mouth. She reached up to tear it off, then paused, a thrill of inspiration shooting through her. The mask! The mask was the answer!

She turned in the direction of the Novygrad and limped down the roof with renewed purpose. It would take a little time, but if done right, she would hopefully be able to face Stefan no matter when he struck, night or day.

* * *

ULRIKA FOUND A worthy victim on her way through the
city, a pimp who did business out of an abandoned
butcher-shop, then, feeling stronger, but by no means
strong, she raced back to the bakery. She reached it only
steps ahead of the dawn, and the first slanting shafts of
sunlight were already lancing through the darkness of
the basement before she had finished taking off her
doublet and shirt to examine the wound Stefan had
given her.

After a night's rest and two feedings, the entry point
was no more than a scabbed, star-shaped scar, but she
knew from the swelling and stiffness of her abdomen
that all was not yet well inside. It felt as if someone had
inflated a balloon under her ribs. She had no idea how
to fix this, or if it would heal itself, so she just bandaged
her waist as tightly as she could with the ruined shirt,
then set about preparing for battle.

First she donned her last whole shirt, then bound it
tightly at wrist and neck with strips from the other. Next
she put on her grey doublet and breeches, lacing them
up as closely as she could, and on top of them, the
leather jerkin she had worn when travelling. After that,
she pulled on her thigh-high riding boots and tucked
the cuffs of the breeches securely down into them.

Then came the most difficult part. The mask of
tragedy would hide her face, and her heavy travelling
cloak had a hood that would cover her head, but neither
kept off the sun entirely. There was still her neck and
forehead and the eye and mouth holes of the mask.
What she needed was something like the veil the cultists
wore, and she cursed herself for not having the fore-
thought to take one while she had the opportunity.

She upended her pack and pawed through her few
meagre belongings. She could drape the rest of her torn
shirt over her head, but it was white. In the sun, it would
be almost impossible to see through. She needed

something black and thin. Then she remembered. The slaver Stefan had brought her to feed upon. He had worn a black bandana under his hat!

She hurried to the room they had disposed of him in. His body was still there. She pulled the bandana from his head and sniffed it with distaste. It smelled of three-day-old corpse and pomade, but there was nothing for it. She draped it over her face then bound it tight at her forehead and throat and tucked the ends down under her collar.

Finally, she fitted the mask down over the veil and threw on her heavy cloak, pulling the voluminous hood as far forwards as she could, then tugged on her riding gloves and unfolded the long cuffs so that they overlapped the ends of her sleeves. Her costume was complete. It was constricting, and stiflingly hot, and she was certain she would get her fair share of looks, even in as wild a city as Praag, but she had succeeded in arming herself against the sun – or so she hoped. The proof was in the doing.

She turned to the stairs and squared her shoulders, then marched up and stepped into the daylight.

ULRIKA SUPPOSED HERSELF fortunate the day was dark and overcast, but nevertheless, after less than a minute under the open sky, she almost turned around and gave it all up as a mistake. Alone, the clothes were hot; under the sun, filtered by clouds though it was, she felt as if she were wearing full plate in the middle of the Nehekharan desert. She was broiling, even when she clung to the shadows, and strength seemed to leech from her with every step, making her dizzy and confused, but there was no option. Finding her way through the sewers and avoiding the things that lived there would take too much time, and she couldn't risk letting Stefan reach the safe house before her.

Praag seemed as fatigued and disoriented as she was. The manic euphoria Ulrika had noticed since arriving in the city was gone. No one was singing. No one was laughing. The soldiers and merchants and beggars she saw on the street shuffled listlessly by, drab and dispirited, like hung-over revellers trudging home after a party. All the gossip in the markets was of the madness and death at the Opera House, and the cultists who had been burned before it – and the fear that there might be still more lurking in the shadows.

Ulrika wondered if the destruction of the Fieromonte had something to do with their mood. Perhaps the awakened violin had somehow sparked a madness for music in the city, and now that it was gone, and the daemon within it returned to the void, perhaps its melodic mania had died with it.

Or perhaps it was only morning. Ulrika didn't often see mornings any more.

At last she reached the quiet cul-de-sac where the safe house sat, and went more carefully, circling around the small dry fountain with the statue of Salyak in its centre, and looking for Stefan or signs he had already visited. She saw nothing, and the house looked as undisturbed and unassuming as before. She stepped to the front door and knocked, then leaned against the door wearily.

There was no answer.

She knocked again, and after a long while, at last heard footsteps.

'Go away,' came a voice Ulrika recognised as one of Evgena's men. 'The mistress is not receiving.'

'I only want to know she is well,' said Ulrika. 'That she has had no… visitors.'

'I am not at liberty to say. Go away.'

Ulrika growled in her throat, the pain of the sun making her impatient. 'Fool! You know who I am! I want to know if she's safe! I want to know if she still lives!'

The footsteps went away.

She pounded on the door. 'Tell me, curse you!'

'She lives,' said a voice behind her. 'But not for long.'

Ulrika whipped around. Stefan von Kohln stood by the fountain in the middle of the cul-de-sac, a broad hat shading his face, and his rapier drawn.

CHAPTER THIRTY-FOUR
DUEL IN THE SUN

ULRIKA DREW HER rapier and dagger, cursing under her breath. This was not how she had wanted this to play out. She had hoped Galiana would let her in. She had hoped to fight him inside. The day had fortunately grown darker still, with lowering clouds, but the light was still cruel. She could not fight Stefan out here. It would kill her.

'I am pleased to see you alive,' said Stefan, stepping forwards. 'I feared what would happen to you at the hands of the authorities.'

Ulrika snorted and stepped away from the door, giving herself some room to move. 'They were very considerate,' she said. 'They removed your wooden sword. I wish I had it with me, so I could return it to you.'

Stefan sighed. 'I know you won't believe me, but I acted in self defence. I still have no wish to harm you.'

'Then why is your sword drawn?'

'I am here to kill Galiana,' said Stefan. 'Step aside and we need not fight.'

Ulrika shook her head, edging closer to him. She had to strike quickly, before all her strength was gone. The daylight was like an anvil sitting on her shoulders. 'I have already allowed you to kill Raiza and Evgena through my gullibility. You will not trick me into betraying my vow a third time.'

'It is no trick,' he said. 'I admit I used you to reach them. It was only my duty. But I meant what I said before. I have grown to… admire you. I wish us to be together.'

Ulrika snarled and lunged. 'Only if we share a grave!'

Stefan beat her blade aside and stepped back, angry. 'I don't understand you. You said you wanted to be the defender of Praag. That is what I offer you. We can rule it together. We can be the good stewards you spoke of – preying on the predators and defending the weak.'

Ulrika sneered. 'You don't care about that.'

'I have come to,' he said. 'Fighting the cult has proven to me the stake we must have in human affairs. If we are to rule, then we must rule well.'

Ulrika hesitated. Was he saying these things only to fool her? He sounded sincere. Perhaps he *had* changed his mind. But did it matter? He might love her, he might share her philosophy, but he had also betrayed her, lied to her, manipulated her into betraying her sworn mistress, stabbed her with a wooden stake and left her to die!

On the other hand, who among her new family had not hurt her in some way? Hermione had named her conspirator, Evgena and Galiana had branded her assassin, Famke had chosen the coward's path, even Countess Gabriella, who had nurtured her through her infancy, had proved herself a fickle, untrustworthy mother. Only Raiza had remained true, and Raiza was dead – worse than dead.

Ulrika thought back to the morning she had shared

blood with Stefan. She had felt no greater pleasure in her life or death. Would she deny herself an eternity of such pleasure for the sake of honour, when it seemed honour had no value in her new life?

She looked at him, standing there strong and proud, and the longing for him and what he could give her was overwhelming. She wanted to drop her rapier and step into his arms. She wanted to beg his forgiveness and have him take her away from the pain of the sun, but a thorn of pride caught her and held her back. Honour might have no value for her sisters, but hadn't she left their society for precisely that reason? If she went to him, if she allowed pleasure to trump honour, she would be giving up her last vow – the most important one, the one she had made to herself – and would be no better than they. She might as well never have left Nuln.

'I'm sorry, Stefan,' she said at last. 'I do not believe one can be a good ruler while standing on the corpse of one's predecessor.'

She lunged with her rapier. Again he turned it, but still did not follow through.

'You are a fool to spurn me,' he said. 'You will die here.'

Ulrika shrugged. 'I am overdue.'

Stefan's lip curled in disgust. 'Then I will oblige you.'

And with that he attacked at last – a thrust right at her heart. She tipped it aside with her dagger and came under with her rapier, aiming for his stomach, but he blocked it with something in his left hand – a jagged length of black onyx.

Ulrika stumbled back, wide-eyed and gasping.

'What's the matter?' said Stefan, slashing furiously at her with it. 'I thought you were ready to die.'

'That is not death,' she growled, edging away from the thing. She could not imagine being trapped and conscious forever in such a prison, with nothing to do, no one to talk to, no air, no wind, no movement. If there was a hell on earth, that was it. And it Stefan's hands, it might be worse, much worse.

'Do you know what happens to vampires when they die?' asked Stefan as he pursued her. 'This is preferable.'

'That depends on who holds the shard, doesn't it?' said Ulrika.

A movement in a window above caught her eye and she glanced up. Someone in the safe house was watching the fight from behind a heavy curtain.

'True,' said Stefan. 'A cruel man could torture you for eternity. That is why my master bid me use them on the Lahmians – so he could have them for his "experiments". He will be angry I killed the boyarina with mere silver, but I had to hide the shards before revealing myself at her mansion, and had no chance to recover them before the concert.'

'And so you will make up for it by giving him my essence instead,' said Ulrika.

Stefan shook his head, grave. 'I would not do that. If you will not be with me, I will keep your shard next to my heart.'

'I hope it cuts you,' said Ulrika, and hacked at the hand that held the onyx blade.

He avoided the stroke and came in again, slashing with both weapons. She blocked the shard, but his rapier tore open her left sleeve just above the glove. The cut barely grazed her, but it didn't matter, for the rip in the cloth bared her flesh to the day.

Ulrika staggered back, yelping in pain, as the exposed skin boiled and steamed like white stew. Stefan darted in again, and in her panic, she fumbled her parry. His sword found her shoulder, and another line of molten agony seared her.

She stumbled to the other side of the fountain, hissing and cursing. She had been so afraid of the Blood Shard it hadn't occurred to her that simple steel was just as deadly in a daytime duel. What a fool! The sun wouldn't just weaken her. It was going to kill her. It would do Stefan's work for him!

She pulled her cloak forwards, covering the hole on her shoulder, but there was nothing to be done about her left arm. If she held it out to attack or parry, she would show it to the sun and it would burn again, and even out of the sun, the pain of the wounds did not fade. It felt like swords, glowing from the forge, pressing against her flesh.

'Please, Ulrika,' said Stefan, coming around the fountain. 'Give this up. I don't want to hurt you further.'

'You couldn't,' she snarled, then charged, slashing and thrusting though every move exposed more skin to the sun.

He parried it all easily and forced her back, lunging for her eyes with his sword and slashing for her arms with the shard. She retreated before the onslaught, and tripped over the coping of the fountain. His rapier chopped her thigh as she fell, splitting cloth and flesh.

She screamed and crashed into the dry pool, her vision blurring as the sunlight cooked the wound. He stepped in and slashed down at her. She rolled behind the statue of Salyak, sobbing with rage. It was impossible. She was too weak, and he was too strong. She couldn't win. She would either have to flee or give in, and in either case, Galiana would die, and Stefan would have his victory. The liar and manipulator would win. The bitterness she felt at that hurt almost worse than the sun.

Stefan stepped around the statue, his face hard and sad. He seemed truly reluctant to kill her. Ulrika almost smiled to see it. In that at least, she was strong and he was weak. As much as she lusted for him, it would not keep her from finishing him. She froze at the thought. That was how she could win!

Stefan stood over her, lowering his point to thrust at her throat.

With a sobbing wail, Ulrika crabbed back, dropping her rapier and dagger. 'Stop!' she cried. 'No more. It hurts too much! I don't want to die!'

Stefan paused, suspicious. 'You have changed your mind, then?'

Ulrika held out her arm, showing the boiling wound, then snatched it back as it began to smoulder. 'Do you wonder at it? Nothing is worth this!' She cradled her arms against her chest, trying to hide all of herself under her cloak. 'Please. Take me out of the sun. Share your blood with me. I will be yours if you stop the pain.'

Stefan stood over her, still hesitant, then put the tip of his rapier to her neck. The hand that held the Blood Shard hung at his side.

'Stand,' he said. 'We will go into the house. I will lock you up until I have dealt with Mistress Galiana.'

Ulrika nodded and pushed up to one knee, then lost her balance and grabbed for the statue of Salyak to catch herself, and for a brief second, Stefan's point left its place at her throat. That was all she needed. With a grunt, she drove forwards, grabbing for the shard and shouldering him back.

Stefan barked in surprise and slashed her across the shoulders with his rapier as they fell against the base of the statue. Burning agony striped her back, but she kept her focus, slamming Stefan's hand against the statue's stone feet.

The shard leapt free. Ulrika snatched it up and pressed it against his throat, just under the jaw. 'Now you know how it feels,' she rasped, 'to be betrayed.'

'Wait!' he said, his eyes showing white as he tried to look down at the black knife. 'You don't want this.'

'More than anything in the world,' said Ulrika.

'You don't understand,' Stefan cried. 'You have nothing without me. There will be nowhere for you to go. Only I can keep you safe!'

Ulrika sneered and pressed the shard harder against his flesh. She was enjoying his squirming. 'Can you keep yourself safe?'

'Listen to me!' he said. 'The world is changing for our kind. My master sends his agents to every city in the Old World, readying them for his coming. Your mistress may have foiled his Strigoi dupe in Nuln, and you may foil me here, but others will come, and he will win eventually, as he has already won in many other places.'

Ulrika frowned. What was this about Nuln? What was he talking about?

'There will be no rebels in my master's empire,' Stefan continued. 'No lone wolves. All will be brought to heel or killed. Only I can protect you. Under my wing, no harm will come to you, but if you kill me, there will be nowhere for you to run. Please. Let me save you.'

Ulrika pulled herself up and knelt on his sword arm. The sun burned into her back and shoulder, but the pain was suddenly faraway. 'The Strigoi in Nuln was a dupe, you say? There will be others? Mistress Gabriella is in danger?'

Stefan nodded. 'Even now, my master's agents begin his greatest play there. The decapitating stroke.'

'Not if I can stop them,' Ulrika growled. 'Who is this master of yours?'

'Don't be a fool,' hissed Stefan. 'Your mistress will be dead before you reach her. You will have no home to return to. Stay here with me as my consort. I will shield you from what is to come.'

Ulrika shook him and raised the Blood Shard threateningly. 'Enough! Who is your master?'

Stefan wrenched his arm from under her knee and

swung his rapier. She ducked as the hilt struck her ear, and stabbed reflexively with the shard, burying it in his throat. Stefan bucked and shrieked, eyes wide, as the black onyx did its work. His face collapsed in on itself and his clutching hands shrivelled to bony claws. His body, under her, shrank inside his clothes.

Ulrika staggered to her feet, horrified, and gripped the statue for support, watching as the light in Stefan's sunken eyes died and he fell still at last. A wave of pain washed over her that had nothing to do with the sun. She wished... But it was always foolish to wish things had been different.

She reached down and pulled the now-glowing Blood Shard from his withered throat. It throbbed through her gloves as she tucked it into her belt pouch. There was only one more thing to do. She recovered her rapier and cut off Stefan's skeletal head, just to be sure, then picked it up and stepped wearily from the fountain.

The door to the safe house opened as she approached it, and a man-at-arms bowed her in. Ulrika shuffled past him, then groaned with relief as he closed it behind her and shut out the merciless sun.

Galiana was standing on the bottom step of the stairs to the upper floor, her face and figure once again wizened and doll-like. Ulrika dropped Stefan's head at her feet, then tore off her mask and veil and threw them on top of it.

'The assassin is dead,' she said. 'The comedy is finished. I...' She weaved, dizzy with pain, then continued. 'I apologise for not seeing through him before he killed Sister Raiza and Mistress Evgena. I have failed in my vow.'

Galiana stepped down and took her arm, then guided her to a chair in the hall. 'You have done much to repair the fault,' she said, 'and fought bravely just now in my defence. Now rest, I will summon someone so you may drink.'

'Thank you,' said Ulrika, and closed her eyes.

SOMETIME LATER, ULRIKA woke naked in a cool, clean bed. She did not remember having fed, but she must have, for her wounds, though still blistered and painful, were greatly healed, and she felt strong enough to move.

After a while a maid came in and offered her her neck, and a while after that, when the sun had gone down, Galiana entered, carrying her freshly laundered and mended clothes. She set them on a table, then came and sat by Ulrika's bed.

'I owe you an apology for the way we treated you, sister,' she said. 'And if Mistress Evgena lived, I am sure she would apologise as well. You were right about the cult. We should have listened. I'm afraid we have grown too insular in the last centuries.'

Ulrika shook her head. 'And you were right about Stefan. I should have listened, too.'

Galiana smiled and patted her hand. 'We have all made mistakes of that nature, at one time or other.' Then she looked down, suddenly subdued. 'It – it seems I am our Queen's sole representative in Praag now, and… I have never led before. I have always been Mistress Evgena's pet – an advisor sometimes – but never more than that.' She looked up at Ulrika. 'I don't think I can do it alone. I want you, therefore, to be my second-in-command – my Raiza.'

Ulrika blinked, nonplussed, then bowed as best she could while in bed. 'You honour me, sister,' she said. 'But I cannot. I have urgent business in Nuln. In fact, I had hoped to beg a coach from you, so I might speed there as quickly as possible.'

Galiana's face hardened. 'It was not a request,' she said. 'You are still bound here by your oath.'

'But – but Boyarina Evgena is dead,' said Ulrika.

'And as I have inherited her properties,' said Galiana, 'so have I inherited her vassals. You are now beholden to me.'

Ulrika stared, panic rising in her throat. 'But I must go back! My mistress is in danger!'

'What's this?' barked Galiana. 'You have no mistress but me.'

'No.' Ulrika pushed back the covers and tried to get out of the bed, but fell to the floor, still dizzy from her wounds and her time in the sun. 'I shared no blood with you! You cannot hold me!'

Galiana stepped to her and pulled her to her knees with just her left hand, then let out the claws of her right. 'Can I not?'

Ulrika spread her arms. 'You will have to kill me then, for I will not stop trying to run. Sylvania threatens my mistress, just as it threatened you, and all Lahmians. I must return and protect her.'

'What do you say?' asked Galiana, her clawed hand lowering unconsciously. 'What is this threat?'

'Stefan von Kohln told me of it before he died,' said Ulrika. 'Sylvania has sent agents to all the cities of the Old World and set them to destroying the Lahmian influence there – the Strigoi in Nuln, Stefan here – and many others, all in preparation for some great invasion or attack.'

Galiana's hand sank to her side. 'This is true?'

'I fear it is,' said Ulrika. 'He said his master makes his greatest play in Nuln as we speak, and that my mistress will die of it. That is why I cannot stay.'

Galiana let go of her and stepped back, her face clouded. 'This is calamity,' she said. 'The Queen must be warned. The sisterhood must ready itself.'

'Then – then, you'll release me?'

Galiana turned back to Ulrika, eyes flashing. 'Release

you? Are you mad? With Sylvania attacking? This is precisely when I need you most. No. You must stay by my side.'

Ulrika stood, stiff with pain, then bowed to her. 'Mistress, if you allow me to return to Nuln, I will praise you to your sisters, and through them, to the Queen. I will tell them of your bravery and foresight in our battle against the cultists and Stefan von Kohln. I will tell them you saved Praag, and deserve every assistance in keeping it safe in the future. But if you try to hold me, I will give you no help. I will fight to leave with all the strength I have left. I will kill you, if necessary, for I will allow nothing to stand between me and my true mistress.' She shrugged. 'The choice is yours: glory and the promise of help, or strife and the possibility of death. Which will it be?'

Galiana glared up at her like an angry doll, her tiny fists balling at her sides, but at last, after a long, simmering moment, she turned away with a disgusted snort and stepped to the table where she had set Ulrika's clothes.

'How do I know you will really do this?' she asked. 'How do I know you will speak well of me when you are beyond my reach?'

Ulrika bowed again. 'I'm afraid, mistress, that I can give you no assurance but my word.'

A FEW HOURS later, Ulrika left Praag by the south gate in a closed coach, with a driver and a change of clothes and a maid to feed upon, all reluctantly provided by Galiana. Faced with Ulrika's unwavering determination to defy her, the vampiress had eventually agreed to let her go, but she had only sneered when Ulrika had asked for help in returning swiftly to Nuln. Fortunately, Ulrika had another weapon in her arsenal.

In the end it had taken everything in her purse – fifty-six golden Reikmarks, plus a fistful of rings, necklaces and bracelets, all taken from the highwaymen Ulrika had preyed upon on the road to Praag – to get Galiana to part with the coach, driver and willing maid. Ulrika doubted the price would have been sufficient had Galiana not been in such reduced circumstances, but the loss of Boyarina Evgena's mansion and all the treasure stored in its coffers had left her bankrupt, and so she had made the trade at last.

Now, as her coach rumbled south, Ulrika put thoughts of Praag behind her, and began to think what awaited her in Nuln. She felt somewhat hypocritical running back to Gabriella after calling her despicable and dishonourable, and setting off to start a new life in order to prove that the Lahmian way was not the only way, but how could she not? No matter their differences, Gabriella was still the woman who had been mother to her, and protected her when she would have died, and the thought of her facing unknown dangers with no one to watch her back was more than Ulrika could bear. Her rebellion could wait. Family came first.

Her thoughts grew black with wild imaginings as she wondered what form the Sylvanian attack upon Nuln would take. Would it be an army of the night? Would it be a witch hunt? Would it be some new Stefan, kissing Gabriella's hand while poisoning her blood with ancient magics? Would the countess fall for such a ruse? Would she allow herself to be lulled by soft words of love and promises of an eternity without loneliness?

Ulrika shuddered and threw open the window to banish the vision and to feel the bracing air of the cold Kislev night on her face. The road paralleled the River Lynsk here, and she watched the moonlight rippling on its waters, then shivered as the sight brought back memories of plunging below the waves of the Reik. The pain of her recent wounds had been nothing compared to the agony she had felt as the river had torn at her soul.

The thought sparked another, and she paused. She must return home as quickly as she could, but there was time for this. She rapped on the wall of the coach.

'Driver! Pull up by the river.'

'Aye, mistress.'

The coach slowed and stopped as her maid blinked and woke on the bench opposite.

'Is everything all right, mistress?'

'Yes, Svetka. Go back to sleep.'

Ulrika stepped out of the coach, then crossed a swathe of dead grass and scrub to the bank of the river. She opened her belt pouch and took out the pulsing Blood Shard that contained Stefan's essence. There were many reasons for wishing him an eternity of excruciating, eviscerating pain – for using her, for lying to her, for killing Raiza – but one stood out over all the others.

'This is for showing me the dream,' she said, holding up the shard. 'Then taking it away.'

And with that, she drew back and threw it as far as she could. It glittered in the light of the two moons as it spun, then plopped into the waves and was gone. Ulrika stood and watched the river drift by for a moment, then returned to the coach and got under way again, racing through the night on the long road to Nuln.

ABOUT THE AUTHOR

Nathan Long was a struggling screenwriter
for fifteen years, during which time he had
three movies made and a handful of live-
action and animated TV episodes
produced. Now he is a novelist, and is
enjoying it much more. For Black Library
he has written three Warhammer novels
featuring the Blackhearts, and he took over
the Gotrek and Felix series, starting with
the eighth instalment, *Orcslayer*.
He is currently writing the Ulrika
the Vampire series.